About the Authors

Lynne Graham lives in Northern Ireland and has been a keen romance reader since her teens. Happily married, Lynne has five children. Her eldest is her only natural child. Her other children, who are every bit as dear to her heart, are adopted. The family has a variety of pets, and Lynne loves gardening, cooking, collecting all sorts and is crazy about every aspect of Christmas.

Cathy Williams is a great believer in the power of perseverance as she had never written anything before her writing career, and from the starting point of zero has now fulfilled her ambition to pursue this most enjoyable of careers. She would encourage any would-be writer to have faith and go for it! She derives inspiration from the tropical island of Trinidad and from the peaceful countryside of middle England. Cathy lives in Warwickshire with her family.

USA TODAY bestselling author **Lynn Raye Harris** burst onto the scene when she won a writing contest held by Mills & Boon. The prize was an editor for a year – but only six months later, Lynn sold her first novel. A former finalist for the Romance Writers of America's Golden Heart Award, Lynn lives in Alabama with her handsome husband and two crazy cats. Her stories have been called 'exceptional and emotional,' 'intense,' and 'sizzling.'

The Secret Heirs

COLLECTION

Secret Heirs: Price of Success

LYNNE GRAHAM

CATHY WILLIAMS

LYNN RAYE HARRIS

MILLS & BOON

First Published in Great Britain 2020
By Mills & Boon, an imprint of HarperCollins*Publishers*
1 London Bridge Street, London, SE1 9GF

SECRET HEIRS: PRICE OF SUCCESS © 2020 Harlequin Books S.A.

The Secrets She Carried © 2012 Lynne Graham
The Secret Sinclair © 2012 Cathy Williams
The Change in Di Navarra's Plan © 2013 Lynn Raye Harris

ISBN: 978-0-263-28086-9

0220

MIX
Paper from
responsible sources
FSC® C007454

This book is produced from independently certified FSC™ paper to ensure responsible forest management.

For more information visit: www.harpercollins.co.uk/green

Printed and bound in Spain
by CPI, Barcelona

THE SECRETS
SHE CARRIED

LYNNE GRAHAM

CHAPTER ONE

CRISTOPHE DONAKIS opened the file on the Stanwick Hall Hotel group, which he expected to become the latest addition to his luxury hotel empire, and suffered an unanticipated shock.

Ironically, it took a great deal to shock Cristophe. At thirty years of age, the Greek entrepreneur and billionaire had seen a lot of bad behaviour and when it came to women in particular he was a complete cynic with low expectations. Orphaned at the age of five, he had survived several major setbacks in life, not the least of which had included foster parents whom he loved but with whom he had not a single thought in common, and a divorce, which still rankled for he had entered his marriage with the best of good intentions. No, what caused Cristophe to vault upright behind his desk and carry the file over to the window to avail of the best possible light was a glimpse of a startlingly familiar face in a photograph of the Stanwick executive staff ... a face from his past.

Erin Turner...a pocket Venus with pale hair that glittered like polished silver gilt and eyes the colour of amethysts. Straight off, his lean, darkly handsome features clenched into forbidding angles. Erin occupied a category all of her own in his memories, for she had been the only woman ever to betray him and, even though almost three years had to have passed since their last meeting, the recollection could still sting. His keenly intelligent gaze devoured the photograph of his former mistress standing smiling at the elbow of Sam Morton, the elderly owner of Stanwick Hall. Clad in a dark business suit with her eye-catching hair restrained by a clip, she looked very different from the carefree, casually clad young woman he remembered.

His tall, powerful body in the grip of sudden tension, Cristo's dark-as-night eyes took on a fiery glow. That fast he was remembering Erin's lithe form clad in silk and satin. Even better did he recall the wonderfully slippery *feel* of her glorious curves beneath his appreciative hands. Perspiration dampened his strong upper lip and he breathed in deep and slow, determined to master the near instantaneous response at his groin. Regrettably, he had never met another Erin, BUT then he had married soon afterwards and only in recent months had he again enjoyed the freedom of being single. He knew that a woman capable of matching his hunger and even of occasionally exhausting his high-voltage libido was a very rare find indeed. He reminded himself that it was very probably that same hunger that had led her to betray his trust and take another man into her bed. An unapologetic workaholic, he had left her alone for weeks while he was abroad on business and it was possible that he had invited the sordid conclusion that had ultimately finished their affair, he conceded grudgingly. Of course, had she agreed to travel with him it would never have happened but regrettably it had not occurred to him at the time that she might have excellent, if nefarious, reasons for preferring to stay in London.

He studied Sam Morton, whose body language and expression were uniquely revealing to any acute observer. The older man, who had to be comfortably into his sixties, could not hide his proprietorial protective attitude towards the svelte little manager of his health spas. His feelings shone out of his proud smile and the supportive arm he had welded to her spine in a declaration of possession. Cristo swore vehemently in Greek and examined the photo from all angles, but could see no room for any more innocent interpretation: she was at it again…bedding the boss! While it might have done him good to recognise Erin's continuing cunning at making the most of her feminine assets, it gave him no satisfaction at all to acknowledge that she was still happily playing the same tricks and profiting from them. He wondered if she was stealing from Morton as well.

Cristo had dumped Erin from a height when she let him down but the punishment had failed to soothe an incredulous bitterness that only increased when he had afterwards discovered that she had been ripping him off. He had had faith in Erin, he had trusted her, had even at one point begun to toy with the idea that she might make a reasonable wife. Walking into that bedroom and finding another man in the bed he had planned to share with her, along with the debris of discarded wine glasses and the trail of clothes that told its own sleazy story, had knocked him sideways. And what had he done next?

Lean, strong face rigid, Cristo grudgingly acknowledged his own biggest mistake. In the aftermath of his discovery that Erin had cheated on him, he had reached a decision that he was still paying for in spades. He had made a wrong move with long-term repercussions and for a male who almost never made mistakes that remained a very humbling truth. With hindsight he knew exactly why he had done, what he had done but he had yet to forgive himself for that fatal misstep and the fall-out those closest to him had suffered. Handsome mouth compressed into a tough line at that reflection, he studied Erin closely. She was still gorgeous and doubtless still happily engaged in confidently plotting and planning how best to feather her own nest while that poor sap at her elbow gave her his trust and worshipped the ground her dainty feet trod on.

But Cristo knew that he had the power to shift the very ground in an earthquake beneath those same feet because he very much doubted that the reputedly conservative and morally upright Sam Morton had any awareness of the freewheeling months that Erin had enjoyed in her guise as Cristo's mistress, or of the salient fact that at heart she was just a common little thief.

That bombshell had burst on Cristo only weeks after the end of their affair. An audit had found serious discrepancies in the books of the health spa Erin had been managing for him. Products worth a considerable amount of money had gone missing. Invoices had been falsified, freelance employees invented to receive pay cheques for non-existent work. Only Erin had had full access to that paperwork and a reliable long-term employee had admitted seeing her removing boxes of products from the store. Clearly on the take from the day that Cristo hired her, Erin had ripped off the spa to the tune of thousands of pounds. Why had he not prosecuted her for her thieving? He had been too proud to

parade the reality that he had taken a thief to his bed
and put a thief in a position of trust within his business.

Erin was a box of crafty tricks and no mistake, he
acknowledged bitterly. No doubt Morton was equally
unaware that his butter-wouldn't-melt-in-my-mouth employee played a very creditable game of strip poker. That
she had once met Cristo at the airport on his birthday
wearing nothing but her skin beneath her coat? And
that even the coat had gone within seconds of entering
his limousine? Did she cry out Morton's name and sob
in his arms when she reached a climax? Seduce him as
only a very sensual woman could while he tried to give
the business news his attention instead? Most probably
she did, for she had learned from Cristo exactly what
a man liked.

Disturbed that he still cherished such strong memories of that period of his life, Cristo poured himself a
whisky and regrouped, his shrewd brain swiftly cooling
the tenor of his angry reflections. The phrase, 'Don't get
mad, get even' might well adorn Cristo's gravestone, for
he refused to waste time on anything that didn't enrich
his life. So, Erin was still out there using her wits and
her body to climb the career and fortune ladder. How
was that news to him? And why was he assuming that
Sam Morton was too naïve to know that he had caught
a tiger by the tail? For many men the trade-off of as
much sex as a man could handle would be acceptable.

And Cristo registered in some surprise at his predict
ability that he was no different from that self-serving
libidinous majority. I could go there again, he thought
fiercely, his adrenalin pumping at the prospect of that
sexual challenge. I could really *enjoy* going there again.
She's wasted on an old man and far too devious to be

contained by a male with a conventional outlook. He began to read the file, discovering that Erin's wealthy employer was a widower. He could only assume that she had her ambition squarely centred on becoming the second Mrs Morton. Why else would a scheming gold-digger be working to ingratiate herself and earn a fairly humble crust? He was convinced that she would not have been able to resist the temptation of helping herself to funds from Sam Morton's spas as well.

Her healthy survival instincts and enduring cunning offended Cristo's sense of justice. Had he really believed that such a cool little schemer might turn over a new leaf in the aftermath of their affair? Had he ever been that naïve? Certainly, he had compared every woman he had ever had in his bed to Erin and found them all wanting in one way or another. That was a most disconcerting truth to accept. Clearly, he had never got her out of his system, he reflected grimly. Like a piece of baggage he couldn't shed, she had travelled on with him even when he believed that he was free of her malign influence. It was time that he finally stowed that excess baggage and moved on and how better to do that than by exorcising her from his psyche with one last sexual escapade?

He knew what Erin Turner was and he also knew that memory always lied. Memory would have embellished her image and polished her up to a degree that would not withstand the harsh light of reality. He needed to puncture the myth, explode the persistent fantasy and seeing her again in the flesh would accomplish that desirable conclusion most effectively. A hard smile slashed Cristo's handsome mouth as he imagined her dismay at his untimely reappearance in her life.

'Look before you leap,' his risk-adverse foster mother

had earnestly told him when he was a child, fearing his adventurous, rebellious nature and unable to comprehend the unimaginably entertaining attraction of taking a leap into the unknown. In spite of all his foster parents' efforts to tame his passionate temperament, however, Cristo's notoriously hot-blooded Donakis genes still ran true to form in his veins. His birth parents might not have survived to raise their son but he had inherited their volatile spirits in the cradle.

Without a second thought about the likelihood of consequences, indeed merely reacting to the insidious arousal and sense of challenge tugging at his every physical sense, Cristo lifted the phone. He informed the executive head of his acquisitions team that he would be taking over the next phase of the negotiations with the owner of the Stanwick Hall Hotel group.

'Well, what do you think?' Sam prompted, taken aback by Erin's unusual silence by his side. 'You needed a new car and here it is!'

Erin was still staring with a dropped jaw at the top-of-the-range silver BMW parked outside the garages for her examination. 'It's beautiful but—'

'But *nothing*!' Sam interrupted impatiently as if he had been awaiting an adverse comment and was keen to stifle it. Only marginally taller than Erin's five feet two inches, he was a trim man with a shock of white hair and bright blue eyes that burned with restive energy in his suntanned face. 'You do a big important job here at Stanwick and you need a car that suits the part—'

'Only not such an exclusive luxury model,' she protested awkwardly, wondering what on earth her colleagues would think if they saw her pulling up in a vehicle that undoubtedly cost more than she could earn in several years of employment. 'That's too much—'

'Only the best for my star employee,' Sam countered with cheerful unconcern. 'You're the one who taught me the importance of image in business and an economical runabout certainly doesn't cut the mustard.'

'I just can't accept it, Sam,' Erin told him uncomfortably.

'You don't have a choice,' her boss responded with immoveable good humour as he pressed a set of car keys into her reluctant hand. 'Your old Fiesta is gone. Thanks, Sam, is all you need to say.'

Erin grimaced down at the keys. 'Thanks, Sam, but it's too much—'

'Nothing's too good for you. Take a look at the balance sheets for the spas since you took over,' Sam advised her drily. 'Even according to that misery of an accountant I employ I'm coining it hand over fist. You're worth ten times what that car cost me, so let's hear no more about it.'

'Sam…' Erin sighed heavily and he filched the keys back from her to stride over to the BMW and unlock it with a flourish.

'Come on,' he urged. 'Take me for a test drive. I've got some time to kill before my big appointment this afternoon.'

'What big appointment?' she queried, shooting the sleek car into reverse and filtering it out through the arched entrance to the courtyard and down the drive past the immaculate gardens.

'I'm having another bash at the retirement thing,' her boss confided ruefully.

Erin suppressed a weary sigh. Sam Morton was al-

ways talking about selling his three country-house hotels, but she believed that it was more an idea that he
toyed with from time to time than an actual plan likely
to reach fruition. At sixty-two years of age, Sam still
put in very long hours of work. He was widowed more
than twenty years earlier and childless; his thriving hotel
group had become his life, consuming all his energy
and time.

Thirty minutes later, having dropped Sam off at his
golf club for lunch and gently refused his offer to join
him in favour of getting back to work, Erin walked back
into Stanwick Hall and entered the office of Sam's secretary, Janice, a dark-haired fashionably clad woman
in her forties.

'Have you seen the car?' she asked Janice with a self-
conscious wince.

'I went with him to the showroom to choose it—
didn't I do you proud?' the brunette teased.

'Didn't you try to dissuade him from buying such an
expensive model?' Erin asked in surprise.

'Right now, Sam's flush with the last quarter's profits
and keen to splurge. Buying you a new car was a good
excuse. I didn't waste my breath trying to argue with
him. When Sam makes up his mind about something
it's set in stone. Look at it as a bonus for all the new clients you've brought in since you reorganised the spas,'
Janice advised her. 'Anyway you must've noticed that
Sam is all over the place at the moment.'

Erin fell still by the other woman's desk with a frown.
'What do you mean?'

'His moods are unpredictable and he's very restless.
I honestly think that he's really intending to go for re-

tirement this time around and sell but it's a challenge for him to face up to it.'

Erin was stunned by that opinion for she had learned not to take Sam's talk of selling up seriously. Several potential buyers had come and gone unmourned during the two years she had worked at Stanwick Hall. Sam was always willing to discuss the possibility but had yet to go beyond that. 'You really think that? My word, are half of us likely to be standing in the dole queue this time next month?'

'Now that's a worry I *can* settle for you. The law safeguards employment for the staff in any change of ownership. I know that thanks to Sam checking it out,' Janice told her. 'As far as I know this is the first time he's gone that far through the process before.'

A slight figure in a dark brown trouser suit, silvery blonde hair gleaming at her nape in the sunlight, Erin sank heavily down into the chair by the window, equal amounts of relief and disbelief warring inside her, for experience had taught her never to take anything for granted. 'I honestly had no idea he was seriously considering selling this time.'

'Sam's sixtieth birthday hit him hard. He says he's at a turning point in his life. He's got his health and his wealth and now he wants the leisure to enjoy them,' Janice told her evenly. 'I can see where he's coming from. His whole life has revolved round this place for as long as I can remember.'

'Apart from the occasional game of golf, he has nothing else to occupy him,' Erin conceded ruefully.

'Watch your step, Erin. He's very fond of you,' Janice murmured, watching the younger woman very closely for her reaction. 'I always assumed that Sam looked on you as the daughter he never had but recently I've begun to wonder if his interest in you is quite so squeaky clean.'

Erin was discomfited by that frankly offered opinion from a woman whom she respected. She gazed steadily back at her and then suddenly helpless laughter was bubbling up in her throat. 'Janice…I just can't even begin to imagine Sam making a pass at me!'

'Listen to me,' the brunette urged impatiently. 'You're a beautiful woman and beautiful women rarely inspire purely platonic feelings in men. Sam's a lonely man and you're a good listener and a hard worker. He likes you and admires the way you've contrived to rebuild your life. Who's to say that that hasn't developed into a more personal interest?'

'Where on earth did you get the idea that Sam was interested in me in that way?' Erin demanded baldly.

'It's the way he looks at you sometimes, the way he takes advantage of any excuse to go and speak to you. The last time you were on leave he didn't know what to do with himself.'

Erin usually respected the worldly-wise Janice's opinions but on this particular issue she was convinced that the older woman had got it badly wrong. Erin was confident that she knew her boss inside out and would have noticed anything amiss. She was also mortified on Sam's behalf, for he was a very proper man with old-fashioned values, who would loathe the existence of such rumours on the staff grapevine. He had never flirted with Erin. Indeed he had never betrayed the smallest sign that he looked on Erin as anything other than a trusted and valued employee.

'I think you're wrong but I do hope that nobody else has the same suspicions about us.'

'That car will cause talk,' Janice warned her wryly. 'There's plenty people around here who will be happy to say that there's no fool like an old fool!'

Erin's face flamed. She was suddenly eager to bring the excruciating discussion to an end. She had grown extremely fond of Sam Morton and respected him as a self-made man with principles. Even talking about Sam as a man with the usual male appetites embarrassed her. Not only had the older man given her a chance to work for him when most people wouldn't have bothered, but he had also promoted and encouraged her ever since then. It was purely thanks to Sam that she had a decent career, a salary she could live on and good prospects. Only how good would those prospects be if Sam sold up and she got a new employer? A new owner would likely want to bring in his own staff and, even if he had to wait for the opportunity, she would not have the freedom to operate as she currently did. It was a sobering thought. Erin had heavy responsibilities on the home front and the mere thought of unemployment made her skin turn clammy and her tummy turn over sickeningly with dread.

'I'd better get on. Owen's interviewing therapists this afternoon,' Erin said ruefully. 'I don't want to keep him waiting.'

As Erin drove the sleek BMW several miles to reach the Black's Inn, the smallest property in Sam's portfolio—an elegant Georgian hotel, which incorporated a brand-new custom-built spa—she was thinking anxiously about how much money she had contrived to put by in savings in recent months. Not as much as she had hoped, certainly not nearly enough to cover her expenses in the event of job loss, she reflected worriedly. Unfortunately she could never forget the huge struggle she had had trying to get by on welfare benefits when her twins, Lorcan and Nuala, were newly born. Back then her mother, once so proud of her daughter's achievements, had been aghast at the mess Erin had made of her seemingly promising future. Erin had felt like a total failure and had worked out the exact moment that it had all gone belly up for her. It would have been great to have a terrific career *and* the guy of her dreams but possibly hoping for that winning combination had been downright greedy. In actuality she had fallen madly in love with the wrong guy and had taken her life apart to make it dovetail with his. All the lessons she had learned growing up had been forgotten, her ambitions put on hold, while she chased her dream lover.

And ever since then, Erin had been beating herself up for her mistakes. When she couldn't afford to buy something for the twins, when she had to listen in tolerant silence to her mother's regrets for the youthful freedom she had thrown away by becoming a single parent, she was painfully aware that she could only blame herself. She had precious little excuse for her foolishness and lack of foresight. After all, Erin had grown up in a poor home listening to her father talk endlessly and impressively about how he was going to make his fortune. Over and over and over again she had listened and the fortune had never come. Worse still, on many occasions money that could not be spared had been frittered away on crazy schemes and had dragged her family down into debt. By the time she was ten years old and watching her poorly educated mother work in a succession of dead-end jobs to keep her family solvent, she had realised that her father was just a dreamer, full of money-making ideas but lacking the work ethic required to bring any of those ideas to fruition. His vain belief that he was set on earth to shine as brightly as a star had precluded him from seeking an ordinary job. In any case working to increase someone else's profit had been what her idle father called 'a mug's game'. He had died in a train crash when she was twelve and from that point on life in her home had become less of a roller-coaster ride.

In short, Erin had learned at a young age that she needed to learn how best to keep herself and that it would be very risky to look to any man to take care of her. As a result, she had studied hard at school, ignored those who called her a nerd and gone on to university, also ignoring her mother's protestations that she should have moved straight into a job to earn a wage. Boyfriends had come and gone, mostly unremarked, for Erin had been wary of getting too involved, of compromising her ambitions to match someone else's. Having set her sights on a career with prospects, she had emerged from university with a top-flight business management degree. To help to finance her years as a student she had also worked every spare hour as a personal trainer, a vocation that had gained her a raft of more practical skills, not least on how best to please in a service industry.

Later that afternoon, when she returned from her visit to Black's Inn, the Stanwick receptionist informed Erin that Sam wanted to see her immediately. Realising in dismay that she had forgotten to switch her mobile phone back on after the interviews were finished, Erin knocked lightly on the door of her boss's office and walked straight in with the lack of ceremony that Sam preferred.

'Ah, Erin, at last. Where have you been all afternoon? There's someone here I want you to meet,' Sam informed her with just a hint of impatience.

'Sorry, I forgot to remind you that I'd be over at Black's doing interviews with Owen,' Erin explained, smiling apologetically until a movement by the window removed her attention from the older man. She turned her head and began to move forward, visually tracking the emergence of a tall powerful male from the shadows. Then she froze as though a glass wall had suddenly sprung into being around her, imprisoning her and shutting her off from her companions.

'Miss Turner?' a sleek cultured drawl with the suggestion of an accent purred. 'I've been looking forward to meeting you. Your boss speaks very highly of you.'

Erin flinched as though a thunderclap had sounded within the room without warning, that dark-timbred voice unleashing an instant 'fight or flight instinct she had to struggle to keep under control. She would have known that distinctive intonation laced with command had she heard it even at a crowded party. It was as unforgettable as the male himself.

'This is—' Sam began.

'Cristophe Donakis…' Cristo extended a lean brown hand to greet her as if they had never met before.

And Erin just stared in consternation at that wicked fallen-angel face as if she couldn't believe her eyes. And she *couldn't*. Cropped black hair spiky with the short curls that not even the closest cut could eradicate entirely, ebony brows level above stunning dark deep-set eyes that could turn as golden as the sunset, high cheekbones and, as though all the rest was not enough to over-endow him with beauty, a mouth that was the all-male sensual equivalent of pure temptation. The passage of time since their final encounter had left no physical mark on those lean dark features. In a split second it was as if she had turned her head and stepped back in time. He remained defiantly drop-dead gorgeous. Something low down in her body that she hadn't felt in years clenched tightly and uncomfortably, making her press her slender thighs together in dismay.

'Mr Donakis,' Erin pronounced woodenly, lifting her chin and very briefly touching his hand, determined to betray no reaction that Sam might question. Sam's 'big appointment' was with Cristo? She was horrified, fighting to conceal her reactions, could feel a soul-deep trembling begin somewhere in the region of her wobbly knees. That fast she was being bombarded by unwelcome images from their mutual past. Cristo grinning with triumph and punching the air when he finally beat her in a swimming race; Cristo serving her breakfast in bed when she was unwell and making a production of feeding her grapes one by one, long brown fingers caressing her lips at every opportunity, teaching her that no part of her was impervious to his touch. Cristo, sex personified night or day with an unashamedly one-track mind. He had taught her so much, *hurt* her so much she could hardly bear to look at him.

'Make it Cristo. I'm not a big fan of formality,' Cristo murmured levelly and even the air around him seemed cool as frost.

Just as suddenly Erin was angry, craving the power to knock him into the middle of next week for not being surprised by her appearance. Evidently he had known in advance that she worked for Sam and he was not prepared to own up to their previous relationship, which suited Erin perfectly. Indeed she was grateful that he had pretended she was a stranger, for she cringed at the idea of Sam and her colleagues learning what an idiot she had once been. One of Cristo Donakis' ex-girlfriends, *what*? That guy who changed women as he changed socks? *Really*? Inside her head she could already imagine the jeers and scornful amusement that that revelation would unleash, for Erin already knew that she had the reputation of being standoffish with the staff for keeping her private life private while others happily told all. Was Cristo the prospective buyer of Sam's hotels? For what other reason would he be visiting the Stanwick hotel? Cristo owned an international hotel and leisure empire.

'Erin…I'd like you to give Cristo a tour of our facilities here and at the other spas. His particular interest lies with them,' Sam told her equably. 'You can give him the most recent breakdown of figures. Believe me when I tell you that this girl has a mind like a computer for the important details.'

Erin went pink in receipt of that compliment.

'Looks *and* brains— I'm impressed,' Cristo pronounced with a slow smile that somehow contrived to freeze her to the marrow.

'You own the Donakis group,' Erin remarked tightly, trying to combat the shocked blankness of her mind with a shrewd take on what Cristo's source of interest could be in a trio of comparatively small hotels, which while luxurious could not seriously compare to the opulence of the elite Donakis hotel standards. 'I thought you specialised in city hotels.'

'My client base also enjoy country breaks. In any business there's always room for expansion in a new direction. I want to provide my clients with a choice of custom-made outlets so that they no longer have to patronise my competitors,' Cristo drawled smoothly.

'The beauty market is up-and-coming. What was once a treat for special occasions is now seen as a necessity by many women and by men as well,' Erin commented, earning an appreciative glance from her boss.

'You surprise me. I've never used a spa in my life,' Cristo proclaimed without hesitation.

'But your nails are filed and your brows are phenomenally well groomed,' Erin commented softly, earning a startled appraisal from Sam, who clearly feared that she was getting much too personal about his guest's grooming habits.

'You're very observant,' Cristo remarked silkily.

'Well, I have to be. One third of our customer base is male,' Erin fielded smoothly.

CHAPTER TWO

ERIN escorted Cristo to the fitness suite that connected with the spa.

'You *can't* buy Sam's hotels,' she said tightly in an undertone, the words framed by gritted teeth. 'I don't want to work for you again.'

'Believe me, I don't want you on my payroll either,' Cristo declared with succinct bite.

Well, she knew how she could take that. If he took over, she would be out in the cold as soon as the law allowed such a move and, appalling as the prospect of unemployment was, it was a welcome warning at a moment when she was feeling far too hot and bothered to think straight. What was it about Cristophe Donakis? That insidious power of his that got to her every time? Sheathed in a charcoal grey pinstripe suit, fitted to his lean powerful body with the flare that only perfect tailoring could offer, Cristo looked spectacular and, although she very much wanted to be, she was not indifferent to his high-voltage sexual charge. Cristo was a very beautiful man with the sleek dark good looks of a Greek god. As she turned to look at him, eyes as blank as she could make them, there was a lowdown buzz already feeding through her every limb like poison. She knew what that buzz was and feared it deeply. It was the burn of excitement, gut-deep, breathtaking *excitement*.

'I wasn't expecting to find a gym here,' Cristo remarked, eying the banks of machines and their sweating occupants, swivelling his handsome head to glance through the glass partition to where a couple of men were training with heavy weights. He returned his attention to her just as Erin slicked her tongue across her white teeth as if she was seeking to eradicate a stray smudge of lipstick. She wasn't wearing very much, just a hint of pale pearlised gloss that added unnecessary voluptuousness to the full swell of that sultry mouth, which he was working very hard not to imagine moving against his... Don't go there, his cool intelligence cautioned him, acting to suppress the kind of promptings that would interfere with his concentration.

'An exercise suite dovetails perfectly with the spa. The customers come here to train and attend classes, treat themselves to a massage or a beauty treatment and go home feeling spoiled and refreshed.' As Erin talked she led the way into the spa and gave him a brief look at those facilities that were free for his appraisal. 'People have less free time these days. It makes sense to offer a complete package at the right price. The profits speak for themselves.'

'So, how much are you creaming off in reward for your great moneymaking ideas?' Cristo enquired smoothly.

Her brow furrowed, amethyst eyes flickering in confusion across his strong bronzed face. 'I don't get commission for bringing in more business,' she responded uncertainly.

'That wasn't what I meant and you know it. I've seen

enough of the premises here. We'll move on to Blacks now and fit in the last place before dinner,' he told her arrogantly.

Cristo strode out to the front of the hotel and the silver Bugatti Veyron sports car that was his pride and joy. Erin followed more slowly, her agile brain struggling to work out what he had meant. 'I'll take my own car,' she called in his wake, crossing to the BMW. 'Then I can go home without needing a lift.'

Cristo wheeled back in his tracks, brilliant dark eyes gleaming between lush curling lashes. He was quick to note the premium model that she drove and he wondered with derision just how she afforded such a vehicle. 'No, I'll take you. We have business to discuss.'

Erin could think of nothing she wanted to discuss with him and she wanted him nowhere near the home she shared with her mother but, as Sam's right-hand woman, keeping Cristo happy was paramount. She wanted Cristo to vanish in a puff of black smoke like the fallen angel he resembled but she did not want Sam to lose out because she hadn't done her job right: she owed the older man too much for his faith in her and could not have looked him in the eye again if she scared off Cristo to suit her own personal preferences. Yet was she capable of scaring him off? There was an air of purpose about Cristo that said otherwise. To be fair, Sam's busy hotels would make a good investment. She pulled out her phone to ring Owen, the manager at Black's, to give him notice of their intended visit.

With pronounced reluctance she climbed into Cristo's boy-toy car, trying not to recall the time she had attended the Motor Show with him where the beautiful models draped over the latest luxury cars had salivated every time Cristo came within touching distance. Women always *always* noticed Cristo, ensnared by his six-foot-four-inch height and breadth and the intensity of dark eyes that could glitter like black diamonds.

Out of the corner of his gaze, Cristo watched her clasp her hands on her lap and instantly he knew she was on edge, composing herself into the little concentrated pool of calm and silence she invariably embraced when she was upset. She was so damn small, a perfect little package at five feet two inches calculated to appeal to the average testosterone-driven male as a vulnerable female in need of masculine protection. His shapely mouth took on a sardonic slant as he accelerated down the drive. She could look after herself. He had once enjoyed her independent streak, the fact she didn't always come when he called. Like most men he preferred a challenge to a clinging vine but he knew how tricky she could be and had no intention of forgetting it.

Erin wanted to keep her tongue pinned to the roof of her mouth but she couldn't. 'What you said back there—that phrase you used, "creaming off," —I didn't like the connotations—'

'I didn't think you would,' Cristo fielded softly, his dark accented drawl vibrating low in his throat.

Gooseflesh covered the backs of her hands and suddenly she felt chilled. 'Were you getting at something?'

'What do you think?'

'Don't play games with me,' she urged, breathing in deep and slow, nostrils flaring in dismay at the familiar spicy scent of his designer aftershave.

The smell of him, so familiar, so *achingly* familiar, unleashed a tide of memories. When he was away from her she used to sleep in one of his shirts but she would never have done anything so naff and revealing when he was around. Sometimes when she was at his city apartment she used to wash his shirts as well, she recalled numbly, eager to take on any little homely task that could made her feel more like one half of a committed couple. But Cristo had *not* made a commitment to her, had not done anything to make her feel secure and had never once mentioned love or the future. Recalling those hard facts, she wondered why she had once looked back on that phase as being the happiest of her life. Admittedly that year with Cristo had been the most exciting, varied and challenging of her twenty-five years of existence but the moments of happiness had often been fleeting and she had passed a great deal more time worrying about where their affair was going and never daring to ask. She had worked so hard at playing it cool with him, on not attaching strings or expectations that might irritate him. Her soft full mouth turned down at the recollection—much good all that anxious stressing and striving had done her! At the end of the day, in spite of all her precautions, he had still walked away untouched while she had been crushed in the process. She had had to accept that all along she had only been a Miss All-Right-For-Now on his terms, not a woman he was likely to stay with. No, she was just one more in a long line of women who had contrived to catch his eye and entertain him for a while until the time came for him to choose a suitable wife. The knowledge that she had meant so little to him that he had ditched her to marry another woman still burned like acid inside her.

'Maybe I'm hoping you'll finally come clean,' Cristo murmured levelly.

Erin turned her head, smooth brow indented with a

frown as she struggled to recall the conversation and get back into it again. 'Come clean about what?'

Cristo pulled off the road into a layby before he responded. 'I found out what you were up to while you were working for me at the Mobila spa.'

Erin twisted her entire body round to look at him, crystalline eyes flaring bright, her rising tension etched in the taut set of her heart-shaped face. 'What do you mean, what I was up to?'

Cristo flexed long brown fingers round the steering wheel and then turned to look at her levelly, ebony dark eyes cool and opaque as frosted glass. 'You were helping yourself to the profits in a variety of inventive ways but I employ a forensic accounting team, who have seen it all before, and they traced the transactions back to you. You were *stealing* from me.'

For a split second, Erin was pinned to the seat by the sheer weight of her incredulity and her eyes were huge. 'That's an outrageous and disgusting lie!' she slammed back at him, her voice rising half an octave with a volume stirred by simple shock.

'I have the proof and witnesses,' Cristo breathed in a tone of cutting finality that brooked no argument, igniting the engine again and filtering the car back onto the main road without batting an eyelash.

'You can't have proof and witnesses for something that never happened!' Erin launched at him furiously. 'I can't believe that you can accuse me of something like that—I've never stolen anything in my life!'

'You *stole* from me,' Cristo shot back at her with simmering emphasis, his bold bronzed profile hard as iron. 'You can't argue with hard evidence.'

Erin was stunned, not only by the accusation coming

so long after the event and out of nowhere at her, but by the rock-solid assurance of his conviction in her guilt.

'I don't care what evidence you think you've got. As it never happened, as I never helped myself to anything I wasn't entitled to, the evidence can only have been manufactured!'

'Nothing was manufactured. Face facts. You got greedy and you got caught,' Cristo asserted grittily. 'I'd have had you charged with theft if I'd known where to find you but by the time I found out you were long gone.'

Trembling with frustrated fury, every nerve jangling with adrenalin, Erin waited impatiently for him to park outside the nineteen-thirties black and white frontage of the Black's Inn hotel. Then she wrenched at the handle on the passenger door and leapt out. Cristo watched her through the windscreen, bleakly amused by the angry heat in her shaken face. She was shocked that he had found her out and not surprisingly frantic to convince him that she was as innocent as a newborn lamb of the charges. Naturally she wouldn't want him to label her a thief with her current employer. Even if she *had* resisted temptation this time around, mud stuck and no boss could have a faith in a member of staff with such a fatal weakness.

Slowly and with the easy moving fluidity of a natural athlete, Cristo climbed out of the car and locked it.

Erin's small hands clenched into fists at her side as she squared up to him. 'We're going to have this out!'

Infuriatingly in control, Cristo cast her a slumberous glance from below his ridiculously long lashes. 'Not a good idea in a public place—'

'We'll borrow Owen's office.' Erin stalked into the hotel and saw the lanky blond manager already on his way out to welcome them. She hurried over to him. 'We'll do the tour in ten minutes. Right now we need somewhere private to talk. Could we use your office?'

'Of course.' Owen spread the door wide and as she passed him smiled down at her and whispered, 'By the way, thanks for the heads-up.'

Cristo noticed that friendly little exchange but not its content and wondered at the precise nature of Erin's relationship with the handsome young manager. Generally she liked older men, Cristo reflected until he recalled the youth barely, if even, into his twenties that he had surprised in her hotel bed and his expressive mouth clenched hard. He recalled Sam Morton's gushing praise of his beautiful area manager and his derision rose even higher. He doubted that he'd ever met a man more in a woman's thrall. Sam thought the sun, the moon and the stars rose on Erin Turner.

Erin closed the door on Cristo's entry and spun back to him, amethyst eyes dark with anger. 'I am not a thief, so naturally I want to know exactly why you're making these allegations.'

He studied her with narrowed eyes. She was breathing fast, her silky top sliding tantalisingly against the rounded bulge of her breasts. Creamy lickable mounds topped by succulent strawberry nipples, he remembered lasciviously, his desire firing at that imagery as a bolt of lust shot through him in a flash, leaving him hard as a rock. What she lacked in height she more than made up for with wonderfully feminine curves. He had loved her body. Even worse, he had dreamt of her passion when he was away from her, craving the unparalleled sexual satisfaction he had yet to find with anyone else.

'I'm not an idiot,' Cristo informed her coldly, forcing

his keen mind back to a safer pathway. 'At the Mobila spa, you sold products out of the beauty store on your own behalf, falsified invoices and paid therapists who didn't exist. Your fraudulent acts netted you something in the region of twenty grand in a comparatively short time frame. How could you think that that level of deceit would go unnoticed?'

'I am not a thief,' Erin repeated doggedly although an alarm bell had gone off in her head the instant he mentioned the theft and sale of products from the store.

She knew someone who had done that for she herself had actually caught the woman putting a box of products into her car. Sally, her administrative assistant in the office, whom she had relied on heavily at the time, had been stealing and selling the exclusive items online. Unfortunately Erin had no proof of that fact because she had neither called in the police to handle the matter nor shared the truth that Sally had been stealing with another member of staff. Instead she had sat a distraught Sally down to talk to her. Together the two women had then done a stocktake and Erin had ended up replacing the missing products out of her own pocket. Why? She had felt desperately sorry for the older woman, struggling to cope alone with two autistic children after her husband had walked out on her. But had she only scraped the tip of the iceberg when it came to Sally's dishonesty? Had Sally even then been engaged in rather more imaginative methods of gaining money by duplicitous means?

'I have the proof,' Cristo retorted crisply.

'And witnesses, you said,' Erin recalled. 'Would one of those witnesses be Sally Jennings?'

His lean strong face tightened and she knew she had

hit a nerve. 'You can't talk or charm your way out of this, Erin—'

'I'm not interested in charming you. I'm not the same woman I was when we were together,' Erin countered curtly, for what he had done to her had toughened her. There was nothing like surviving an unhappy love affair to build self-knowledge and character, she reckoned painfully. He had broken her heart, taught her how fragile she was, left her bitter and humiliated. But she had had to pick herself up again fast once she discovered that she was pregnant. Choice and self-pity hadn't come into that challenging equation.

Erin stared back at him, pale amethyst eyes searching his darkly handsome features, blocking her instinctive response to that beautiful bone structure. Had he truly not read a single one of her letters? What had happened to human curiosity? Her phone calls had gone unanswered and his PA had told her she was wasting her time phoning because Cristo wouldn't accept a call from her. Even when she had got desperate enough to call his family home in Greece she had run into a brick wall erected by his spiteful foster mother, who had proudly told her that Cristo was getting married and wanted nothing more to do with, 'a woman like her'. As if she were some trollop Cristo had picked up in the street for a night of sex, rather than the woman who had been his constant companion for a year.

Although, perhaps it hadn't been his foster mother's fault. After all, while she might have seen herself in the light of a serious relationship, it was clear that Cristo had seen her entirely differently. He had never let her meet his family and, even though he'd known that she wanted him to meet her mother, he had found it inconvenient every time she'd tried to set up even a casual encounter. She might have been part of his private life but he had walled her off from everyone else in it, for she had only occasionally met his friends and never again after the evening when one of his mates had made a point of commenting on how long he had been with Erin.

'I think you'll change your tune once you appreciate how few choices you have,' Cristo responded softly. 'Now let's view the facilities here. I have a tight schedule.'

Her mouth tightening, she followed him out of the office. How did he expect her to change her tune? Certainly, he hadn't listened to a word she'd said. Had Sally Jennings lied about her? What else could she think? Had her abrupt departure from her job at the Mobila spa played right into the older woman's hands when the irregularities were exposed by the accounting team? Change her tune? What had he meant by that comment? Her brain engaged in working out what she could possibly do to combat such allegations, Erin realised that she would have to see the evidence he had mentioned to work out her own defence and how to nail the real culprit. Had she been a total idiot to let Sally off the hook when she caught her stealing? She was appalled that her sympathetic and supportive treatment of the older woman might have been repaid with lies calculated to make Erin look guilty in her place. Confronting Sally, appealing to her conscience—if she had one—might well be the only course she could take. But what had Cristo meant about choices?

Owen brimmed with enthusiasm as he showed them round the spa, describing the latest improvements and special offers as well as the upsurge in custom that had resulted. He finished by offering them coffee but Cristo demurred, pleading time constraints as he whisked Erin back out to the car and angled it back out onto the road to make their last call. Brackens was Sam's most exclusive property. A Victorian house set in wooded surroundings, it was very popular with couples in search of a romantic weekend and the spa was run as a member's only club.

Erin watched Mia, the elegant brunette in her thirties who managed Brackens, melt at Cristo's first smile and allowed the knowledgeable manager to do most of the talking as she showed them round her impressive domain. Erin was struggling to concentrate on the job at hand. There was too much else on her bemused mind. So, for almost three years, Cristo had been under the impression that she had stolen a fat wad of cash from him. Why hadn't he contacted her? Why had he virtually let it go instead of informing the police? Cristo never let people get away with doing the dirty on him. He was a man few would wish to cross but he did reward loyal, hardworking staff with generous bonuses and opportunities.

Watching Mia laugh flirtatiously with Cristo made Erin feel slightly nauseous. She could recall when she had been even more impressionable. One glance at that lean dark face of sharp angles and creative hollows and those stunning black diamond eyes and she had been enamoured, her interest caught, her body humming with unfamiliar thrills. Her wariness with men, her long hours of study while others partied, had made her more than usually vulnerable for a young woman of twenty-one. She slammed down hard on the memory, award-

ing Cristo a veiled glance when he ushered her back
to his Bugatti with a fleeting remark on her quietness.

'May I go home now?' she enquired as he turned
the sports car.

'We're having dinner together at my hotel,' Cristo
informed her. 'We have things to talk about.'

'I have nothing to talk to you about. Sam does his
own negotiating,' Erin volunteered drily. 'I'm just the
hired help.'

'If rumour is to be believed, you're not *just* anything
when it comes to Sam Morton.'

Erin went rigid in the passenger seat at the suggestion. 'Do you listen to rumours?'

'You slept with me while I was employing you,'
Cristo reminded her without heat.

Her teeth ground together. For two pins she would
have slapped him. 'That's different. We were already
involved when I began working for you.'

Cristo compressed his beautifully shaped mouth, his
thoughts taking him back even though he didn't want
to go there. He had never had to work so hard to get a
woman into bed. Her elusiveness, her surprising inhi-
bitions had heightened his desire, persuaded him that
she was different. Yes, she *had* been different, she had
lined her pockets at his expense throughout their affair,
he recalled grimly. She had taken him for a fool just as
she was taking Morton.

'Sam and I are only friends—'

His eloquent mouth quirked. 'The same sort of
friendship you had with that other friend of yours, Tom?'

Erin stiffened, remembering how suspicious Cristo
had become of her fondness for Tom's company towards

the end of their affair. 'Not as familiar. Sam's from a different generation.'

Tom was a mate from her university days, more like a brother than anything else and still an appreciated part of Erin's life. Unfortunately Cristo didn't believe that platonic friendships could exist and Erin had eventually given up trying to convince him otherwise, reasoning that she was entitled to her own friends regardless of his opinions.

'Morton's old enough to be your grandfather—'

'Which is why there's nothing else between us,' Erin slotted in flatly. 'I'm not sleeping with Sam.'

'He's besotted with you. I don't believe you,' Cristo framed succinctly.

'That's your prerogative.' Erin dug out her mobile phone and tapped out her home number.

Her mother answered. In the background she could hear a child crying. Lorcan, she guessed. Her son sounded tired and cross and her heart clenched, for she felt guilty that she couldn't be there with him. It hurt that she got to spend so little time with her children during the week and she cherished her weekends with the twins when she tried to make up for her absence during working hours.

'I'm sorry but I'll be late home tonight,' she told Deidre Turner.

'Why? What are you doing?' the older woman asked.

'I have some work to deal with before I can leave.'

Tight-lipped and knowing she still had a maternal interrogation to face, Erin put her phone back in her bag. The very last thing she could afford to tell her parent was that Cristo had reappeared in her life. She would never hear the end of it, much as she had yet to hear the end of the reproaches about bringing two children into the world without first having acquired a wedding ring on her finger. But she didn't blame her mother for her attitude. Educated in a convent school by nuns and deeply devout, Deidre had somewhat rigid views. At the same time, however, she was a very loving and caring grandmother and Erin could not have coped as a single parent without the older woman's support.

'I still don't know what this is about,' Erin complained as Cristo parked outside the foremost hotel in the area. 'I didn't steal from you three years ago but until you give me more facts I can't defend myself.'

'One of the transactions was traced right back to your bank account. Don't waste your time trying to plead innocence,' Cristo shot back at her very drily.

'I don't want to have dinner with you. It's not like we parted on good terms,' Erin reminded him doggedly.

Cristo climbed gracefully out of the car. 'It's like this. Either you dine with me and we talk or I go straight to your boss with my file on your thefts.'

He spoke so levelly, so unemotionally that for several taut seconds Erin could not quite accept that he had threatened her without turning a hair. The blood drained from below her fair skin and she froze until she recognised that he had given her a choice. She could tell him to take his precious file of supposed evidence and put it where the sun didn't shine. She could call his bluff. But, unhappily for her, she *knew* Cristophe Donakis and she knew what he was capable of.

He didn't bluff and he was very determined. He would push to the limits and beyond to gain a desired result. He was tough, sufficiently volatile to be downright dangerous and a merciless enemy. If Cristo truly believed that she had stolen from him, he would not settle until he had punished her for her offence.

For the first time in a very long time, Erin felt utterly helpless. She had too much at stake to risk her children's future. She had worked very hard to get to where she was and she would fight just as hard to retain it…

CHAPTER THREE

ERIN walked into the cloakroom of the hotel and ran
her wrists below the cold water tap until the panicked
thump of her heartbeat seemed to slow to a tolerable
level. Get a grip on yourself, she told her tense reflection as she dried her hands. Why should Cristo come
back into her life now and try to wreck it? On his part
it would be a pointless exercise...

Unless he *was* after revenge. At the vanity counter
she tidied her hair and noticed with annoyance that her
hands were no longer steady. He had already contrived
to wind her up like a clockwork toy, firing all her self-
defence mechanisms into override. And she needed to
watch out because panic would make her stupid and
careless. She breathed in slow and deep, fighting to stay
calm. He didn't know about the children so evidently he
had not read a single one of her letters. Had he known
about the twins he would have left her in peace, she
was convinced of it. What man went out of his way to
dig up trouble?

Cristo did, a little voice piped up warningly at the
back of her head, and all of a sudden time was taking
her back to their first encounter.

At the time Erin was employed in her first job as a

deputy manager at a council leisure centre. Elaine, one of her university friends, was from a wealthy home and her father had bought her an apartment in an exclusive building. When Elaine realised what a struggle Erin was having trying to find decent accommodation on a budget, she had offered Erin her box room, a space barely large enough for a single bed with storage beneath. But Erin hadn't cared how small the room was, she had enjoyed having Elaine's company, not to mention daily access to the residents' fancy leisure complex on the ground floor.

Erin had always been a keen swimmer and had won so many trophies for her school that she could have aspired to an athletic career had her parents been of a different ilk. Regretfully, in spite of her coach's efforts at persuasion, Erin's parents had been unwilling to commit to the time and cost of supporting a serious training schedule for their talented daughter. However, Erin still loved the sport and swam as often as she could.

The first time she had seen Cristo he had been scything up and down the pool with the sleek flow of a shark. His technique had been lazy, his speed moderate, she had noted, overtaking him without effort as she pursued her usual vigorous workout.

'Race me!' he had challenged when he caught up with her.

And she still recalled those dark deep-set gorgeous eyes, gleaming like polished bronze, electrifying in his lean, darkly handsome features.

'I'll beat you,' she warned him ruefully. 'Can you take that?'

The dark golden eyes had flashed as though she had lit a fire inside him. 'Bring it on...' he had urged.

And just like him, she had loved the challenge, skimming through the water with the firing power of a bullet, beating him to the finish line and turning to cherish his look of disbelief. Afterwards she had hauled herself out of the water and he had followed suit, straightening his lean powerful length to tower over her diminutive frame, water streaming down over his six-pack abs, drawing her attention to his superb muscular development. It was possibly the very first time that she had ever *seriously* noticed a man's body.

'You're tiny. How the hell did you beat me?' he demanded incredulously.

'I'm a good swimmer.'

'We have to have a retrial, *koukla mou*.'

'OK, same time Wednesday night but I warn you I train every day and your technique is sloppy—'

'Sloppy…' Cristo repeated in accented disbelief, an ebony brow quirking. 'If I wasn't tired, I'd have beaten you hollow!'

Erin laughed. 'Sure you would,' she agreed peaceably, knowing what the male ego was like.

He extended a lean brown hand. 'I'm Cristophe Donakis…I'll see you Wednesday and I'll whip your hide.'

'I don't think so,' she told him cheerfully.

'Cristophe Donakis? You met Cristophe in the residents' pool where us ordinary people swim?' Elaine later gasped in consternation. 'What on earth was he doing there? He owns the penthouse and he has a private pool on the roof.'

'Well, he was slumming this evening. Who is he?'

'A spoilt rotten Greek tycoon and playboy with pots of money and a different woman on the go every week. I've seen him taking them up there in the lift. He's very fond of decorative beauties. Stay clear. He'd gobble you up like a mid-morning snack,' Elaine warned her drily.

But that same night the recollection of Cristo's flawless male perfection got Erin all hot and bothered in her dreams and she marvelled that he could have that effect on her, for her strict upbringing had made her reserved and wary about all things sexual. Even at a glance she had recognised that Cristophe Donakis was a very sexual animal. On the Wednesday she beat him a second time, albeit with a little more effort on her part.

'Join me for a drink,' he suggested afterwards, his hungry gaze wandering at leisure over her slim curves in the plain black and red suit she wore, rising to linger on her soft full mouth, the sexual charge of his interest blatant and bringing self-conscious colour to her cheeks.

'No, thanks.' Fear of getting out of her depth and of somehow making a fool of herself made Erin especially cautious

'A rematch, then…third time lucky?' he prompted, amusement dancing in his stunning eyes below the fringe of black curling lashes.

'My flatmate tells me you have your own pool.'

'It's in the process of being replaced. Rematch?' he pressed again, pure challenge gleaming in those bronzed eyes. 'The next time the loser buys dinner. Give me your phone number and we'll arrange a date for it. I'm about to leave for the US for a week.'

She admired his persistence and had never been able to resist a dare. The third time he beat her, punching the air with uninhibited triumph. And that was also the moment she fell for Cristo, loving the naturally dramatic streak that he kept concealed below the surface in favour of cool assurance and the gloriously wicked grin that could burnish his hard dark features with adorably boyish enthusiasm.

She fed him in an American-style diner down the street in the sort of basic unsophisticated setting that she could tell was unfamiliar to him, but he proved a good sport and an entertaining raconteur, who drew her out about her job and her ambitions. He assumed that she would accompany him back to his apartment after the meal, looked at her in frank surprise when she refused, for he was very much a male accustomed to easy conquests. After that rebuff it took him two whole weeks to phone her again.

'He'll hurt you,' Elaine forecast. 'He's too handsome, too rich, too arrogant. You're very down to earth. What have you got in common with a guy like that?'

And the answer was…*nothing*. But like a moth drawn to a candle flame she had refused to acknowledge the obvious and eventually she had got burned, badly enough burned to avoid getting involved ever since. From time to time other men had made a play for her but she had resisted, reluctant to entertain such a complication in her life. In any case living under the same roof as her mother was almost as good as wearing a chastity belt, she reflected with sheepish amusement.

Cristo was already seated in the elegant restaurant. He levered upright as she approached, his keen dark gaze welded to her delicate features. She looked like an angel, fragile, pure, amethyst eyes luminous as jewels in her heart-shaped face. He noticed the other men following her progress and the seductive image of her spread across his silk sheets flashed through his head, instantly hardening him. He marvelled at the effect she had on him even though he knew that she was both dishonest and untrustworthy, a thoughtless, foolish little slut below the patina of that perfection. No truly clever woman would have tossed him and what he could buy her away for the cheap thrill of a casual encounter and what he considered to be a paltry sum of money.

Erin felt the heat of his appraisal and flushed, her spine stiffening, her bone structure tightening as she exerted fierce self-discipline. Willing herself not to react, she sat down and immediately lifted the menu to peruse it. She picked a single course, told him that she didn't want any wine and sat as straight as a child told to sit properly at table.

'So, tell me what you want and get it over with,' she suggested, eager to take charge of the conversation rather than sit there quailing like a victim.

His dark golden eyes rested on the hands she had clasped together on the table top and his beautiful mouth took on a sardonic twist. 'I want you,' he countered levelly.

Her smooth brow indented. 'In what way?'

Cristo laughed, raw amusement lightening his stunning eyes to a shade somewhere between amber and honey. 'In the most obvious way that a man wants a woman.'

But she couldn't credit that, for hadn't he ditched her and moved on to marry an exceptionally beautiful Greek woman, a socialite called Lisandra, within weeks of their split? She hadn't been able to hold him then, hadn't been important enough to him to retain his interest. He had moved on with his life without her at breathtaking speed. Now he was divorced and it was mean of her to reflect that his marriage had barely lasted long enough for the ink to dry on the licence. Maybe he had got bored with his wife and being married in the same way that he had got bored with Erin. Maybe he didn't have what it took to really *care* about any woman.

'That's the price of my silence,' Cristo drawled smooth as silk.

Blackmail? Erin was shocked, so shocked that her teeth settled into the soft underside of her lower lip and she tasted the faint coppery tang of blood in her mouth. 'The silence relating to this supposed thieving you believe me to be guilty of—'

'*Know* you to be guilty of,' Cristo traded.

'You can't possibly be serious,' Erin breathed tightly.

Lean bronzed face radiating raw assurance, Cristo ran a lean brown forefinger down over the back of her hand and every skin cell in her body leapt into tingling awareness. 'Why would you think that? We had a very good time between the sheets.'

Assailed by unwelcome memories, Erin went rigid but that fast, still shockingly attuned to a certain dark intimate note in his deep drawl, her body reacted. Inside her bra, her breasts swelled, her nipples tightening into prominent points, and her breath rasped in her tight throat. She blinked, lashes lowering, shutting out the hot dark golden gaze pinned to her. He could still get to her and that shocked her but was it so surprising? She had lived like a nun since her children were born, grateful just to have a job and a roof over her head in the wake of the struggle to survive while she was pregnant and unemployed. *A good time.* That phrase cheapened her, made light of what she had once believed they had shared. Was a good time all she had been? Or was the very fact that he was back in her life, trying to force her to give him her time and her body again, proof that she had actually meant something more to him? It was a heady suspicion. Not that she still cared about him, she reflected, but like any woman she had her pride.

'So what are you suggesting?' Erin queried, resolving to play him along for a while until she better understood her position. 'Are you asking me to come back to you?'

'*Na pas sto dialo*...go to hell!' Cristo growled, incredulity flashing across his spectacular bone structure at that explosive suggestion. 'I'm talking about one weekend.'

Her delicate face froze tight. She felt the painful sting of that contempt right down to her marrow bone and inwardly swore that somehow, some way, some day he would pay for insulting her like that. Had the waiter not arrived with their meals she could not have trusted herself not to say something unwise. Forced to hold her tongue, she studied her plate fixedly, her hackles raised, bitterness poisoning her. How dared he? How dared he treat her like some hooker he could rent for an hour or two?

'A dirty weekend,' she framed through compressed lips. 'That does fit your MO.'

Those lustrous amber eyes shimmered below his thick sooty lashes, the leashed power of his strong personality and masculine virility creating an aggressive aura. Another punch of awareness slid through her. It was like poking a tiger through the bars of a cage and shockingly exciting, a welcome respite from the hard little knot of humiliation he had inflicted.

'One weekend in return for my silence and the twenty grand you stole...cheap at the price,' Cristo quipped cool as ice.

Erin wanted to thump him for that crack and restraining that natural urge made her slender hands clench into fists where she had placed them on her lap, out of view of his shrewd notice. The only way to play it with Cristo was cool. If she lost her temper she was lost and he would walk all over her.

'Stop playing the ice goddess. That may be a turn on for Morton but it doesn't rev my engine at all,' Cristo informed her drily. 'One weekend—that's the deal on the table—'

'Was this whole thing a set-up? Have you no intention of buying Sam out?' Erin pressed shakily.

'That is a question for me and my acquisitions team to decide. If it's a good investment your presence on the staff will not deter me, although obviously I'd be bringing back the forensic accounting team to run a check on your activities.'

Her chin came up. 'They'll find nothing because I have done nothing dishonest. Neither at Sam's company nor at yours. Furthermore I will not accept blackmail.'

'I think you'll end up eating those words,' Cristo forecast gently, spearing a chunk of succulent steak, primal male to the bone in his unspoilt appetite.

'You have to show me the evidence you say you have before I can make any kind of a decision.'

'After we've eaten. It's in my suite,' he responded equably.

His easy acquiescence on that score shook Erin. Clearly he was confident about the proof he had of her deceit. But, dismayed though she was by that suspicion, she brought her chin up, amethyst eyes glinting with challenge. 'We'll see.'

And she ate even though she wasn't hungry, for to push her food round her plate and leave it virtually untouched would only highlight the reality that she was sick with nerves.

'I have to go home for a week,' Cristo told her smoothly. 'My foster father's company is in trouble and he needs my advice. You must be aware of the state of the Greek economy.'

Erin nodded grudgingly. 'Aren't you suffering from the same effects?'

'My businesses are primarily here and in North America. I saw the way things were going a couple of years back but Vasos is stubborn. He dislikes change and he wouldn't listen to me when I tried to warn him.'

'And you are telling me this...*because*?'

'To help you to pen that weekend slot into your no doubt busy social calendar.'

Her teeth gritted behind her closed lips, her aggrieved sense of outrage building higher. He was so confident of winning that it was an affront. For a split second she was tempted to tell him that two young children took a heavy toll on what free time she had, but common sense kept her quiet, not to mention pride. She did not want him to know that a night out for her these days would most likely encompass a trip to the cinema or a modest meal with friends.

'So what is the state of play with Morton?' Cristo enquired quietly.

As Cristo was rarely quiet, she glanced up suspiciously. 'My relationship with Sam is none of your business.'

'I'm divorced,' he murmured flatly.

Erin shrugged a slim shoulder as if the information meant nothing to her. 'I read about it in the papers. Your marriage didn't last very long.'

He frowned, black brows drawing together. 'Long enough.'

And as his darkly handsome features shadowed and hardened Erin made a discovery that stung her. His broken marriage was still a source of discomfort to him. She sensed his regret and his reserve and the latter was nothing new. Cristo had always played his cards close to his chest, keeping his feelings under cover, and he had played it that way right to the end of their affair when he had told her it had run its course without drama or remorse. The recollection stiffened her backbone because she had been so shocked and unprepared for that development. This time around, she knew who and what she was dealing with: if he wanted a fight, one way or another, she would give him one!

They travelled up in the lift in a tense silence. She could not credit the situation she found herself in. Was she to be the equivalent of a rebound affair in the wake of his divorce? It occurred to her that a sleazy one-off weekend scarcely qualified for that lofty description and mortified pink highlighted her cheeks. Cristo studied her, picturing her silver gilt hair loose, a party dress to replace the business suit, high heels to show off those shapely legs. His body quickened to the image and was swiftly encouraged by far more X-rated images from the past. When he had her in his bed again, she would disappoint him, of course she would. It would not be as good as he remembered, he told himself urgently. That was the whole point of the game, that and, of course, a well-deserved dose of retribution. She had changed though. Those amethyst eyes no longer telegraphed every reaction making her easily read and she was more controlled than he recalled. Once she saw that he had definitive evidence of her thefts, she would surely study to please…

Erin had not quite bargained on the silent isolation of a hotel suite and she hovered in the centre of the reception room, having refused a drink. She watched him stride into the bedroom to retrieve whatever he was after, that long, lean, powerful body that had once haunted her dreams and ensured that other men could not compare so graceful in movement that she compressed her lips into a tight line, infuriated by the fact that she had noticed. But Cristo was a very noticeable guy. Every female head turned when he walked by and their attention lingered. But, Elaine had been right about him, he was a predator to the backbone and she was now simply a target with an X marked on her back. She wondered what his wife had done to him. Did Cristo have a score to settle against the female sex? And why, after almost three years had passed, was she on the menu again?

Cristo extended a file. 'Go ahead and take a look.'

Once again his self-assurance ignited her anxiety level. She took the file over to a sofa and sat down, determined not to be hurried or harassed. There were copies of many documents she had signed off while she worked for him, payments to suppliers and therapists, invoices attached to other copies that differed to show altered figures on the base lines. Her heart sank like lead in her chest and she felt as though someone were sitting on her lungs. It was very comprehensive stuff and shatteringly straightforward in its presentation.

Her knees developed an irritating tremor below the file on her lap but she still fought for a clear head. 'And

according to your investigation these particular therapists didn't exist?'

'You know they didn't,' Cristo responded flatly.

Erin came to the final document and stared down
at the evidence of a single large payment of a thousand pounds heading into a bank account in her name
and nausea stirred in her stomach. Had she ever bothered to close that old bank account? She had intended
to but couldn't remember. Only one payment but one
was enough to damn her. In her opinion only Sally
Jennings could be responsible for such duplicity. She
had pretty much automatically signed anything that the
older woman put on her desk. With hindsight she knew
she had been too trusting. Unhappily managing the spa
had been her first serious job and she had had no deputy
to stand in for her when Cristo wanted her to make time
for him. Torn between too much work, hostile staff, who
loathed working for the owner's girlfriend, and a deep
driving desire to impress Cristo with her efficiency, she
had relied a lot on Sally, who had worked at the spa since
it had opened ten years earlier and knew the business
inside out. No such thing as a free ride, Erin told herself heavily now. Even Sam would doubt her innocence
in the face of such damning proof as the file contained.

Erin stood up and dropped the file down with a dis-
tasteful clunk of dismissal on the coffee table. 'Very
impressive, but I didn't *do* it! You gave me a great opportunity when you put me in that job and I wouldn't
have gone behind your back to steal from you.'

Cristo continued to stare at her, eyes like chips of
bright gold below his luxuriant lashes, and all of a sudden she was struggling to breathe evenly and something
inside her seemed to speed up as if her blood were rac-

ing through her veins and the buzz of forbidden excitement in the pit of her tummy were spreading like contagion to her entire body.

'You still want me, *koukla mou*,' Cristo purred, revelling in the charge in the atmosphere, the awareness in her clear gaze. It was the first time he had been able to read her again and it satisfied him.

'No! That is absolutely not true!' Erin shot back at him vehemently, wishing she had not asked to see that evidence in his presence as she recognised how much it had unnerved her and damaged her self-discipline. Now she was all shaken and stirred, a state to be avoided in a predator's radius.

Cristo reached out a hand and curled his fingers around her slender wrist, edging her out from behind the table. The storm of reaction inside her rose to hurricane force, suppressing her caution and defensiveness.

'No…' she said in a small choked voice, fighting just to get air back into her lungs.

Nevertheless he drew her close, banding strong arms round her like a prison, and the heat and strength of him acted like an aphrodisiac on her disturbed senses. She tried to keep distance between them, her slender body rigid as a rock, but he closed the gap with inexorable purpose.

'It's OK,' he rasped in the most frighteningly soothing tone. 'I want you too.'

And Erin did not want to hear that from the male who had dumped her and gone straight off to marry another woman. He had never wanted her enough to love her or keep her and that was the only wanting she had ever needed from him. He meant sex, only sex, she told herself feverishly while the reassuring warmth of him filtered through their clothing to warm her chilled limbs. But far more insidious was the insanely familiar smell of him that close, her nostrils flaring on the faint aroma of the same designer cologne he had always worn, never forgotten, and she was breathing him headily in as though he were a forbidden drug.

'Stop it, Cristo!' she told him tartly. 'I am not going there again. I am never going there again with you!'

'We'll see…' And, golden eyes blazing down at the fiercely conflicted expression on her heart-shaped face, his beautiful mouth swooped down on hers to claim the kiss she would have done almost anything to deny him.

And the taste of him was instantly addictive even as her hands swept up to strike in fists against his broad shoulders while he hauled her closer. Hot, hungry need roared through her in a storm that made her knees shake and she didn't know whether it was her or him behind it, or if, indeed, both of them were equally responsible. His tongue delved and she shuddered, so awake and defenceless against his every seductive move that it hurt, hurt to feel anything so strongly after so long without it. She wanted that kiss then with a sudden ferocity that terrified her. Nothing else mattered but the forceful power of that lean strong body against her own, the pulsing prominence of her nipples and the liquid burn between her thighs driving her on. His mouth bore down on hers with a seething, sizzling urgency that zinged through her slight length like an electric shock, stunning every sense into reaction. Nothing had ever tasted so good, nothing had ever felt so necessary and answering the shrill shriek of warning firing at the back of her brain took every atom of her inner strength.

'No!' she said in fierce rebuttal, thrusting him away

from her with an abruptness that almost made him lose that famous catlike balance of his as he backed into a chair.

In a daze, Cristo blinked. She packed a punch like a world-class boxer. He shook his handsome dark head, dark eyes instantly veiling as he fought the bite of unsated hunger clawing through his big powerful frame. 'You're right…this is not the moment. I have a flight to catch,' he retorted thickly.

Erin's breasts heaved as she frantically breathed in deep in an effort to emulate his fast recovery. Her amethyst eyes were dark with strong emotion as she studied his lean, darkly handsome features with a loathing she couldn't hide. 'I meant no as in *never*,' she contradicted shakily. 'Leave me alone, stay out of my life and stop threatening me.'

His black diamond eyes flared brilliant gold again, for there was nothing in life that Cristo enjoyed so much as a challenge. 'I won't go away.'

'You're going to get burned if you keep pushing me,' Erin warned him angrily, her small face set like a stone, all emotion but anger repressed. 'Get back out of my life or you'll regret it.'

'No, I won't. I rarely regret anything that I do,' Cristo fielded, visibly savouring the admission. 'Are you worried that I'll screw up your future with Morton? Sorry, *koukla mou*. I'll be doing him a favour. You're toxic.'

Her hands clenched into tight fists. 'I think you'll feel the toxic effect more strongly by the time this is over.'

Cristo shot her a grimly amused appraisal. 'I could handle you with one hand tied behind my back.'

'You always did like to believe your own publicity,' Erin countered tightly, her spine as straight as an arrow as she walked to the door. 'I'll catch a taxi back to Stanwick.'

In the lift, she had what felt like a panic attack, her heart beating too fast for comfort, cold clamminess filming her skin. That kiss? Total dynamite! How could that be? How had that happened? She was not in love with him any more, had believed she was fully cured of all that foolishness…until the instant she laid eyes on him again and his mesmerising attraction gripped her as tightly as steel handcuffs.

Maybe she'd succumbed to that kiss because she had been upset after reading that file. Is that the best excuse you can find? a little voice sneered inside her brain. She reddened, hating herself almost as much as she now hated him. Her response to him had qualified as weak and that was something she could not accept.

CHAPTER FOUR

In the early hours of the following morning, Erin rocked her son, Lorcan, on her lap. A nightmare had wakened him and it always took a while to comfort him and soothe him back to sleep.

'Mum…' he framed drowsily, fixing big dark eyes on her as she smoothed his short tousled curls back from his brow, lashes lowering again as tiredness swept him away again.

Much like her son, Erin was utterly exhausted. When she had arrived back at Stanwick to collect her car Sam had wanted a briefing on Cristo's impressions, which had stretched into a meeting that lasted a couple of hours. Sam was keen for his properties to join the Donakis empire because he sincerely believed that a businessman of Cristo's standing could take his three hotels—his life's work—to a higher level. For the first time Erin had felt uncomfortable with the older man, too aware that she was not being entirely honest with him. He didn't know she had had a previous relationship with Cristo Donakis and she did not want him to know. If Sam were to realise that Cristo was the guy who had ditched her and ignored her letters and calls for assistance when she found herself pregnant, he would automatically distrust the younger man. And why should her messy personal life interfere with Sam's plans for retirement? Letting that happen, she felt, would be more wrong than continuing to keep her secrets.

Lorcan shifted against her shoulder, his curly black hair tickling her chin, a warm weight of solid sleeping toddler.

'Tuck him back into bed quickly,' a voice advised quietly from the doorway.

As Deidre Turner, a small blonde woman, moved past to hastily flip back the bedding and assist her daughter in settling the little boy back into his cot, Erin sighed and stood up. 'I'm sorry Lorcan wakened you again.'

'Don't be silly. I don't have to get up as early as you do in the morning,' her mother replied. 'Go back to bed. You look like you're sleepwalking. I don't know what Sam's thinking of, keeping you at work so late. He has no appreciation of the fact that you want to spend time with your family in the evening.'

'Why should he have? He's never had children to worry about,' Erin murmured soothingly, twitching the covers back over her son's small prone body. 'Sam always likes to wind down with a chat at the end of the day and he's very excited about the possibility of selling up.'

'That's all right for him, but if he does sell up where's it going to leave you and the rest of the employees?' Deidre questioned worriedly. 'We couldn't possibly manage on my pension.'

Erin patted her mother's tense shoulder gently. 'We'll survive. Apparently the law protects our jobs in a take-over. But I'll find work somewhere else if need be.'

'It won't be easy with the state the economy's in.

There aren't many jobs out there to find,' the older woman protested.

'We'll be all right,' Erin pronounced with a confidence that she didn't feel and a guilty conscience that she had not felt able to tell her mother that Cristo Donakis was Sam's potential buyer.

But that news would only inflame Deidre Turner, who would also demand to know why her daughter had not made instant use of her access to Cristo to finally tell him that he was a father. In addition her mother was a constant worrier, always in search of the next black cloud on the horizon, and Erin only shared bad news with the older woman if she had no other choice. Checking that her daughter, Nuala, Lorcan's twin sister, was still soundly asleep, curled up in a little round cosy ball inside her cot, Erin returned to bed and lay there in the darkness feeling every bit as anxious as her mother, if not more, as she struggled to count blessings rather than worries.

They lived in a comfortable terraced house. It was rented, not owned. Deidre, predictably imagining less prosperous times ahead, had decided that Erin borrowing money to buy a property for them was far too risky a venture. Her mother's attitude had irritated Erin at the time, but now, with the future danger of unemployment on her mind again she was relieved to be a tenant living in modest accommodation. Sam had reassured her about her job, reminding her that the current legislation would protect his staff with guaranteed employment under the new ownership. But there was often a way round such rules, Erin ruminated worriedly, and, when she was already aware that Cristo didn't want her on his staff, it would only be sensible to immediately begin looking for a new position. Unhappily that might take months to achieve but it was doable, wasn't it? She had to be more positive, stronger, fired up and ready to meet the challenges ahead.

But, Cristo was not a challenge. He was like a great big massive rock set squarely in her path and she didn't know how to get round such an obstacle. He believed she had stolen from him. But why hadn't he pursued that at the time? Why hadn't he called in the police? Erin was thinking back hard, reckoning that by the time Cristo received proof of her supposed theft he would have been married. Had he put the police on her, the fact that she was his ex would soon have emerged and perhaps got into the newspapers. Would that have embarrassed him? She didn't think that the Cristo she recalled would have embarrassed that easily. But that publicity might have embarrassed or annoyed his bride. Was it even possible that Lisandra and Erin had both been in a relationship with Cristo *at the same time*? And that he had feared having that fact exposed? After all, Cristo had got married barely three months after ditching Erin and few couples went from first meeting to marrying that fast. Had he been two-timing both of them? She had never had cause to believe that he was unfaithful to her but refused to believe that he would be incapable of such behaviour. After all, what had she ever really known about Cristo when she had not even suspected that he was about to dump her?

Erin had always liked things safe and certain and she never took risks. The one time she had—Cristo—it had gone badly wrong. On that level she and Cristo were total opposites because nothing thrilled Cristo more than taking a risk or meeting a challenge. So when he had started calling her to ask her out after finally beating her at swimming she had said no, sorry, again and again and again until he had finally manoeuvred her into attending a party at his apartment, urging her to bring friends as her guests.

Her presence bolstered by the presence of Elaine and Tom, it had proved a strangely magical evening with Cristo, she later appreciated, on his very best behaviour. At the end of the night Cristo had kissed her for the first time and that single kiss had been so explosive, it had blown the lid off her wildest dreams…and terrified her. She had known straight off that Cristo Donakis was a high-risk venture: lethally dangerous to her peace of mind.

'I like you…I do like you,' she had told Cristo lamely while still shaking like a leaf in the aftermath of the intense passion that had flared up between them. 'Why can't we just be friends?'

'Friends?' Cristo had echoed as though that word had never come his way before.

'That's what I'd prefer,' she had said brightly.

'I don't do that,' he had told her drily.

With those reservations she'd had more sense at the outset of their affair than she had shown later on, she acknowledged painfully. And once she had had the twins, her life had been turned upside down. She was ashamed to realise that she had been so angry with Cristo in that hotel suite that she had actually been threatening to tell him she was the mother of his children. What aberration had almost driven her to that insane brink? He would not want her children, would never agree to take on the role of father, would only angrily resent the position she put him in and make her feel small and humiliated, a burden he resented. Surely she was entitled to retain some pride when there was no perceptible advantage to telling him the truth?

Cristo had, after all, once confided in her that one of his friends' girlfriends had had a termination. 'It broke them up,' he had commented flatly. 'Few couples survive that sort of stress. I'm not sure I'll ever be ready for children. I prefer my life without baggage.'

And she had got the not exactly subtle message he had taken the trouble to put across, his so clever dark eyes pinned to hers: *Don't do that to me!* Revealingly, it had been the one and only time he ever chose to make her a party to confidential information about someone he knew for Cristo was, by instinct, very discreet. She had taken it as a warning that if she fell pregnant, he would want her to have a termination and their relationship would be over. It still infuriated her that it had actually been entirely his fault that she had conceived and, although she had later grown desperate enough to try and contact him to ask for financial help, she had known even then that the announcement she had to make of his impending fatherhood would infuriate him. Cristo was too arrogant and controlling to appreciate surprises from any source. That a woman could give birth to a baby without a man's prior agreement to accept the responsibility would no doubt strike him as very unfair. No, she saw no point whatsoever in telling Cristo that he was the father of two young children.

Even so, what was she planning to do about his threat to reveal that file of impressive evidence? Cristo was threatening the security of her entire family. Everything she had worked to achieve could vanish overnight. Not only Erin, but her mother and her children would pay the cost of her losing her job and salary. On the other hand, if she could sink her pride enough to play Cristo's cruel game, that file would never see the light of day and at the very least she would have another year of safe employment and plenty of time in which to search for an alternative position. What was one weekend out of the rest of her life, really? She pictured her mother's face earlier, drawn and troubled as she fretted about the hotel group even changing hands. Life had taught Deidre Turner to fear the unknown and the unexpected. She did not deserve to be caught up in the upheaval that was gathering on her daughter's horizon and there was little Erin would not have done to protect her children from the instability she had suffered growing up.

Unhappily, Erin believed that the entire situation was her own fault. Hadn't she ignored everybody's advice in getting involved with Cristo in the first place? Nobody had had a good word to say about Cristo, pointing out that his reputation as a womaniser spoke for him. And why had she made herself even more dependent by agreeing to go and work for him? Was that wise? her friends had asked worriedly. And no, nothing she had done that year with Cristo had been wise. Hadn't she hung on in there even when the going got rough and her lover's lack of commitment was blatantly obvious? He had not even managed to make it back into the UK to celebrate her last birthday with her. She had asked for trouble and now trouble had well and truly come home to roost. Cristo was not going to agree to play nice. Cristo had had over two years to fester over the conviction that she had dared to steal from him. Cristo was out for blood.

* * *

As the sun went down in a blaze of glory, Cristo was staring out at the shaded gardens of his foster parents' much-loved second home away from the smog and heavy traffic in Athens. On his terms, it was homely rather than impressive and it might be situated on the private island of Thesos, which Cristo had inherited at the age of twenty-one, but that was its sole claim to exclusivity.

Vasos and Appollonia Denes had always been extremely scrupulous when it came to enriching themselves in any way through their custodianship of a very wealthy little boy. Both his parents saw life in black and white with no shades of grey, which made them difficult to deal with, Cristo reflected in intense frustration. He had spent three very trying days locked in an office with Vasos, struggling to pull his father's company back from the edge of bankruptcy without the escape route of even being able to offer the firm a cheap loan. They would not touch his money in any form. Yet his father was suffering from so much stress that he had fallen asleep in the middle of dinner and his mother was still worryingly quiet and troubled, in spite of all her protestations to the contrary. She had never quite recovered from the nervous breakdown she had gone through eighteen months earlier.

Had they had any idea what he was engaged in with Erin Turner they would have been sincerely appalled, Cristo acknowledged grudgingly. They adored him, always thought the best of him, and firmly believed that with the conservative upbringing they had given him he must have absorbed their values, their decent principles. But even as a child Cristo had understood what it took to please his parents and he had learned how to pretend as well as accept that it wasn't always within his power to cure the evils of the world for them… His lean strong face hardened fiercely as a particularly unpleasant instance of that impossibility twanged deep in his conscience. He poured himself another drink and shook the memory off again fast.

When life was full of eighteen-hour days and the constant demands of his business empire, Erin was a wonderful distraction to toy with, that was *all*. If she didn't phone him within the next twenty-four hours, however, they would be entering round two of their battle of wits and he would play hardball. He was already figuring out his next move, no regrets whatsoever. Plainly he lacked the forgiving gene. That was becoming obvious even to him and he was not a man given to self-examination. But the lust driving him was on another plane altogether. One kiss…hell, what was he, a teenager to have got so hot and bothered?

And why did it disturb him that right this very minute she might be lying in a bed with Sam Morton, ensuring his continuing devotion in the easiest and most basic way a woman could? Why should that matter to him? Why, in fact, did that mental vision make him seethe? It should turn him off, douse the fire she roused…*disgust* him. But all Cristo could think about just then, indeed the only blindingly blue stretch of sky in his immediate future, was the prospect of that weekend. A weekend of the most perfect fantasy. Of course, it went without saying that fantasy would inevitably turn out to be dross, he pondered cynically. And then it would be over and he would be cured of this inconvenient, incomprehensible craving for her cheating little carcass for all time.

Done and dusted. He savoured that ideal prospect, increasingly keen to reach that moment of equilibrium.

Erin picked up the phone, her blood solidifying like ice in her veins. Caving in *hurt;* it was something she didn't do any more. Show weakness and people often fell on you like vultures. She was not the woman she had been three years earlier. But while she might be tougher, it was useless because Cristo had put her in the no-win corner, giving her no choice other than to try and protect those that she loved by whatever means were within her power.

'Yes, Miss Turner,' some faceless PA trilled at the end of the line. 'Mr Donakis mentioned that you would be calling. I'll put you through.'

His sheer certainty that she would surrender struck another blow to her already battered pride while she thought painfully of all the other times she had tried to speak to Cristo two and a half years earlier and had run into an endless brick wall of refusals. Of course, a call from an ex would not have been welcome to a newly engaged male but the potential offer of sex, it seemed, occupied a whole other plane of acceptability.

'Erin,' Cristo drawled smoothly. 'How may I help you?'

'Will the weekend of the fifth suit?' Her voice was breathless with strain and something very like anguish was rising inside her, for she had lost control of the situation. In the back of her mind something was shrieking that she just could not be doing this, could not possibly be contemplating such a sleazy arrangement, but her brain was mercifully in control as she pictured her children and her mother and once again acknowledged what was most important.

'That's two weeks away,' Cristo growled.

'And it's the soonest I can manage,' Erin said as coolly as if it were a business appointment she was setting up.

'Agreed. Someone will be in touch about the arrangements. Have a current passport available.'

'Why? Where on earth are you planning to go?' she gasped.

'Somewhere discreet. I'll see you on the fifth,' he murmured, the guarded quality in his tone letting her know that he was not alone.

Dry-mouthed, she replaced the phone, pure hatred strong and immovable as a concrete block forming inside her. What had she ever done to him that he should seek her out and threaten to destroy her life? So, he thought she was a thief. *Get over it*, she wanted to shriek at him. When they had been together she had refused to accept expensive gifts and clothes from him—did that telling fact count for nothing? In every way possible she had tried to make their relationship one of equals and her mind slid back into the past...

Surprisingly, he had banished her reluctance to enter a relationship with him with the use of romantic gestures. He had sent her flowers, occasional witty texts to keep her up to date with his life and on Valentine's Day he had sent her the most exquisite card and invited her out to dinner again. As there had not been a glimmer of him showing any interest in any other female during that period, Erin didn't know a woman alive who would have not succumbed to so persuasive an onslaught from a very handsome male. So, she had finally gone out with

him, just the two of them, thoroughly enjoyed herself
and that was how it had begun: date after date but just
kissing, nothing more because she wouldn't agree to
anything more. And, no fan of the celibate life, Cristo
had protested, persisting with his need for an explanation until she finally admitted that he would be her first
lover. Disconcerted by that admission, he had surprised
her by agreeing to wait until *she* felt that the moment
was right and she had loved him all the more for not
putting pressure on her.

And in the end she had slept with him because she
couldn't say no to her own craving any longer and the
experience, the connection she had felt with him from
the outset of true intimacy, had been unutterably wonderful. Four months into their affair, probably tiring of
the number of times she was not available through work
or the extra hours she put in as a personal trainer to a
few select clients, he had offered her the job of manager at the Mobila spa in his flagship London hotel. She
had thought long and hard before she accepted but as
she was already working as a deputy manager she had
believed that the position was well within her capabili-
ties. She had been more afraid that working for Cristo
might change their relationship but it had not occurred
to her that her new colleagues might resent her inescap-
ably personal ties to their employer.

At the time she had been taking the contraceptive pill
but, in spite of trying several different brands, she had
suffered mood changes that made her feel like a stranger
inside her own skin. Ultimately, Cristo had suggested
that he take care of precautions and soon after had come
that disturbing little chat about the friend's girlfriend,
who had had a termination, that same possibility ob-

viously having awakened Cristo's concern on his own account. After six months she had virtually lived in Cristo's apartment when he was there and he had begun asking her to join him on his travels. She had pointed out that she couldn't just walk out on her job and expect her staff to take her seriously. He had understood that but he hadn't *liked* it and around the same time he had started to question the amount of time she spent with Tom while he was abroad. Tom Harcourt was the closest thing Erin had ever had to a brother. They had met on the same university course and had stayed close friends when Tom also found work in London. There had never been a sexual spark between Erin and Tom but they got on like a house on fire, something Cristo had witnessed on several occasions and had evidently resented or found suspicious. Eight months into their relationship Cristo and Erin had had a huge, horrible row about Tom and Erin had stormed home in a temper.

'How would you like it if I had a female friend that close?' Cristo had demanded.

And in truth she wouldn't have liked it at all, but she loved Tom like a brother and refused to give him up.

'You're too possessive for me,' she had told Cristo, inflaming him as he furiously denied the charge.

'You're a very beautiful woman—Tom has to be aware of that. Truly platonic relationships don't exist,' Cristo had insisted. 'One party or the other always feels something more.'

'Either you trust me or you don't,' Erin had reasoned, stripping the dispute back to the bare bones while resisting the dangerous temptation to inform him that he had a shockingly jealous streak.

'Cristo is in love with you,' her more experienced

flatmate, Elaine, had pronounced with amusement. 'I didn't think it would happen but in my opinion men only get that possessive when they're keen.'

And that heartening forecast was why Erin had extended an olive branch to Cristo after a two-week silence while they both smouldered after that argument. In any case, by that stage Tom was already taking a back seat in her life because he had met the woman, Melissa, whom he would eventually marry. She had then waited hopefully for Cristo to demonstrate a more serious attitude towards her but it had never happened. They had spent Christmas and even his birthday apart while he went home to Greece without even dropping a hint that he might consider asking her to accompany him. Only one element of their affair had stayed the same: his passion for her body had never ebbed right to the very last night they had ever spent together and that same night was the one during which she was convinced she had fallen pregnant.

One week later, after bailing on her birthday party at his hotel, he had dumped her. He had had no qualms about the way he did it either, for he had walked into the spa, asked for a moment alone with her in her office and strolled away five minutes later, the deed done.

'You and I?' he had said drily. 'We've run our course and I'd like to move on.'

And he had moved on at supersonic speed to a wife, Erin recalled, settling back into the present with a dazed look on her delicate face. What she couldn't grasp was why, after that emotion-free affront of a dismissal almost three years ago, he should want to revisit the past. It didn't make sense to her. Yes, he might want to pun-

ish her for supposedly thieving from him, but how did
the act of sex, anything but retribution with a guy like
Cristo Donakis, encompass that ambition?

CHAPTER FIVE

Two weeks later, Erin stepped out of the car that had collected her at the airport and breathed in slow and deep. Italy, Tuscany in fact, not at all the setting that she had dimly expected Cristo to provide. In truth she had assumed the weekend would take place in London at his apartment, if he still lived there in the city, or even in one of his hotels. A grand fortified house presiding over an incredibly scenic hidden Italian valley had not featured at all.

Even with the sun starting to set in a golden blaze, the views of grape terraces, arrow-shaped cypresses, pine-forested slopes and silver-grey olive trees were magnificent; almost as much so as the wide graceful house with its shallow terracotta red roof and twin lines of tall elegant windows. Bells tinkled while sheep grazed on stretches of lush green grass in a timeless pastoral scene. It was not the backdrop she would have given to Cristo, whom she had once believed could only thrive on the often insane pace of city life.

A small balding manservant was already grasping the small case she had travelled with and with an expansive wave of one hand he welcomed her in English, introduced himself as Vincenzo and invited her to follow him indoors to an imposing marble hall that echoed with their footsteps. He escorted her straight up the sweeping marble staircase to a beautifully furnished bedroom decorated in masculine shades of gold and green. Her cheeks flared as she gazed at the wide gold-draped bed and hastily she glanced away again, preceding Vincenzo into the superb modern bathroom and politely smiling in admiration.

Did the wretched man know what she was here for? Or did he simply assume that she was yet another one of Cristo's women? And whatever he thought, what did it matter? She studied her taut reflection with self-loathing. Get over yourself, she told herself urgently. It might feel like a lifetime since she had had sex but at the end of the day sex was just sex even with Cristo and not worth risking her security over. She was being practical, choosing the safest option...

Over the past two weeks negotiations over the buyout of Sam's hotels had speeded up to reach agreement. The deal was signed, sealed and delivered and, whether she liked it or not, she was going to be working for Cristo Donakis again, although presumably only after that forensic accounting team he had mentioned had convinced him that she was to be trusted after all. The sting of his conviction that she was a thief still lingered though, not to mention the necessity of having had to lie outright to her trusting mother to travel to Italy. That latter act sat like a giant stone on her conscience.

Her face and her heart troubled, Erin doffed her light raincoat and agreed to come downstairs to enjoy the coffee that Vincenzo was offering. She had told her mother that she was catching the train up to Scotland to stay with Tom and his wife, Melissa, and their new baby, Karen. What else could she have told the older woman? Deidre Turner would have had a heart attack had she known the truth of what her wayward daughter was about to do and guilt nagged at Erin. Surely sometimes a lie was kinder than the truth, she reasoned uncertainly. But that was of little comfort to a young woman raised to 'tell the truth and shame the devil'.

Coffee was served on the terrace in the warmth of early evening and she thought about Lorcan and Nuala, resenting the loss of a weekend that she had expected to spend with her twins. As she abstractedly took in the fabulous view shadowing into dark hills and tree tops her phone buzzed and she drew it from her bag.

Wear your hair loose, the text told her.

Cristo was reducing her to the level of a toy with a starring role in *his* fantasy. The taste of her coffee soured in her mouth. She was sick with nerves. Cristophe Donakis was the man she had once loved beyond belief. Although she had worked hard to hide it, she had absolutely adored him and their intimacy had only added another dimension to that love. This demeaning emotion-free encounter would destroy even the good memories. Though perhaps that would be a godsend? Was Cristo getting a kick out of having her at his disposal? Cristo enjoyed power. Teeth gritting, she finished the coffee and went back upstairs to change. Was she supposed to dress as if this were a date or await his arrival in that vast bed? Tears stung her eyes and she blinked them away furiously as she headed for a shower. No, absolutely no way was she going to wait in the bed! Swathed in a towel, she tugged a silky blue dress from her case.

Cristo leapt out of the helicopter and strode up to the

villa, impatience and hunger burning through him. He hadn't been worth a damn all day, all week for that matter! Just the thought of Erin being there had wiped out his wits, Vincenzo's call to confirm her arrival catching him in the middle of a board meeting. How many times had he told himself he shouldn't be doing this? What the hell, he reasoned furiously, why shouldn't he be a bastard for a change? He had let her off the hook too lightly three years ago. This— being with her one more time—was an indulgence but it was also an exorcism, and when it was done he would be done with her as well.

The pulse in Erin's neck was beating like crazy as she hovered by the bedroom window, refusing to look outside while her tummy twisted into knots. She had heard the helicopter landing, knew Cristo liked to fly himself, and knew it would be him and that within minutes he would walk through the bedroom door. She clasped her hands tightly together, willing back her nerves, striving for calm and cool.

And then the door flew open, rocking back on its hinges to frame Cristo, brilliant black diamond eyes snaking across the room to rest on her, his tall well-built body casting a long shadow in the lamp light. And there she was, silvery pale hair tumbling round her shoulders, something pretty and blue swirling round her petite little body, *waiting* for him just as he remembered from times gone by. *Erin.* He savoured her, noting the glow of self-consciousness that coloured the beautiful delicacy of her features. He experienced such a charge of hunger at the first glance that a predatory smile crossed his mobile male mouth.

'Cristo…' Erin contrived to enunciate with admirable clarity, only the breathy quietness of her voice letting her down.

'Erin,' he breathed thickly, closing the distance between them and hauling her straight into his arms.

He said something in Greek as he gazed down at her and she would have given anything to know what it was. 'What—?'

'Don't want to talk, *koukla mou,*' Cristo husked, his breath fanning her cheek as he bent his handsome dark head.

His eyes, those beautiful beautiful eyes, lion gold surrounded by spiky black lashes, held hers fast and she literally stopped breathing because the clean designer scent of him was drenching her with every mouthful of air. He looked so good, so irretrievably, undeniably good that his pure impact overwhelmed her. He kissed the corner of her mouth in a tiny teasing caress and she shivered, her thoughts blanking out, her body taking over and she wanted more, wanted more so badly that it hurt. His mouth found hers with a sudden urgency that she welcomed. Her tongue slid against his and the pressure of his lips increased in a deep hot kiss that blew her away. In the midst of it he wrenched free of his jacket and dropped it, yanked at his tie and she trailed it free, her fingers releasing the shirt button at his strong brown throat.

And it took no thought to do any of those things and she was shaken by the instinct driving her at a level she didn't understand. Her fingers curved to one high cheekbone as she struggled to stay upright with her heart slamming against her breastbone as hard as though she were in race. Her legs felt weak, insufficient to support her and she was fiercely aware of the empty ache in her pelvis and the swelling tightness of her breasts as he spread his big hands over her buttocks and crushed her into his hard erection.

'I'm burning alive for you,' Cristo growled almost accusingly, spinning her round to find the zip on her dress and taking care of it with efficiency.

'Me too,' Erin admitted with a bitterness she couldn't hide, her whole body throbbing with uncontrollable desire as deft fingers brushed the straps of her dress off her slight shoulders and the garment pooled in a silky heap round her feet.

Breathing audibly, Cristo spun her back to him and bent to curve his hands round her slim thighs, hitching her up against him and bringing her down on the bed with a sound of satisfaction that started deep in his broad chest. It's just sex, *amazing* sex, he adjusted helplessly, but the burn, the burn of excitement was indescribable. He slid a hand beneath her to unclasp her bra and stared down into her amethyst eyes, purple blue like precious gems. Thief, he told himself, liar, *cheat* but that little mantra of reminders didn't work its desired magic. He ripped off his shirt, felt her hands sweeping up, up over his chest and honestly wondered if he could hold it together long enough to get inside her.

'How can you still do this to me?' he demanded in a fierce undertone, shimmering hot golden eyes pinned to the flushed triangle of her face and then sinking down a level to concentrate on the pale breasts he had uncovered, firm little mounds adorned with large pink nipples that magnetised his attention.

Claiming a straining bud with his mouth, Cristo suckled strongly, using his hands, his lips and the edge of his teeth because he knew how sensitive she was there. As her slim length jackknifed under him, spine arching on a strangled moan, his sense of achievement increased and he let his lips rove hungrily over her dainty breasts, lingering on the swollen straining peaks to torment them with pleasure. His attention glued to her prone body, he backed off the bed again and unzipped his trousers.

Her face hot pink with shame and discomfiture, Erin sat up and clasped her knees. She didn't want to enjoy anything they did. She wanted to lie there like a stone statue and stay inwardly untouched and detached from him. But Cristo was far too expert a lover to allow her that kind of escape route and he was seducing a response out of her resistant body.

'I didn't intend to fall on you like a wild animal the minute I came through the door,' he volunteered impatiently. 'I was planning on having dinner first.'

Erin averted her gaze, the victim of unwelcome memories of a passion that had never gone off the boil. 'You were never very good at waiting. It was always like this for us—'

'There is no "us" any more.'

Erin lowered her lashes. He was wrong. Lorcan and Nuala were a wonderful combination of their respective genes and unless she was very much mistaken her toddlers had inherited his volatile nature. Lorcan was wilful and hot-tempered and Nuala was sharp as paint and mercurial, neither of them demonstrating an iota of their mother's quieter, more settled personality. But she was grateful that Cristo didn't know about them. Lorcan and Nuala would never get the chance to emulate their father's tough cynical outlook on the world, where what he wanted always came ahead of what was best for other people. He would not get the chance to turn them into spoilt, selfish children and, after the manner in which he had corralled her back into his bed, she refused to feel guilty about the fact.

She glanced up in the silence.

'You look like you're plotting,' Cristo remarked thoughtfully.

He towered over her, naked and aroused, gazing down at her with hot golden eyes of appreciation. She was appalled when her body reacted deep down inside, her nipples tingling as dampness formed at the heart of her.

'What on earth would I be plotting?'

'I don't know.' He stroked the tight set of her sultry mouth with a considering fingertip. 'But you're wearing the same face you wore when you found out I'd taken business associates to a lap-dancing club, *koukla mou*.'

Erin flushed as he came down beside her. 'Not one of my better memories.'

Cristo unclasped the hands she had tightened round her knees and pulled her back against his warm, hair-roughened torso. 'Nor mine, but unfortunately that kind of venue is par for the course with certain men.'

Her breath scissored in her throat as he found her breasts again, gently, surely shaping and tugging at the swollen tips. He pressed her back against the pillows, long brown fingers dipping below the waistband of her knickers, moving across bare smooth skin to stroke her clitoris. As the ache between her thighs intensified, she shut her eyes tight. He kissed her with hot driving force, skimmed off that last garment and pressed his lips to the smooth slope of her belly. Her eyes flew wide because she had silvery stretchmarks there from her pregnancy and she quivered as he trailed his expert mouth over her abdomen and then lower, startling her with that move. He found her with his mouth and his fingers, delving into the honeyed heat of her until she moaned, hips squirming as the pleasure built. He tipped her back, drowning her in sweet sensation that sent her out of control. Her breath sounded in audible gasps as she shifted helplessly up to him, wanting, *needing* and then response took over to send her racing into an explosive climax.

'I love watching you come…it must be the only time in your life that you let go of control,' Cristo husked, looking down at her with an unusually reflective light in his keen gaze. 'You're so different from me.'

Emerging dizzily from the tremors of ecstasy still rocking her body, Erin looked up into his lean dark face and the stunning eyes engaged in tracking her every change of expression. She felt exposed, vulnerable, shaken that he had already seduced her so thoroughly that she could barely recall what day it was, never mind how they had ended up in a bed at such indecent speed. 'I don't want to be here doing this with you,' she said fiercely.

'Liar.' He brought his mouth down on hers and her tongue slid against his again and that single kiss was so passionate she shivered.

Cristo donned a condom and came over her like a one-man invasion force, tipping her legs over his shoulders and driving into her so hard and deep that her head fell back in a curtain of shiny silver blonde hair, neck arching feverishly in reaction. It was good, hell it was *amazing*, she thought furiously, angry with herself, enraged that she hadn't found it possible to lie there without responding and destroy his desire for her. She knew him well enough to know that if she had held back and failed to respond he wouldn't have persisted. He shifted position and ground into her faster with hungry pounding strokes that made her heart race as though she were in a marathon. He groaned with unashamed pleasure as she cried out, bucking up to him, reacting helplessly to the delicious friction of his fluid rhythm. And she felt the heat mushrooming up from her pelvis again until an explosion of light shot through her like a flash of white-hot fire, shooting wild hot tension along every limb. He pulsed inside her and groaned as she came apart at the seams in another shattering orgasm.

By the time she came free of that shattering onslaught of raw pleasure, she was trembling and, surprisingly, he still had his arms round her, one hand splayed across her stomach as he pressed his sensual mouth to her damp cheek. 'You're amazing. That was *so* worth waiting for, *koukla mou*.'

But she hadn't made him wait; they had ended up in bed five minutes after his arrival. *I'm easy*, she decided painfully, marvelling that she was still lying in his arms and revelling in that unbelievable sense of closeness with him again. How could she possibly feel connected to Cristophe Donakis again? It felt as if almost three years had vanished in a time slip to deposit her back to when she had cherished such private and vulnerable moments with the man she loved. Only she didn't love him any more, she told herself bitterly, and he had never loved her and, what was more, he had ruthlessly blackmailed her back into his bed. As she began to reclaim her wits and pull away Cristo pulled away from her to disappear into the bathroom.

She listened to the shower running and wondered how she would live with the victory she had given him, how she would ever look in the mirror and like herself again. It was all right to tell herself that she had done what she had to do to protect her life and her children's, but what she had just allowed to happen went against her every principle. It was a punishment to appreciate that she had participated in and enjoyed her own downfall.

Lithe, bronzed and truly magnificent, Cristo reappeared with a towel wrapped round his lean hips just as a knock sounded on the bedroom door. 'I told Vincenzo to bring up dinner,' he remarked carelessly.

Erin scrambled out of bed naked and vanished into the bathroom to use the shower. She was on automatic pilot, desperate to escape his presence lest she lose what little distance she had contrived to achieve. Stepping out of the shower again, she saw the black towelling robe hanging on the back of the door and made use of it because she hadn't packed anything that practical. She rolled up the sleeves, tied the sash tight.

Cristo had donned close-fitting jeans and a black tee. A heated trolley now stood beside the small table in the corner.

'How did Vincenzo get all that food up here?' she asked stiffly.

'There's a lift. The last owner was an elderly lady with mobility problems.'

'When did you buy this place?'

'About a year ago. I wanted somewhere to relax between business trips,' Cristo said, sounding amazingly calm and distant after what they had just shared. 'What would you like to eat?'

'I'll see to myself.' Her tummy rumbled as, maintaining a scrupulous distance from his lean, powerful body, she studied the tempting array of dishes. She was surprised that she was so hungry but then nervous tension had pretty much killed her appetite over the previous forty-eight hours while she was forced to pretend to everyone around her that life was normal. She chose meat-stuffed *tortelloni* and *Panzanella* salad and lifted a slice of home baked bread.

His lean, darkly handsome face composed, Cristo poured wine for them both and sat down in a fluid movement. His assurance set her teeth on edge. He had blasted her pride and confidence out of existence because all of a sudden she didn't know who she was any more. She was not the mature, self-contained woman she had believed she was and that acknowledgement hurt.

'Doesn't it bother you that you blackmailed me into bed?' Erin shot at him abruptly.

'It might have started out that way, but that's not how it concluded,' Cristo fielded smooth as glass, his gaze welded to her. Gleaming silvery fair hair tumbled loose round her slight shoulders, accentuating her flawless features. He had burned for her from the first moment he saw her standing wet and tousled beside the swimming pool where they had met. He had burned the same way when he met her again in Sam Morton's office. He wasn't happy that she set him on fire. He wasn't happy that one wildly exciting taste of her had only primed him to want the next. *Toxic,* he reminded himself grimly.

Erin met cool, measuring, dark golden eyes that contained not an ounce of remorse and gritted her teeth, afraid to utter a word in her own defence, for what exactly could she say? They both knew that she had not played the part of an unwilling victim. 'I don't understand why you wanted me here,' she admitted tightly. 'After all, when we split up, you made it clear that you were bored with our relationship.'

Cristo became very still. 'I never said I was bored.'

Barely forgotten frustration invaded Erin afresh. It was a throwback to the bewilderment of the past when she had tormented herself for months in the aftermath of their breakup wondering what she had done or not done to make him want his freedom back. Suddenly that old curiosity was biting into her like a knife point. 'Then why did you ditch me?'

His lean, strong face was impassive. 'I doubt that you want the answer to that question.'

Erin stabbed a piece of juicy tomato with her fork. 'It's a long time ago, Cristo,' she said drily.

'Precisely,' he slotted in sardonically.

'But I would *still* like to know why,' Erin completed doggedly.

Cristo set down his wine glass, brilliant dark eyes pinned to her and she felt the chill like ice water spilling across her skin. 'You cheated on me...'

Erin stared back at him in astonishment. 'No. I didn't.'

'I caught the guy in your bed in your hotel room the night after your birthday bash,' Cristo countered flatly. 'You cheated on me.'

Erin was frowning. 'Who did you see in my hotel room?'

Cristo shrugged a broad shoulder and dealt her a satiric glance. 'I have no idea who he was. I let myself into the room intending to surprise you and instead *I* got the surprise.'

Erin was stunned. 'But I wasn't there—you didn't see me.'

Cristo dealt her a scornful look. 'I saw the man, the discarded clothes, the wine glasses and I could hear the shower running in the bathroom. I didn't need to see you as well.'

Erin was so tense she was barely breathing. In a sudden movement she pushed back her chair and stood upright, her amethyst eyes bright with anger. 'Well, actually you did because that *wasn't* me in the bathroom! I didn't even stay in London that night.'

Cristo gave her an unimpressed look. 'It was your room and he was in your bed—'

Anger coursed through her in a torrent of incredulous rage. 'And you're only telling me this now, nearly three *years* later? Why didn't you mention it at the time?'

'I didn't see any point in staging a messy confrontation. I had seen all I needed to see,' Cristo derided with harsh assurance.

CHAPTER SIX

ERIN genuinely wanted to strangle Cristo at that moment. In the space of seconds she was reviewing the misery she had endured after their parting and finally grasping why he had dumped her with so little fanfare. Hostility at his latest misjudgement roared through her, her facial bones drawing taut below her fine skin. 'You had seen all you needed to see—is that a fact?' she snapped back furiously.

An ebony brow elevated with sardonic cool. 'What more evidence would I have required?'

'*Proper* evidence!' Erin fired back at him quick as a flash with more than a hint of his own intensity. 'Because that wasn't me in that bathroom. I didn't stay in London that night. I got a call from the hospital to tell me that my mother had been rushed to Casualty with a suspected heart attack. Tom and his girlfriend offered to run me home—Tom's kid brother, Dennis, asked if he could use my hotel room to stay in town with his girlfriend. I said yes, why wouldn't I have? I wasn't expecting you to turn up. When you told me you couldn't make it home to my party, you also said that you probably wouldn't make it back to London for at least another twenty-four hours.'

His darkly handsome features set like stone, Cristo gave her an unyielding look. 'I don't believe your explanation.'

At that inflammatory admission, Erin simply grabbed up the bottle of wine and poured it over his head, watching with satisfaction as the golden liquid cascaded down over his black hair and granite-hard masculine features. Startled by the assault, he leapt up with an irate Greek curse and wrenched the bottle from her grasp. 'Have you gone insane?' he raked back at her in ringing disbelief.

Untouched by any form of guilt, Erin grimly watched him dry his face with a napkin. 'I must've been when I got involved with you. How dare you assume that I slept with some other guy? How dare you just accept that and judge me for it? After the amount of time I was with you, I deserved more respect. How could you condemn me without a hearing?'

'I'm not having this conversation with you—I'm going for a second shower,' Cristo declared, striding towards the bathroom door.

Erin moved liked lightning to get there ahead of him and leant back in the doorway, daring him to shift her out of his path. 'You are so stubborn. But I could put my hand on a bible and *swear* that I wasn't in the Mobila hotel that night.'

'You were there!' Cristo breathed rawly, wrathful challenge scored into every hard angle and hollow of his breathtakingly handsome face.

'No, I wasn't!' Erin snapped back at him angrily. 'How could you even credit that I'd spent the night with another man?'

'Why not? I couldn't make it back in time for your birthday party and I knew you had to be furious with me—'

'Not so furious that I would have got into bed with someone else! I can't believe that you thought that of me and just walked away from it.'

His eyes hostile, his hard jaw line squared and he said nothing.

'Of course, I understand why now,' Erin continued thinly. 'You are so full of ego and pride. Walking away was the easiest thing to do—'

'That's not why I said nothing,' Cristo argued, his Greek accent roughening every vowel sound, anger glittering in the golden blaze of his eyes. 'I had had doubts about you for a while. There had been other...things that made me suspicious—'

'Name them,' she challenged.

'I will not discuss them with you—'

'You unreasonable, *arrogant*...' she slammed back, so enraged with him that she was trembling. 'In all the time we were together I never so much as looked at another man but that wasn't good enough for you, was it? You're jealous and possessive to the bone—you couldn't even stand me spending time with Tom!'

Eyes glowing like the heart of a fire between black spiky lashes, Cristo closed his hands to her waist and lifted her off her feet to set her to one side. 'I've told you. We're not having this discussion.'

Erin followed him into the bathroom. 'We definitely are, Cristo. You can't accuse me of infidelity and expect me to accept it in silence! What's wrong with you? You think I'm a thief as well but you said nothing about that either at the time. In retrospect don't you find all this muck being flung at me a little strange?'

Cristo was engaged in stripping off his wine-stained clothing. 'In what way strange?' he queried curtly.

'It's beginning to look to me like someone set out to deliberately discredit me in your eyes.'

His handsome mouth took on a sardonic curve as he peeled off his jeans and left them in a heap. 'That sounds like paranoia.'

Erin averted her attention as he stripped off his boxers and discovered that she was studying his long, powerful, hair-roughened thighs instead. The colour in her cheeks heightened as she lifted her head again, struggling to blot out the sight of the lean ropes of muscle banding his powerful torso. 'There's nothing paranoid about my suspicions—'

'You cheated on me and I found out…get over it,' Cristo advised witheringly as he switched on the shower and stepped in, utterly unconcerned by the nudity of his lean bronzed body. But then he had never been shy. 'It's ancient history. Don't try to resurrect it.'

'I wish I'd hit you with that bottle.'

Cristo rammed back the shower door and rested cold dark eyes of warning on her angry, defiant face. 'Don't you ever do anything like that again or I won't be responsible for what I do.'

Erin clashed with scorching golden eyes and her tummy lurched. Rage washed over her again because butterflies were leaping in her pelvis. Infuriatingly her body was reacting to him with all the control of an infatuated adolescent. 'I wish I had cheated on you…the way you treated me, I might as well have done!'

She stalked out of the bathroom. He had knocked her for six with that accusation. He had also taught her that she didn't know him as well as she had always believed she did. Although she had recognised his reserve she had never dreamt that he might have the capacity to keep such big secrets from her. What else didn't she know about Cristo? And what else had happened that had caused him to doubt her loyalty? What were those other 'things' he had grudgingly mentioned? Yanking the bedspread off the bed, and lifting a pillow, she made up the sofa on the far side of the room for her occupation.

'You're not sleeping over there,' Cristo told her tautly.

'I'm certainly not getting back into a bed with a man who thinks I'm a slut as well as a thief!' Erin replied with spirit, pale hair bouncing on her shoulders as she spun round to face him.

Stark naked, Cristo was hauling fresh clothing from drawers. He shot her a censorious appraisal from brilliant dark eyes. 'We have a deal—'

'But I intend to add my own conditions,' Erin declared thinly. 'I'll keep to our agreement *if*—'

'Too late—we already have a deal.'

'If that's your attitude I'm sleeping on the sofa.'

His thick sooty lashes lowered on stunning golden eyes while he surveyed her. 'Do you cheat at cards too?'

'You ought to know—you taught me to play,' she reminded him.

The silence buzzed like an angry wasp. Cristo continued to watch her, his attention locked to the sultry pink pout of her mouth. He wished he had kept his own shut and could not think why he had admitted that he knew of her betrayal. Everything had been going so well until she decided that honour demanded she now prove that she was pure as the driven snow. In exasperation he scored long brown fingers through his damp black hair. 'What conditions?' he demanded impatiently.

'I'll get back into that bed if—and only *if*—you agree to talk to Tom, who will verify that he passed the key card for the room to his brother and later dropped me off at the hospital a hundred miles away to be with my mother.'

Cristo looked pained. 'That's ridiculous.'

Erin tilted her chin. 'No, it's the least of what you owe me.'

'I owe you nothing.' He was poised there insolently, still half naked but for the jeans he had pulled on. Just looking at Cristo made her heartbeat pick up speed and her breathing quicken: he was so physically gorgeous. White-hot sex appeal was bred into his very bones. Even more disturbingly, the wilful line of his beautiful mouth was remarkably like her son, Lorcan's, she registered in dismay, rushing to suppress that unnerving sense of familiarity. Inside himself Cristo was seething with anger, she *did* know that, but Cristo rarely revealed anger on the surface, deeming that a weakness. And one thing Cristophe Donakis did not do was weakness.

'I deserve that you check out my side of the story,' Erin proclaimed as regally as a queen. 'You didn't give me the opportunity three years ago, so the least you can do is take care of the omission now.'

A winged ebony brow quirked. 'And if I agree, you'll get back into bed?'

'I have just one more thing to say.'

'You're pricing yourself out of the market.'

Erin gazed back at him, remembering when she had loved him, when she had simply lived for his quick easy smile and attention and shrinking from the recollection, fearful of ever laying her heart out again. 'No, I'm worth waiting for.'

Cristo dealt her a hungry appraisal that made her triangular face burn as though he had turned an open flame on her skin. 'Speak…'

'Ask yourself why I would commit fraud and put myself at risk of a prison sentence while refusing to accept the valuable diamond jewellery you tried to give me on several occasions,' she advised softly. 'If I wanted money that badly, keeping the diamonds and selling them would have been much more sensible.'

Cristo held her eyes coolly without reaction and then released his breath on a slow measured hiss. 'Get back in bed,' he breathed.

Erin retrieved her pillow and undid the tie on the robe, letting it fall as she scrambled onto the divan. Cristo watched, desire igniting almost simultaneously to raise his temperature. Surely there had never been any woman with paler, more perfect skin or more delicate yet highly feminine curves? He lay down on the bed beside her with a sense that all was right in his world for the first time in a long time. Erin studied the stark beauty of his features, knowing why no other man had tempted her, knowing why she was still heart whole. Nobody had ever come close to comparing to Cristo either in looks or passion. Eyes drowsy, she lifted a hand in the simmering silence and with her forefinger gently traced the volatile curve of his full lower lip. His gaze smouldered and his hand came up to entrap hers, long fingers wrapping round her smaller hand with precision.

'Go to sleep,' he breathed ruefully, noting the shadows that lay below her eyes like bruises. 'You're exhausted.'

Why should it bother him that she looked so tired? Why had he even noticed? His expressive mouth tightened. They were enjoying the equivalent of a two-night stand: finer feelings of any kind were not required. Nor had he any intention of getting caught up in discussing their previous relationship. There was nothing to discuss. But Erin had looked so shocked when he accused her of cheating on him. Perhaps she had been shocked that he had found her out. Clearly her partner that night had stayed silent about Cristo's entry to the hotel room. And Erin had always had a talent for playing innocent and naïve. Once that had charmed him, fooled him. Now it merely set his teeth on edge with suspicion.

What was Erin hoping to get out of this weekend? She was a survivor. As was he and he didn't like the fact that he was enjoying her company so much.

The next day they had breakfast on the terrace mid-morning. Erin had slept so late she was embarrassed. Sleeping in, after all, was a luxury she no longer enjoyed at home. The twins woke up at the crack of dawn demanding attention and since their birth Erin had learned to get by on short rations of sleep. Casually garbed in white cotton trousers teamed with a colourful silk top, she spread honey on her toast and enjoyed the picturesque landscape of rolling hills covered with mature chestnut and oak woods at the rear of the villa. It occurred to her that she might as well have been on a pleasure trip, for the accommodation and food were superb and even the company was acceptable.

Acceptable, jeered a little mocking voice in her head as she glanced at Cristo, lean and darkly magnificent in a black polo shirt and tailored chinos, predictably pacing the terrace as he ate and drank, the restive spirit that drove him unable to keep the lid on his sheer energy this early in the day. He had let her sleep undisturbed, had already been up and dressed when he finally wakened her. As his spectacular dark golden eyes surged her she went pink, something akin to panic assailing her as she felt her treacherous body's instant response to his powerful masculinity. There was an ache at the heart of her, a physical reminder of the wild passion they had shared. Yes, *shared*, she labelled, refusing to overlook her own behaviour. The sleazy weekend of her worst imaginings had come nowhere near reality and it had also proved surprisingly informative, she acknowledged wryly as she continued to think deeply about Cristo's admission that he had believed she had cheated on him. How could he not have confronted her about that? And yet she knew why not, she understood the bone-deep unforgiving pride that was so much a part of his nature. He had successfully hidden his anger from her at the time, refusing to vent it, something she could not have done in his place. He had accepted her supposed betrayal and, even now, his lack of faith in her when she had loved him appalled her. As Cristo had reminded her, though, it was the past and she thought it was wiser not to dwell on it.

He took her out for a drive in an open-topped sports car. Such freedom felt strange to her. She was accustomed to taking the twins to the park on Saturday mornings. Guilt weighed her down for she knew that her children would be missing out on that outing because Erin's mother found it difficult to watch over her grandchildren alone in a public place. Lorcan loved to explore and he wandered off, often followed by his sister. Erin had twice found her son standing up to his knees in the boating lake and had carried him kicking and scream-

ing back to dry land where Nuala waited to enrage him
with the toddler version of, 'I told you so.'

'How did you end up working for Sam Morton?'
Cristo prompted.

'Pure good luck. I was living at home and working
as a personal trainer again. My best client was a friend
of Sam's. That kind lady talked me up to him when he
was looking for a spa manager and he phoned me and
offered me an interview.'

'What made you leave London to return to Oxford?'

Erin shot him a taut glance and opted for honesty. 'I
couldn't afford city life when I was living on benefits.
I should never have resigned from my job at the Mobila
spa—that was rash and short-sighted of me.'

'I was surprised when you resigned,' Cristo admitted. 'Later I assumed it was because you'd been dipping
into the till and you thought it would be safer to stage
a vanishing act.'

Erin stiffened at that reminder but said nothing, resigned to the fact that she could not combat that charge
until she had, at least, tackled Sally Jennings. 'I left because I didn't want to keep running into you and I assumed you'd feel the same way but I was over-sensitive.
Leaving after working there such a short time blighted
my CV. It was also much harder to find another job than
I thought it would be.' Especially once she had realised
that she was pregnant and no longer feeling well, she
completed inwardly.

A hundred memories of their time together were assailing Cristo and lending a brooding edge to his mood.
He remembered her twirling in the rain with an um-
brella. She had preferred nights in watching DVDs to
nights out at a club but the horror movies, which she

loved, gave her nightmares. He had learned not to mind being used as a security blanket in the middle of the night. They had virtually lived together at weekends when he was in London, his innate untidiness driving her wild while her love of pizza had left him cold. Now he asked himself how well he had ever known her.

The sun beat down on them as they walked around a little hill village, packed with stone houses and narrow twisting alleys. In the cool quiet interior of the tiny ancient church, she lit a candle and said a little prayer for peace while Cristo waited outside for her. Around him she couldn't think straight and the level of her emotional turmoil was starting to scare her. She needed to hate him but what she was feeling was *not* hatred. That she knew, but what she did feel beyond the pull of his magnetic attraction was much harder to pin down and she abandoned the challenge. In twenty-four hours she would be heading home and this little episode would be finished, she reasoned doggedly, keen to ground herself to solid earth again. What was the point in tormenting herself with regrets and foolish questions?

They had a simple lunch in the medieval piazza where Cristo stretched like a lion basking in the midday heat while Erin sat back in the shade, aware that without it her winter pale skin would burn. The waitress, a young woman in her twenties, couldn't take her eyes off the striking beauty of Cristo's classic features or the sizzling effect of his honey-coloured gaze when he smiled. With a sinking heart Erin recalled when she had been even more impressionable.

Even now, she flushed beneath his disturbingly intent scrutiny. '*What*?'

'You look beautiful and you didn't even have to make an effort. It only took you ten minutes to get dressed.'

'You're accustomed to more decorative women… that's all.'

'You always turn aside compliments as though they're insincere,' Cristo murmured, his attention lodging revealingly on the voluptuous curve of her raspberry-tinted lips.

Erin knew that look, recognised his sexual hunger and *felt* the raw pull of it deep inside her body. Her nipples tingled and a pool of liquid heat formed in her pelvis, making her instantly ashamed of her lack of self-discipline. Breathing rapidly in the warm still air in an attempt to suppress those unwelcome reactions, she tensed but she remained insanely aware of his appreciative scrutiny. The atmosphere positively smouldered. Cristo laughed with husky satisfaction and her heart hammered like a trapped bird in her chest.

'Time for us to leave, *koukla mou,*' he murmured, silkily suggestive, sliding fluidly upright to take care of the bill.

Tomorrow could not come soon enough for her, Erin told herself. The weekend would be over and she could pretty much slip back into the comforting routine of her very ordinary life. But she would also be working for Cristo again and in the wake of this forty-eight-hour break from reality that would be no easy challenge.

They walked back downhill, Erin moving a few steps in Cristo's wake. It was the hottest hour of the day and even her light clothing was clinging to her damp skin but she loved the sunshine. He caught her hand as he drew level with the car and drew her closer, hot, hungry eyes with the pure lustre of gold connecting with hers.

He bent his dark head and claimed her lips in a searing kiss. Every response she had fought since leaving the villa bubbled up in a fountain of need. The erotic charge between them was delirious, devastating her defences as he fed hungrily from the sweetness of her mouth. She could feel the leashed demand in his lean, hard body as he bent her back against the car bonnet, the tremor in the long fingers clasping her cheek as her tongue tangled with his. She wanted to eat him alive. With a ragged groan, he stepped back from her.

'Let's go,' he rasped.

Her legs were as bendy and unreliable as twigs as she stumbled into the passenger seat. With her heart thundering and her head swimming after that lusty exchange her thoughts ran blood red with guilt and shame. This was not how she had expected the weekend to turn out: she had never counted on still being so attracted to Cristo that every barrier between them dropped.

Snatching in a steadying breath, Cristo drove off. He felt out of control and he didn't like that. When had 'just sex' become 'must-have sex'? And what had happened to the exorcism goal? *This* was getting her out of his system? He thought of his marriage, an infallible reminder of the danger of undisciplined impulses, and straight away the electrifying heat in his blood cooled, his arousal subsiding to a more bearable level.

Erin's mobile phone started ringing as she entered the villa. She snatched it out of her bag with a frown and answered it. 'Mum?' she queried into the excited barrage of her mother's too fast hail of words. 'Calm down. What is it?'

Cristo watched Erin begin to pace the hall in quick short steps. 'What sort of an accident?' she was asking urgently, her triangular face lint white with shock and dismay. 'Oh m-my…word…how bad is it?'

Erin pressed a concerned hand to her parted lips and turned in a clumsy uncoordinated circle. Nuala had had an accident at the playground and had broken her arm. It was a fracture and required surgery. Erin's heart was beating so fast with worry that she felt sick. Assuring her mother that she would be at the hospital as soon as possible, she ended the call.

'Bad news?' Cristo prompted.

'It's an emergency—you've got to get me home as fast as you can. I'm sorry. I'll go and pack.'

Erin fled upstairs, nothing in her head but the thought of her daughter suffering without her mother's support. She had never felt so guilty in her life. Nuala was hurt and about to have an operation and Erin couldn't be with her. It would never have happened if Erin had stayed at home. Deidre Turner had tried to take the twins to the park in her daughter's place. Nuela had squirmed to the top of the climbing frame and hung upside down in spite of her grandmother's pleas for her to come down. When the child fell she might have broken her arm but she was exceedingly lucky not to have broken her neck. Knowing that her daughter had to be in pain and frightened, Erin felt her tummy churn with nausea. She should have told Cristo that she couldn't make the weekend because she now had children, *responsibilities*. Staying silent on that score had been the act of an irresponsible parent.

'What's going on?' Cristo questioned from the bedroom doorway.

Erin paused in the act of flinging clothes back into her case and twisted her head round. 'How quickly can you get me back home?'

'Within a few hours—we'll leave as soon as you're ready, but I'd appreciate an explanation.'

Erin folded her lips, eyes refusing to meet his, and turned back to her packing. 'I can't give you one. A relative of mine has had an accident and I need to get home…urgently.'

Cristo released an impatient sigh. 'Why do you make such a song and dance about even simple things? Why can't you tell me the whole story?'

Erin dealt him a numb, distanced look. 'I don't have the words or enough time to explain.'

Within fifteen minutes they had left the house to travel to the airport. Erin was rigid with tension and silent, locked in her anxiety about her daughter, not to mention her guilt that her mother was being forced to deal with a very stressful situation alone. This was her punishment for deceiving her mother about where she was staying for the weekend, she thought painfully. Her children needed her but she was not within reach to come quickly to their aid. Instead their next-door neighbour, Tamsin, a young woman with kids of her own, had come to the hospital to collect Lorcan so that her mother could stay on there and wait for Nuala to come out of surgery.

They were walking through the airport when Cristo closed a hand to Erin's wrist and said curtly. 'We have to talk about this.'

'Talking isn't what you brought me here for,' Erin countered tartly. 'I appreciate that you feel short-changed but right now there's nothing I can do about it.'

'That's not what I meant,' Cristo said glacially, frustration brightening his black diamond gaze to brilliance in his lean, strong face. 'I'll get you back to Oxford as quick as I can but you have to tell me what's going on.'

Erin nodded agreement and bit her lip. 'Once we're airborne.'

Tell him—he made it sound so simple. She thought of those phone calls she had made, desperate to tell him, desperate for his support in a hostile world. When she'd realised she was pregnant she had reached out in panic, not thinking about what she would have to say or how he would react. Those kinds of fears would have been luxuries when she was struggling just to survive. Now she was older, wiser, aware she was about to open a can of worms with a blunt knife and make a mess. But why not? Why shouldn't Cristo know that he was a father? How he reacted no longer mattered: she already had a job, a roof over her head. She didn't *need* him any more.

Ensconced in the cream-leather-upholstered luxury of Cristo's private jet, Erin struggled to regain her composure but she was too worried about Nuala and her mother. Deidre Turner didn't deal well with the unexpected and suffered from panic attacks. How could she have left her mother with the burden of the twins for the weekend when the older woman had already looked after them all week long? Her mother would have been tired, tested by the daily challenge of caring for two lively toddlers, who didn't always do as they were told, a combination that was an accident waiting to happen.

Cristo released his seat belt and stood up, six feet four inches of well-groomed male, in a dark business suit that made the most of his lean, powerful physique. Shrewd dark golden eyes below sooty lashes welded to her, he dealt her an expectant look.

'I have children now,' Erin declared baldly, breaking the tense silence. 'Twins of two and a bit, a boy and a girl—'

Unsurprisingly, Cristo was stunned. '*Children*?' he repeated the plural designation in a tone of astonishment. 'How could you possibly have children?'

CHAPTER SEVEN

'The usual way. I fell pregnant. I became a mother eight months later,' Erin told him flatly.

'Twins?' Cristo bit out a sardonic laugh to punctuate the word.

'Yes, born a little early. And my daughter, Nuala, got hurt in a playground accident this morning. She broke her arm and she has to have surgery on it. That's why I have to get home asap,' Erin completed in the same strained tone.

'And you didn't feel that you could mention the little fact that you're a mother before this point?' Cristo derided grimly.

Erin studied the carpet. 'I didn't think you'd be interested.'

'I'm more interested in finding out who the father of your twins might be,' Cristo admitted, his stubborn jaw line clenching hard. 'Is it Morton?'

'No,' Erin fielded without hesitation. 'My children were very young when I first met Sam.'

'Why is this like pulling teeth?' Cristo demanded with ringing impatience.

'Because you're going out of your way to avoid the most obvious connection.' Erin lifted her chin and studied him with cool amethyst eyes, an ocean of calm co-cooning her as she moved towards the final bar she had set herself to clear. 'Lorcan and Nuala are your children and don't you dare complain about only finding that out now! It's your fault that I made endless attempts to get in touch with you and failed.'

His stunning dark eyes widened, his beautiful mouth twisting. '*My* children —don't be ridiculous. How could they possibly be mine?'

'The traditional way, Cristo. You turned over in bed one night shortly before we broke up and made love to me without using a condom. Of course I can't be a hundred per cent certain about the exact timing, but certainly that's when I assume that I conceived,' she explained curtly.

Beneath his bronzed skin, Cristo had grown pale as if such nit-picking detail added a veracity to her claim that nothing else could have done. 'You're saying that I got you pregnant?'

'There wasn't anyone else in the picture, in spite of all your misconceptions about Tom's little brother.' Erin rose to her feet with determination. 'You are the father of my children. You can do DNA tests, whatever you like to satisfy yourself. I really don't care. That side of things is immaterial to me now.'

Cristo poured himself a drink from the built in bar. His hand wasn't quite steady as he raised the glass to his lips and drank deep. 'This is inconceivable.'

He wheeled back round to stare at her with cloaked intensity, momentarily stepping outside the dialogue while with every fibre of his being he relived that last sweet taste of her in sunlight as her tongue tangled with his. The burn of that hunger had electrified him. She was a sexual challenge that never waned. That was what she meant to him, a high of satisfaction he craved every time he looked at her. He hated what she was but he wanted to bed her over and over again. That was easier to think about than the fantastic idea that he might have accidentally got her pregnant in the past. Hadn't he only just emerged from a nightmare in that category? A nightmare that had comprehensively blown his marriage and his family apart? And now, the least likely mother of all was telling *him* that he was immaterial? He would never let another woman deny him his paternal rights.

'I'll take a soda and lime,' Erin told him pointedly.

Frowning, his black brows drawing together, Cristo turned back to the bar to prepare her drink. His movements were deft and precise. He handed her a tall moisture-beaded glass, turning his arrogant dark head to study her afresh as he did so. He was so deep in shock at the concept of being a father that he felt as if the passage of time had frozen him in his tracks. 'You said you made endless attempts to get in touch with me.'

'Your PA finally told me that she had instructions not to put my calls through to you and that I was wasting my time.'

Cristo set his glass down on the bar with a sharp little snap of protest. 'I never issued any such instruction!'

'Well, maybe it was the bad fairy who issued it.' Erin lifted and dropped a slight shoulder, unimpressed by his plea of innocence. All too well did she remember how humiliated she had felt having to make those repeated and clearly unwelcome phone calls. 'I also sent a couple of letters.'

'Which I never received.'

Erin ignored that comeback. 'You had changed your

private cell phone number. I had no choice but to try and contact you through your office. At the last, I even phoned your family home in Athens…'

'You contacted my…*parents*?' Cristo queried with frank incredulity.

'And your mother refused to pass on a message to you. She said you were getting married and that you wanted nothing more to do with "a woman like me",' Erin grimaced as she repeated that lowering description.

'I don't believe you. My foster mother is a kind, gentle woman. She would never be so offensive, particularly to a pregnant woman—'

'Oh, I didn't get as far as telling her that I was pregnant during our conversation. I could hardly get a word in edgeways once she realised who I was.'

'She would not have known who you were,' Cristo countered with conviction. 'I never once mentioned your existence to my parents.'

Erin tried not to wince. She had often wondered and he had just confirmed her deepest suspicions. While evidently his foster mother had known her son did have a relationship with a woman in London, she had not received that information from him. Evidently, Erin had never been important enough to her lover to warrant being discussed with his family 'I wrote to your office as well. The letters were returned to me unopened,' she confided doggedly 'That's when I gave up trying to contact you.'

Cristo drained his glass, set it down, shook his head slightly. 'You say I'm the father of your children. I cannot accept that.'

Erin shrugged and sank back into her seat. At least he wasn't shouting at her or calling her a liar…*yet*. Time might well take care of that oversight. In truth, though, she had never seen him so shaken, for Cristo was strong as steel and given to rolling with the punches that life dealt out. But right now he was in a daze, visibly shattered by her revelation.

'It's OK if you can't accept it. I'll understand. But at least I've finally told you. How you feel about it, whether or not you believe me, isn't relevant any more.'

Cristo shot her an exasperated look that hinted at the darker, deeper emotions he was maintaining control over beneath his forbidding reserve. 'How can it not be relevant?'

'Because it doesn't matter any longer. When I first fell pregnant, life was tough. I needed your help then and I didn't get it,' Erin pointed out ruefully. 'Now, thanks to my mother's support, the kids and I are quite self-sufficient as long as I have a reasonable salary to rely on.'

In the strained silence, Cristo poured himself another drink. She watched the muscles work in his strong brown throat and then recalled how only hours earlier she had wanted to eat him alive and she cringed at that reminder of how weak she could be around him. On the other hand, he was a sophisticated man and he had the sexual experience to make her burn—that was *all*! It would be foolish to punish herself just because she had sunk low enough to enjoy their intimacy on his terms. She was a healthy, warm-blooded woman who had suppressed her natural needs for too long. In the end, if anything, too much self-control had made a victim of her. Of course she had never met a man she wanted as she wanted Cristo, never known a man who, even in the midst of the most emotional scene she had ever endured, could still make her mind wander down undisciplined paths. For there he stood, shocked but unbowed, gorgeous dark eyes smouldering with raw reaction in his even more gorgeous face.

'If this story of yours is true, why didn't you tell me the instant I came back into your life?' he pressed, lifting his proud dark head high, a tiny muscle pulling tight at one corner of his unsmiling mouth.

Erin compressed her lips, shook her head. 'I didn't want anyone to know that we'd even had a past relationship, never mind that you're the father of my kids.'

'I don't follow that reasoning. Would Morton have turned against you had he known the truth?'

'Stop dragging Sam into everything. He's nothing to do with any of this,' Erin said vehemently. 'I owe Sam. He took a risk on me. The job with his hotel group made it possible for me to survive. As for other people knowing about our…er…past connection, I would have found that embarrassing.'

Embarrassing? Cristo gritted his even white teeth while resisting the urge to bite back. Why would she lie now? After all, if he was the father of her twins, he had to owe her thousands of pounds in child support. Nor, until he had made checks, could he disprove her claim that she had tried to contact him to tell him that she was pregnant. If it was true and if she had continued with the pregnancy rather than seeking a way out of her predicament, he owed her a debt, didn't he? While his intelligence urged caution, he would be careful of uttering any disparaging comments.

'I'll accompany you home,' Cristo announced in a tone of finality.

Disconcerted, Erin frowned. 'But why would you do that?'

'Perhaps I would like to see these children whom you insist are my flesh and blood.'

Her triangular face froze, long lashes sweeping down over her eyes while she processed an idea that seemed to strike her as extraordinary.

'Surely you expected that?'

Erin glanced up and clashed with eyes that burned like a furnace in Cristo's hard masculine face. 'I hadn't thought that far ahead.'

'I'm coming to the hospital with you,' Cristo decreed.

Erin winced at the prospect, picturing her mother's astonishment, not to mention the prospect of explaining that she had lied about going to Scotland and had gone to Italy to be with Cristo instead.

'There's nothing else that I can do,' Cristo added grimly.

Erin was mystified. Was curiosity or a sense of duty driving him? But then how on earth had she expected him to react to her revelation? Had she really believed that he might just walk away untouched by the news that he was a father?

'I'm not expecting you to get involved with the twins,' Erin muttered uncomfortably.

'It is more a matter of what I expect of myself,' Cristo countered with a gravity she had never seen in him before.

Oh, my word, what have I done? Erin wondered feverishly. What did he expect from himself in the parenting stakes? His own upbringing, after all, had been unusual. And he was a non-conformist to the marrow of his bones, shrugging off convention if it made no sense to him.

It was nine in the evening before they made it to the hospital. Deidre Turner was seated in a bland little side ward next to a bed in which a small still form lay. The older woman, her face grey with exhaustion and her eyes marked pink by tears, scrambled upright when she saw her daughter. 'Erin, thank goodness! I was scared you mightn't make it back tonight and I was worried about leaving Lorcan with Tamsin,' she confided, only then noting the presence of the tall black-haired male behind Erin.

'Mum?' Erin murmured uncertainly. 'This is Cristo Donakis. He insisted on coming with me.'

For once shorn of his social aplomb, Cristo came to a dead halt at the foot of the bed to gaze down at the little girl with the white-blonde curls clustered round her small head. She looked like Erin but her skin was several shades darker than her mother's fair complexion. His attention rested on the small skinny arm bearing a colourful cast and he swallowed a sudden unfamiliar thickness in his throat. She was tiny as a doll and as he stared in growing wonderment her feathery lashes lifted to reveal eyes as dark a brown as his own.

'Mummy...' Nuala whispered drowsily.

'I'm here.' Erin hastily pulled up a seat and perched on the edge of it, leaning forward to pat Nuala's little hand soothingly. 'How did the surgery go, Mum?'

'Really well. The surgeon was very pleased,' Deidre confided. 'Nuala should regain the full use of her arm.'

'That's a relief,' Erin commented, turning her gaze back to her daughter's small flushed face. 'How are you feeling, pet?'

'My arm's sore.' The little girl sighed, her attention roaming away from her mother to lock to the tall powerful man stationed at the foot of her bed. 'Who is that man?'

'I'm Cristo,' Cristo muttered not quite steadily.

'He's your daddy,' Deidre Turner explained without hesitation, a broad smile of satisfaction chasing the exhaustion from her drawn face.

Shock at that announcement trapped Erin's breath in her throat and she shot the older woman a look of dismay.

'Honesty is the best policy,' Deidre remarked to noone in particular, rising from her seat to extend a hand to Cristo. 'I'm Erin's mother, Deidre.'

'Daddy?' Nuala repeated wide-eyed at the description. 'You're my daddy?'

In the simmering silence, Erin frowned. 'Yes. He's your daddy,' she confirmed. 'Mum? Could I have a word with you in private?'

A nurse came in just then to check on Nuala and, after mentioning that her daughter was complaining of pain, Erin stepped outside with her mother. 'You must be wondering what's going on,' Erin began awkwardly.

'What's there to wonder? Obviously you've finally told the man he's a father and that's not before time,' the older woman replied wryly.

Erin breathed in deep. 'I'm afraid I lied to you about where I was this weekend—I wasn't in Scotland with Tom and Melissa. I was with Cristo.'

'And you didn't know how to tell me, I suppose. Did you think I would interfere?' Deidre enquired astutely. 'He's the twins' father. Naturally you need to sort this situation out but you've taken the first step towards that and I'm proud of you.'

Surprised by that assurance, Erin gave her parent a quick embarrassed hug. 'I'm sorry I wasn't honest with you. Look, now I'm here, you should go home—'

'And collect Lorcan and put him to bed,' Deidre completed. 'He was upset about Nuala. Will you stay the night here with her or will you come home later?'

'I'll see how Nuala is before I decide.'

'She'll be fine. She's a tough little article,' Erin's mother pronounced fondly. 'Lorcan cried when she fell because he got a fright and she called him a baby. By the time I got Nuala to the hospital they were fighting—at least it took her mind off the pain of the break.'

Erin saw the older woman into the lift and returned to the side ward.

'What do daddies do?' Nuala was asking plaintively.

'They look after you.'

Erin's daughter was unimpressed. 'Mummy and Granny look after me.'

'And now you have me as well,' Cristo told his daughter quietly.

'You can fix my arm with magic,' Nuala told him in a tone of complaint.

'Daddy doesn't have his magic wand with him,' Erin chipped in from the foot of the bed.

Nuala's dark eyes rounded. 'Daddy has a magic wand?'

Cristo skimmed Erin a pained glance. 'I'm afraid I don't.'

'Never mind,' Nuala said drowsily. 'My arm hurts.'

'The medicine the nurse gave you will start working soon,' Cristo asserted soothingly.

Within minutes, Nuala had drifted off to sleep.

'I'm sorry Mum just leapt in with her big announcement,' Erin muttered uncomfortably.

'Obviously she believes the twins are mine and, if that's true, there are no regrets on my part,' Cristo responded with a quality of calm she had not expected to see in him after the bombshell she had dropped on him. 'It's a bad idea to lie to children.'

Erin fell asleep in her chair and only wakened when the nurses began their morning round. She was surprised that Cristo had remained through the night, for she had expected him to leave late and make use of a hotel. Instead he had stayed with them and she was grudgingly impressed by his tenacity. His black hair was tousled, his tie loose where he had undone the top button of his shirt. A heavy dark shadow of stubble covered his strong jaw line, accentuating the sensual perfection of his mobile mouth. It shook her to open her eyes and see him and for her first thought to be that he was absolutely gorgeous. Her face flamed as his stunning dark golden eyes assailed hers. Her skin prickled with awareness, her breasts swelling and making her bra feel too tight. She tore her attention from him with a sense of mortification that she had so little control over her reactions to him.

'Apparently the canteen opens soon. We'll go down for breakfast once Nuala has had hers,' Cristo said decisively.

The night had been long and his reflections deep and interminable, Cristo acknowledged heavily, fighting off the exhaustion dogging him. He had watched Erin and the child who might be his daughter sleep. He had remembered the early years of his own childhood with the fortitude of an adult, processing what he had learned from those unhappy memories, already knowing what he must do while striving to greet rather than flinch from the necessity.

Erin took Nuala into the bathroom to freshen up. She was stiff from spending the night in the chair and slow to respond to her daughter's innocent chatter. She did what little she could to tidy herself but her raincoat, silk top and linen trousers were creased beyond redemption and without make-up she could do nothing to brighten her pale face and tired, shadowed eyes.

'Obviously you'll want DNA tests done,' Erin said over breakfast, preferring to take that bull by the horns in preference to Cristo feeling that he had to make that demand. 'I'll agree to that.'

'It would make it easier to establish the twins as my legal heirs,' Cristo agreed, his expression grave. 'But I believe that that is the only reason I would have it done.'

'You're saying that you believe me now?' Erin prompted in a surprised undertone.

Cristo gave her a silent nod of confirmation and finished his coffee. By the time they returned to Nuala's bedside the doctors' round had been done and the ward sister informed them that they could take Nuala home as soon as they liked.

Lorcan, already prepared by his grandmother for the truth that he was about to meet his father, was in full livewire mode, behaving like a jumping bean from the instant Cristo entered the small sitting room of Deidre and Erin's terraced home. Lorcan scrambled onto a stool and stood up to get closer to the tall black-haired male but, dissatisfied with the height differential, leapt off the stool and clambered onto the coffee table instead.

'Get down, Lorcan,' Erin instructed, stooping to gather up the pile of magazines that her son had sent flying to the floor while her mother cooed over Nuala like a homing pigeon. 'Right now...'

When Cristo focused on the little boy he felt as if he had been punched in the stomach. With his coal-black curls and impish dark eyes, Lorcan was a dead ringer for every photograph Cristo had ever seen of himself at the same age. His stare darkened in intensity, shock reverberating through his big powerful length as he made that final step towards accepting what he was seeing as fact: he was a father.

'I'm going to count to five, Lorcan,' Erin warned, her tension level rising. 'One...two...'

Lorcan performed a handstand and grinned with delight at Cristo from upside down. 'Daddy do this?' he asked expectantly.

'*Don't*!' Erin gasped as Cristo bent down.

But, mercifully, Cristo had not been about to perform a handstand. He had merely bent to lift his son off the coffee table and turn him the right side up while Lorcan shrieked with excitement. 'Hello, Lorcan,' Cristo murmured evenly. 'Calm down.'

Unfortunately Lorcan was in no mood to calm down. When Cristo returned him to the floor, Lorcan began to scramble over every piece of furniture in the room at high speed while loudly urging Cristo to watch what he could do. Erin almost groaned out loud as Nuala bounded from her side to try and join in the ruckus. Cristo snatched his daughter out of harm's way. 'Show Lorcan your arm,' he instructed her.

Nuala showed off her cast, small mouth pouting.

'Hurts,' she informed her brother, who moved closer to inspect the injured arm.

Erin crouched down. 'And we have to be *very* careful with Nuala's sore arm,' she told her son.

Lorcan touched the cast enviously. 'Want it,' he said.

'You should take them out to the park to let off some steam,' Deidre Turner suggested, beaming at Cristo, who was returning the cushions Lorcan had knocked off the sofa. 'Oh, never mind about that—I'm used to tidying up every five minutes!'

Erin swallowed a yawn. 'The park? That's a good idea. I'll just go and get changed first.'

Hurtling upstairs to her small bedroom, Erin could not quite come to grips with the knowledge that Cristo was in her home. It felt like some crazy dream but there was something horribly realistic about the fact that both her children were acting up like mad and revealing their every wild and wonderful fault. What did Cristo really think about them? How did he really feel? And why did she care about that side of things? After all, naturally he wanted to see both children to satisfy his curiosity, but she doubted that his interest went much deeper than that. Respecting the cool temperature of a typical English spring, Erin donned straight-leg jeans, knee-length boots and a blue cable knit sweater. She brushed her hair, let it fall round her shoulders and made use of a little blusher and mascara before she felt presentable. Presentable enough for what? *For Cristo?* Shame engulfed her like a blanket. Why was she so predictable? Why was she always worrying about what Cristo thought of her? Only last month she had seen Cristo in a gossip column squiring a beautiful model with hair like gold silk and the glorious shape of a Miss World!

Cristo specialised in superstar women with the kind of looks that stopped traffic. His ex-wife, Lisandra, was an utterly ravishing brunette. Erin had never been in that class and had often wondered if that was why he had lost interest in her.

But now she knew different, she reminded herself wretchedly as she went downstairs. Now she knew that Cristo had dumped her because he believed she was a total slut who had gone behind his back and slept with another man. Was it better to know that or *worse*?

A twin apiece, they walked a hundred yards to the park. Cristo had sent his limo driver off to locate and buy car seats for the children. Lorcan took exaggerated big steps as he concentrated on stepping only on the lines between the flagstones. Nuala hummed a nursery rhyme and pulled handfuls of leaves off the shrubs they passed until Cristo told his daughter to, 'Stop it!'

Without hesitation, Nuala threw herself down on the pavement and began to kick and scream.

'You shouldn't have said that,' Erin hissed in frustration. 'She's tired and cross and her arm's hurting her. Of course she's not in a good mood.'

'You can't let her vandalise people's gardens,' Cristo replied drily and he bent down and picked Nuala up. Her daughter squirmed violently, flailed her fists and screamed full throttle.

Cristo took a couple of fists in the face before he restored order. 'No,' he said again.

'Yes!' Nuala shrieked back at him, unleashing the full tempest of her toddler temper.

Erin was trying not to cringe and cave in to her daughter's every demand as she saw faces appearing at windows overlooking the street.

'Want slide,' Lorcan whinged, tugging at his mother's jacket. 'Want swings.'

'So, this is what it feels like to be a parent,' Cristo commented, flexing his bruised jaw with a slight grimace, his stunning eyes pure black diamond brilliance as if on some weird level he was actually enjoying the challenge.

'They're a handful sometimes…not *all* the time,' Erin stressed, walking on, keen to reach the park where noisy childish outbursts commanded less attention.

Lower lip thrust out, Nuala told Cristo, 'Want down.'

'Say please,' Cristo traded.

'No!' Nuala roared.

'Then I'll carry you the rest of the way like a baby.'

Nuala lost her head again and screamed while her brother chanted delightedly, 'Nuala's a baby!' as he walked by his mother's side.

Silence fell only as they reached the gates of the park.

'Please,' Nuala framed as if every syllable hurt.

Cristo lowered his daughter slowly back onto her own feet.

'I hate you!' Nuala launched at him furiously, snatching her hand free of his and grabbing her mother's free hand in place of it. 'I don't want a daddy!'

As Cristo parted his lips to respond Erin cut in, 'Just ignore it…*please.*'

Once she sat down on the mercifully free bench in her accustomed spot, Erin murmured, 'The best way to handle the twins is with distraction and compromise. Going toe to toe with them simply provokes a tantrum.'

'Thanks for the heads-up. I'm going to need it. I believe I used to throw tantrums,' Cristo confided. 'According to my foster mother, I too was a challenging child.'

'Tell me something I couldn't have guessed.' Erin laughed, abstractedly watching the breeze ruffle his cropped hair into half curls, so very similar to his son's. As she met his spectacular amber and honey coloured eyes framed by sooty lashes, it was as if a hand grabbed her heart and squeezed and possibly that was the moment that she understood that she would never be entirely free of Cristo Donakis. That was not simply because she had given birth to children who had inherited his explosive personality. It was because she enjoyed his forceful character, his strength of purpose and persistence and the very fact he could sit on an old bench in a slightly overgrown and rundown park and seem entirely at home there in spite of his hand-stitched shoes, gold cufflinks and a superbly well-cut suit that still looked a million dollars even after he had sat up all night in it. He might be arrogant but he was hugely adaptable, resourceful and willing to learn from his mistakes.

'I should tell you about my marriage,' Cristo said flatly.

'You never mention your ex-wife,' she remarked helplessly, disconcerted by the sudden change of subject and the intimacy of the topic as she watched Lorcan play on the swings and Nuala head down to the sandpit, her cast protected by the cling film Erin had wrapped round it. It wasn't like Cristo to volunteer to talk about anything particularly private.

'Why would I? We were only married for five minutes and now we're divorced,' Cristo fielded coolly.

'Have you stayed friends?'

'We're not enemies,' Cristo stated after a moment's

thought on that score. 'But we move in different social circles and rarely see each other.'

'Was it a case of marry in haste and repent at leisure?' Erin pressed tautly. 'Did you know her well before you married her?'

'I thought I did.' Cristo bit out a sardonic laugh. 'I also thought it was time I got married. My foster parents, Vasos and Appollonia, had been urging me to marry for a couple of years. It was the only thing they had ever tried to influence in my life and I did want to please them,' he admitted gruffly. 'I met Lisandra at a dinner party at their home. I already knew her but not well. We seemed to be at the same stage in life, bored with the single scene. We got married three months later.'

'So what went wrong?' she almost whispered, recognising the shadow that crossed his lean, darkly handsome face.

'About a year after we married, Lisandra decided that she wanted a child. I agreed—it seemed like the natural next step.' His shapely mouth tightened and compressed. 'When she got pregnant, she was ecstatic and she threw a party to celebrate. Both our families were overjoyed at the prospect of a first grandchild.'

'And you—how did you feel about it?' Erin prompted hesitantly.

'I was pleased, happy Lisandra was happy, grateful she had something new to occupy her. She got bored easily,' Cristo admitted stonily. 'And a couple of months into the pregnancy Lisandra got cold feet.'

'Cold feet?' Erin queried with a frown, her attention locked to the air of harsh restraint etched in his lean strong face that indicated that, while his voice might sound mild, his inner feelings were the exact opposite.

'My wife decided she wasn't ready to have a child after all. She felt too young for the responsibility and trapped by her condition. She decided that the only solution to her regrets and fears was a termination.'

Erin released her pent up breath in a sudden audible hiss. 'Oh, Cristo—'

'I tried to talk her out of it, reminding her that we could afford domestic staff so that she need never feel tied down by our child.' He breathed in slow and deep and bitter regret clouded his dark eyes. 'But I failed to talk her round to my point of view. She had a termination while I was away on business. I was devastated. Our families had to be told. My foster mother, who was never able to have a child of her own, had a nervous breakdown when she found out—she just couldn't handle it. Lisandra's parents were distressed but they supported their daughter's decision because they had never in their entire lives told her that, no, she couldn't have everything and do anything she wanted…'

'And you?' Erin prodded sickly, feeling guilty that she had not even suspected that a truly heartbreaking story might lie behind his divorce.

Cristo linked lean brown hands and shrugged a fatalistic broad shoulder. 'I suppose I couldn't handle it either. Intellectually I don't know what Lisandra and I would have done with a child whose mother didn't want it and resented its very existence but I still couldn't forgive my wife for the abortion. I tried, she tried, we both *tried* but it was just there like an elephant in the room every time we were together. I made her feel guilty, she made me feel angry. I saw too much in her that I didn't like and I didn't think she would ever change, so I asked her for a divorce.'

'I'm so sorry, Cristo…really, very sincerely sorry,' Erin murmured shakily, a lump forming in her throat as she rested a slender hand briefly on his arm in a gesture of support. 'That must have been a shattering experience.'

'I only told you because I want you to understand why I can't walk away from Lorcan and Nuala. If that's what you're expecting or even hoping for, I'm afraid you're going to be disappointed.'

Erin paled, wondering what he was telling her and fearfully insecure about what his next move might be.

CHAPTER EIGHT

CRISTO wasn't accustomed to feeling powerless but that was exactly how he felt after his consultation with a top London lawyer.

An unmarried father, he learned at that crucial meeting, had virtually no rights over his children under English law and even a married father, lacking his wife's support and agreement, might well have to fight through the courts to gain any access to his offspring. Furthermore he had no grounds on which to complain about any aspect of the twins' upbringing. In spite of the fact that he had not contributed to his children's upkeep they were currently living within the security of their mother and grandmother's home with all their needs adequately provided for.

'Marrying the twins' mother is really the only remedy for a man in your position,' he was told succinctly.

It was not good news on Cristo's terms for he loathed any situation outside his control. The DNA testing, achieved and completed within ten days of his first meeting with Lorcan and Nuala had merely confirmed what Cristo already knew and accepted. He was a father and the twins were his flesh and blood, a connection he was incapable of ignoring or treating lightly. He could not move on with his life without them. While he knew that Erin had done her best he also recognised that the twins would require firmer boundaries before they got much older. Yet did that mean that he was to overlook the less acceptable elements in Erin's character? A woman who had stolen from him? For the first time ever he acknowledged grudgingly that that charge did not quite add up. If Erin was mercenary why hadn't she taken more advantage of his financial generosity while she was with him? Why on earth would a woman who craved more money have refused to accept valuable diamond jewellery from him? That made no sense whatsoever. He resolved to take a fresh look at the irregularities that had been found in the accounts of the Mobila spa during Erin's employment there. But before the press got hold of the story—as he was convinced they inevitably would—he required a decent solution, not only to his and Erin's current predicament but also for the future. Some arrangement that would endure for as long as the children needed their parents' support. Recognising the direction his thoughts were taking him in, Cristo felt anger kicking in again.

On the exact same day, Erin was tackling a difficult personal matter with Sam. They were standing in his temporary office, the larger original room having been taken over by a team from Donakis Hotels, who were working to ensure a smooth changeover of ownership. The sale was complete. Sam was only still making himself available for consultation out of loyalty to his hotel group and former employees.

The older man knitted his brows, a shocked look in his blue eyes. 'Cristo Donakis is the twins' father?' he repeated in astonishment.

'I felt I should mention it. My mother has been telling people and I wanted you to hear it from me, rather than as a piece of gossip,' Erin admitted stiffly.

'But when you met here neither of you even admitted that you knew each other.'

'I hadn't seen Cristo since we broke up and my natural inclination was to keep my personal life private.'

Sam Morton dealt her a hurt look that made her flush with discomfiture. 'Even from me?'

'When I walked into your office that day and saw Cristo standing there it was such a shock that I wasn't exactly thinking straight,' she said apologetically. 'I'm sorry. Maybe I should have come clean afterwards but it was very awkward.'

'No, you're quite right. Your private life should be private. I assume it was Cristo you were working for in London?'

Erin nodded. 'I resigned when we split up.'

'I should have made that connection from your original CV. But Donakis let you down badly when you were pregnant,' Sam completed drily.

'There was a misunderstanding,' Erin declared, her eyes evasive. 'Cristo had no idea I was pregnant and there was no further communication between us.'

'But you tried very hard to get in touch with him,' Sam reminded her.

'It was just one of those things, Sam.'

Sam's nostrils flared. 'So, he's forgiven for putting you through hell.'

'It's not like that. Cristo knows about the children now and we're trying to work through that as best we can.'

'Are you getting involved with him again? No, scratch that!' Sam advised abruptly. 'I have no right to pry.'

Erin thought about Italy and screened her expressive eyes. 'I don't know how to answer that question—it's complicated?' she joked uneasily.

'I hope it's the right thing for you. I'd *hate* to see you unhappy again,' Sam pronounced feelingly. 'You gave Donakis one chance. Who's to say he deserves another?'

Well, her mother for one thing, Erin reflected wryly as she caught up with her emails ten minutes later. In her mother's eyes, Cristo had gone from being the most reviled womanising male in Europe to being a positive favourite. And all within the unlikely space of a mere ten days! His regular visits, his interest in the twins, his good manners, his tactful ability to defer to her mother's greater knowledge when it came to the children, his insistence that Deidre Turner join them when they went out to eat had all had an effect. Cristo had shone like a star at every opportunity and was piling up brownie points like a miser with a barn full of treasure chests. Erin, on the other hand, was finding the new order confusing and hard to adapt to.

Cristo was no longer her lover. That weekend in Italy, that single night of passion, did in retrospect seem more like the product of her imagination than anything that had actually happened. Now Cristo visited their home to see Lorcan and Nuala and stayed in one of his newly acquired hotels when he was in the area. He was wary and deep down inside that fact hurt Erin. She could remember another Cristo, a guy who had raced through the door to greet her eagerly when he'd been away for a while, unashamedly passionate, openly demonstrative, not picking his words, not hiding behind caution. This new Cristo was older and much cooler. He was polite, even considerate, but reserved when it came to

more personal stuff. Even the confidences he had unex-
pectedly shared with Erin in the park still troubled her.

His wife's termination had deeply wounded Cristo
and possibly made him think more deeply than many
men about what a child might mean to him. Now Erin
was seeing the results of that more solicitous outlook in
practice, for Cristo undoubtedly wanted to do as much
as possible to help her with their children. When he visited, he played with them, took them out with Erin in
tow and had even helped to bathe them one evening after
Erin fell asleep on the sofa after work. He was demonstrating that he could be a hands-on father and the kids
were already very partial to his more energetic presence.
Erin was impressed but more than a little concerned as
to where all this surprising attention was likely to lead.

What did Cristo really want from her? Acceptance of
his role? Could it be that simple? Could Cristo, for possibly the very first time in his life, be playing it straight?
Or was there a darker, more devious plan somewhere
in the back of his mind? Cristo Donakis did not dance
to other people's tunes. He always had an agenda. Unfortunately for Erin she was unable to work out what
that agenda might be and what it might entail for her
and her children. In addition she was especially worried that Cristo still harboured serious doubts about her
honesty. It was time she tackled Sally Jennings, she reflected ruefully. Somehow she had to prove her innocence of theft. But would Sally even agree to speak to
her? It occurred to her that it might well be wiser to arrive to see Sally at Cristo's flagship London spa without a prior announcement of her intent. She decided to
take a day's leave and tackle Sally. Would she get any-

where? She didn't know but it was currently the only idea she could come up with.

The phone by her bed rang at six the following morning and, ruefully knuckling the sleep from her eyes, Erin sat up in bed. '*Yes*?'

It was Cristo. 'Erin?'

'Why are you waking me up at this time of the morning?'

'A deputy editor I'm friendly with has just called me with a tip-off. Apparently there's a story in the pipeline about you, me and the twins. The publication he named is particularly sleazy so I don't think the article will contain anything that your family or mine would want to read.'

Erin's face froze. 'But why? Who on earth would be interested in reading about us?'

'Erin…' Cristo sighed, mustering patience for he was more accustomed to dealing with people who took tabloid attention in their stride and even courted it for the sake of their careers or social status. 'I'm a very wealthy man, recently divorced…'

Lorcan darted through the bedroom door, scrambled under the duvet with his mother and tucked cold feet against her slim thighs. His sister was only a few steps behind him.

Erin was squashed up against the wall as Nuala joined them in the bed. 'If it's true, if there is going to be a story, there's nothing we can do to prevent it.'

'Yes, there is,' Cristo contradicted. 'I can get you and the children out of that house and put you somewhere the paparazzi can't get near you for a photo opportunity. Then I can organise a PR announcement concerning my new status as a father and, once that's done, the press will lose interest.'

Erin breathed in deep. She certainly didn't fancy the press on her doorstep, but she was much inclined to think that he was taking the matter too seriously. 'Cristo, I have a job. I can't just drop everything and disappear.'

'Of course you can. You work for me now,' he reminded her. 'Pack. I'll make the arrangements. A car will pick you up to take you to the airport.'

'But I haven't agreed yet.'

'I will do whatever it takes to protect you and the twins from adverse publicity,' Cristo cut in forcefully, exasperation lending his dark deep drawl a rougher edge. 'I don't want some innuendo-laden piece appearing in print about us.'

'We had an affair. I got pregnant. It's not that unusual—'

'Trust me,' Cristo breathed. 'You'll be accused of having been a married man's mistress and that is not a possibility I want to appear in print.'

A flash of temper and distaste at that prospect rippled through Erin because that was also a humiliating label that she did not want to be lumbered with. 'OK. Where are you planning to send us…assuming I agree, which I haven't yet,' she reminded him.

'Greece…specifically, my island.'

Erin rolled her eyes. 'Oh, so you now have an island all your own?'

'I inherited Thesos from my father when I was twenty-one.'

'Well, you never mentioned it before,' Erin remarked curtly, wondering how much else she didn't know about him while trying to think frantically fast. 'Look, I'll consider going to Greece for a few days if you really think it's necessary—'

'I do.'

'But before I leave I want the chance to speak to Sally Jennings. She does still work for you, doesn't she?'

There was a moment of silence before Cristo responded expressionlessly, 'She does. She's now the deputy manager at the spa. Why?'

'And I'm sure she's very efficient. She was when I was working there,' Erin commented stiffly. 'I'll call in on the way to the airport. I don't want her to know I'm coming. I'll drop the twins off with you at your office.'

'There's no need. I'll meet you in the hotel foyer. But I don't think this is a good idea, Erin. Very few people know about the money that went missing. I handled it very discreetly. I don't think it's wise to start making enquiries again this long after the event.'

'This is the price of me going to Greece,' Erin countered flatly. 'I see Sally in London before I go or I don't go at all.'

'But that's bl—' Cristo retorted in a seething undertone.

'Blackmail?' Erin slotted in with saccharine sweetness. 'You're preaching to the converted, Cristo. Guess who taught me the skill?'

'If I facilitate this meeting at the spa, you'll come to Greece with me?'

'Of course I will. I keep my promises.' Erin came off the phone a minute later, feeling re-energised, and swept the twins out of bed to get dressed. It was past time she began calling some of the shots. Cristo became unbearable when he got his own way too much.

But she was rather touched that he was willing to go to so much trouble to whisk them away from the perils of too much press interest. Honestly, Erin thought ruefully, sometimes Cristo could be naïve. Did he really think she couldn't cope with journalists on the doorstep or some nasty article that tried to make her sound more exciting and wicked than she was? She was not that vulnerable. Life had taught her to roll with the punches. In any case the idea of travelling to Cristo's private island intrigued her. He was *finally* going to take her to his real home and naturally she was curious.

Her mother got up while the twins were eating their breakfast and, when she realised that her daughter was to leave the house in little more than an hour to travel abroad, she urged Erin to go and start packing. Before she did so, Erin rang work and requested a week's leave.

'Do you think you'll meet Cristo's parents?' Deidre asked hopefully.

Erin grimaced, in no hurry to meet Appollonia Denes, who had cut her off on the phone while making it very clear that she did not think Erin was good enough for the little boy she had raised to adulthood. Cristo had been born into a substantial fortune, the only child of two young, rich and beautiful Greeks, both from socially prominent families. Vasos and Appollonia had become Cristo's guardians when he was orphaned at the age of five, after his birth parents died in a speedboat accident. Vasos had been a trusted employee in the Donakis empire and Cristo's godfather. The older couple had had no children of their own. Erin recalled that Cristo had mentioned Appollonia having a nervous breakdown and during that phone call she had decided that the older woman was more than a little off the wall.

So, she hoped she wouldn't be meeting the older couple. Things would be challenging enough without having to deal with people who had disliked and disapproved of her even before they had met her. No doubt Vasos and Appollonia would find the news that she was the mother of Cristo's twins a source of severe embarrassment and dissatisfaction.

The twins fell asleep in the limo that carried them to London, waking up with renewed energy to bounce up the steps of the Mobila hotel. Garbed in a grey pinstripe dress and jacket, her pale hair curving round her cheekbones, Erin was apprehensive as she walked into the opulent foyer.

'Daddy!' Lorcan cried, tearing his hand free of his mother's to pelt across the open space.

'Kisto!' Nuala exclaimed, for she would not call her father Daddy, even though he had asked her to do so.

Erin focused on Cristo, seeing the manager of the renowned hotel anchored to his side and reckoning that so public a greeting from his secret children could scarcely be welcome to him. But Cristo was grinning, that wide wonderful smile she had almost forgotten flashing across his lean bronzed features in a transformation that took her breath away as he swung Lorcan up into his arms and smoothed a comforting hand over Nuala's curly head as she clung to his trouser leg with toddler tenacity.

As Erin looked at the drop-dead gorgeous father of her children a tingle of heat pinched the peaks of her breasts to tightness and arrowed down into her pelvis to spread a sensation of melting warmth. All her hormones, she registered in dismay, were in top working order and threatening to go into overdrive.

'Miss Turner.' The hotel manager shook hands with every appearance of warmth. 'What beautiful children.'

'Erin, I've arranged for Jenny to look after the twins in the crèche while we're visiting the spa,' Cristo explained, and a young woman stepped forward with a smile and proceeded to chat to Nuala.

'So, you've opened a crèche here now,' Erin remarked, her professional interest caught by that idea because she had first floated it to Cristo.

'It's very popular with our clients,' the manger advanced with enthusiasm. 'Many of them have young children.'

'The facility pays for itself,' Cristo explained, a lean hand resting to Erin's taut spine to lead her in the direction of the spa. She was filled with dismay at the realisation that he intended to accompany her, for she had not thought that far ahead and she was convinced that his intimidating presence could only injure her chances of success.

Momentarily. Erin glanced back anxiously at the twins. Lorcan was making a phenomenal noise with the toy trumpet the wily Jenny had produced while Nuala was trying her hardest to get her hands on the same toy.

'Are you certain you want to go ahead with talking to Sally?' Cristo pressed in a discouraging undertone. 'I don't agree with it. What the hell can you expect to gain but embarrassment from such a meeting?'

'Sally is the only person who knows the whole story. I don't have a choice,' Erin replied tightly, her nervous tension rising as Cristo bent down to her level and the rich evocative smell of his cologne and him ensnared her on every level.

'Don't do this for me, *koukla mou*,' Cristo urged suddenly, staring down at her as they came to a halt outside the door that now bore Sally's nameplate. 'It doesn't matter to me now. A lot of water has gone under the bridge since then. You were young. You made a mistake and I'm sure you learned from it—'

'Don't you dare patronise me, you...you...you *toad*!' Erin finally selected in her spirited retort. 'And don't interfere.'

'Toad?' Cristo repeated blankly.

'I'd have called you something a good deal more blunt if I hadn't trained myself not to use bad words around the children!' she told him curtly, hastily depressing the door handle of the office before she could lose what little remained of her momentum.

Sally, a tall middle-aged woman with red hair and light blue eyes, was standing behind her desk talking on the phone. When she saw Erin, she froze, her previous animated expression ironed flat as she visibly lost colour.

'Erin, my goodness,' she breathed in astonishment, dropping the phone back on its cradle in haste and bustling round the desk. 'And Mr Donakis...'

'I would like your assurance that anything that is said in this room remains between these four walls,' Cristo said quietly.

Sally looked bewildered and then she smiled. 'Of course, Mr Donakis. Take a seat and tell me what I can help you with.'

Erin was so nervous that she could feel her knees trembling and she linked her hands tightly together as she sat down. 'I'm sure that you're aware that the audit two and a half years ago threw up certain anomalies in the spa accounts...'

If possible, Sally went paler than ever and she dropped rather heavily back down behind her desk. 'Mr Donakis did ask me to keep that problem confidential.'

'Sally,' Erin muttered, suddenly filled with a sense of utter hopelessness. What craziness had brought her here to this pointless encounter? There was no way Sally was going to offer up a belated confession of fraud with her employer present. 'Perhaps you could leave us alone, Cristo.'

'No, I have news to share first. I'm planning to have the account irregularities looked at again.'

The older woman's face went all tight. 'But, Mr Donakis, I thought that matter was done and dusted. You said you were satisfied.'

'I'm afraid I wasn't. And bearing in mind how helpful you were during the first investigation, I thought you should be informed before the experts arrive to go over the books again,' Cristo completed.

Sally had turned an unhealthy colour, her dazed eyes flickering between the two of them, and suddenly she spoke. 'You're a couple again, aren't you?' she exclaimed, her attention lodging almost accusingly on Erin. 'And you've told him about me, haven't you?'

'Told me what?' Cristo enquired lazily.

Taking on board the reality that Cristo was piling the pressure on Sally to admit that she had lied and offering Erin a level of support she had not expected to receive from him, Erin squared her shoulders in frustration. She had always fought her own battles.

Sally compressed her lips in mutinous silence as if daring Erin to answer that question.

'While I was working here I discovered that Sally had been taking products from the store and selling them on online auctions.' Erin turned her attention back to the older woman, who had once been a trusted colleague. 'I know I promised that that was our secret but sometimes promises have to be broken.'

'You were stealing?' Cristo prompted Sally forbiddingly.

Tears spilled from Sally's eyes and she knocked them away with her hand and fumbled for a tissue, which she clenched tightly in one hand.

'I guarantee that whatever you tell me there will be no prosecution now or in the future.' Lean, strong face taut, Cristo stood up, a lithe powerful figure of considerable command. 'I very much regret that you felt unable to be honest with me when this business was first discovered but I'm hoping that for Erin's sake you will now tell me the truth.'

'No prosecution?' Sally queried uncertainly.

'No prosecution. I only want the truth,' Cristo confirmed.

'One lunchtime shortly before Erin resigned a man came to see me,' Sally related in a flat voice. 'He said he was a private detective and he offered me a substantial amount of money if I could give him information that would damage Erin's reputation.'

'*What*?' Cristo positively erupted into speech, his disbelief unhidden.

'His name was Will Grimes. He worked at an agency in Camden. That's all I know about him. At first I said no to him. After all there wasn't any information to give!' Sally pointed out with a wry grimace. 'You hadn't done anything but work hard here, Erin, but then you suddenly resigned from your job and just like that I realised how I could get myself out of the trouble that I was in.'

'Will Grimes,' Cristo was repeating heavily.

'I was in a great deal more financial trouble than I admitted when you found me helping myself to that stuff from the store,' Sally told Erin tautly. 'I had set up a couple of other scams in the books—'

'The payments to therapists that didn't exist, the altered invoices?' Cristo specified.

'Yes, and then you organised the audit and I started to panic,' Sally confided tearfully. 'Erin had left the spa by then.'

'And you decided to let me take the blame for it?' Erin prompted while she wondered how on earth she had ever attracted the attention of a private detective.

'I *wanted* to stop taking the money,' the older woman stressed in open desperation.' I knew it was wrong but I had got in too deep. Once the fraud was uncovered and I set up things so that you got the blame I could go back to a normal life again and, of course, I still had my job. I knew you would be safe from prosecution with Mr Donakis—he wasn't likely to trail his own girlfriend into court!'

'You got me right on that score,' Cristo derided.

'Will you prosecute me now?' Sally asked him shakily.

'No. I gave you my word and I thank you for finally telling me what really happened,' Cristo responded.

Clearly limp with relief, Sally braced her hands on the desk to stand up. 'I'll clear my desk immediately and leave—'

'No, work out your notice here as normal,' Cristo

urged, resting a hand on Erin's taut shoulder to ease her slowly upright.

'Erin?' Sally breathed stiltedly. 'I'm sorry. When you were so kind to me, you deserved better from me.'

Erin nodded, even tried to force her lips into a forgiving smile, but couldn't manage it for she was all too well aware how the false belief that she was a thief had affected Cristo's opinion of her. In any case, she was deeply shaken by what Sally had confessed and she couldn't hide the fact. She had been fond of the older woman, had only lost contact with her because she had fallen pregnant and on hard times. Pride had ensured that she did not pursue ongoing contact with anyone at her former workplace. She stole a veiled glance at Cristo's profile. He was pale, his facial muscles taut below his dark complexion.

Cristo paused at the door on his way out. 'Did you collect the reward money from the private detective and give him the supposed evidence of Erin's dishonesty?'

Sally winced and nodded slowly. 'It got me out of debt and gave me a fresh start.'

Erin gritted her teeth, disgusted by Sally's selfishness.

Cristo felt as if the walls of his tough shell were crumbling around him. Astonishingly, Erin's seemingly paranoid suspicion that she was being set up for a fall by persons unknown had been proven correct. He, who rarely got anything wrong, had been wrong. He had made an appalling error of judgement. But more than anything at that moment he wanted to know who could possibly have hired a detective to discredit Erin in his eyes by fair means or foul.

CHAPTER NINE

ERIN picked at the perfectly cooked lunch served on board Cristo's private jet without much appetite. She was still angry at Sally and bitter that the older woman had got away with destroying Erin's reputation rather than her own. How many other people were suffering from the mistaken assumption that she was a con woman, who had escaped her just deserts solely because she was the owner's ex-girlfriend? As someone who had always worked hard with scrupulous honesty and pride in her performance of her duties, she deeply resented the false impression that Sally had created to hide her own wrongdoing.

'We have to talk,' Cristo remarked flatly.

'I don't think I've ever heard that phrase from you before,' she parried waspishly, recalling that once upon a time Cristo had been the first out of he door when such a suggestion was laid before him. That had certainly been his all-too-masculine reaction on every occasion when she'd tried to corner him for a *serious* conversation.

From the cabin next door she could hear the sounds of the children playing and talking. Jenny, the charming young brunette nanny, had turned out not to work for the spa crèche after all. No, indeed, Jenny had been specifically hired by Cristo to take care of the twins while they were in Greece.

'That's so unnecessary and extravagant,' Erin had criticised when she found out about the arrangement at the airport.

'You can't look after them 24-7,' Cristo had informed her authoritatively.

'Why can't I?' she had asked.

'Why shouldn't you have a break?' he had responded arrogantly.

'If Jenny is your concept of responsible parenting you need to buy another handbook,' she had retorted curtly, annoyed that he had taken such a decision over her head. He was Lorcan and Nuala's father: all right, she accepted that, however that didn't mean that she would accept his interference in matters about which he was scarcely qualified to have an opinion. She was no more in need of a break than any other working mother, she thought thinly, which she supposed meant that, rail as she had at him, the prospect of the occasional hour in which she could relax and think of herself again was disturbingly appealing and made her feel quite appallingly guilty.

Returning to the present and the tense atmosphere currently stretching between them, Erin shot Cristo a glance from cool amethyst eyes. 'You think we should talk? I'll be frank—only if you crawled naked over broken glass would I think you had redeemed yourself.'

A wicked grin very briefly slashed Cristo's lean bronzed features, his dark eyes shot with golden amusement below his thick sooty lashes, making him spectacularly handsome. 'Not much chance of that,' he admitted.

'So, where's my apology?' Erin demanded truculently to mask the effect of her dry mouth and quickened heartbeat because, no matter how furious he made her, she could still not remain impervious to his stunning good looks, a reality that mortified her. 'It's taking you long enough!'

'I was trying to come up with the right words.'

'Even if you swallowed a dictionary, it wouldn't help you!'

Lean strong face taut, Cristo sprang out of his seat. 'I am sincerely sorry that I ever entertained the suspicion that you had stolen from me, *koukla mou*.'

'You didn't just entertain it,' she objected. 'You fell for it hook, line and sinker!'

'My security team are even at this moment checking into this Will Grimes angle. I can't understand why a private detective would have been interested in you.' Indeed, having thought deeply about that particular issue, Cristo could only think that someone *he* knew had hired a detective in an apparent effort to disgrace Erin. But who would have wasted their money on such a pursuit and what had been the motivation? It still made no sense to him. Erin had not been his wife or fiancée? Why would anyone have wanted to harm her and, through her, him?

Erin tilted her chin, eyes glinting pure lavender. 'Seems I wasn't paranoid, after all. I'm still waiting on that apology too.'

His strong jaw line hardened, dark eyes gleaming. 'And you'll be waiting a long time because you're not getting a second. If you hadn't been so direct about your expectations I might have soft-pedalled for the sake of peace, but now I'll be equally direct: you brought that theft accusation down on your own head!'

Erin stared at him aghast, totally wrong-footed by that condemnation coming at her out of the blue when she had expected a grovelling apology. *Really*? Well, possibly not of the grovelling variety, but, yes, she had assumed he would be embarrassed by his misjudgement and eager to soothe her wounded feelings. Now, deprived of that development and outraged by his attitude, Erin leapt out of her seat to face him. 'And how do you work that out?'

'As far as I was aware Sally Jennings was an exemplary long-term employee with no strikes against her and no reason to lie. Had I known she had already been caught thieving at work I would have known to take a closer look at her activities,' Cristo shot back at her levelly.

Erin stiffened, feeling she was on weaker ground when it came to the decision she had once made over Sally and defying the reflection. 'Sally was going through a divorce and she has two autistic sons. At the time, I believed she needed compassionate handling rather than punishment.'

Cristo expelled his breath in a hiss, his brilliant eyes cracking like whips. 'Compassion? If I'd known then how you mishandled her dishonesty I would have sacked you for incompetence!'

'*Incompetence?*' Erin bleated incredulously, rage jumping up and down inside her like a gushing fountain suddenly switched on.

'Yes, incompetence,' Cristo confirmed with succinct bite. 'How would you feel about a manager who left a thief in a position of power in your business and chose not to warn anyone about her dangerous little weakness?'

'I dealt with the situation as I saw fit back then. Looking back, I can see I was too trusting—'

'Correction…bloody naïve!' Cristo shot back at her witheringly. 'I didn't hire you to be compassionate. Plenty of people lead tough lives but few of them steal. I hired you to take care of part of my business and that was your sole responsibility. Listening to sob stories and letting a clever calculating woman get off scot-free with her crimes was no part of your job description!'

It took enormous will power but Erin managed to restrain her temper and the urge to snap back at him because she knew that he was making valid points. 'It's not a decision I would make now. Unfortunately I liked Sally and believed she was a wonderful worker. I was naïve—I'll admit that—'

'Why the hell didn't you consult me about it or at least approach someone with more experience for their opinion on what to do about her?' Cristo demanded angrily. 'At the very least, once you knew Sally was a thief, all her activities at work should have been checked out thoroughly and she should have been moved to a position where she had no access to products, account books or money.'

As he made those cogent decrees Erin lifted her head high, refusing to go into retreat. 'You're right but I thought I could deal with the situation on my own. I didn't want you to think that I couldn't cope. But I was hugely overworked and stressed at the time. I notice the current manager has a deputy and I saw at least two administrators in the general office. I didn't have anyone but Sally to rely on.'

'Then you should have asked for more help,' Cristo fielded without hesitation.

'My biggest mistake was accepting a position from someone I was involved with. I was too proud, too busy trying to impress you about what a great job I was doing. I didn't have enough experienced staff around me and those that were there kept their distance because I was too close to the boss. I was very focused on building the business, bringing in more custom, increasing productivity. It made me far too dependent on Sally for support. I can see that now,' Erin concluded that honest statement curtly.

'At least you can now see what that inappropriate decision cost you. Sally didn't hesitate when it came to setting you up to take the blame for her acts of fraud or when she got the chance to reap financial benefits from her disloyalty,' Cristo pointed out.

'Don't forget that Sally Jennings fooled you as well. The role she played was very convincing,' Erin reminded him tightly. 'You didn't smell a rat in her performance either.'

'But I would have done had you tipped me off about her stealing. Right, we've aired this for long enough, subject closed,' Cristo pronounced decisively.

'Now that you've had your say and blamed me for everything?' Erin countered tautly, amethyst eyes dark and unwittingly vulnerable, for that word, 'incompetence', had cut deep as a knife. 'Was it too much for me to expect that after knowing me for a year you would question the idea that I might have been filling my pockets at your expense?'

'After certain suspicions had been awakened and the man I saw in your hotel-room bed I will concede that I was predisposed to think the worst of you,' Cristo derided, compressing his wide sensual mouth into a tough line. 'What's that cliché about the easiest explanation usually being the right one? In this case, the easiest explanation was the wrong one.'

Erin sank back down in her seat. 'Am I finally getting a clean slate on the score of the one-night stand with the toy boy?' she asked grittily. 'Tom's brother, Dennis, was only nineteen back then.'

'That's not quite so clear cut. My suspicions in that quarter were first awakened by other indications, which I will discuss with you when we get to the island,' he added as her triangular face tensed into a frown of bemusement. 'I am sincerely sorry that I misjudged you and that I didn't dig a little deeper three years back.'

Erin said nothing. What other evidence of her infidelity did he imagine he had? She hadn't a clue what he was talking about and had no time for more mysteries. In addition her mind was being bombarded with thoughts after that heated exchange of views. He had shot her down in flames and it rankled and that was precisely why she had not approached him for advice after she had caught Sally stealing. She had known he would take the toughest stance and would call in the police. She had feared that he would blame her for the inadequate security in the products store, which had made Sally's thefts all too easy. If she was honest she had also worried about how she would cope without Sally at her elbow. My mistake, she acknowledged painfully. A wrong decision that had cost her more than she could ever have dreamt.

Cristo watched in frustration as Erin made a weak excuse and went off to join Jenny and the twins. It had been right to tell her the truth, he told himself angrily. He was damned if the fact that she was the mother of his children would make him start lying just to please her! Did shooting from the hip mean he had also shot himself in the foot? Almost three years ago, he had not talked to Erin about important issues and this time around he was determined not to repeat that mistake. Blunt speech had to be better than minimal communication and misunderstandings, he decided impatiently.

Shielded by the need to keep the twins occupied for what remained of a journey that entailed a final helicopter flight to the island of Thesos, Erin licked her wounds in private. From the air she had a fantastic view of Cristo's island. It was bigger than she had imagined and the southern end was heavily forested with pine trees. She spied a cluster of low-rise structures on what appeared to be a building site on the furthest coast and a picturesque little town by the harbour before the helicopter flew level again and began to swoop down over the tree tops to land.

Lorcan was asleep and Cristo hoisted his son out of Erin's arms and carried him off. They had landed about twenty yards from a magnificent ultra-modern villa surrounded by terraces and balconies to take advantage of the land and sea views.

'This all looks new,' Erin remarked.

'I demolished my parents' house and had this one designed about three years ago. It made more sense than trying to renovate the old place,' he commented casually.

Three years ago, while they had still been a couple, Erin had known nothing about his island or the new house he was having built. Not for the first time Erin appreciated that Cristo had shut her out of a large section of his life and she wondered why. Obviously he had never considered her important enough to include her in the Greek half of his existence, which encompassed home and family. And that, whether she liked it or not, *hurt*, most particularly when he had married a Greek woman within months of dumping Erin.

A short brunette with warm brown eyes was introduced as Androula, the housekeeper. Straight away Androula cooed over the children in their arms and hurried off to show Erin and Jenny to the rooms set aside for their use. Erin was taken aback to discover that Cristo had already had accommodation specially prepared for his son and daughter, each complete with small beds, appropriate decoration and an array of toys. Leaving the capable Jenny to put the drowsy children to bed, Erin explored her own room with its doors opening onto the terrace and superb view through the trees to a white beach and a turquoise sea over which the sun was sinking in a display of fiery splendour.

'Will you be comfortable here?'

Erin spun to find Cristo behind her, poised between the French windows. 'How could I fail to be? It's the height of luxury,' she said awkwardly.

Cristo searched her shuttered face and breathed almost roughly, 'I was tough on you on the plane. I was angry that you let that scheming woman make you pay the price for her crimes.'

'But at least that's sorted out now. The rooms organised for the children are beautiful,' she told him stiffly, suppressing the discomfiture she was still feeling. 'You must have organised that almost as soon as you found out about them.'

Cristo inclined his dark head. 'Yes, even before I asked you if they could visit Thesos. I still tend to act first and ask later.'

Not even questioning that arrogant assumption of power, Erin turned away and rested her elbows back on the low wall girding the terrace. She had intended to get her revenge on Cristo for what he had done to her in Italy, but it had gradually dawned on her that angering or hurting Cristo would most probably damage his relationship with their children. Their own relationship was irrevocably meshed with the ties and responsibilities of also being parents. And how, in conscience, could she take that risk of weakening those links?

'You never ever told me that this place existed,' she said.

'What would have been the point if I wasn't planning to bring you here?' he murmured wryly. 'When I was with you I wasn't quite ready to move our affair on to the next stage. I was simply enjoying the place we had reached until it blew up in both our faces. I'm sorry.'

'No need to apologise.' Erin fought the just-slapped-in-the-face sensation of humiliation that his piece of plain speaking inspired and wondered why on earth he was suddenly telling her such things. In the past she had loved him and longed for a secure future with him but he had not felt the same. Why did that news still make her feel so gutted? That time was gone and she didn't love him any longer. She just lusted after him, enjoyed his energising company, respected his business prowess, intelligence and strength of principle. Enumerating that unacceptably long list of his supposed attributes, Erin gritted her teeth together. Why was she doing this to herself? Dwelling on things that no longer had any place between them? She was the mother of his children and that was all.

'In those days…' Cristo, engaged in watching the tense muscles in her slender back and the vulnerable piece of pale nape exposed by her bent head, floundered. 'I wasn't exactly in touch with my feelings.'

'I'm not sure you had any…above your belt,' Erin specified shakily.

'That is *so* wrong!' Cristo growled, lean hands closing forcefully to her shoulders to tug her back round to face him. 'I was sick to the stomach when I thought you'd gone to bed with another man! It turned my whole life upside down!'

'Try being pregnant by a man you can't even get to speak to you on the phone!' Erin lanced back at him with unconcealed bitterness.

His dark golden eyes shone amber bright at the challenge. 'I would never have knowingly allowed that to happen. What reason would I have to treat you like some demented stalker? I intend to get the full story out of Amelia when I'm next in Athens where she works now.'

'I'll still never forgive you.'

His superb bone structure was taut and he gazed steadily back at her. 'Was being pregnant so bad?'

'I had to live on welfare benefits. It was a struggle I'll never forget,' Erin admitted truthfully. 'My home was a damp tenth-floor council flat barely fit for human habitation. It was only when my mother came to see me and realised how I was living that she invited me to go home with her. There was also the not so little matter of me being pregnant and unmarried, which really did upset Mum. She's an old-fashioned woman and as far as she's concerned decent girls don't have babies until they have a ring on their wedding finger. We were estranged for most of my pregnancy.'

His concern was unfeigned. 'You had no support at all? What about your friend, Elaine? Did she ask you to move out of her apartment?'

'No, I made that decision— I couldn't pay my way any more,' Erin explained ruefully. 'But Tom and Melissa helped out as best they could.'

'Melissa?'

'Now Tom's wife but at the time they were living together and I couldn't have had better friends,' Erin declared. 'They were very good to me.'

His keen gaze was screened by his luxuriant black lashes, his eloquent mouth set in a forbidding line. 'I owe them a debt for that.'

'Yes, you do,' Erin told him bluntly. 'They didn't have much either but what they had they shared.'

His lashes swept up on breathtakingly beautiful golden eyes from which all anger had vanished. 'But I owe the biggest debt of all to you for bringing my children into the world. Don't think I don't appreciate that and know how lucky I was that you chose not to have a termination. I *do* know—I *do* appreciate it,' he completed in a rare display of unmistakable emotion.

Cristo took the wind out of Erin's sails with that candid little speech, but her anger with him was not so easily soothed. 'When I was pregnant I assumed that if you had a choice you would have preferred me to have a termination. You once told me about that friend of yours whose girlfriend got pregnant,' she reminded him.

'I didn't say that I approved of what they chose to do. Maybe it was right for them but I would not have reacted the same way that he did.'

'Easy to say,' she needled. 'Hindsight is a wonderful device with which to rewrite the past. You also said that you preferred your life without baggage.'

'Don't judge me for what I did and didn't do almost three years ago. I've grown up a lot since then,' Cristo spelt out tautly.

His marriage to Lisandra, she thought ruefully, thinking it was sad that she apparently owed this rather less arrogant and reserved version of Cristo to the machinations of another woman. Even so, her heart could only be touched by his gratitude that she had given birth to Lorcan and Nuala. She had felt his sincerity and it meant a great deal to her. Cristo had, after all, taken to fatherhood with enthusiasm and energy. He seemed neither resentful of the responsibility he had had thrust on him, nor ill-at-ease with it. That awareness tore more than one brick out of Erin's defensive wall.

Walking back indoors, she noticed a trio of large envelopes lying on an occasional table. Already opened, they were addressed to Cristo at his London office. 'What are these?'

Cristo hesitated and then frowned, his restive pacing coming to a sudden halt. 'The evidence I promised to show you once we got here. Take a look at what's in those envelopes…'

'Why? What's in them?'

'Photos which were sent to me during the latter months we were together in London.'

Erin extracted a large, slightly blurred photograph of a couple walking hand in hand. The man was her friend, Tom Harcourt, and the face on the woman was hers. As she had never held hands with Tom in her life she was astonished until she studied the body and the cloth-

ing of the female depicted. In a frantic rush, she leafed
through the other photos, one showing the same couple
kissing and another of them hugging. 'That may be my
face but it's not my body—it's Melissa's. These photos
are all of Tom with his wife, Melissa, but they've been
digitally altered to make it look as though the woman
is me!' she murmured in disbelief.

'*Altered*?' Cristo stood by her side as she fanned out
the photos and one by one proceeded to verbally pick
them apart. 'How altered?'

'Whoever sent these photos to you grafted my face
onto Melissa's body,' she told him angrily. 'All we have
in common is that we're both blondes but I'd recognise
that sweater from a mile away! How on earth could you
think that was me, Cristo? Melissa is much smaller, well
under five foot tall. Didn't you notice how small she
seems beside Tom, who isn't that tall? And since when
did I have a bust as big as that?'

Peering down at the photos, Cristo noted every point
of comparison. 'None of them are of you with Tom,' he
finally breathed in bewilderment. 'Why didn't I notice
those differences for myself?'

It might as well have been a rhetorical question because Erin had no intention of pursuing that pointless
line of enquiry. 'As you said, you act first and ask later.
But I just don't believe how secretive you can be! You
received these rotten lying photos on three separate occasions and didn't once mention them to me. No wonder
you became so suspicious of my friendship with Tom!'

In retrospect she could recall the surprisingly sudden alteration in Cristo's attitude towards her spending
time with Tom while he was away on business. Cristo
had gone from accepting that friendship without com-

ment to suddenly questioning her every meeting with the other man, but only now was she discovering that genuine disquiet had provoked that change of heart.

Erin was struggling to understand why he had remained silent in the face of such provocation and failing. It was cruel to realise that she had gone through so much pain just because some hateful individual had decided to destroy Cristo's trust in her, ensuring that he would reject her. He had walked away from her and almost straight away gone on to marry another woman. The wound inflicted by that decision of his had never left her. He had got over her so quickly and she believed that he must always have viewed her as not being good enough to marry. His choice of a rich Greek wife from a background similar to his own had been revealing.

'Why didn't you show these photos to me at the time?' Erin demanded.

Lean, strong face shuttered, Cristo clenched his jaw. He walked away a few paces, his long, lean body as fluid and graceful as running water, his black hair gleaming like polished jet in the fading daylight above his bold bronzed profile. Sometimes he looked so incredibly handsome that she couldn't take her eyes off him, she thought rawly, anguish for what they had lost engulfing her.

'I had too much pride,' Cristo grated the admission. 'I could not make my mind up about whether you were cheating on me or whether your relationship with Tom had simply become too close and affectionate. I didn't know what to think but it did make me doubt your loyalty—'

'And when you walked into that hotel room and saw a strange man in the bed, you were in exactly the right frame of mind to assume that I was cheating on you,' Erin completed with fierce resentment. 'How could you not give me a single chance to defend myself?'

'I will always regret it,' Cristo confessed in a driven undertone, piling the photos together and cramming them into a single envelope. 'We are now living with the consequences. I've missed more than two years of my children's lives as a result. I would not like to be in the shoes of whomever I find is responsible for deliberately setting out to destroy us.'

'But the hotel-room thing was just an unlucky co-incidence,' Erin reasoned heavily, shaken that anyone could have gone to such lengths to discredit her in his eyes. 'I do understand after seeing those photos that you honestly believed you didn't need to see me in the flesh in the same room to believe that I was cheating on you. Do you have a bunny-boiling ex-girlfriend somewhere in your past? Jealous women can be vicious. Who else would take so much time and trouble and put so much money into trying to split us up?'

'I don't know but I have every intention of finding out,' he swore, a hostile expression stamped on his hard features. He cast the envelopes aside and drew her back to him with determined hands.

He lowered his head and caressed her parted lips slowly with his own in a move that completely disconcerted her. Her entire body tingled with electrified awareness. Coming alive to his sensual call, she was shamefully aware that the peaks of her breasts were straining into bullet points and her thighs pressing together to contain the ache of emptiness there. 'I want a fresh start with you,' he breathed in a raw undertone, his breath fanning her cheek. 'Let's get all the rubbish out of the way and leave it behind us.'

'A lot of what you call rubbish messed up my life,' Erin replied defensively, her eyes prickling with tears behind her eyelids, and she didn't even understand why she so suddenly felt screamingly vulnerable and unsure of herself. *I want a fresh start with you.* She hadn't seen that coming, didn't know what to say.

'We both screwed up,' Cristo contradicted, gravity hardening his high cheekbones to make him look tougher and stronger than ever. 'We can't change the past but we can begin again…'

Erin looked up into his lean, tense features. 'Can we?' she whispered.

Long brown fingers framed her cheekbone and intent dark golden eyes flamed over her troubled face. 'I say we can,' he declared, curving a hand to her hip to ease her closer.

She wanted to believe it; she wanted to believe it so badly. He wanted her back. He *still* wanted her. A powerful tide of relief rolled through her, closely followed by a flood of happiness. Dark eyes glinting sensually below his lashes, he melded her to his big powerful length and desire flared through her like a hungry fire ready to blaze out of control. The heat of him against her, the glorious scent of his skin and the hungry thrust of his erection were a potent inducement and when he crushed her sultry mouth beneath his she was with him every step of the way.

Cristo peeled off her blouse with wildly impatient hands and then released her bra to bury his mouth urgently in the sweet sloping swell of her breasts. 'You're so beautiful, so perfect—'

'Not perfect,' she pro[...]
lowered her down on the [...]
impatience she could not r[...]

'You're perfect for me, k[...]
tered, determined to have the [...]
were.'

The passionate kiss that followe[...]
confines of her mouth with devourin[...]
Her nipples were hard and swollen and [...] there
with his mouth and his fingers to reduce [...] to gasping
compliance with the hot sensuality that was so much
a part of him. The remainder of her clothes were discarded and Cristo undressed in haste, returning to claim
her with his lean, strong body boldly aroused. Her heart
raced as she stroked the long, hard thickness of his shaft
and she rejoiced when he groaned and arched his hips
up to her in supplication. He flipped her back against
the pillows, searching out the slick sensitive folds and
the tiny knot of nerve-endings above to stroke her with
teasing, tender skill. The tide of pleasure swept her out
of her control, each touch of his fingers making her
burn and writhe and finally sob with anticipation and
need. And only then did he reach for protection and
sink deep into her damp sheath, telling her huskily of
his pleasure as her inner muscles tightened convulsively
around him. Excitement gripped her when he withdrew
and then plunged deep into her again, ripples of delight rising higher and higher inside her as the fire in
her pelvis burned hotter than ever. And when she finally reached a climax and he reached the same point
with her, he lay sated and uncharacteristically silent in
the protective circle of her arms afterwards and she felt
gloriously happy.

onderful, *koukla mou*,' Cristo husked, slight damp body, to him with possessive I don't know how I contrived to keep my hands off you for so long.'

'I should've said no,' Erin lamented, studying his lean, darkly handsome features with dazed eyes. 'You blackmailed me into bed in Italy—'

'You wanted me.' Cristo punctuated that claim with a soothing kiss on her reddened lips, smouldering golden eyes scanning her flushed face with unashamed satisfaction. 'I wanted you. I found a way round the difficulties so that we could be together again. Now that I have you back in my arms where you belong I would be a liar if I pretended to have regrets.'

'The end justifies the means?' Erin pressed drily.

'You know that you want me just as much,' he argued with unashamed assurance. 'When we burn, we burn together.'

It was true and even with that frantic need fulfilled she could not lie in contact with that compellingly masculine body of his without experiencing the first little quivers of yet another sensual awakening. As the liquid warmth at the heart of her began to melt he ran the edge of his teeth down the extended length of her neck and she shivered violently. He reached for another condom and then pulled her over to him, watching as her lashes dipped low in a cloaked expression of intense pleasure that he savoured.

'Will you marry me?' he murmured tautly.

Eyes flying wide, Erin stared down at him, wondering if she had imagined that question.

'It seemed like the right moment,' Cristo asserted, his hands clasping to her hips to rock her gently up on him and then down in a controlling rhythm that was impossibly exciting. 'Don't laugh—'

'I'm not going to laugh!' she riposted, offended by the suggestion and studying him with troubled amethyst eyes. 'Are you serious?'

'I want you and the twins to be a proper part of my life.' His breathing fractured as she made a subtle circling movement above him, pale silvery fair hair streaming down over her shoulders to allow tantalising glimpses of her small pert breasts. 'I don't think it can get better than this, *koukla mou*.'

And when only minutes later yet another orgasm took Erin by storm, she decided she agreed with him. She lay in the relaxed circle of his arms, breathing in the hot damp smell of him like a hopeless addict, too long deprived of the source of her fix. He wanted her. He wanted their children. What more was there? *Love*? Cristo hadn't offered her love the last time she was with him and he likely never would. It was wiser to focus on what she could have rather than what she couldn't. Wasn't it the question she had always wanted him to ask? And did it really matter that he hadn't made an occasion of the proposal? Aside of the few gestures he had made when in initial pursuit of her, Cristo didn't have a romantic bone in his body. He was probably being practical. They were very much attracted to each other and it made sense for them to marry and share the children, she conceded ruefully, but she was slightly amazed that he was willing to surrender his freedom again after his first unhappy marriage.

'Are you sure about this?'

His sooty lashes swept up on his level gaze. 'I know what I want.'

'But is it really us as a family unit?'

'Do I get to wake up to you almost every morning?' Cristo raised a mocking brow. 'That's my sole demand. That's what I want and need.'

Erin was not quite convinced of that when two little wriggling noisy bodies tried to get into bed with them at dawn the next morning. Aghast, Cristo snatched up his boxers to make himself presentable and looked on in disbelief as the twins cuddled up between them, providing as effective a barrier as a wall.

'What are you doing in Mummy's bed?' Lorcan demanded curiously.

'Your mother and I are getting married very soon,' Cristo announced instantly.

Erin stiffened in dismay. 'Cristo, I didn't say yes.'

Cristo sent her a shocked look, his eyes dancing with wicked amusement. 'Are you saying that you took repeated gross advantage of me last night without any intention of making an honest man of me and doing the decent thing?'

Erin reddened at his mockery, the ache of her well-used body reminding her that after the enthusiasm she had demonstrated between the sheets he naturally took her agreement to marry him somewhat for granted. 'No, I'm not saying that.'

'Then I can go ahead and make the wedding arrangements?'

Erin nodded uncertainly, thoroughly shaken by the concept of becoming his bride. 'Shouldn't we have a living-together trial first?'

'Nope. You might change your mind. I refuse to be put on trial. And on a more serious note, it's time I told my parents about you and the twins. I don't want them to hear from another source,' he imparted wryly. 'I'll go and see them after breakfast.'

'They live here on the island?' Now she grasped why he had never offered to bring her to Thesos for a visit.

'They have a second home here. They use it weekends, holidays.' He shrugged. 'They're here right now.'

'How do you think they'll react?'

'I suspect my foster mother will be overjoyed—she's crazy about children.'

'Just not so crazy about me?' Erin remarked uncomfortably as the twins scampered out of bed and she followed suit.

'Some misunderstanding must've lain behind the strange impression you received of my foster mother during that phone call you made while you were pregnant. Appollonia had no reason to think badly of you. She knew nothing about you.'

The four of them enjoyed breakfast on the terrace and then Cristo left to visit his parents and Erin changed into a swimsuit, packed a bag and took the children down to the beach As the morning ticked slowly past she wondered anxiously what sort of a reception Cristo was receiving from his parents. His foster parents, she reminded herself again, having studied a picture on the wall of a glamorous young couple standing on the deck of a yacht and guessed that the glossy pair were Cristo's birth parents. When she came back from the beach, she let Jenny take the exhausted twins and went for a shower, emerging to phone her mother and describe the island and the house and, finally, their plans to marry. Her parent was very pleased by her news.

Choosing a book from the well-stocked, handsome library to entertain her until lunchtime, Erin relaxed in a cushioned lounger in the shade below the trees. She was drowsing in the heat when a slight sound alerted her to the awareness that she was no longer alone. Taking off her sunglasses, she sat up and frowned at Cristo, who looked grim. Lines of strain were indented between his nose and mouth, his black hair was tousled and stubble darkened the revealing downward curve of his beautiful mouth.

'What's up?' Erin demanded worriedly, checking her watch. He had been gone for hours. It was two in the afternoon.

As he sank down heavily opposite her Erin leant a little closer and sniffed. 'Have you been drinking?'

'I might have had a couple while I was waiting on the doctor's arrival with Vasos,' he volunteered half under his breath. 'It's been such a ghastly morning that I don't really remember.'

'Who needed a doctor?' she exclaimed.

'My mother.'

'Appollonia's taken ill?'

Cristo dealt her a troubled appraisal. 'It was her…she was the one who hired the private detective. I wouldn't have believed it if she hadn't known enough to convince me. My father is in shock—he had no idea what was going on.'

Erin was bemused. 'What are you talking about?'

'My mother hired Will Grimes.'

Her eyes widened while she recognised how much that staggering discovery had upset him. There was enormous sorrow in his unshielded eyes that made her wince and long to hold him close, for she knew how deeply attached he was to the couple who had raised him. In fact it hurt her so much to see him wounded in such a way that she stopped lying to herself in that same moment: all her proud pretences and defences fell away and she was left to face the inescapable truth that she still loved Cristophe Donakis and had never stopped loving him.

CHAPTER TEN

'APPOLLONIA learned that you and I had been together for at least a year from one of my friends. She was always ridiculously eager for me to settle down and have a family and she became convinced that you were holding me back from that development. She was obsessed with the idea of me marrying another Greek and spending more time here in Greece,' Cristo explained with a heavy sigh as he sat opposite Erin, who was studying him fixedly. 'She paid a private detective to investigate you and eventually told him that she would pay him a bonus if he would use whatever means were within his power to break us up.'

'But that's crazy,' Erin whispered, reeling from the unexpected tale he was telling her. 'You're an adult. How could your mother interfere in your life like that?'

'Appollonia seems honestly to have believed that she was doing it for the sake of my future happiness, *koukla mou*. How I might feel about it or how much damage she might do in the process to me or you never seems to have entered her head until it was too late.'

'How on earth did you realise that it was your foster mother who had hired the detective?'

'I was telling her about you and the twins and she

suddenly made a rather scornful reference to the thefts from the spa. That immediately made me suspicious because she did not get that information from me. It could only have come from the detective she hired. Once she grasped that you were the mother of my children she was very shocked and guilty and in that state she blurted out the whole story. My father, Vasos, was appalled and he asked her what she had been thinking of...'

'Did you tell her that I wasn't the thief?' Erin asked ruefully.

'Of course. She didn't ask the detective what weapons he used to bring about our split, in fact she didn't want to know the dirty details, and once it was achieved she invited Lisandra to dinner and dangled her under my nose. I told her about the doctored photos and Sally being rewarded for identifying you as the thief. I also told her that it was her fault that Lorcan and Nuala were strangers until I met them two weeks ago. She remembered your phone call. She did honestly believe that you had been stealing from me and that was how she justified her interference—you were a wicked woman and I needed help to break free of your malign influence. That had become her excuse and when that excuse was taken from her she became extremely distressed. Vasos was shouting at her and it all got very hysterical and overheated.' Cristo groaned, luxuriant black lashes almost hitting his exotic cheekbones as he briefly closed his eyes in frustration. 'In the end we called the local doctor to administer a sedative to calm her down...'

'Oh, my goodness, is this the reason she had a nervous breakdown when your marriage went wrong?'

'Yes, although none of us appreciated that at the time.

But she felt hugely guilty at having encouraged me to marry Lisandra.'

'No offence intended, Cristo, but right now Appollonia sounds like the mother-in-law from hell,' Erin remarked with an apologetic grimace.

'I think it is good that the truth has come out at last.' Cristo was seemingly determined to find a positive angle. 'Possibly Appollonia's secret arrangement with the detective has been the burden on her conscience which damaged her recovery from the breakdown she suffered. She is still a fragile personality but she wasn't always like that.'

'Was your PA got to by the detective as well? Was that why my calls were never put through and my letters were returned unread?'

Cristo sighed, 'My foster mother told her you were stalking me and that she'd be grateful if Amelia shielded me from nuisance calls and letters. Amelia probably believed she was doing me a favour.'

'Bloody hell!' Erin erupted furiously, standing up and walking away, only to spin back. 'No wonder I couldn't get hold of you!'

Cristo appraised with appreciation her slim, pale, delicately curved body in the brief red bikini she wore. 'If it's any consolation, Appollonia is the party most punished by the fallout from all this.'

Turning pink at the intensity of the gaze resting on her heaving breasts, Erin crossed her arms to interrupt his view. She hated the way he could just look at her and her body would have an involuntary reaction while her brain fogged over. 'And how do you make that out?'

'You're the one in possession of grandchildren she has never seen. Had she known you were carrying my child she would never have targeted you and she would have supported you in every way possible. I told her how alone you had been and she felt guiltier than ever,' he completed wryly.

'So, what happens now?'

'We go down to the village and see the priest and fill out the forms for our wedding.'

'You want to get married here on the island?' Erin was taken aback by the idea.

'I'll fly out your mother along with any friends you want to attend.' Seeing that that assurance had no visible effect, Cristo unfolded to his full impressive height, adding, 'We've been apart a long time—I don't want to wait long for the wedding.'

'I didn't realise it would be happening so soon,' Erin responded tentatively. 'When I agreed to come here it was only for a week to escape the press because you got so hot and bothered about them.'

A faint smile softened the harsh curve of his shapely mouth. 'Everything has changed between us since then, *koukla mou.*'

It had changed in the bedroom, Erin reflected guiltily, recalling how easily she had succumbed to his hot-blooded hunger for her. She had said yes where she should have said no and that was the only green light that a male with Cristo's high voltage libido required.

'I barely remember my birth parents. They're just a stylish photo on the wall,' Cristo remarked tautly. 'The first five years of my life I was raised by nannies. I was always being told not to *bother* my parents because they were such *busy* people. They had no time for me and little interest.'

Erin was frowning. 'Go on…'

'I didn't know what a normal home and parents were like until Vasos and Appollonia took charge of me. They spent time with me, talked to me, took an interest in my small achievements and gave me love. I owe everything I am today to them. I want to do the same thing for Lorcan and Nuala.'

She had not realised that his early years had been so bleak and she understood his attitude, for her own childhood had been almost as troubled and insecure. Marrying Cristo made sense, she reasoned ruefully. She wanted her children to have a full-time father and the chance of a happy family life. Cristo was offering her that option and she put as high a value on that lifestyle as he apparently did. But he would not have wanted to marry her had she not had the twins and that hurt. It hurt that he didn't love and want her with the same intensity that he wanted their children.

That evening Sam Morton phoned her. 'Your mother told me you were in Greece. I was shocked.'

'We're getting married, Sam.'

'Yes, she told me that as well. Of course that's the safest choice for Donakis if he wants access to his children. I understand that he consulted an expert in family law in London to find out exactly where he stood. Watch your step, Erin. In a Greek court, he could gain custody of the kids.'

Erin's blood ran cold at that forecast. 'Are you trying to scare me? We're getting married, not divorced.'

'I think it's very convenient for Donakis to marry you now but he wasn't interested in marrying you three years ago. Don't forget that.'

Sadly that was a fact that Erin never forgot and she

could have done without the second opinion. Had Cristo consulted a legal expert? How had Sam found that out? No doubt someone knew someone in the legal field who also knew Sam and word had got back to him in that way. Ought she to be worried? She supposed it was understandable that Cristo should have sought advice when he first found out that he was a father. That was not in itself wrong. Even so, the knowledge sent a little buzz of insecurity through her that she could not shake.

'Cristo,' she said towards the end of the evening while she worried about whether it was foolish of her to trust Cristo to such an extent. 'Would you mind very much if I slept on my own until the wedding?'

Cristo frowned. 'Not if it's important to you.'

'With Mum arriving a few days before the wedding, it would really be more comfortable for me,' she told him stiffly.

One week later, Cristo and Erin were married in the little church overlooking the town harbour. She wore a white lace dress, tight on the arms and fitted to make the most of her slender figure, obtained from a designer in Athens. Her mother had thought her daughter was being controversial buying into the whole white wedding fantasy when she already had two young children but Erin had seen no reason why her special day should not live up to her girlhood dreams. After all, she loved Cristo Donakis and preferred to be optimistic about their future.

The Greek Orthodox service presided over by the bearded priest in his long dark robe was traditional and meaningful. The church was crammed with well-wishers and filled with flowers. The scent of incense and the fresh-orange-blossom circlet placed on her head mingled headily and, strange as it all was to her, she loved it, loved Cristo's hand in hers, the steadiness of his lion-gold gaze and utter lack of nerves. For the first time she felt that they were meant to be together and she fought off downbeat thoughts about what his wedding to Lisandra might have been like as it was clearly not on his mind.

The days running up to their wedding had been exceptionally busy. She had had to take Nuala to an Athens hospital to have her cast checked. Mercifully everything had been in order and the little girl had not required a replacement. That appointment had been followed by a shopping trip to buy Erin's wedding gown. The next day she had first made the acquaintance of Cristo's father, Vasos Denes, when he came over to meet the twins. Initially appearing stern and quiet, Vasos had slowly shaken off his discomfiture over his wife's interference in Cristo's private life and its disastrous side effects to relax in his son's home and Erin had decided that he was a lovely man. She had been surprised when Cristo explained that his father's company was on the edge of bankruptcy but that the older man refused to accept his financial help. She had soon grasped from whom Cristo had learned his principles and even if his volatile nature warred against them and occasionally won—as in when he had blackmailed her into going to Italy with him—she knew Cristo did try to respect scruples and operate accordingly.

In a gesture made purely for Cristo and his foster father's sake, Erin had volunteered to take the children to visit Appollonia Denes at their villa on the outskirts of the town. Even on the medication her doctor had advised to help her with her low mood, the older woman had been stunned to see the twins and tears had trailed slowly down her cheeks while she attempted awkwardly to express her regret for the actions she had taken almost three years earlier. That she absolutely adored Cristo had shone out of her and her wondering delight in Lorcan and Nuala had inspired pity in Erin. She knew it would take time before she could forgive Appollonia for what she had done but she was willing to make the effort.

Cristo had thrown himself into spending every afternoon with the twins. Watching her children respond to his interest, noting the shocking similarity in their lively demanding personalities, Erin had known that marrying Cristo was the right step to take. Lorcan was already learning that when his father said no he meant it and Nuala's tantrums had become less frequent. The first time she condescended to call Cristo, 'Daddy', he admitted to Erin that he felt as if he had won the lottery.

Her mother had travelled to Thesos in the company of Tom and Melissa. Sam had turned down his invitation but had sent a lavish present. The day before the wedding, Cristo had taken them all out sailing. He was a wonderful host and had been in the very best of moods. Erin had taken that as a compliment: Cristo was happy that they were getting married. And she had during the week that had passed learned to regret her request that they sleep apart until the ceremony. Intimacy brought a special closeness to their relationship and she missed it, disliking the new distance that her demand had wrought in Cristo. He was too careful to give her space. A couple of times she had lain awake into the early hours, her body taut with frustration and longing, trying to summon up the courage to go and join Cristo in the opulent master suite at the top of the stairs. Why was she still punishing herself for wanting him? Why had she let Sam's sour suspicious comments make her doubt Cristo's sincerity?

Cristo lifted her hand in the car on the way back to the house from the church and touched the shiny new platinum ring on her finger with approval. 'Now you're mine.'

'That sounds exceedingly caveman-type basic,' Erin remarked.

'I suppose carrying you upstairs *before* we entertain our guests would be even more basic?' Cristo rested scorching golden eyes on her face as she turned fire-engine red with sexual awareness and embarrassment.

'You're scaring me because I know you're capable of behaving like that,' she admitted ruefully.

'I was pure caveman when I blackmailed you into meeting me in Italy,' Cristo conceded with a sardonic laugh. 'I do crazy things with you that I've never done with any other woman. Italy was supposed to be an exorcism—'

Erin gave him a blank look while trying not to picture how wickedly exciting it would be if Cristo was were to trail her straight off to his bedroom. That was the real problem. He might be pure caveman but on some level she liked that side of him and responded to it. There was something uniquely satisfying about knowing she was such an object of desire to him.

'An exorcism?' she repeated.

'I couldn't stop thinking about you and how incredible we were in bed. It infuriated me. I thought that if I saw you again, slept with you again I'd be disappointed and I could get you out of my system. My, didn't that work well?' he said with rich self-mockery. 'Here we are just three weeks later and we're married!'

'Did you and Lisandra get married in the same church?' Erin asked, no longer able to stifle her curiosity.

'Of course not. We had a massive society wedding staged in Athens. Lisandra likes to make a big splash in public.'

'But the church here and the simple service were lovely,' Erin commented softly.

His handsome mouth twisted. 'You and Lisandra are very different.'

Did he have regrets? A little ache set in somewhere in the region of Erin's heart. Erin had seen photos of his ex-wife in glossy magazines and Lisandra was much more sophisticated than she was. Most people would reckon that Cristo had married 'down' in choosing Erin and when they realised that the twins were his they would put another construction altogether on their marriage. Did that matter to her? Was she too sensitive? Expediency, rather than love, made the world go round. She didn't *need* him to love her. Evidently she didn't have that essential spark that would inspire such feelings in him or he would have fallen in love with her when they were first together and everything was all shiny and new.

'Visiting my mother in spite of what she did, allowing her to be present today and treating her like one of the family,' Cristo specified wryly. 'Lisandra would never have forgiven her.'

'I haven't forgiven Appollonia either.'

'But you're willing to *try*. I'm very grateful for that,'

Cristo told her quietly. 'You had the opportunity to get your own back by excluding her from our lives but you didn't take it. That was generous of you.'

'She truly regrets what she did. We all make mistakes.'

Cristo grasped her hand, curved lean fingers to the side of her face and brought his mouth down on hers with a hungry urgency that sent pure energy winging through her trembling body. 'I'm wrecking your make-up,' he groaned against her sultry mouth.

'Doesn't matter,' Erin proclaimed breathlessly, looking up at him with starry eyes and a thundering heart-beat.

Cristo handed her a tissue for the lipstick he had smeared. 'Our guests await us but first…I have a gift for you.'

He handed her a tiny jewellery box, which she flipped open. It contained a band of diamonds, an eternity ring. 'Cristo, it's beautiful but I haven't got you anything.'

'My gift is having you back in my bed again,' he murmured lazily.

The burning intensity of the look that accompanied that statement was like a blowtorch. She tottered out of the car on wobbling knees, struggling to pin a social smile to her lips. He really *really* wanted her and that was good, a healthy sign for a very practical marriage, she told herself earnestly, striving hard to be sensible while she admired the new rings sparkling on her finger. Cristo for eternity would be paradise, she thought dizzily, barely able to credit that he was finally hers. She watched as the twins ran to him and he scooped them up in both arms in a movement that made Lorcan and Nuala break into fits of laughter.

'He's so good with them,' her mother remarked approvingly from the front door that stood open. 'I expect you're planning on more children.'

'Not at the minute,' Erin told her mother frankly. 'I think we'll be getting used to being married for quite a while.'

'Cristo looks happier and more relaxed than I've seen him in years,' Vasos commented approvingly at her elbow. 'You're good for each other. I only wish that my wife's interference hadn't parted you when you should have stayed together.'

'It's water under the bridge now,' Erin said lightly as she looked up at the older man.

'I had an argument with my son when he said he couldn't possibly take a honeymoon while my company was failing. Don't worry,' Vasos urged comfortably. 'I soon talked sense into him. Of course you're having a honeymoon.'

Erin swallowed uncomfortably. She knew how hard Cristo had worked in his efforts to support his father's business, which had suffered badly in the difficult economic climate in Greece, but she also knew that Vasos' stubborn independent streak had made it an almost impossible challenge. 'He worries a lot about you.'

'He'll get over it,' Vasos replied staunchly.

'No, he won't actually,' she told him in a low voice. 'He'll feel like the worst failure if your business goes down. Why won't you let Cristo help you?'

'I could never accept money from Cristo.'

'But you're his family.'

'When he came to us as a child he was a fantastically rich little boy and I swore never to take advantage of that.'

'Times change. For a start, he's an adult, not a child any more. He loves you very much. Isn't it selfish to force him to stand by and do nothing while you go bankrupt? He'll be devastated.'

Vasos frowned.

'Please don't be offended with me,' Erin begged. 'I just wanted you to know what it's like for him not to be allowed to help when you're in trouble. In the same situation wouldn't you want to help him no matter what?'

'I will consider that angle,' Vasos replied after a long minute of silence, his stern face troubled. 'You can be very blunt, Erin…but you do understand Cristo.'

'Hopefully.' With a warm smile, Erin moved away to greet other guests, praying she hadn't said too much to Cristo's foster father. Cristo would probably be furious if he knew she had said anything, but negotiations between him and the older man were currently at a standstill and she had decided that she might as well speak up on Cristo's behalf.

Late afternoon, Cristo informed her that they were leaving. 'To go where?' she pressed.

'It's a surprise.'

'I haven't even packed—'

'There's no need. A new wardrobe awaits you at our destination. You don't need to worry about the twins either because your mother has agreed to stay on here until we return. Let's go—'

'Like…*right now*?' Erin exclaimed. 'I need to get changed—'

'No. I want to be the one to take off that dress,' Cristo confessed, gazing down into her eyes with a sensual look of anticipation that sparked fire in her bloodstream.

They flew to the airport in the helicopter and, having

presented their passports, boarded the jet straight away. By then, having been up at the crack of dawn, Erin was smothering yawns and the drone of the engines sent her into a sound sleep. When she wakened, she was embarrassed by the poor showing she was making as a bride and barely had time to tidy her mussed hair and repair her make-up before they landed.

'You've brought me back to Italy,' she registered in surprise, recognising the airport. 'Why Italy?'

'It's where we began again even if we didn't appreciate it that weekend.'

And alighting from the limo that brought them to the villa and struggling to walk in the high-heeled sandals that were now pinching horribly, she decided that he had made a good point. Her emotions had rekindled along with her desire for him. It had been time out of time and wonderful in the strangest way of happiness coming when you least expected it to do so.

'I gave the housekeeper the weekend off.'

Cristo swept her up in his arms to carry her through the door he had unlocked.

It was a romantic gesture she hadn't expected from him and, eyes widening, she smiled up at him, colliding with dark golden eyes that made her heart race. They walked up the stairs, though, hand in hand and she almost giggled, unfamiliar as she was with such signs from Cristo, who was usually cooler than cool in that department. In the bedroom doorway she stilled, scanning the room, which had been transformed with lush arrangements of white flowers and dozens of candles with little flames that leapt and glowed in the darkness: she was transfixed.

'Good heavens,' she murmured, totally stunned by the display. 'You organised this?'

'I wanted it to be perfect for you.'

Hugely impressed, Erin smiled again and walked on in, kicking off her tight shoes with a sigh of relief.

'Now you've shrunk,' Cristo teased, uncorking the bottle of champagne awaiting them and handing her an elegant flute bubbling with the pale golden liquid.

Erin sipped. 'Did you do something like this for Lisandra?'

He frowned. 'Why do you keep on asking about her?'

'Well, *did* you?' Erin persisted.

'No, I didn't. It wasn't that kind of marriage. I thought you would have worked out by now that I married Lisandra on the rebound,' Cristo imparted with a rueful twist of his mouth. 'I reeled away from the wreckage of our relationship and made the biggest mistake of all.'

On the rebound? She liked that news. She liked it even better that he was willing to admit that his first marriage had been a mistake. It soothed the hurt place inside her that had formed when she had realised he had taken a wife within months of their split. An extraordinary urge to move closer and hug him also assailed Erin. She might want to wrap that confession in fairy lights and laugh and smile over it but an aching sadness afflicted her at the same time. Three years back, he must have cared about her more than she had realised but she had still lost him through no fault of her own.

'You weren't in love with your wife?' she prompted stiffly.

'I thought I'd made that clear.'

'Why did you marry her, then?'

'After losing faith in you I had no heart for dating.

My marriage pleased my family, gave me something to focus on other than you, but it was a catastrophe.' Cristo shifted a broad shoulder in a fatalistic shrug and gave her a wry look. 'This is our wedding night. I don't want to talk about this now.'

Something to focus on other than you. And suddenly Erin understood something that she had never quite believed in before. When they broke up, he had been badly hurt too, he had suffered as well. He had rushed into a marriage that he had hoped would cure him of his unhappiness. But now she was suddenly reflecting on the eternity ring and the beautiful bower of flowers and candles he had had prepared for their arrival and her heart swelled with warmth and forgiveness. He was doing things he had never done before. He was trying to show her that he had feelings for her and naturally he didn't want her rabbiting on about Lisandra in the middle of it.

'I love you,' he told her in a roughened undertone, detaching the champagne glass from her nerveless fingers and setting it aside so that he could pull her close. His eyes were bright with emotion in the flickering candlelight. 'I was in love with you when we broke up but I didn't know it. You've haunted me ever since. When I saw you in that photo with Sam and his staff, all I could think about was seeing you again. I lied to myself. I told myself that it was only sex and that I wanted to get over the memory of you, but I was still in love with you when I brought you here that weekend. When I woke up beside you the next morning I knew I didn't ever want to let you go again.'

Tears welled up in Erin's amethyst eyes and any strand of lingering resentment over that weekend vanished, for they had found each other again in this peaceful house, re-establishing the connection they had forged years earlier. That he loved her meant so much that she could barely contain the huge surge of happiness spreading inside her. 'We've lost so much time when we could have been together,' she sighed.

'But we're still young enough to make up for that and maybe while we were apart we both learned stuff we needed to know,' Cristo countered more thoughtfully. 'But if we had stayed together I would have eventually married you. I just wasn't in a hurry.'

'And this time around you probably felt like you didn't have a choice,' Erin completed.

Cristo spun her round to run down the zip on her gown. 'No, I thought very carefully about that decision. I didn't have to live with you to play a part in the twins' lives and my financial support would have taken care of any problems you had. No, I asked you to marry me because I wanted *you* in my life every day.'

Smiling widely at that assurance, a glow of pleasure lighting up her eyes, Erin turned back to help him out of his jacket. 'And there I was thinking that you had only married me because you thought it was the *practical* thing to do!'

Cristo curved long fingers to her cheekbones and groaned. 'I know it was a useless proposal. I should never have asked you when we were in bed but I couldn't hold back any longer. Wives are a lot harder to lose than girlfriends and I needed to know that you were mine again for ever, *pethi mou.*'

'I like the sound of for ever,' Erin savoured, shimmying out of her lace gown and standing in her frivolous silk and lace bra and panties, a blue garter adorning one slim stocking-clad thigh.

'I like the underpinnings,' Cristo teased, fiery dark eyes welded to her scantily clad figure as he appraised her with lingering intensity. 'But I'll like you out of them even better and after a week of celibacy it's overkill.'

'Is it?' Her brows lifted, her uncertainty visible.

Laughing, Cristo picked her up and dropped her down on the gloriously comfortable bed. 'You look gorgeous but I did notice that the separate bedrooms made your mother more comfortable in our home, *latria mou*.'

'I wanted tonight to be special,' Erin whispered, running a possessive hand up a shirt-clad arm.

He sat up and discarded his shirt with alacrity, revealing a hard brown torso taut and roped with muscle. She spread her fingers there instead, revelling in the solid reassuring beat of his heart. 'I forgot to tell you that I loved you.'

'And as punishment you have to tell me at least ten times every day,' Cristo delivered, lowering his head to claim a long passionate kiss that sent her hands up to clasp his head. 'You know, I thought it might take you much longer to forgive me for not being there when you needed me…and even worse marrying another woman.'

Erin smiled 'No, I know you've been through tough times too. What I didn't understand io why you were suddenly doing all the romantic stuff you never did before. Do you remember what our first ever row was about?'

'I forgot Valentine's Day once we were dating. Well, actually I didn't. I'd always avoided the mushy stuff as it raises unfair expectations and I was embarrassed about the one I sent you before you agreed to go out with me.'

'A card?' Erin scorned. 'A *card* would rouse expectations?'

Cristo winced. 'I thought that sort of thing, like meeting each other's families, should be kept for someone you're serious about. We had only been together eleven months and twenty three days…'

Her eyes widened. 'You counted how long we were together?'

'I was always a maths whizz,' Cristo fielded deadpan.

Erin was impressed. She glanced around her candlelit flower-bedecked bower and smiled happily at what that display said: she had finally made the grade for the mushy stuff! He would never ignore Valentine's Day again. She gazed up at him, enthralled by his lean, darkly handsome features and the tender look in his beautiful dark eyes.

'I missed you *so* much!' he breathed suddenly. 'Something would remind me and then, boom, all these images would flood my head. And then I would remember what I thought you had done and get really angry that I was thinking about you again.'

Erin reached up and kissed him. 'That time is gone. Now we've got something better and stronger, something that will last—'

'For ever,' he slotted in with determination.

Her eyes slid shut as he claimed her parted lips in another hungry, demanding kiss. Heat spread inside her with tingling, burning energy and she gave herself up to desire and happiness without any sense of fear at all.

* * *

Two years later, Erin hosted the grand opening of Cristo's first spa hotel on Thesos. Built beside a secluded beach and surrounded by lush pine forest, it provided a back-to-nature retreat with luxury on tap for the discerning traveller, and as the latest must-have place to go it was already fully booked six months in advance. As Cristo had been held up, Vasos and Appollonia Denes were by her side.

A sea change had taken place in her relationship with the older couple. The passage of time had soothed the bad memories of the past and Erin's natural resentment. Appollonia had grown stronger and calmer and as she recovered from her excessive nervousness and fatal tendency to apologise for everything had confided that her greatest fear had always been that Cristo would discover what she had done and refuse to forgive her. Once the secret was out, Appollonia had had to deal with her guilt, and forging a healthy, normal relationship with Erin and the twins had gone a long way to achieving that.

Vasos had ultimately accepted a loan from Cristo to save his business but had insisted that Cristo accept a partnership in the firm, an arrangement that had left both men with their pride and principles intact. Cristo had been overjoyed that Erin's intervention had wrought a change in his foster father's stubborn outlook.

For the first year of her marriage Erin had spent a great deal of time checking out the spa facilities in her husband's hotel empire and travelling a great deal. Jenny and the twins had often accompanied her while her mother was a frequent visitor to Thesos. During the second year Erin had begun supervising the final touches to the new island spa, which was providing much needed work for the locals and had already prompted the opening of several tourist-type businesses in the village.

Sheathed in a shimmering silver evening gown, she posed for photographers and waved back as Sam and his former secretary, Janice, raised their glasses to salute her from across the room. Sam Morton was about to embark on a worldwide cruise with his recently acquired bride. Erin smiled warmly at the other couple, currently engaged in chatting to her mother, Deidre, thinking that she had been blind not to appreciate that Janice cared about Sam and that her removal from the scene would make it easier for Sam to see Janice in a different light. Sam had had to retire before he could appreciate how much he missed Janice's company and a friendly dinner date to catch up on news had eventually resulted in his second marriage.

'You look amazing, Mrs Donakis,' a rich dark drawl purred above her head as a possessive hand curved to her hip.

Erin whirled round. 'Cristo, when did you get back?'

'Half an hour ago. I had the quickest shower and change on record,' he confided. 'That's it, though. I won't be off on another trip for at least six weeks.'

Erin feasted her eyes on her handsome husband. He looked spectacular in his dark designer suit. The female photographer was watching him as though dinner had just walked through the door, but Erin was accustomed to the buzz that Cristo brought to the women in a room and it didn't bother her. Jenny came through the door with Lorcan and Nuala. Nuala, adorable in a fancy party dress, skipped over to show it off to her father, little hands holding out the skirt as if she were about to perform a curtsy.

Lorcan took his hands out of his pockets at his father's request and then ran off to try and climb the huge palm tree in the centre of the foyer.

'Lorcan!' Cristo yelled, and he strode over to lift his squirming son off the trunk and imprisoned him under one arm, talking to the little boy before setting him down again.

'Lorcan's such a boy,' Nuala pronounced, rolling her eyes with pained superiority.

Erin's mother held out her hands to the children and they latched onto her immediately, begging her to take them down to the beach.

'I wonder what the third one will be like,' Cristo commented, his dark golden gaze dipping briefly to the barely perceptible bump visible below Erin's dress.

'A mix of our genes, some good, some bad.'

'I can't wait to see our baby,' Cristo confessed.

A warm sense of tenderness filled Erin, and only their public location stopped her leaning in to hug him. She hadn't initially been sure about how another child would fit into their busy lives, but one of the main reasons she'd come round to the idea had been the awareness that Cristo had missed out on the experience of the twins as babies. While she had conceived faster than she had expected, she had thoroughly enjoyed having a supportive, interested male by her side to share every development in her pregnancy and the sight of Cristo with tears in his eyes when he saw the first scan of their child was one she would never forget.

The evening wore on in chats with influential people and business associates. The twins were whisked home to bed and Cristo, his attention consistently returning to his wife's lovely face and smile, was unashamedly relieved when they could finally take their leave of their guests.

'I hate being away from you now,' he confided, lifting her out of the four-wheel drive he had taken her home in.

'You're not away half as much as you used to be.'

'I can do a lot of my work at home.' At the foot of the stairs he swung her up in his arms and insisted on carrying her the rest of the way in spite of her protests. 'I know your feet are killing you, *latria mou.*'

She kicked her shoes off when he put her down, holding up the skirt of her gown so that she didn't trip on the trailing hem. 'But the shoes did look gorgeous,' she pointed out.

Cristo framed her laughing face with tender hands. 'You don't need to suffer to look beautiful.'

'Only a man could say that. I still can't believe that you were *born* with eyebrows that stay in shape,' Erin lamented. 'It's so unfair.'

'I would love you even without all the waxing,' Cristo intoned huskily.

Erin tried to imagine getting into bed with a pair of hairy legs and barely repressed a shudder. 'The things you say.'

'I'm trying to impress you with how crazy I am about you.' Cristo sighed with a long-suffering look belied by the amusement dancing in his dark golden eyes. 'It's an uphill challenge.'

'No, it's not. I love you too, naturally perfect brows included,' his wife informed him, gazing up at him with an appreciation she couldn't hide. *Mine*, every natural instinct said and she adored the fact.

He bent his handsome dark head and kissed her softly

with all the skill at his disposal, and her head swam and
her knees wobbled and the glory of loving Cristo swept
over her like a consuming tide, filled with happiness
and acceptance and pure joy.

* * * * *

THE SECRET SINCLAIR

CATHY WILLIAMS

PROLOGUE

RAOUL shifted as quietly as he could on the bed, propped himself up on one elbow and stared down at the woman sleeping contentedly next to him. Through the open window the sultry African night air could barely work itself up into a breeze, and even with the fan lethargically whirring on the chest of drawers it was still and humid. The net draped haphazardly over them was very optimistic protection against the mosquitoes, and as one landed on his arm he slapped it away and sat up.

Sarah stirred, opened her eyes sleepily and smiled at him.

God, he was beautiful. She had never, ever imagined that any man could be as beautiful as Raoul Sinclair. From the very first moment she had laid eyes on him three months ago she had been rendered speechless—and the effect still hadn't worn off.

Amongst all the other people taking their gap years, he stood head and shoulders above the rest. He was literally taller than all of them, but it was much more than that. It was his exotic beauty that held her spellbound: the burnished gold of his skin, the vibrancy of his black, glossy hair—long now; almost to his shoulders—the latent power of his lean, muscular body. Although he was only a matter of a few years older than the rest of them, he was a man amongst boys.

She reached up and skimmed her hand along his back.

'Mosquitoes.' Raoul grinned, dark eyes sweeping over her smooth honey-gold shoulders down to her breasts. He felt himself stirring and hardening, even though they had made love less than a few hours ago. 'This net is useless. But, seeing that we're now both up and wide awake...'

With a little sigh of pleasure Sarah reached out and linked her hands around his neck, drawing him to her and wriggling restlessly as his mouth found hers.

A virgin when she had met him, she knew he had liberated her. Every touch had released new and wonderful sensations.

Her body was slick with heat and perspiration as he gently pulled down the thin sheet which was all they could endure out here.

She had the most wonderful breasts he had ever seen, and with a sudden pang of regret for things to come Raoul realised that he was going to miss her body. No—much more than that. He was going to miss *her*.

It was a situation he had not foreseen when he had decided to take three months off to work in Mozambique. At the time, it had seemed a fitting interlude between the conclusion of university—two hard-won degrees in Economics and Maths—and the start of what he intended to be the rest of his life. Before he threw himself into conquering the world and putting his own personal demons to rest he would immerse himself in the selflessness of helping other people—people as unfortunate as he himself had been, although in a completely different way.

Meeting a woman and falling into bed with her hadn't been on his radar. His libido, like everything else in his life, was just something else he had learnt to control ruthlessly. He had intended to spend three months controlling it.

Sarah Scott, with her tangled blonde hair and her fresh-faced innocence, was certainly not the sort of woman he fancied himself drawn to. He generally went for tougher, more experienced types—women with obvious attractions, who were as willing as he was to have a brief, passionate fling. Women who were ships passing in the night, never dropping anchor and more importantly, never expecting *him* to.

One look at Sarah and he had recognised a girl who would be into anchors being dropped, but it hadn't been enough to keep him away. For two weeks, as they'd been thrown together in circumstances so far removed from reality that it was almost like living in a bubble, he had watched her broodingly out of the corner of his eye, had been aware of her watching him. By the end of week three the inevitable had become reality.

They made love now—quietly and slowly. The house they shared with six other occupants had walls as thin as tracing paper, and wooden floors that seemed to transmit sound with ruthless efficiency.

'Okay,' Raoul whispered, 'how close do you think I can get before you have to stifle a groan?'

'Don't,' Sarah whispered back with a giggle. 'You know how hard it is...'

'Yes, and it's what I like about you. One touch and I can feel your body melt.' He touched her accordingly, a feathery touch between her generous breasts, trailing a continuous line to circle her prominent nipples until she was squirming and breathing quickly, face flushed, her hand curling into his over long hair.

As he delicately licked the stiffened, swollen tip of her nipple he automatically placed a gentle hand over her mouth, and half smiled as she tried very hard not to groan into the palm of his hand.

Only a handful of times had they taken the beaten up Land Rover and escaped to one of the beaches, where they had found privacy and made love without restraint. Between work and down-time on the compound, however, they were confined to a type of lovemaking that was as refined and guarded as a specialised dance.

Sarah half opened her eyes, simply because she could never resist watching Raoul—the dark bronze of his body against the paler gold of hers, the play of sinew and muscle as he reared up over her, powerful and strong and untamed.

Although it was after midnight, the moon was bright and full. Its silvery light streamed through the window, casting shadows on the walls and picking up the hard angles of his face as he licked a path along her stomach, down to where her legs were parted for his eventual caress.

Quite honestly, at times like this Sarah thought that she had died and gone to heaven, and it never failed to amaze her that her feelings for this man could be so overwhelming after only a matter of three months…less! She felt as though, without even realising it, she had been saving herself for him to come along and take possession of her heart.

As their lovemaking gathered urgency the uneasy tangle of thoughts that had been playing in her head for the past few days were lost as he thrust into her and then picked up a long, steady rhythm that became faster and harder, until she felt herself spiralling towards orgasm, holding on so that their bodies became one and they climaxed. The only sounds were their fast-drawn breaths, even though she wanted to cry out loud from the pleasure of fulfilment.

As she tumbled back down to earth the moonlight illuminated his suitcases, packed and standing to attention by the single old-fashioned wardrobe.

And then back came the disquieting thoughts.

Raoul sank against her, spent, and for a few seconds neither of them spoke. He draped his arm over her body. The sheet had managed to work itself into a heap at the foot of the bed, and he idly wondered just how long it would take for the mosquitoes to figure out that there was a new and much bigger entrance available to get inside.

'Can…can we talk?'

Raoul stiffened. Past experience had taught him that anyone who wanted to *talk* invariably wanted to say things he didn't want to hear.

'Okay, I can tell from the way you're not jumping with joy that you don't want to talk, but I think we should. I mean…your cases are all packed, Raoul. You're leaving in two days' time. And I…I don't know what's going to happen to us.'

Raoul swung off her to lie back. He stared at the ceiling in silence for a few seconds. Of course he had known that this was where they would end up, but he had conveniently chosen to ignore that because she had bewitched him. Every time he had considered giving her one of his little speeches about expecting nothing from him he had looked into her bright green eyes and the speech had melted away.

He reluctantly turned to face her and stroked the vanilla blonde hair off her face, neatly tucking loose strands behind her ears.

'I know we need to talk,' he admitted heavily.

'But you still don't want to…'

'I'm not sure where it's going to get us.'

Hearing that was like having ice cold water thrown in her face, but Sarah ploughed on bravely—because she just couldn't see that what they had could possibly come to *nothing* the minute he departed. They had done a thousand things together. More than some people packed into a lifetime. She refused to concede that it could all melt away into nothingness.

'I never intended to come out here and start any kind of relationship,' he confessed, his eloquence for once gone, because he was just not accustomed to having emotional conversations with anyone. He never had. He just didn't think that he had it in him. But there she was, staring at him in the darkness with those big, questioning eyes... waiting.

'Nor did I. I mean, I just wanted to get some experience and live a little—do something a bit different before starting university. You know that. How many times did I tell you that—?' She'd very nearly said *falling in love*, but an innate sense of self-preservation held her back. Not once had he ever told her what he felt for her. She had only deduced from the way he looked at her and touched her, and laughed at the things she said, and when she teased him. 'That meeting someone wasn't part of my agenda either. The unexpected happens.'

Did it? Not to him. Never to him. He had endured a childhood that had been riddled with the unexpected— all of it bad. Top of his list of things to avoid was *The Unexpected*, but she was right. What had blossomed between them had taken him by surprise. He drew her against him and searched for the right words to explain just why the future staring them in the face would be one they each faced on their own.

'I shouldn't have given in, Sarah.'

'Shouldn't have given in to what?'

'You know what. To you.'

'Please don't say that,' she whispered with heartfelt dismay. 'Are you saying that what we did was all a big mistake? We've had so much fun! You don't have to be serious all the time.'

Raoul took her hand and kissed the tips of her fingers, one by one, until the radiant smile reappeared on her face. She smiled easily.

'It's been fun,' he agreed, with the heavy feeling of someone about to deliver a fatal blow to an unsuspecting victim. 'But this isn't reality, Sarah. This is time out. You pretty much said it yourself. Reality is what's in front of us. In your case three years at university. In my case...' *The world and nothing less.* 'A job. I really hoped that we wouldn't have to have this conversation. I hoped that you would see what's pretty clear to me. This has been great, but it's...a holiday affair.'

'A holiday affair?' Sarah repeated in a small voice.

Raoul sighed and ran his fingers through his too-long hair. He would get rid of it the second he made it back to civilisation.

'Don't make me out to be an ogre, Sarah. I'm not saying that it hasn't been...incredible. It has. In fact, it's been the most incredible three months of my life.' He hesitated. His past had never been something he chose to discuss with anyone, least of all a woman, but the urge to go further with her was overpowering. 'You've made me feel like no one else ever has...but then I suppose you know that...'

'How can I when you've never told me?' But it was something for her to hang onto.

'I...I'm not good with this kind of emotional drama. I've had a lot of emotional drama in my life...'

'What do you mean?' She knew only the barest of facts about his past, even though he pretty much knew everything about hers. She had waxed lyrical about her childhood—her very happy and very ordinary childhood—as an only child of two parents who had always thought that they would never have kids until her mother became pregnant at the merry age of forty-one.

He had skirted round the subject aside from telling her that he'd had no parents, preferring to concentrate on the future which, as time went on, suited her very well—even though any mention of *her* in that future hadn't actually been voiced. She liked the thought of him forging his way with her at his side. Somewhere.

'I grew up in a foster home, Sarah. I was one of those kids you read about in the newspapers who get taken in by Social Services because their parents can't take care of them.'

Sarah sat up, lost for words. Then her natural warmth took over and she felt the prickle of tears, which brought a reluctant smile to his lips.

'Neither of your parents could look after you?'

'Just the one parent on the scene. My mother.' It was not in his nature to confide, and he picked carefully at his words, choosing to denude them of all potency. It was a trick he had learnt a long time ago, so his voice, when he spoke, was flat and detached. 'Unfortunately she had a problem with substances, which ended up killing her when I was five. My father... Who knows? Could have been anyone.'

'You poor soul!'

'I prefer to think of my background as character-building, and as foster homes went mine wasn't too bad. Where I'm going with this...' For a second he had to remind himself where he *was* going with it. 'I'm not looking for a relationship. Not now—probably not ever. I never meant to string you along, Sarah, but...you got under my skin... And all *this* didn't exactly go the distance in bringing me back to my senses.'

'All what?'

'Here. The middle of nowhere. Thrown together in the heat…'

'So nothing would have happened between us if we hadn't been out here?' She could hear her voice rising and had to control it, because she didn't want to wake anyone—although there was only one other English speaking person on the compound.

'That's a purely hypothetical question.'

'You could try answering it!'

'I don't know.' He could feel the hurt seeping out of her, but what could he do about it? How could he make it better without issuing promises he knew he wouldn't keep?

Frustration and anger at himself rushed through him in a tidal wave. Hell, he should have known just by looking at her that Sarah wasn't one of those women who were out to have a good time, no strings attached! Where had his prized self-control been when he had needed it most? Absent without leave! He had seen her and all trace of common sense had deserted him.

And when he had discovered that she was a virgin? Had that stopped him in his tracks? The opposite. He had felt unaccountably thrilled to be her first, had wanted to shout it from the rooftops. Instead of backing away he had rushed headlong into the sort of crazy quasi-romantic situation that he had always scorned. There hadn't been chocolates and jewellery—not that he could have afforded either—but there had been long, lazy conversations, a great deal of laughter… Hell, he had even cooked her a meal on one occasion, when the rest of the crew had disappeared for the weekend to camp on the beach, leaving the two of them in charge.

'You don't know? Is that because I'm not really your type?'

He hesitated just long enough for her to bitterly assume the obvious.

'I'm not, am I?' She slung her legs over the bed, kicking away at the mosquito net and finally shoving it aside so that she could crawl under it.

'Where are you going!'

'I don't want to be having this conversation.' In the darkness she hunted around for her clothes, located them, and began putting them on. An old tee shirt, a pair of denim shorts, her flipflops. 'I'm going outside. I need to get some air.'

Raoul debated the wisdom of following her for a few seconds, then leapt out of the bed, struggling with his jeans, not bothering with a shirt at all, as he watched her flying out of the room like a bat out of hell.

The bedroom was small, equipped with the most basic of furniture, and cluttered with all the bits and pieces of two occupants. He came close to tripping over one of his shoes and cursed softly under his breath. He shouldn't be following her. He had said all there was to say on the subject of any continuing romance. To prolong the conversation would be to invite a debate that would be stillborn, so what was the point? But watching her disappear through the bedroom door had galvanised him into instant, inexplicable action.

The house was a square concrete block, its front door accessed by sufficient steps to ensure that it was protected against flooding during the cyclone season.

He caught up with her just as she had reached the bottom of the steps.

'So, what *are* your types!' Sarah swung round to glare at him, hands on her hips.

'Types? What are you talking about?'

'These women you go for?'

'That's irrelevant.'

'Not to me it isn't!' Sarah stared up at him. She was shaking like a leaf, and she didn't know why she was getting hung up on that one detail. He was right. It was irrelevant. What did it matter if he went for tall brunettes and she was a short blonde? What mattered was that he was dumping her. Throwing her out like used goods. Tossing her aside as though she was just something insignificant that no longer mattered. When he was *everything* to her.

She literally shied away from the thought of waking up in three days' time in an empty bed, knowing that she would never lay eyes on him again. How on earth was she going to survive?

'You need to calm down.' He shook his head and raked his fingers through his hair, sweeping it back from his face. God, it was like an oven out here. He could feel the sweat beginning to gather on his body.

'I'm perfectly calm!' Sarah informed him in a shrill voice. 'I just want to know if you've had fun *using* me for the past three months!'

She swung round, began heading towards the central clearing, where the circular reed huts with their distinctive pointed roofs were used as classrooms for the twenty local children who attended every day. Raoul didn't teach. He and two of the other guys did brutally manual labour— building work in one of the communities further along, planting and harvesting of crops. He gave loads of advice on crop rotation and weather patterns. He seemed to know absolutely everything.

'Were you just making the best of a bad job out here? Sleeping with me because there was no one else around to your taste?'

'Don't be stupid!' He reached out and stopped her in her tracks, pulling her back to him and forcing her to look up.

'I know I'm not the most glamorous person in the world. I know you're probably accustomed to landing really gorgeous girls.' She bit her lip and looked away, feeling miserable and thoroughly sorry for herself. 'I knew it was odd that you even looked at me in the first place, but I suppose I was the only other English person here so you made do.'

'Don't do this, Sarah,' Raoul said harshly. He could feel her trembling against him, and he had to fight the impulse to terminate the conversation by kissing that lush, full mouth. 'If you want to know what kind of women I've always gone for, I'll tell you. I've always gone for women who wanted nothing from me. I'm not saying that's a good thing, but it's the truth. Yes, they've been good looking, but not in the way that you are...'

'What way is that?' Sarah asked scornfully, but she was keen to grasp any positive comment in these suddenly turbulent waters. She realised with a sinking heart that she would be willing to beg for him. It went against every grain of pride in her, but, yes, she would plead for him at least to keep in touch.

'Young, innocent, full of laughter...' He loosened his fingers on her arm and gently stroked her. 'That's why I should have run a mile the minute you looked at me with those big green eyes,' he murmured with genuine regret. 'But I couldn't. You summed up everything I wasn't looking for, and I still couldn't resist you.'

'You don't have to!' Before he could knock her last-ditch plea down in flames she turned away brusquely and walked towards the clearing, adopting a position on one of the fallen tree trunks which had been left as a bench of sorts.

Her heart was beating like a jackhammer and she could barely catch her breath. She didn't look at him as he sat down on the upturned trunk next to her.

The night was alive with the sounds of insects and frogs, but it was cooler out here than it had been in the stifling heat of the bedroom.

Eventually she turned to him. 'I'm not asking you to settle down and marry me,' she said quietly—although, really, who was she kidding? That was exactly what she wanted. 'But you don't have to walk away and never look back. I mean, we can keep in touch.' She threw him a watery, desperate smile. 'That's what mobile phones and e-mails and all these social networking sites are all about, you know.'

'How many times have we argued about the merits of throwing your personal life into a public arena for the world to feed on?'

'You're such a dinosaur, Raoul.' But she smiled. They'd argued about so many things! Light-hearted arguments, with lots of laughter. When Raoul took a stand it was impossible to deflect him, and she had enjoyed teasing him about his implacability. She had never known anything like it.

'And you'd be happy to do that?' Raoul thought that if she were the kind of girl who could be happy with that kind of distant, intermittent contact then they wouldn't be sitting here right now, having this conversation, because then she would also be the kind of girl who would have indulged in a three-month fling and been happy to walk away, without agonising about a future that wasn't destined to be.

For a fleeting moment he wondered what it would be like to take her with him, but the thought was one he discarded even before it had had time to take root. He was a product of his background, and that was something he was honest enough to acknowledge.

Deprived of stability, he had learnt from a very young

age that he had to look out for himself. He couldn't even really remember when he had made his mind up that the world would never decide his fate. He would control it, and the way he would do that would be through his brains. Foster care had honed his single-minded ambition and provided him with one very important lesson in life: rely on no one.

Whilst the other kids had been larking around, or pining for parents that failed to show up at appointed times, he had buried his head in books and mastered all the tricks of studying in the midst of chaos. Blessed with phenomenal intelligence, he had sailed through every exam, and as soon as he'd been released from the restrictions of a foster home had worked furiously to put himself through college and then later university.

Starting with nothing, he had to do more than just *be clever.* A degree counted for nothing when you were competing with someone who had family connections. So he had got two degrees—two high-powered degrees—which he intended to use ruthlessly to get where he wanted to go.

Where, in his great scheme of things, would Sarah fit in? He was no carer and never would be. He just didn't have it in him. And Sarah was the sort of soft, gentle person who would always need someone to take care of her.

Heck, she couldn't even bring herself to answer his question! When she spoke of keeping in touch, what she really meant was having an ongoing relationship. How responsible would he be if he told her what she wanted to hear?

Abruptly Raoul stood up, putting some vital immediate distance between them—because sitting next to her was doing crazy things to his thoughts and to his body.

'Well?' he asked, more harshly than he had intended, and he sensed her flinch as she bowed her head. He had to use every scrap of will-power at his disposal not to go across and put his arms around her. He clenched his hands into fists, wanting to hit something very hard. 'You haven't answered my question. *Could* you keep in touch with me with the occasional e-mail? When you should be moving on? Putting me behind you and chalking the whole thing up to experience?'

'How can you be so callous?' Sarah whispered. She had practically begged and it hadn't been enough. He didn't love her and he never would. Why should she waste her time lamenting the situation? He was right. E-mails and text messages would just prolong the hurt. She needed to cut him out of her life and leave no remaining bits to fester and multiply.

'I'm not being callous, Sarah. I'm sparing you the pain of building false hopes. You're young, with stars in your eyes…'

'You're not exactly over the hill, Raoul!'

'In terms of experience I'm a thousand years older than you, and I'm not the man you're looking for. I would be no good for you…'

'That's usually the coward's way out of a sticky situation,' she muttered, having read it somewhere and thought that it made sense.

'In this case it's the truth. You need someone who's going to take care of you, and that person is never going to be me.' He watched her carefully and wondered if he would ever again be in the business of justifying himself to another human being. *Walk alone,* that was what he had taught himself, *and you don't end up entangled in situations such as this.* 'I don't want the things that you do,' he continued softly.

Sarah would have liked to deny that she wanted any of those things he accused her of wanting, but she did. She wanted the whole fairytale romance and he knew it. It felt as if he knew her better than anyone ever had.

Her shoulders slumped as she struggled to look for the silver lining in the cloud. There always was one.

'I'm not equipped for playing happy families, Sarah…'

She eventually raised her eyes to his and looked at him coldly. 'You're right. I want all that stuff, and it *is* better for you to let me down so that I can have a fighting chance of meeting someone who isn't scared of commitment.' Her legs felt like jelly when she stood up. 'It would be awful to think that I might waste my time loving you when you haven't *got it in you* for the fairytale stuff!'

Raoul gritted his teeth, but there was nothing to say in response to that.

'And by the way,' she flung over her shoulder, 'I'll leave your clothes outside the bedroom door, because I'll be sleeping on my own tonight! You want your precious freedom so badly? Well, congratulations—you've got it!'

She kept her head held high as she covered the ten thousand miles back to the house. At least it felt like ten thousand miles.

Memories of their intense relationship flashed through her head like a slow, painful slideshow. Thinking about him could still give her goosebumps, and she hugged herself as she jogged up the flight of stone steps to the front door.

In the bedroom, she gathered up some of his clothes and buried her face in them, breathing in his musky, aggressively male scent, then duly stuck them outside—along with his cases.

Then she locked the bedroom door, and in the empty quiet of the bedroom contemplated a life without Raoul in it and tried to stop the bottom of her world from dropping out.

CHAPTER ONE

CAUGHT in the middle of crouching on the ground, trying to get rid of a particularly stubborn stain on the immaculate cream carpet that ran the length, breadth and width of the directors' floor of the very exclusive family bank in which she had now been working for the past three weeks, Sarah froze at the sound of voices emerging from one of the offices. Low, unhurried voices—one belonging to a man, the other to a woman.

It was the first time she had been made aware of any sign of life here. She came at a little after nine at night, did her cleaning and left. She liked it that way. She had no wish to bump into anyone—not that there would have been the slightest possibility of her being addressed. She was a cleaner, and as such was rendered instantly invisible. Even the doorman who had been allowing her entry ever since she had started working at the bank barely glanced up when she appeared in front of him.

She could barely remember a time when she had been able to garner a few admiring glances. The combined weight of responsibility and lack of money had rubbed the youthful glow from her face. Now when she looked in the mirror all she saw was a woman in her mid-twenties with shadows under her eyes and the pinched appearance of someone with too many worries.

Sarah wondered what she should do. Was there some special etiquette involved if a cleaner come into contact with one of the directors of this place? She hunkered down. In her blue checked overalls and with her hair scraped back under a matching scarf, she figured she might easily have passed for a heap of old clothes dumped on the ground, were it not for the elaborate trolley of cleaning materials by her side.

As the hushed voices got closer—just round the corner—Sarah put her all into the wretched stain on the carpet. But with a sinking heart she was aware that the voices had fallen silent, and the footsteps seemed to have stopped just in front of her.

In fact, sliding her eyes across, she could make out some hand-made Italian shoes just below charcoal-grey trousers, sharply creased, a pair of very high cream stilettos, and stockings with a slight sheen, very sheer.

'I don't know if you've done the conference room as yet, but if you have then you've made a very poor job of it. There are ring marks on the table, and two champagne glasses are still there on the bookshelf!'

The woman's voice was icy cold and imperious. Reluctantly Sarah raised her eyes, travelling the length of a very tall, very thin, very blonde woman in her thirties. From behind her she could hear the man pressing for the lift.

'I haven't got to the conference room yet,' Sarah mumbled. She prayed that the woman wouldn't see fit to lodge a complaint. She needed this job. The hours suited her, and it was well paid for what it was. Included in the package was the cost of a taxi to and from her house to the bank. How many cleaning jobs would ever have included *that*?

'Well, I'm relieved to hear it!'

'For God's sake, Louisa, let the woman do her job. It's

nearly ten, and I can do without spending the rest of the evening here!'

Sarah heard that voice—the voice that had haunted her for the past five years—and her mind went a complete blank. Then it was immediately kick-started, papering over the similarities of tone. Because there was no way that Raoul Sinclair could be the man behind her. Raoul Sinclair was just a horrible, youthful mistake that was now in the past.

And yet…

Obeying some kind of primitive instinct to match a face to that remarkable voice, Sarah turned around—and in that instant she was skewered to the spot by the same bitter chocolate eyes that had taken up residence in her head five years ago and stubbornly refused to budge. She half stood, swayed.

The last thing she heard before she fainted was the woman saying, in a shrill, ringing voice, 'Oh, for God's sake, that's the *last thing we need*!'

She came to slowly. As her eyelids fluttered open she knew, in a fuddled way, that she really didn't want to wake up. She wanted to stay in her peaceful faint.

She had been carried into an office and was now on a long, low sofa which she recognised as the one in Mr Verrier's office. She tried to struggle upright and Raoul came into her line of vision, taller than she remembered, but just as breathtakingly beautiful. She had never seen him in anything dressier than a pair of jeans and an old tee shirt, and she was slowly trying to match up the Raoul she had known with this man kneeling over her, who looked every inch the billionaire he had once laughingly informed her he would be.

'Here—drink this.'

'I don't want to drink anything. What are you doing here? Am I seeing things? You can't be here.'

'Funny, but I was thinking the very same thing.' Raoul had only now recovered his equilibrium. The second his eyes had locked onto hers he had been plunged into instant flashback, and carrying her into the office had re-awakened a tide of feeling which he had assumed to have been completely exorcised. He remembered the smell of her and the feel of her as though it had been yesterday. How was that possible? When so much had happened in the intervening years?

Sarah was fighting to steady herself. She couldn't believe her eyes. It was just so weird that she had to bite back the desire to burst into hysterical, incredulous laughter.

'What are you doing here, Sarah? Hell…you've changed…'

'I know.' She was suddenly conscious of the sight she must make, scrawny and hollow-cheeked and wearing her overalls. 'I have, haven't I?' She nervously fingered the checked overall and knew that she was shaking. 'Things haven't worked out…quite as I'd planned.' She made a feeble attempt to stand up, and collapsed back down onto the sofa.

In truth, Raoul was horrified at what he saw. Where was the bright-eyed, laughing girl he had known?

'I have to go… I have to finish the cleaning, Raoul. I…'

'You're not finishing anything. Not just at the moment. When was the last time you ate anything? You look as though you could be blown away by a gust of wind. And *cleaning*? Now you're doing cleaning jobs to earn money?'

He vaulted to his feet and began pacing the floor. He could scarcely credit that she was lying on the sofa in this office. Accustomed to eliminating any unwelcome emotions and reactions as being surplus to his finely tuned and highly controlled way of life, he found that he couldn't control the bombardment of questions racing through his brain. Nor could he rein in the flood of unwanted memories that continued to besiege him from every angle.

Sarah was possibly the very last woman with whom he had had a perfectly natural relationship. She represented a vision of himself as a free man, with one foot on the ladder but no steps actually yet taken. Was that why the impact of seeing her again now was so powerful?

'I never meant to end up like this,' Sarah whispered, as the full impact of their unexpected meeting began to take shape.

'But you have. How? What happened to you? Did you decide that you preferred cleaning floors to teaching?'

'Of course I didn't!' Sarah burst out sharply. She dragged herself into an upright position on the sofa and was confronted with the unflattering sight of her sturdy work shoes and thick, black woollen tights.

'Did you ever make it to university?' Raoul demanded. As she had struggled to sit up his eyes had moved of their own volition to the swing of her breasts under the hideous checked overall.

'I...I left the compound two weeks after you left.'

Her strained green eyes made her look so young and vulnerable that sudden guilt penetrated the armour of his formidable self control.

In five years Raoul had fulfilled every promise he had made to himself as a boy. Equipped with his impressive qualifications, he had landed his first job on the trading floor at the Stock Exchange, where his genius for making money had very quickly catapulted him upwards. Where colleagues had conferred, he'd operated solely on his own, and in the jungle arena of the money-making markets it hadn't been long before he'd emerged as having a killer streak that could make grown men quake in their shoes.

Raoul barely noticed. Money, for him, equated with freedom. He would be reliant on no one. Within three years he had accumulated sufficient wealth to begin the process of acquisition, and every acquisition had been bigger and more impressive than the one before. Guilt had played no part in his meteoric upward climb, and he had had no use for it.

Now, however, he felt it sink its teeth in, and he shoved his fingers through his hair.

Sarah followed the gesture which was so typically him. 'You've had your hair cut,' she said, flushing at the inanity of her observation, and Raoul offered her a crooked half-smile.

'I discovered that shoulder-length hair didn't go with the image. Now, of course, I could grow it down to my waist and no one would dare say a word, but my days of long hair are well and truly over.'

Just as she was, she thought. She belonged to those days that were well and truly over—except they weren't, were they? She knew that there were things that needed to be said, but it was a conversation she'd never expected to have, and now that it was staring her in the face she just wanted to delay its onset for as long as possible.

'You must be pleased.' Sarah stared down at her feet and sensed him walk towards her until his shadow joined her feet. When he sat down next to her, her whole body stiffened in alarm—because even through the nightmare of her situation, and the pain and misery of how their relationship had ended, her body was still stirring into life and reacting to his proximity. 'You were always so determined...' she continued.

'In this life it's the only way to go forward. You were telling me what happened to your university career...'

'Was I?' She glanced across at him and licked her lips nervously. For two years she had done nothing but think of him. Over time the memories had faded, and she had learnt the knack of pushing them away whenever they threatened to surface, but there had been moments when she had flirted with the notion of meeting him again, had created conversations in her head in which she was strong and confident and in control of the situation. Nothing like this.

'I...I never made it to university. Like I said, things didn't quite work out.'

'Because of me.' Raoul loathed this drag on his emotions. Nor could he sit so close to her. Frustrated at the way his self-control had slipped out of his grasp, he pulled a chair over and positioned it directly in front of the sofa. 'You weren't due to leave that compound for another three months. In fact, I remember you saying that you thought you would stay there for much longer.'

'Not all of us make plans that end up going our way,' she told him, with creeping resentment in her voice.

'And you blame me for the fact that you've ended up where you have? I was honest with you. I believe your parting shot was that you were grateful that you would have the opportunity to find Mr Right... If you're going to try and pin the blame for how your life turned out on me, then it won't work. We had a clean break, and that's always the best way. If the Mr Right you found turned out to be the sort of guy who sits around while his woman goes out cleaning to earn money, then that's a pity—but not my fault.'

'This is crazy. I...I'm not blaming you for anything. And there's no *Mr Right*. Gosh, Raoul...I can't believe this. It feels like some kind of…of…nightmare… I don't mean that. I just mean…you're so *different*…'

Raoul chose to ignore her choice of words. She was in a state of shock. So was he. 'Okay, so maybe you didn't find the man of your dreams…but there must have been someone…' he mused slowly. 'Why else would you have abandoned a career you were so passionate about? Hell, you used to say that you were born to teach.'

Sarah raised moss-green eyes to his and he felt himself tense at the raw memory of how she'd used to look up at him, teasing and adoring at the same time. He had revelled in it. Now he doubted that any woman would have the temerity to tease him. Wealth and power had elevated him to a different place—a place where women batted their eyelashes, and flattered…but *teased*? No. Nor would he welcome it. In five years he had not once felt the slightest temptation to dip his toes into the murky waters of commitment.

'Did you get involved with some kind of loser?' he grated. She had been soft and vulnerable and broken-hearted. Had someone come along and taken advantage of her state of mind?

'What are you talking about?'

'You must have been distraught to have returned from Africa ahead of schedule. I realise that you probably blame me for that, but if you had stuck it out you would forgotten me within a few weeks.'

'Is that how it worked for you, Raoul?'

Pinned to the spot by such a direct question, Raoul refused to answer. 'Did you get strung along by someone who promised you the earth and then did a runner when he got tired of you? Is that what happened? A degree would have been your passport, Sarah. How many times did we have conversations about this? What did he say to you to convince you that it was a good idea to dump your aspi-rations?'

He didn't know whether to stand or to sit. He felt pe-culiarly uncomfortable in his own skin, and those wide green eyes weren't helping matters.

'And why cleaning? Why not an office job somewhere?'

He looked down at his watch and realised that it was nearing midnight, but he was reluctant to end the conver-sation even though he queried where it was going. She was just another part of his history, a jigsaw puzzle piece that had already been slotted in place, so why prolong the catch-up game? Especially when those huge, veiled, ac-cusing green eyes were reminding him of a past for which he had no use?

If he politely ushered her to the door he was certain that she would leave and not look back. Which was clearly a good thing.

'You can't trust people,' he advised her roughly. 'Now perhaps you'll see my point of view when I told you that the only person you can rely on is yourself.'

'I've probably lost my job here,' Sarah intoned distract-edly.

She had seen him look at his watch and she knew what that meant. Her time was coming to an end. He had moved onwards and upwards to that place where time was money. Reminiscing, for Raoul, would have very limited interest value. He was all about the future, not the past. But she had to plough on and get where she needed to get, horrible though the prospect was.

'I couldn't countenance you working here anyway,' Raoul concurred smoothly.

'What does this place have to do with you?'

'As of six this evening—everything. I own it.'

Sarah's mouth dropped open. 'You own *this*?'

'All part of my portfolio.'

It seemed to Sarah now that there was no meeting point left between them. He had truly moved into a different stratosphere. He literally owned the company whose floors she had been scrubbing less than two hours ago. In his smart business suit, with the silk tie and the gleaming hand-made shoes, he was the absolute antithesis of her, with her company uniform and her well-worn flats.

Defiantly she pulled off the headscarf—if only to diminish the image of complete servility.

Hair the colour of vanilla, soft and fine and unruly, tumbled out. He had cut his hair. She had grown hers. It tumbled nearly to her waist, and for a few seconds Raoul was dazzled at the sight of it.

She was twisting the unsightly headscarf between her fingers, and that brought him back down to earth. She had been saying something about the job—this glorious cleaning job—which she would have to abandon. Unless, of course, she carried on cleaning way past her finishing time.

He'd opened his mouth to continue their conversation, even though he had been annoyingly thrown off course by that gesture of hers, when she said, in such a low voice that he had to strain forward to hear her, 'I tried to get in touch, you know...'

'I beg your pardon?'

Sarah cleared her throat. 'I tried to get in touch, but I...I couldn't...'

Raoul stiffened. Having money had been a tremendous learning curve. It had a magnetism all of its own. People he had once known and heartily wished to forget had made contact, having glimpsed some picture of him in the financial pages of a newspaper. It would have been amusing had it not been so pathetic.

He tried to decipher what Sarah was saying now. Had she been one of those people as well? Had she turned to the financial news and spotted him, thought that she might get in touch as she was down on her luck?

'What do you mean, *you couldn't*?' His voice was several shades cooler.

'I had no idea how to locate you.' Her heart was beating so hard that she felt positively sick. 'I mean, you disappeared without a trace. I tried checking with the girl who kept all the registration forms for when we were out there, and she gave me an address, but you'd left...'

'When did all this frantic checking take place?'

'When I got back to England. I know you dumped me, Raoul, but...but I had to talk to you...'

So despite all her bravado when they had parted company she had still tried to track him down. It was a measure of her lack of sophistication that she had done that, and an even greater measure of it that she would now openly confess to doing so.

'I came to London and rented a room in a house out east. You would never have found me.'

'I even went on the internet, but you weren't to be found. And of course I remembered you saying that you would never join any social networking sites...'

'Quite a search. What was that in aid of? A general chat?'

'Not exactly.'

Sarah was thinking now that if she had carried on searching just a little bit longer—another year or so— then she would have found him listed somewhere on the computer, because he would have made his fortune by then. But she had quickly given up. She had never imagined that he would have risen so far, so fast, and yet when she thought about it there had always been that stubborn, closed, ruthless streak to him. And he had been fearless. Fearless when it came to the physical stuff and fearless when it came to plans for his future.

'I wish I had managed to get through to you. You never kept in touch with your last foster home, did you? I tried to trace you through them, but you had already dropped off their radar.'

Raoul stilled, because he had forgotten just how much she knew about him—including his miserable childhood and adolescence.

'So you didn't get in touch,' he said, with a chill in his voice. 'We could carry on discussing all the various ways you tried and failed to find me, or we could just move on. *Why* did you want to get in touch?'

'You mean that I should have had more pride than to try?'

'A lot of women would have,' Raoul commented drily. She turned her head and the overhead light caught her hair, turning it into streaks of gold and pale toffee. 'But I suppose you were very young. Just nineteen.'

'And too stupid to do the sensible thing?'

'Just…very young.' He dragged his eyes away from the dancing highlights of her hair and frowned, sensing an edginess to her voice although her face was very calm and composed.

'You can't blame me if I couldn't find you…'

Raoul was confused. What was she talking about?

'It's getting late, Sarah. I've worked through the night, hammering out this deal with lawyers. I haven't got the time or the energy to try and decipher what you're saying. Why would I *blame* you for not being able to find me?'

'I'll get to the point. I didn't *want* to get in touch with you, Raoul. What kind of a complete loser do you imagine I am? Do you think that I would have come crawling to you for a second chance?'

'You might have if you'd been through the mill with some other guy!'

'There *was* no other guy! And why on earth would I come running to *you* when you had already told me that you wanted nothing more to do with me?'

'Then why *did* you try and get in touch?' He felt disproportionately pleased that there had been no other guy, but he immediately put that down to the fact that, whether they had parted on good terms or not, he wouldn't have wanted her to be used and tossed aside by someone she had met on the rebound.

'Because I found out that I was pregnant!'

The silence that greeted this pooled around her until Sarah began to feel dizzy.

Raoul was having trouble believing what he had just heard. In fact he was tempted to dismiss it as a trick of the imagination, or else some crazy joke—maybe an attention-seeking device to prolong their conversation.

But one look at her face told him that this was no joke.

'That's the most ridiculous thing I've ever heard, and you have to be nuts if you think I'm going to fall for it. When it comes to money, I've heard it all.' Like a caged beast, he shot up and began prowling through the room, hands shoved into his pockets. 'So we've met again by chance. You're down on your luck, for whatever reason, and you see that I've made my fortune. Just come right out and ask for a helping hand! Do you think I'd turn you away? If you need cash, I can write a cheque for you right now.'

'Stop it, Raoul. I'm not a gold-digger! Just listen to me! I tried to get in touch with you because I found out that I was having your baby. I knew you'd be shocked and, believe me, I did think it over for a while, but in the end I thought that it was only fair that you knew. How could you think that I'd make something like that up to try and get money out of you? Have you ever known me to be materialistic? How could you be so insulting?'

'I couldn't have got you pregnant. It's not possible! I was always careful.'

'Not always,' Sarah muttered.

'Okay, so maybe you got yourself pregnant by someone else...'

'There *was* no one else! When I left the compound I had no idea that I was pregnant. I left because...because I just couldn't stay there any longer. I got back to England and I still intended to start university. I *wanted* to put you behind me. I didn't find out until I was nearly five months along. My periods were erratic, and then they disappeared, but I was so... I barely noticed...'

She had been so miserable that World War III could have broken out and she probably wouldn't have noticed the mushroom cloud outside her bedroom window. Memories of him had filled every second of every minute of her every waking hour, until she had prayed for amnesia—anything that would help her forget. Her parents had been worried sick. At any rate, her mother had been the first to suspect something when she'd begun to look a little rounder, despite the fact that her eating habits had taken a nosedive.

'I'm not hearing this,'

'You don't *want* to hear this! My mum and dad were very supportive. They never once lectured, and they were there for me from the very minute that Oliver was born.'

Somehow the mention of a name made Raoul blanch. It was much harder to dismiss what she had said as the rantings of an ex-lover who wanted money from him and was prepared to try anything to get it. The mention of a name seemed to turn the fiction she was spinning into something approaching reality, and yet still his mind refused to concede that the story being told had anything to do with him.

He'd never been one to shy away from the truth, however brutal, but the nuts and bolts of his sharp brain now seemed to be malfunctioning.

Sarah wished he would say something. Did he really believe that she was making up the whole thing? How suspicious of other people had he become over the years? The young man she had fallen in love with had been fiercely independent—but to this extent? How valuable was his wealth if he now found himself unable to trust anyone around him?

'I…I lived in Devon with them after Oliver was born,' she continued into the deafening silence. 'It wasn't ideal, but I really needed the support. Then about a year ago I decided to move to London. Oliver was older—nearly at school age. I thought I could put him into a nursery parttime. There were no real jobs to be had in our village in Devon, and I didn't want to put Mum and Dad in a position of being permanent babysitters. Dad retired a couple of years ago, and they had always planned to travel. I thought that I would be able to get something here—maybe start thinking about getting back into education…'

'Getting back into education? Of course. It's never too late.' He preferred to dwell on this practical aspect to their conversation, but there was a growing dread inside him. There had been more than one occasion when he had not taken precautions. Somehow it had been a different world out there—a world that hadn't revolved around the usual rules and regulations.

'But it was all harder than I thought it was going to

be.' Sarah miserably babbled on to cover her unease. He thought she had lied to try and get money out of him. There was not even a scrap of affection left for her if he could think that. 'I found a house to rent. It's just a block away from a friend I used to go to school with. Emily. She babysits Oliver when I do jobs like these…'

'You mean you've done nothing but mop floors and clean toilets since you moved here?'

'I've earned a living!' Sarah flared back angrily. 'Office jobs are in demand, and it's tough when you haven't got qualifications or any sort of work experience. I've also done some waitressing and bar work, and in a month's time I'm due to start work as a teaching assistant at the local school. Aren't you going to ask me any questions about your son? I have a picture… In my bag downstairs…'

Raoul was slowly beginning to think the unimaginable, but he was determined to demonstrate that he was no push-over—even for her. Even for a woman who still had the ability to creep into his head when he was least expecting it.

'I grant that you may well have had a child,' he said heavily. 'It's been five years. Anything could have happened during that time. But if you insist on sticking to this story, then I have to tell you that I will want definite proof that the child is mine.'

Every time the word *child* crossed his lips, the fact of it being his seemed to take on a more definite shape. After his uncertain and unhappy past, he had always been grimly assured of one thing: no children. He had seen first-hand the lives that could be wrecked by careless parenting. He had been the victim of a woman who had had a child only to discover that it was a hindrance she could have well done without. Fatherhood was never going to be for him. Now, the possibility of it being dropped on him from a very great height was like being hit by a freight train at full speed.

'I think you'll agree that that's fair enough, given the circumstances,' he continued as he looked at her closed, shocked face.

'You just need to take one look at him... I can tell you his birth date...and you can do the maths...'

'Nothing less than a full DNA test will do.'

Sarah swallowed hard. She tried to see things from his point of view. An accidental meeting with a woman he'd thought left behind for good, and, hey presto, he discovered that he was a father! He would be reeling from shock. Of course he would want to ensure that the child was his before he committed himself to anything! He was now the leading man in his very own worst nightmare scenario. He would want proof!

But the hurt, pain and anger raged through her even as she endeavoured to be reasonable.

He might not want her around. In fact he might, right now, be sincerely hoping that he would wake up and discover that their encounter had been a bad dream. But didn't he know her at all? Didn't he *know* that she was not the type of girl who would ever *lie* to try and wrangle money out of him?

Unhappily, she was forced to concede that time had changed them both.

Whilst she had been left with her dreams in tatters around her, a single mother scraping to make ends meet and trying to work out how she could progress her career in the years to come, he had forgotten her and moved on. He had realised his burning ambitions and was now in a place from which he could look down at her like a Greek god, contemplating a mere mortal.

She shuddered to think what would have happened had she managed to locate him all those years ago.

'Of course,' she agreed, standing up.

She could feel a headache coming on. In the morning, Oliver would be at playgroup. She would try and catch up on some sleep while the house was empty. It hadn't escaped her notice that Raoul still hadn't shown any appetite for finding out what his son was like.

'I should go.'

In the corner of her eye, the cleaning trolley was a forlorn reminder of how her life had abruptly changed in the space of a few hours and suddenly become much more complicated. She doggedly reminded herself that whatever the situation *between them* it was good that he knew about Oliver. She sneaked a glance at him from under her lashes and found him staring down at her with an unreadable expression.

'I'm very sorry about this, Raoul.' She dithered, awkward and self-conscious in her uniform. 'I know the last thing you probably want is to have bumped into me and been told that you've fathered a child. Believe me, I don't expect you to do anything. You can walk away from the situation. It's only going to clutter up your life.'

Raoul gave a bark of derisive laughter.

'What planet are you living on, Sarah? If...if I am indeed a father, then do you really think I'm going to walk out on my responsibility? I will support you in every way that I can. What possible choice would I have?'

Tacked on at the end, that flat assertion said it all. He would rise to the occasion and do his duty. Having wanted nothing in life but to be free, he would now find himself chained to a situation from which he would never allow himself to retreat. She wondered if he had any idea how that made her feel, and felt painful tears push their way up her throat.

She found a clean white handkerchief pressed into her hand, and she stared down at the floor, blinking rapidly in an attempt to control her emotions. 'You never owned a hankie when I knew you,' she said in a wobbly voice, reaching for anything that might be a distraction from what she was feeling.

Raoul gave her a reluctant smile. 'I have no idea why I own one now. I never use it.'

'What about when you have a cold and need to blow your nose?'

'I don't get colds. I'm as healthy as a horse.'

It was only a few meaningless exchanged words, but Sarah felt a lot better as she stuck the handkerchief in the pocket of her overall, promising to return it when it had been washed.

'I'll need to be able to contact you,' he told her. 'What's your mobile number? I'll write mine down for you, and you can contact me at any time.'

As they exchanged numbers, she couldn't help but think back to when he had walked out on her with no forwarding address and no number at which he could be contacted. He had wanted to be rid of her completely—a clean cut, with no loose threads that could cause him any headaches later down the road.

'I'll be in touch within the week,' he told her, pocketing his mobile, and then he watched as she nodded silently and walked out of the room. He saw her yank off the overall and dump it in the trolley, along with the headscarf. She left it all just where it was in a small act of rebellion that brought a smile to his lips.

Alone in the office, and alone with his thoughts, Raoul contemplated the bomb that had detonated in his life.

He had a son.

Despite what he had said about wanting evidence, he knew in his gut that the child was his. Sarah had never cared about money, and she had always been the least manipulative woman he had ever known. He believed her when she said that she had tried to contact him, and he was shaken by the thought of her doing her utmost to bring up a child on her own when she had been just a child herself.

The fact was that he had messed up and he would have to pay the price. And it was going to be a very steep price.

CHAPTER TWO

SARAH was at the kitchen sink, finishing the last of the washing up, when the doorbell went.

The house she rented was not in a particularly terrific part of East London, but it was affordable, public transport was reasonably convenient, and the neighbours were nice. You couldn't have everything.

Before the doorbell could buzz again and risk waking Oliver, who had only just been settled after a marathon run of demands for more and more books to be read to him until finally he drifted off to sleep, Sarah wiped her hands on a dishcloth and half ran to the front door.

At not yet seven-thirty she was in some faded tracksuit bottoms and a baggy tee shirt. It was her usual garb on a weekend because she couldn't afford to go out. Twice a month she would try and have some friends over, cook them something, but continually counting pennies took a lot of the fun out of entertaining.

She had spent the past two days caught up in trying to find herself some replacement shift work. The cleaning company that had hired her had been appalled to find that she had walked out on a job without a backward glance, and she had been sacked on the spot.

Her heart hadn't been in the search, however. She'd been too busy thinking about Raoul and tirelessly replaying their unexpected encounter in her head. She'd spent hours trying to analyse what he had said and telling herself that it had all happened for the best. She'd looked at Oliver and all she'd seen was Raoul's dark hair and bitter chocolate eyes, and the smooth, healthy olive skin that would go a shade darker as he got older. He was a clone of his father.

If Raoul saw him there would be no doubt, but she still hadn't heard from him, and her disappointment had deepened with every passing hour.

On top of that, she couldn't make her mind up what she should tell her parents. Should they know that Raoul was Oliver's father and was back on the scene? Or would they worry? She had confessed that she had had her heart broken, and she wasn't convinced that they had ever really believed it to have been fully pieced together again. How would they react if they knew that the guy who'd broken her heart was back in her life? She was an only child, and they were super-protective. She imagined them racing up to London wielding rolling pins and threatening retribution.

She pulled open the door, her mind wandering feverishly over old ground, and stepped back in confusion at the sight of Raoul standing in front of her.

'May I come in, Sarah?'

'I…I wasn't expecting you. I thought you said that you were going to phone…'

She was without make-up, and no longer in a uniform designed to keep all hint of femininity at bay, and Raoul's dark eyes narrowed as he took in the creamy satin smoothness of her skin, the brightness of her green eyes in her heart-shaped face and the curves of her familiar body underneath her tee shirt and track pants.

He recognised the tee shirt, although it was heavily

faded now, its rock group logo almost obliterated. Just looking at it took him back in time to lying on the bed in the small room in Africa, with the mosquito net tethered as best they could manage under the mattress, watching and burning for her as she slowly stripped the tee shirt over her head to reveal her full, round breasts.

Raoul had planned on phoning. He had spent the past two days thinking, and had realised that the best way forward would be to view the situation in the same way he would view any problem that needed a solution—with a clear head. First establish firm proof that the child was his, because his gut instinct might well be wrong, and then have an adult conversation with her regarding the way forward.

Unfortunately he hadn't been able to play the waiting game. He hadn't been able to concentrate at work. He had tried to vent his frustration at the gym, but even two hours of gruelling exercise had done nothing to diminish his urgent need to *do something*.

Sarah read everything into his silence and ushered him into the house.

'I didn't know if I should be expecting a call from… somebody…about those tests you wanted…'

'On hold for the moment.'

'Really?' Her eyes shone and she smiled. 'So you *do* believe me.'

'For the moment I'm prepared to give you the benefit of the doubt.'

'You won't regret it, Raoul. Oliver's the image of you. I'm sorry he's asleep. I *would* wake him…'

Raoul had no experience of children. They weren't part of his everyday existence, and in the absence of any family he had never been obliged to cut his teeth on nephews or nieces. He was utterly bewildered at the notion of being in the presence of a son he had never laid eyes on. What did a four-year-old boy *do*, exactly? Were they capable of making conversation at that age?

Suddenly nervous as hell, he cleared his throat and waved aside her offer. 'Maybe it's best if we talk about this first...'

'Then would you like something to drink? Tea? Coffee? I think I might have some wine in the fridge. I don't keep a great deal of alcohol in the house. I can't afford it, anyway.'

Raoul was looking around him, taking in the surroundings which were a stark reminder of how far he had travelled. Now he lived in a massive two-storeyed penthouse apartment in the best postcode in London, furnished to the very highest standard. Frankly, it was the best that money could buy—although he barely glanced at his surroundings and was seldom in to take advantage of the top-of-the-range designer kitchen and all the other jaw dropping features the high-tech apartment sported.

This tiny terraced house couldn't have been more different. The carpet, the indeterminate colour of sludge, had obviously never been replaced, and the walls, although painted in a cheerful green colour, showed signs of cracks. Standing in the hall with her, he was aware there was practically no room to move, and as he followed her into the kitchen there was no change. A pine table was shoved against the wall to accommodate random pieces of freestanding furniture—a half sized dresser, a chest of drawers, some shelves on which bottles with various cooking ingredients stood.

He had managed to climb up and away from these sorts of surroundings, but it still sent a chill through his body that but for a combination of brains, luck and sheer hard work beyond the call of duty he might very well have still been living in a place very much like this.

This was precisely why, he told himself, he had refused to be tied down. Only by being one hundred percent free to focus on his career had he been able to fulfil his ambitions. Women were certainly an enjoyable distraction, but he had never been tempted to jettison any of his plans for one of them.

The more wealth he accumulated, the more jaded he became. He could have the most beautiful women in the world, and in fact he had had a number of head-turning girlfriends on his arm over the years, but they had always been secondary to his career.

Dim memories of living in a dingy room with his mother while she drank herself into a stupor had been his driving force. This house was only a few steps up from dingy. He imagined the landlord to be someone of dubious integrity, happy to take money from desperate tenants, but less happy to make any improvements to the property.

The notion of *his son* had somehow managed to take root in his head, and Raoul was incensed at the deplorable living conditions.

'I know,' Sarah apologised, following the critical path of his eyes. 'It's not fantastic, but everything works. And it's so much better than some of the other places I looked at. I don't even know where *you* live...'

Raoul, who had been staring at a dramatic rip in the wallpaper above the dresser, met her eyes and held them.

He couldn't understand whether it was her familiarity that was making him feel so *aware of her*—inconveniently, frustratingly, *sexually* aware of her—or whether he had just managed to make himself forget the attraction she had always had for him.

'Chelsea,' he said grimly, sitting on one of the chairs

at the table, which felt fragile enough to break under his weight.

'And…and what's it like?' She could feel hot colour in her cheeks, because he just dominated the small space of the kitchen. His presence seemed to wrap itself around her, making her pulses race and her skin feel tight and uncomfortable.

Coffee made, she handed him a mug and sat on the other chair.

'It's an apartment.' He shrugged. 'I don't spend a great deal of time in it. It works for me. It's low maintenance.'

'What does that mean? Low maintenance?'

'Nothing surplus to requirements. I don't like clutter.'

'And…and is there a woman in that apartment?' She went bright red as she asked the question, but it was one that had only occurred to her after she had left him. Was there a woman in his life? He didn't give the impression of being a married man, but then would he ever?

'What's the relevance of that question?' He sipped some of the instant coffee and looked at her steadily over the rim of the mug.

'It's relevant to this situation,' she persisted stubbornly. 'Oliver's your son, and he's going to have to get used to the idea of having a father around. I'm the only parent figure he's ever known.'

'Which isn't exactly my fault.'

'I know it's not! I'm just making a point.' She glared at him. 'It's going to take time for him to get to know you, and I don't want him to have to deal with a woman on the scene as well. At least I'd rather not. I suppose if you're married…'

Having never had to answer to anyone but himself, Raoul refused to be railroaded into an explanation of his private life—although he could see the validity of her question.

'No. There's no little lady keeping the home fires burning. As for women… I'll naturally strive to ensure that a difficult situation isn't made even more difficult.'

'So there *is* someone.' She tried desperately to take it in her stride, because it really wasn't very surprising. He was sinfully gorgeous, and now wealthy beyond belief. He would be a magnet for any footloose and single woman—and probably for a good few who *weren't* footloose and single.

'I don't think we should get wrapped up in matters that don't really have much to do with this…situation. We just need to discuss what the next step should be.'

'Come upstairs and see him. I can't have this conversation with you when you don't even know the child you're talking about. This isn't a business deal that needs to be sorted out.' She stood up abruptly and Raoul, put on the spot, followed suit.

'He's sleeping. I wouldn't want you to wake him.' Raoul was more nervous than he could ever remember being—more nervous than when he had chased, and closed, his first major deal. More nervous than when he had been a kid and he had stared up at the forbidding grey walls of the foster home that would eventually become his residence.

'Okay. I won't. But you still have to see him, or else he's just going to be a *problem that needs solving* in your head.'

'Since when did you get so bossy?' Raoul muttered under his breath, and Sarah spun around to find him looming behind her.

Standing on the first stair, she could almost look him in the eye. 'Since I ended up being responsible for another human being,' she said. 'I know it's not your fault that you weren't aware of the situation…' *Although it was, because if he had only just given her a contact number she would have been able to get in touch with him.* 'But it was terrifying for me when I discovered that I was pregnant. I kept thinking how nice it would be if you had been around to support me, and then I remembered how you had dumped me because you had plans and they didn't include me, and that if you *had* been around my pregnancy would have been your worst nightmare.'

'My plans didn't include *anyone*, Sarah. I did you a favour.'

'Oh, don't be so arrogant! If you'd cared enough about me you would have kept in touch.' She was breathing heavily as all the remembered pain and bitterness and anger surged through her, but staring into the depths of his fabulous dark eyes was doing something else to her—making her whole body tingle as though someone had taken a powerful electrical charge to it.

Raoul clocked her reaction without even consciously registering it. He just knew that the atmosphere had become taut with an undercurrent that had nothing to do with what they had been talking about. It was a type of non-verbal communication that sent his body into crazy overdrive.

'I don't know why I'm bothering to tell you any of this.' She jerked her hand in clumsy dismissal, but he caught her wrist. The heat of physical contact made her draw in her breath sharply, although he wasn't hurting her—not at all. He was barely circling her wrist with his long fingers. Still…she was appalled to find that she wanted to sink against him.

That acknowledgment of weakness galvanised her into struggling to free herself and he released her abruptly, although when she could have turned around and stalked up the stairs she continued to stare at him wordlessly.

'I know it must have been a bad time for you…'

'Well, that's the understatement of the decade if ever there was one! I felt completely lost and alone.'

'You had your parents to help you.'

'That's not the same! Plus I'd left for my gap year thinking that I was at the start of living my own life. Do you know what it felt like to go back home? Yes, they helped me, and I couldn't have managed at all without them, but it still felt like a retrograde step. I never, ever considered having an abortion, and I was thrilled to bits when Oliver was born, but I was having to cope with seeing all my dreams fly through the window. No university, no degree, no teaching qualification. You must have been laughing your head off when you saw me cleaning floors in that bank.'

'Don't be ridiculous.'

'No? Then what *was* going through your head when you looked down at me? With a damp cloth in one hand and a cleaning bottle in the other, dressed in my overalls?'

'Okay. I was stunned. But then I started remembering how damned sexy you were, and thinking how damned sexy you still were—never mind the headscarf and the overalls…'

His words hovered in the air between them, a spark of conflagration just waiting to find tinder. To her horror, Sarah realised that she wanted him to repeat what he had just said so she could savour his words and roll them round and round in her head.

How could she have forgotten the way he had treated her? He might justify walking out on her as *doing her a favour*, but that was just another way of saying that he hadn't cared for her the way she had cared for him, and he hadn't been about to let a meaningless holiday romance spoil his big plans.

'I've come to realise that sex is very overrated,' Sarah said scornfully, and then flushed as a slow smile curved his beautiful mouth.

'Really?'

'I don't want to talk about this.' But she heard the tell-tale tremor in her voice and wanted to scream in frustration. 'It certainly has nothing to do with what's…what's happening now. If you follow me, I'll show you to Oliver's room.'

Raoul let the conversation drop. He was as astounded as she had been by his own genuine admission to her, and he was busily trying to work out how a woman he hadn't seen in years—a woman who, in the great scheme of things, had not really been in his life for very long—could still exercise such a powerful physical hold over him. It was as though the years between them had collapsed and disappeared.

But of course they hadn't, he reminded himself forcefully. Proof of that was currently asleep in a bedroom, just metres away from where they had been standing.

Upstairs, if anything, seemed more cramped than downstairs, with two small bedrooms huddled around a tiny bathroom which he glimpsed on his way to the box room on the landing.

She pushed open the door to the only room he had seen so far that bore the hallmark of recent decoration. A night-light revealed wallpaper with some sort of kiddy theme and basic furniture. A small bed, thin patterned curtains, a circular rug tucked half under the bed, a white chest of drawers, snap-together furniture, cheap but functional.

Raoul unfroze himself from where he was standing

like a sentinel by the doorway and took a couple of steps towards the bed.

Oliver had kicked off the duvet and was curled around a stuffed toy.

Raoul could make out black curly hair, soft chubby arms. Even in the dim light he could see that his colouring was a shade darker than his mother's—a pale olive tone that was all *his*.

In the grip of a powerful curiosity, he took a step closer to the bed and peered at the small sleeping figure. When it shifted, Raoul instantly took a step back.

'We should go—just in case we wake him,' Sarah whispered, tiptoeing out of the bedroom.

Raoul followed her. The palms of his hands felt clammy.

She had been right. He had a son. There had been no mistaking those small, familiar signs of a likeness that was purely inherited. He wondered how he could ever have sat in his office and concluded that he would deal with the problem with the cold detachment of a mathematician completing a tricky equation. He had a child. A living, breathing son.

The cramped condition of the house in which he was living now seemed grossly offensive. He would have to do something about that. He would have to do something about pretty much everything. Life as he knew it was about to change. One minute he had been riding the crest of a wave, stupidly imagining that he had the world in the palm of his hand, and the next minute the wave had crashed and the world he had thought netted was spinning out of control.

It was a ground-breaking notion for someone whose only driving goal throughout his life had been to remedy the lack of control he had had as a child by conquering the world. A tiny human being, barely three feet tall, had put paid to that.

'You're very quiet,' Sarah said nervously, as soon as they were out of earshot.

'I need a drink—and something stronger than a cup of coffee.'

The remnants of a bottle of wine were produced and poured into a glass. Sarah looked at him, trying to gauge his mood and trying to forget that moment of mad longing that had torn through her only a short while before on the staircase.

'You were right,' he said heavily, having drunk most of the glass in one go. 'I see the resemblance.'

'I knew you would. It'll be even more noticeable when you see him in the light. He's got your dark eyes as well. In fact, there's not much of me at all in him! That was the first thing Mum said when he was born... Would you like to see some of the drawings he's made? He goes to a playgroup two mornings a week...I get help with that...'

'Help? What kind of help?' Raoul dragged his attention away from the swirling wine in his glass and looked at her.

'From the government, of course,' Sarah said, surprised. How on earth could she afford childcare otherwise, when she worked as a cleaner? On the mornings when Oliver was at nursery, she helped out at the school at which she was due to start work, but that was unpaid.

Raoul controlled his temper with difficulty. 'From the government?' he repeated with deadly cool, and Sarah nodded uneasily. 'Do you know what my aim in life was? My *only* aim in life? To escape the clutches of government aid and own my future. Now you sit here and tell me that you're *reliant* on government aid to get you through life.'

'You make it sound like a crime, Raoul.'

'For *me*, it's obscene!'

The force of his personality hit her like a freight train travelling at full speed, but she squared her shoulders and glared at him defiantly. If she allowed him to take control just this once then she would be dancing to his tune as and when he wanted her to. Hadn't she done enough of that years ago? And look where it had got her!

'And I can understand that,' Sarah told him evenly. 'I really can. But your past has nothing to do with my present circumstances. I couldn't afford to put Oliver into a private nursery,' she informed him bluntly. 'You'd be shocked at how little I earn. Mum and Dad supplement me, but every day's a struggle. It's all very well for you to sit there and preach to me about pride and ambition, but pride and ambition aren't very high up in the pecking order when you barely have enough money to put food on the table. So if I can get help with the nursery, then I'll take it.' She wished that she had had some wine as well, because she was in dire need of fortification. 'You were never such a crashing snob before, Raoul,' she continued bitterly. 'I can see that you've changed in more ways than one.'

'Snob? I think you'll find that that's the last thing I am!' He was outraged that she could hurl that accusation at him in view of his past.

'You've moved away from your struggling days of when we first met! I'll bet you can't even remember what it was like, darning those shorts of yours when they got ripped because you couldn't afford to chuck them out!'

'*You* darned them.' He looked at her darkly. He could remember her doing it as if it had been yesterday, swatting mosquitoes and moths away while outside a dull rumble of thunder had heralded heavy rain. She had looked like a girl in a painting, with her hair tumbling around her face as she frowned in concentration.

Sarah bit back the temptation to tell him what an idiot she had been, doing stuff like that, worshipping the ground he walked on, eager to do whatever he wanted.

'And I *haven't* forgotten my past,' he said grimly. 'It's always there at the back of my mind, like a stuck record.'

Her heart softened, but she held her ground with grim determination.

'I may not have planned for this, but I want you to know that things are going to change now. This place is barely fit for habitation!' He caught the warning look in her eyes and offered her a crooked smile. 'Okay. Bit of an exaggeration. But you get where I'm going. Whether you think I've become a monstrous snob or not, I can afford to take you away from here—and that's got to be my number one priority.'

'Your number one priority is getting to know Oliver.'

'I would prefer to get to know him in surroundings that won't challenge me every time I walk through the front door.'

Sarah sighed. It would certainly make life easier not having to worry so much about money. 'Okay. I take back some of the things I said. You haven't completely changed. You still think that you can get your own way all the time.'

'I know. It more than compensates for *your* indecision. Now, you could put up a brief struggle to hold on to your independence, maybe give me a little lecture on things being just perfect here, with your quaint, outdated kitchen furniture and the walls in need of plasterwork, but we both know that you can see my point of view. I can afford to take you out of this, and I consider it my duty to do so.'

The word *duty* lodged in her head like a burr, and she looked down at her anxiously clasped fingers. There was nothing like honesty to really hurt.

'What do you suggest?' she asked. 'Do I have any input

here? Or are you going to just walk all over me because you have lots of money and I have none?'

'I'm going to walk all over you because I have lots of money and you have none.'

'Not funny,' Sarah muttered, remembering his talent for defusing a situation with his sense of humour. Given the conditions years ago, when they had been cooped up on the compound, tempers had occasionally run high and this talent of his had been invaluable. Was he using it now just to get his own way? And did that matter anyway? The prospect of no longer having a daily struggle on her hands was like being offered manna from heaven.

'I intend to take my responsibilities very seriously, Sarah. I think you should know that. It would be very time-consuming to travel out here every time I wanted to see Oliver. Somewhere closer to where I live would be a solution.'

Now that they were discussing things in a more businesslike manner Sarah could actually focus on what was being said—as opposed to fighting to maintain her equilibrium, which showed threatening signs of wanting to fall apart.

'I feel as though I'm suddenly on a rollercoaster ride,' she confessed.

'Spare a thought for me. Whatever rollercoaster ride you're on, mine is bigger, faster, and I'm a hell of a lot less prepared for it than you are.'

And yet he was rising to the occasion. It didn't matter that the only reason they were now even having this conversation was because she had become a responsibility he couldn't shirk. He had taken it all in his stride in his usual authoritative way. That there was no emotion involved was something she would have to deal with. It wasn't his problem, and she wasn't going to let that get in the way of the relationship he had to build with his son.

'So we move to another place… There are still all sorts of other things that need sorting out. I'll have to try and explain to Oliver that he has a…a father. He's only young, though. I should warn you that it might not be that easy.'

'He's four,' Raoul pointed out with impeccable logic. 'He hasn't had time to build up any kind of picture for or against me.'

'Yes, but—'

'Let's not anticipate problems, Sarah.'

Now that he had surmounted the sudden bout of intense nervousness that had gripped him in the bedroom, Raoul was confident he would be able to get Oliver onside. Having had a life of grinding poverty, replete with secondhand clothes and secondhand books and secondhand toys, and frankly secondhand affection, he was beginning to look forward to giving his son everything that he himself had lacked in his childhood.

'We take things one at a time. First the house. Secondly, I suggest you try and explain my role to Oliver. Has he… has he ever asked about his father?'

'In passing,' Sarah admitted. 'When he's been to a birthday party and seen the other kids with their dads. Once when I was reading him a story.'

Raoul's lips thinned but he didn't say anything. 'You will obviously have to tell your parents that you are moving, and why. Will you tell them I'm on the scene? What my position is?'

'Maybe we shouldn't go there just yet,' Sarah said vaguely.

'I won't hide in the shadows.'

'I'm not sure they're going to be overjoyed that you're on the scene, actually.' She flushed guiltily as she remem-

bered their distress when she had told them how she had
fallen hard for a guy who had then chucked her. The hormones rushing through her body had made her all the more
vulnerable and emotional, and she had spared nothing in
her mournful, self-pitying account.

Honestly, she didn't think that Raoul was going to be
flavour of the month if she produced him out of nowhere.
But she knew that she would have to sooner or later. Her
mum always phoned at least three times a week, and always had a chat with Oliver. Sarah wouldn't want her to
find out via her grandchild that the heartbreaker and callous reprobate was now around.

'I'm getting the picture,' Raoul said slowly.

Sarah thought it better to move on quickly from that
topic of conversation. 'I'm sure they'll be very happy.' She
crossed her fingers behind her back. 'They're very conventional. They'll be delighted that Oliver will now have
a father figure in his life.'

He stood up. 'I'll be in touch tomorrow. No—scrap
that. I'll come by tomorrow afternoon so that I can be introduced to my son.'

The formality of that statement brought a rush of colour
to Sarah's face, because it underlined his lack of enthusiasm for the place in which he now found himself.

'Should I buy him something special to wear?' she said
tartly. 'I wouldn't want his appearance to offend you.'

'That's not helpful.'

'Nor is your approach to Oliver!' Tears stung the back
of her eyes. 'How can you be so…so…*unemotional*? This
wasn't how I ever thought my life would turn out. I always
thought that I would fall in love and get married, and when
a baby came along it would be a cause for celebration and
joy. I never imagined that I would have a child with a man
who wasn't even pleased to be a father!'

Raoul flushed darkly. What did she expect of him? He was here, wasn't he? Prepared to take on a task which had been sprung on him. Not only that, but she would be the recipient of a new house to replace her dismal rented accommodation, and also in the enviable position of never having to worry about money in her life again. Were hysterical accusations in order? Absolutely not!

He was very tempted to give her a checklist of all the things she should be thankful for. He settled for saying, in a cool voice, 'I've found that life has a funny way of not playing fair in the great scheme of things.'

'Is that all you have to say?' Sarah cried in frustration. 'Honestly, Raoul, sometimes I could...*hit you*!'

Her eyes were blazing and her hair was a tumbling riot of gold—and he felt a charge race through his system like an uncontrolled dose of adrenaline.

'I'm flattered that I still get you so worked up,' he murmured with husky amusement.

He couldn't help himself as he reached out and tangled his fingers in that hair. The contact was electric. He felt her response slam into him like a physical force and he revelled in the dark sexual hunger snaking through his body. *That* was something no amount of hard-headed logic or cool, calm reason could control.

Her lips had parted and her eyes were unfocused and half closed. Kissing her would halt all those crazy accusations in mid-flow. And he was hungry for her—hungry to remind himself of what her lips felt like.

'Don't you dare, Raoul...'

He pulled her towards him and noted, with a blaze of satisfaction, the unspoken invitation in her darkened eyes.

That first heady taste of him was intoxicating. Sarah moaned and pressed her hands against his chest. He had always been able to make her forget everything with a single touch, and her mind duly went blank. She forgot everything as her body curved sensuously against his, every bit of her melting at the feel of his swollen masculinity pushing against her, straining against the zipper of his trousers. Her breasts ached and she moved them against him, almost fainting at the pleasurable sensation of the abrasive motion on her sensitised nipples.

Raoul was the first to pull away.

'I shouldn't have done that.'

It took a few seconds for the daze in Sarah's head to clear, and then she snapped back to the horrified realisation that after everything she had been through, and hot on the heels of her really, *really* wanting to hit him, she had just *caved in*—like an addict who couldn't control herself. He had kissed her and all the hurt, anger and disappointment had disappeared. She had become a mindless puppet and five years had vanished in the blink of an eye.

'Neither of us should have…'

'Maybe it was inevitable.'

'What do you mean? What are you talking about?'

'You know what I'm talking about. This *thing* between us…'

'There's nothing between us!' Sarah cried, stepping back and hugging herself in an automatic gesture of self-defence.

'Are you trying to convince me or yourself?'

'Okay, maybe we just…just gave in to something *for the sake of old times*.' She took a deep breath. 'And now we've got that out of the way we can move on and…and…'

'Pretend it never happened?'

'Exactly! Pretend it never happened!' She took a few more steps back, but she thought that even if she took a million steps back and fled the country the after-effects of that devastating kiss would still be with her. 'This isn't

about *us*. This is about Oliver and your part in his life, so...
so...'

Raoul looked at her with a brooding intensity that made
her tremble. She didn't have a clue what was going on in
his head. He had always been very good at shielding his
thoughts when it suited him. She worked herself up into
a self-righteous anger, remembering how terrific he had
been at keeping stuff from her—like their lack of future—
until she had fallen for him hook, line and sinker. Never
again would she let him have that level of control!

'So just come here tomorrow. You can meet Oliver, and
we can work out some kind of schedule, and...then we can
both just get on with our own lives...'

CHAPTER THREE

By the time the doorbell went the following afternoon Sarah hoped that she had risen above her physical weakness of the day before and reached a more balanced place. In other words sorted her priorities. Priority number one was Oliver, and she bracingly repeated to herself how wonderful it was that his father would now be there for him, willing to take on a parental role, whatever that might be. A full and frank discussion of that was high on her agenda. Priority number two, on a more personal level, was to make sure that she kept a clear head and didn't get lost in old feelings and memories.

She opened the door to a casually dressed Raoul.

'Oliver's in the sitting room, watching cartoons,' she said, getting down to business straight away.

Raoul looked at her carefully, and noted the way her eyes skittered away from his, the way she kept one hand on the doorknob, as though leaving her options open just in case she decided to shut the door in his face. In fact she had only half opened the door, and he peered behind her pointedly.

'Are you actually going to let me in, or do you want me to forge a path past you?'

'I just want to say that we'll really need to discuss… um…the practicalities of this whole situation…'

'As opposed to what?'

'I've been thinking, Raoul…'

'Dangerous,' Raoul said softly. She was in a pair of jeans and a tight tee shirt that reminded him a little too forcibly of the mysterious physical hold she still seemed to have over him. He had spent the night vainly trying to clear his head of images of her.

'I've been thinking that we should have as little to do with one another as possible. I don't want anything to happen between us. Been there, done that and have the tee shirt. The important thing is that you get to know Oliver, and that should be the extent of our relationship with one another.'

'And have you told him who I am?'

Sarah was startled and a little taken aback at the speed with which he had concluded a conversation she had spent hours rehearsing in her head. Had she hoped that he would at least try and knock down some of her defences? Had she erected her *Keep Off* sign in the expectation that he might just try and steamroller through it? Had she secretly *wanted* him to steamroller through it?

'Not yet,' she said crisply. 'I thought it best that you two get to know one another first.'

'Okay. Well, there's some stuff I'd like to bring in.'

'Stuff? What kind of stuff?'

He nodded to his car, which was parked a few spaces along 'Why don't you go inside? I'll be a few minutes.'

'You haven't bought him presents, have you?' she asked suspiciously, but when she tried to step outside to get a closer look, he gently but firmly prevented her.

'Now, how did I know that you would disapprove?'

'It's not appropriate to show up with an armful of gifts the very first time you meet him!'

'I'm making up for lost time.'

Sarah gave up. You couldn't buy affection, she conceded, but perhaps a small token might help break the ice. Oliver had had no male input in his short life so far aside from her own father, whom he adored. She had been too busy just trying to make ends meet to dip her toes in the dating pool, and anyway she had not been interested in trying to replace Raoul. To her way of thinking she had developed a very healthy cynicism of the opposite sex. So Oliver's sole experience of the adult world, to a large extent, had been *her*.

He was in the process of trying to construct a tower of bricks, with one eye on the manic adventures of his favourite cartoon character, when Raoul appeared in the doorway. In one arm there was a huge box, and in the other an enormous sack.

There was more in the boot of the car, but Raoul just hadn't had the arms to bring it all in. Now he was glad that he hadn't. Oliver appeared to be utterly bewildered, and Sarah… Her mouth had fallen open in what could only be described as an expression of horror. Couldn't she say something?

Feeling like a complete fool for the first time in as long as he could recall, Raoul remained standing in the doorway with what he hoped was a warm smile pasted to his face.

'Oliver! This is…this is my friend, Raoul! Why don't you say hi to him?'

Oliver scuttled over to Sarah and clambered onto her lap, leaving Raoul trying to forge a connection by introducing a series of massively expensive presents to his son.

An oversized remote controlled car was removed from the box. The sack was opened to reveal a collection of games, books and stuffed toys which, Raoul assured a progressively more alarmed Sarah, had come highly recommended by the salesperson at the toy shop. He stooped to Oliver's level and asked him if he would care to try out the car. Oliver, by way of response, shook his head vigorously, to indicate very firmly that the last thing he wanted was to go anywhere near the aggressive silver machine that took up a fair amount of their sitting room space.

The games, books and stuffed toys garnered the same negative response, and silence greeted Raoul's polite but increasingly frustrated questions about playschool, sport and favourite television programmes.

At the end of an agonising forty-minute question and no answer session, Oliver finally asked Sarah if he could carry on with his blocks. In various piles lay the items that Raoul had bought, untouched.

'Well, *that* was a roaring success,' was the first thing Raoul muttered venomously under his breath, once he and Sarah were in the kitchen, leaving Oliver in the sitting room.

'It's going to take time.'

Raoul glared at her. 'What have you told him about me?'

'Nothing. Just that you were an old friend.'

'Hence the friendly way with in I was greeted?'

His own son had rejected him. Over the years, in his inexorable upward march, Raoul had trained himself to overcome every single setback, because every setback could be seen as a learning curve. He needed to speak French to close a deal? He learnt it. He needed intimate knowledge of the gaming market to take over a failing computer company? He acquired sufficient knowledge to get him by, and employed two formidable gaming geeks to do the rest. He had built an empire on the firm belief that he was capable of doing anything. There were no obstacles he was incapable of surmounting.

Yet half an hour in the company of a four-year-old had

rendered him impotent. Oliver had been uninterested in every toy pulled out of the bag and indifferent to *him*. There was no past experience upon which Raoul could call to get him through his son's lack of enthusiasm.

'Most kids would have gone crazy over that toy car,' he imparted in an accusatory tone. 'At least that's what the salesperson told me. It's been their biggest seller for the past four years. That damned car can do anything except carry passengers on the M25. So tell me what the problem was?' He glared at her as she serenely fetched two glasses from the cupboard and poured them some wine. 'The boy barely glanced in my direction.'

'I don't think it was such a good idea to bring so many toys for him.'

'And how do you work that one out? I would have been over the moon if I had ever, as a kid, been given *one* new toy! So how could several new, expensive, top of the range toys fail to do the trick?'

With a jolt of sympathy that ran contrary to every defence mechanism she had in place, Sarah realised that he really didn't have a clue. He had drawn from his own childhood experiences and arrived at a solution for winning his son's affections—except he hadn't realised that there was more to gaining love and trust than an armful of gifts.

'Do you know,' Raoul continued, swallowing the contents of his glass in one gulp, 'that every toy I ever played with as a child had come from someone else and had to be shared? A remote controlled car like the one languishing in your sitting room would have caused a full-scale riot.'

'That's just awful,' Sarah murmured.

'Now you're about to practise some amateur psychology on me. Don't. You should have told me that he liked building things. I would have come armed with blocks.'

'You're missing the point. You need to engage him. Like I said, he's used to only having me around. He's going to view any other adult on the scene with suspicion. What happened on birthdays? Christmas?'

'What are you talking about?'

'With you? Didn't you get birthday presents? What about Father Christmas?'

Raoul looked at her with a crooked smile that went past every barrier and settled somewhere in the depths of her heart.

'I don't see what this has to do with anything, but if you really want to know Father Christmas was tricky. Frankly, I don't think I ever believed in the fat guy with the beard. My earliest memory is of my mother telling me when I was three years old that there was no such person. Thinking about it now, I suspect she didn't want to waste valuable money on feeding that particular myth when the money could have been so much better spent on a bottle of gin. Anyway, even at the foster home there wasn't much room to hold on to stories like that. Father Christmas barely rated a mention.' He laughed without rancour. 'So—you're going to give me a lesson on engagement. If Oliver has no time for anything I bought for him, then how do we proceed?'

'Are you asking for my help?'

'I'm asking for your opinion. If I remember correctly, you have never been short of those…'

'Why don't you go out there and build something with him?' she suggested. 'No. I'll get him to bring his bricks in here, and the two of you can build something on the kitchen table while I prepare supper.'

'Forget about cooking. I'll take you both out. Name the restaurant and I'll ensure the chef is only too happy to whip up something for Oliver.'

'No,' Sarah said firmly. 'This is what normal life is all

about with a child, Raoul. Spaghetti Bolognese, familiar
old toys, cartoons on television, reading books at night before sleep…' Except, she thought, suddenly flustered by
the picture she had been busy painting, that was the *ideal*
domestic situation—one in which two people were happily married and in love. It certainly wasn't *their* situation.
As she had told him—*and she had meant every word of
it*—they had no relationship outside the artificial one im-
posed by circumstance.

'Okay. I'll bring Oliver in and you can start chopping
some onions. They're in the salad drawer in the fridge.
Chop them really small.'

'You want me to *cook*?'

'Well, to help at any rate. And don't tell me that you've
forgotten how to cook. You used to cook on the compound.'

'Different place, different country.'

'So…you just eat out all the time?' Sarah asked, distracted.

'It's more time-efficient.'

'And what about with your girlfriends? Don't you want
to stay in sometimes? Do normal stuff?'

The questions were out before she had the wit to keep
her curiosity to herself, and now that she had voiced them,
she realised that it had been on her mind, poised just beneath the surface, ever since she had laid eyes on him
again. In fact, thinking about it, it was something she had
asked herself over and over again through the years. Had
he found someone else? Had another woman been able to
capture his interest sufficiently for him to make the commitment that he had denied her? He hadn't loved *her*, but
had he fallen in love with someone else? Someone prettier
or cleverer or more accomplished?

'Not that it's any of my business,' she added, and
laughed airily.

'It is now. Haven't you said that yourself? No women in Oliver's presence… Rest assured that the only woman in my life at the moment is *you*…'

'That's not what I was asking and you know it, Raoul!'

'No. You're just curious to know what I've been getting up to these past few years. There's nothing wrong with curiosity. Curiosity's healthy.'

'I don't *care* what you've been getting up to!' It was a lie. She cared. Who were these women he had dated? What had he felt for them? Anything? Had he preferred them to *her*? She was mortified just thinking about that particular question.

'I haven't been getting up to anything of interest,' Raoul replied drily. 'Yes, there have been women. But I've deterred them from doing anything that involved pots, pans, an apron, candlelight and home-cooked food.'

'Oh, Raoul, you're such a charmer.' But a tendril of relief curled inside her. She squashed it. 'Now, I'm going to fetch Oliver.'

'Hey, what about you? Don't I get the low-down on *your* life? No man at the moment, but any temptations? Do you cook your spaghetti Bolognese for anyone else aside from Oliver?'

His voice was light and mildly amused, and he wondered why he felt so tense when it came to thinking of her with another man. He, after all, had never been and would never be a candidate when it came to marriage and rings on fingers. He was now a father, and that was shocking enough, but that was the only derailment to his carefully constructed life on the cards as far as he was concerned.

'Maybe…'

'Maybe? What does *that* mean?' The amusement sounded forced. 'Am I in competition with someone you've got hidden in a cupboard somewhere?'

'No,' Sarah admitted grudgingly. 'I've been too busy being a single mum to think of complicating my life with a guy.' She sensed rather than saw the shadow of satisfaction cross his face, and continued tartly, 'But, as you've pointed out, life is going to get much easier for me now. It's going to make a huge difference with you around, playing a role in Oliver's life. I won't be doing it on my own. Also, it'll be nice not having to think about money, or rather the lack of it, all the time—and it'll be fantastic having a bit of time to myself…time to do what I want to do.'

'Which *doesn't* mean that you've now got carte blanche to do whatever you like.' Raoul didn't care for the direction in which this conversation was now travelling.

'You make me sound like the sort of girl who can't wait to pick someone up!'

She was wondering what right he had to lay down any kind of laws when it came to her private life. Raoul Sinclair didn't want his life encumbered with attachments. True, he had discovered that some encumbrances were beyond his control, but just as he had never contemplated committing to her, so he had never contemplated committing to anyone. It was small comfort. *He* might think that it was perfectly acceptable to lead a life in which he and his son were the only considerations, but it was totally unfair to assume that *she* felt the same way. *He* might want to pick up women and discard them when they were no longer of any use, but *she* needed more than that. For Raoul, a single life was freedom. For her, a single life would be a prison cell.

'I'm not going to suddenly start scouring the nightclubs for eligible men,' she expanded, with a bright, nervous laugh, 'but I *will* be able to get out a bit more—which will be nice.'

'Get out a bit more?'

'Yes—when you have Oliver.'

'I don't think we should start projecting at this point,' Raoul said deflatingly. 'Oliver hasn't even spoken to me as yet. It's a bit premature to start planning a hectic social life in anticipation of us becoming best friends. Let's just take one day at a time, shall we?'

'Of course. I wasn't planning on going clubbing next week!'

Clubbing? What did she mean by that? Other men? Sleeping around? While he kept Oliver every other weekend?

He pictured her dressed in next to nothing, flaunting herself on a dance floor somewhere. Granted, the women he went out with often dressed in next to nothing, but for some reason the thought of *Sarah* in a mini-skirt, high heels and a halterneck top set his teeth on edge.

'Good. Because it won't be happening.'

'Excuse me?'

'Think about it, Sarah. Oliver doesn't even know that I'm his father. Don't you think that he'll be just a little bit confused if *your friend*, who has mysteriously and suddenly appeared on the scene from nowhere, starts engineering outings without you? You're the constant in his life. As you keep telling me. For me to have any chance of being accepted we have to provide a united front. We have to get to a point where he trusts me enough to leave you behind now and again.'

'Exactly what are you trying to say, Raoul?'

'That you have to scrap any crazy notions of us having nothing to do with one another. You're living in cloud cuckoo land if you think that's going to work. The whole bedtime story, spaghetti Bolognese thing is going to have to involve both of us. Of course it'll be a damn sight easier when you get out of this place and move somewhere more

convenient. And less cramped. On the subject of which—
I have my people working on that.'

There were so many contentious things packed into that
single cool statement that Sarah looked at him, staggered.

'When you say *involve both of us*...'

Raoul flushed darkly and dealt her a fulminating look
from under his lashes.

'I don't know the first thing about being a parent,' he
told her roughly. 'You've witnessed my sterling performance out there.'

'I didn't know the first thing about being a parent either,' Sarah pointed out with irrefutable logic. 'It's just a
case of doing your best.'

The thought of doing things with Raoul and Oliver, a
cosy threesome, was enough to bring on the beginnings
of a panic attack in her. Already she was finding it difficult to separate the past from the present. She looked at
him, and who was she kidding when she told herself that
she was no longer attracted to him? Raoul was in a different place, and would be able to take her on board as just a
temporary necessity in his life, easily set aside once he had
what he wanted: some sort of ongoing relationship with
his son. But she was aghast at the prospect of having him
there in *her* life. How on earth was she ever going to get
to that controlled, composed place of detachment if she
was continually tripping over him in the kitchen as he attempted to bond with his son over fish fingers?

Perhaps he had exaggerated, she thought, soothing her
own restless, panicked mind. He was still smarting from
Oliver's less than exuberant reception of him. Right at this
very moment this was the only plan he could see ahead of
him, and Raoul was big on plans. He would not be taking
into account the simple fact that when children were involved plans could never really be made. In a day or two

he would probably revise his ideas, because she very much doubted that he wanted to spend quality time with *her* in the picture.

'And the whole house issue...' she continued faintly. 'You have your *people* working on it?'

'Here's one of the things I've discovered about having money: throw enough of it at a problem and the problem goes away. Right now they're in the process of drawing up lists of suitable properties. I will be giving them until the end of next week. So,' he drawled when she failed to respond, 'are we on the same wavelength here, Sarah?'

'I can't just move into a house *you* happen to choose. I know you probably don't care about your surroundings, but *I* care about mine...'

'Don't you trust me to find somewhere you'd like?'

He'd used to be amused at her dreamy, whimsical ideas. From where he had stood there had been little use for dreams unless you had the wherewithal to turn them into reality, and even then he had never made the mistake of confusing dreams with the attainment of real, concrete goals. What was the point in wishing you could own a small island in the middle of the Pacific if the chances of ever having one were zero? But her dreams of cottages and clambering roses and open fires had made him smile.

'True, the thatched cottage with the roses and the apple trees might be a little troublesome to find in London...'

Sarah blushed, unsettled by the fact that he had remembered her corny youthful notion of the perfect house Which she recalled describing in tedious detail.

'But I've got them working on the Aga in the kitchen, the garden overlooking water, and the fireplaces...'

'I can't believe you remember that conversation!'

She gave a brittle laugh, and went an even brighter

shade of red when he replied softly, 'Oh, there's a lot I re-member, Sarah. You'd be surprised.'

He didn't miss the flare of curiosity in her eyes. She might have made bold statements about not wanting any-thing to do with him, about shoving that kiss they had shared into a box at the back of a cupboard in her head, where she wouldn't have to confront it, but every time they were in each other's company he could feel that undercur-rent of electricity—a low, sizzling hum that vibrated just below the radar.

'Well, I don't actually remember all that much,' Sarah responded carelessly.

'Now, I wonder why I'm not believing you…'

'I have no idea, and I don't care. Now, if you wouldn't mind getting to work on those onions, I'll go and fetch Oliver.'

She disappeared before he could continue the conver-sation. When he looked at her like that she would swear that he could see right down into the very depths of her. It was an uncomfortable, frightening sensation that left her feeling vulnerable and exposed. Once she had gladly opened up to him—had told him everything there was to know about herself. She had taken him at face value and turned a blind eye to the fact that while she had been fall-ing deeper and deeper in love with him, he had pointedly refused to discuss anything that involved a future between them. He had taken everything she had so generously given and then politely jettisoned her when his time on the com-pound was up.

Raoul was a taker, with little interest in giving back. When he looked at her with those lazy, brooding eyes she could sense his interest. Some of his remarks carried just that little hint of flirtation, of deliberately treading very close to the edge. He had possessed her once, much to her shame. Did he think that he could possess her again?

She returned with Oliver to find him at the kitchen counter, dutifully chopping the onions as instructed.

Oliver had brought in a handful of his blocks, and Sarah sat him on a chair and then called Raoul over. She made sure to keep her voice light and friendly, even though every nerve in her body tingled as he strolled towards them, a teatowel draped over one shoulder.

'Blocks…my favourite.'

She had sat at the table, next to Oliver, and now Raoul leaned over her, his strong arms trapping her as he rested his hands on the table on either side of her. Sarah could feel his breath whisper against her neck when he spoke.

'Did you hear that, Oliver? Raoul loves building things! Wouldn't it be fun for you two to build something for me? What about a tower? You love building towers! Do you remember how high your last tower was? Before it fell?'

'Twelve blocks,' Oliver said seriously, not looking at Raoul. 'I can count to fifty.'

'That's quite an achievement!' Raoul leaned a little closer to Sarah, so that the clean, minty smell of her shampoo filled his nostrils.

She shifted, but had almost no room for manoeuvre. Her eyes drifted compulsively to his forearm, to the fine sprinkling of dark hairs that curled around the dull matt silver of his mega-expensive watch.

'Why don't you sit down, Raoul?' she suggested stiltedly. 'You can help Oliver with his tower.'

'I don't need any help, Mum.'

'No, he really doesn't. I sense that he's more than capable of building the Empire State Building all on his own.'

Oliver glanced very quickly at Raoul, and then returned to the task in hand.

Sarah heard Raoul's almost imperceptible indrawn breath as he abruptly stood back, and when she turned to look at him he had removed himself to the kitchen sink, his expression one of frustrated defeat.

'Give it time,' she said in a low voice, moving to stand in front of him.

'How much time? I'm not a patient man.'

'Well, I guess you'll have to learn how to be. Good job with the onions, by the way.'

But she could feel his simmering impatience with the situation for the rest of the evening. Oliver was not so much hostile as wary. He answered Raoul's questions without meeting his eye and, dinner over, finally agreed to go outside with him to test drive the car which had been abandoned in the sitting room.

Through the kitchen window, Sarah watched their awkward interaction with a sinking heart.

She had planned on sitting Oliver down and explaining that Raoul was his father once a bond of trust between them had been accepted. To overload him with too much information would be bewildering for him. But how long was that going to take? she wondered. Raoul was obviously trying very hard.

She watched as Oliver sent the oversized car bouncing crazily into the unkempt bushes at the back of the tiny garden, losing interest fast and walking away as Raoul stooped down to deliver a mini-lecture on mechanics.

The consequences of him missing out, through no fault of his own, on those precious first four years hit her forcibly. Another man, with experience of growing up in a real family, might have had something to fall back on in a situation like this. Raoul had no such experience, and was struggling to find a way through his own shortcomings.

She abandoned her plans to have him read something to

Oliver before bed, which was their usual routine. Instead, she told him to wait for her in the kitchen while she settled Oliver.

'You can help yourself to…um…whatever you can find in the fridge. I know dinner was probably not what you're used to…'

'Because I'm such a snob?'

Sarah sighed heavily, 'I'm just conscious that we're… we're miles apart. When we were working out in Africa there wasn't this great big chasm separating us…'

'You need to move on from the past.'

'*You* haven't moved on from yours!'

'I'm not following you?'

'You thought you could buy Oliver with lots of presents because that's what your past has conditioned you to think! And then you got impatient when you discovered that it doesn't work that way.'

'And *you* can't move on from the fact that—okay… yes—I dumped you!' Raoul thundered. 'You want to find something to argue about—*anything at all*—because you've wrapped yourself up in a little world comprised of just you and Oliver and you can't deal with the fact that I'm around now! Dinner was disappointing because it was stressful! I didn't know how to deal with him.'

Hell, Oliver had played with his food, spread most of it on the table, and had received only the most indulgent scolding from Sarah! His childhood memories of mealtimes were of largely silent affairs, with rowdy behaviour at the table meriting instant punishment.

'I *don't* know how to deal with him.'

Dumbfounded by that raw admission, Sarah was overcome with regret for her outburst. He was so clever, so *all-knowing*, that she hadn't really stopped to consider that now he really was at a loss.

'I'm…I'm sorry, Raoul. I shouldn't have said that stuff about your past…' she mumbled.

'Look, we've found ourselves in this situation, and constantly sniping isn't going to get either of us very far.'

Mind made up, Sarah nodded in agreement. 'I'll take him up for a bath… Yes, you're right…it's difficult for both of us…' She managed a smile. 'I guess we both need to do some adjusting…'

She returned forty-five minutes later and looked as fresh as a daisy. He felt as though he had done ten rounds in a boxing ring.

'I think he's really beginning to warm to you!' she said cheerfully.

Raoul raised his eyebrows in an expression of rampant scepticism. 'Explain how you've managed to arrive at that conclusion?' He raked his fingers through his hair and shook his head with a short, dry laugh. 'There's no need to put on the Little Miss Sunshine act for me, Sarah. I may not know much when it comes to kids, but I'd have to have the IQ of a goldfish not to see that my own son has no time for me. You were right. All those toys were a complete waste of time and money.'

'You're just not accustomed to children. You don't know how they think. Sometimes it's hard to imagine you being a kid at all! Oliver enjoys pushing the boundaries. Most children do, Raoul. He'll fiddle with his food until I have to be firm, and he'll always go for *just another five minutes* or *one more story* or *two scoops of ice cream, please.*'

'Whatever happened to discipline?' Raoul scowled at her laid-back attitude.

'Oh, there's a lot of that. It's just knowing when to decide that it's really needed.'

She looked at Raoul thoughtfully. The man who could move mountains had discovered his Achilles' heel, and she was sure that he would never ask for her help. He was stubbornly, maddeningly proud. To ask for help would be to admit a weakness, and she knew that was something he would find it very hard to do.

But helping him was the only solution—and, more than that, helping him would give her a psychological boost, even out the playing field.

'Okay, well, he's now thrilled with the car. Tonight I'll pack away all the rest of the stuff you brought for him. I can bring bits out now and again as treats.' She folded her arms and braced herself to take control with a guy who was so used to having the reins that he probably had no idea relinquishing them was a possibility.

Raoul sat back and clasped his hands behind his head. He had thought for one crazy moment, when he had laid eyes on her again, that time hadn't changed her. He had been wrong. This was no longer the blindly adoring girl who had yielded to him with such abundant generosity. There was a steely glint in her eye now, and he realised that he had seen it before but maybe hadn't really recognised it for what it was. The molten charge between them was still there, whether she wanted to admit it or not, but along with that was something else...

Raoul felt a certain fascination, and a surge of raw, powerful curiosity.

'Am I about to get a ticking off?' he drawled, his eyes roving lazily over her from head to toe in a way that made it difficult for her not to feel frazzled.

'No,' she said sweetly. 'But I am going to tell you what you need to do, and you're going to listen to me.' She smiled a bit more when she saw his frown of incomprehension. 'You like to think you know everything, but you don't.'

'Oh? You're going to be my teacher, are you?'

'Whether you like it or not!'

Raoul shot her a slow, dazzling smile. 'Well, now,' he said softly, instantly turning the tables on her, 'it's been a while since anyone taught me anything. You might find that I like it a lot more than you expect…'

CHAPTER FOUR

SARAH looked at her reflection in the mirror and frowned. Her cheeks were flushed, and her eyes were glowing. She looked *excited*. Guilt shot through her, because this was just what she didn't want. She didn't *want* to find herself giddy with anticipation because Raoul was on his way over.

For the past four weeks she had kept her manner brisk and impersonal. She had pretended not to notice those occasional sidelong glances of his, when his fabulous dark eyes would rest speculatively on her face. She had taken extra care to downplay what she wore. Anyone would have been forgiven for thinking that the only components of her wardrobe were faded jeans, tee shirts, shapeless jumpers and trainers. Now that the weather was getting warmer, and spring was edging tentatively into summer, the jumpers had been set aside, but the jeans, the tee shirts and the trainers were still fully in evidence.

Sarah was determined to make sure that her relation ship with Raoul remained detached and uninvolved. She knew that she couldn't afford to forget what had happened in the past.

She had thrown herself into the task of helping him get to know his son, and she had to admit that it was no longer the uphill struggle it had initially been. Oliver was gradually opening up and losing some of his restraint, and Raoul, in turn, was slowly learning how to relate to a child. Like a teacher struggling with troublesome pupils and finally seeing the light at the end of the tunnel, she could now cautiously tell herself that her role of mediator had been successful.

And *that* accounted for the glow in her eyes and her flushed cheeks.

Oliver was actually looking forward to seeing Raoul. In fact, he was dressed and ready to go.

She clattered down the stairs as the doorbell buzzed and smiled at the sight of Oliver in the sitting room, kneeling on the chair by the bay window, eyes peeled for Raoul's arrival. He had been treated to several rides in Raoul's sports car, and had gravely told her that he would buy *her* one just as soon as he had saved enough money. He had two pounds, and considered himself well on the way.

'Am I dressed correctly for a day out at a theme park, Miss?' Raoul laughed at her exasperated expression.

'You know I hate it when you call me that.'

'Of course you don't! It makes you feel special. And besides…I enjoy watching the way you blush when I say it.'

On cue, Sarah felt her cheeks pinken.

'You shouldn't say stuff like that.'

'Why not?'

'Because…because…it's not appropriate…'

And because it threatened her. She had been walking on thin ice for the past four weeks as he dug deeper and deeper under her defences with his easy charm, his wit, his willingness to tackle head-on a situation that must have rocked his world. She desperately wanted her one-dimensional memory of him back, because it was so much easier to deal with him as the man who had ruined her life.

'Now you really *are* beginning to sound like a school-teacher,' Raoul said softly. 'Should I expect to be punished any time soon?'

'Stop it!'

He held up his hands in a gesture of surrender and laughed, throwing his head back, keeping his velvety black eyes on her face.

Sarah glared at him. This couldn't continue. Raoul didn't know what he was doing to her, but she was mentally and emotionally exhausted. She would talk to Raoul today. Begin the process of sorting out visiting arrangements. She couldn't foresee any problem with Raoul now taking Oliver out for the day without her having to be there as chaperone.

In other words it was time to acknowledge that her brief stint at usefulness was over and Raoul had been right. It had been essential for them to present a united front to Oliver so that his confidence in Raoul could be built. Would it come as a shock for him to accept Raoul as his father? Certainly it would be a lot easier now than it would have been a month ago, when Raoul had been an intimidating stranger bearing expensive gifts who had landed in their midst from nowhere.

The gifts had all been stowed away and Raoul had not repeated his mistake—although he warned her he would definitely be christening the new house he had bought for them with something spectacular in the back garden.

When Sarah considered the speed with which her life had changed in a matter of a month, her head spun.

Raoul back on the scene. Oliver slowly beginning to bond with his father. A house which she and Oliver had seen only two weeks previously immediately purchased by Raoul on the spot, with enough money thrown at the deal to ensure that it closed with record speed.

'You like it. Why hang around?'

He had shrugged with such casual dismissal of the cost that Sarah had stared at him, open-mouthed. That had been the point when she had thought that the attainment of wealth was the most important thing to Raoul, and instinctively she had shied away from what that implied about his character. Very quickly, however, she had realised that the only thing wealth represented to him was freedom. Money gave him the ability to do as he liked without reference to anyone else. It was the opposite of the way he had grown up.

In fact, and only by accident, she had recently discovered that he gave large sums of his vast fortune to charity—including the very same charity which had originally brought them together all those years ago. She had been in his penthouse with Oliver, waiting for him while he finished a conference call in his office. Oliver had been wandering around, gaping at the high-tech television and then experimenting with the chrome and black leather stools at the granite-topped kitchen counter, swivelling round and round with childish enjoyment, and there on the table by the massive window that overlooked a private park had been a letter of gratitude, thanking Raoul for his contributions over the years.

Sarah had not mentioned a word of what she had inadvertently seen, but she had filed it away in her head, where it jostled for space with all the other bits and pieces she was unconsciously gathering about him. In every way he was the most complex man she would ever meet. He was driven, ambitious, and ferociously single-minded. But the way in which he had applied himself to the task of getting to know his son showed compassion, patience, and an ability to roll with the punches.

There was no question that he used women, and yet

there was nothing manipulative about him. He had big *Keep Out* signs all around him, and yet she couldn't help feeling that she had seen something of the boy who had become the man—even though when he talked about his past it was only through necessity, and in a voice that was utterly devoid of emotion.

Five years on and Raoul Sinclair still fascinated her. Although that was something that Sarah barely recognised. She just knew that she was becoming dangerously addicted to his visits, which were frequent, even though she kept telling him that she didn't want to disrupt his work schedule.

She felt as though she was seeing him through the eyes of an adult as opposed to the romantic young girl she had once been, and she wondered what life would be like when their relationship became normalised. When he popped over on a Wednesday evening and took Oliver out, leaving her behind, or when he had Oliver for a weekend and she had her much espoused free time to do as she liked.

She immediately told herself that it would be brilliant. She would be able to build some kind of life for herself! She no longer had the excuse of lack of money, lack of time and lack of opportunity.

Raoul had insisted on opening a bank account for her, and when she had tried to assert her independence he had turned her determination on its head by quietly telling her that it was the very least he could do, bearing in mind that she had been a single mother for all those years when he had been rapidly building his fortune. Had he been more aggressive she would have taken refuge in an argument. But, brilliant judge of character that he was, he had known the most efficient way to get exactly what he wanted.

Sarah sighed and tried not to think. Aside from the disturbing melee of her own feelings, there was the very simple reality that they would be moving soon, and Oliver would need to be told who Raoul really was.

Today they were going to a theme park. Oliver had never been to a theme park. Nor had Raoul. She had only learned this after a great deal of questioning, during which she had been determined to prise from him what he had longed for as a kid but never had. She had asked him in the crisp voice she made sure to use in order to reinforce that their relationship was entirely impersonal, and he had adopted the slightly sardonic, lazy drawl which he always used when referring to his past. But then he had said, in a voice that contained a certain amount of surprise—maybe because the memory had come from nowhere—that he had missed the big annual treat of the year when he had been nine years old and his age group were taken to a theme park. It had been a celebration of sorts, to mark the fiftieth anniversary of the place, but he had been laid up with flu and had spent the entire weekend cooped up in the sick quarters.

There and then Sarah had decided that a visit to the theme park was essential.

Lagging behind as Raoul and Oliver walked towards the car, Sarah mentally took in the picture they made. Raoul literally towered over his son, who had to walk at a smart pace to keep up with him. From behind, she noted the similarity of their hair colour and the trace of olive in Oliver's skin tone that would burnish and darken over time—just as Raoul's had. Oliver was proudly carrying his backpack, which was a new purchase, and wearing his jeans, also a new purchase.

Her eyes drifted across to Raoul and she felt suddenly dizzy, because he just continued to take her breath away. Without fear of being observed *watching him*, she feasted on the length of his muscular legs, the low-slung faded black jeans, the white shirt, sleeves slightly pushed up even though it was still quite cool. However good she was at being adult and detached when she was in his company, she still knew that her indifference was a long way from being secure.

Raoul popped the boot of his car and Sarah glanced in and said, surprised, 'What's all that?'

Raoul gazed down at her upturned face and shot her a crooked half-smile.

'What does it look like?'

'You've made a *picnic*?'

'*I* haven't made a picnic. My caterer has. I've been assured that there's an ample selection.'

The past few weeks had been a massive learning curve for Raoul. Having never seen himself in the role of father, he had found himself having to adapt in all sorts of ways that were alien to him. Defined through his staggering ability to work, he had had to sideline hours in front of his computer or at the office in favour of the soul-destroying task of trying to edge responses out of his son. Accustomed to having every word he spoke treated with respect, and every order he gave obeyed to the letter, he had had to dig deep and find levels of patience that were foreign to him— because small children frequently disobeyed orders and often lacked focus. Ferociously against ever asking anyone for help, he had found himself in the uncustomary position of having to take guidance from Sarah, so that his path to a relationship with Oliver was eased. He had had to learn how to jettison his very natural inclination to command. But it had all paid enormous dividends because Oliver was gradually warming to him.

And alongside that he'd been witness to a new side of Sarah, so wildly different from the impressionable young girl she had been years ago. There was a core of strength in her now that intrigued him.

'I'm impressed, Raoul,' Sarah murmured, staring down at the wicker basket and the requisite plaid rug, and the cooler which was full of ice-cold drinks.

She imagined that when he decided on a certain course of action he gave one hundred percent of his energy to it. His course of action, in this instance, was winning over the son he'd never known he had, and he had approached the task in hand with gusto. This elaborate picnic was evidence of that. All kids loved a picnic. *She* loved a picnic.

He slammed shut the boot on Sarah's dismayed realisation that in the process of charming Oliver Raoul had inadvertently been doing exactly the same with her.

'Of course I would have been more impressed if you'd prepared it all yourself...' Her voice sounded forced.

'Never satisfied...' But he was grinning in a way that made her skin warm. 'You're a tough taskmaster.'

'You don't need a caterer to prepare food for you. I know that you're perfectly capable of doing it yourself.'

'I'll bear that in mind for next time,' Raoul murmured.

'Next time? There won't be a next time,' she told him in a fast rush. 'Don't forget that all of this is...you know... part and parcel of your learning curve.'

'Theme park—tick. Picnic—tick. Homecooked food eaten at the kitchen table—tick. Fast food restaurant— tick. When did you get so regimented?'

'I'm not regimented. I'm practical. And isn't it time we left? Oliver's already in the car. Have I told you how excited he was about today? He could hardly get to sleep last night!'

'I found sleeping pretty difficult myself.'

Sarah's eyes widened, and she sucked in a shaky breath

as he braced himself against the car, circling her so that she had to half sit on the bonnet.

'What are you doing?' she squeaked.

'I'm tired of trying to kid myself that I don't want you, Sarah.'

'You *don't* want me. I don't want *you*. I know we've been getting along, but it's all because of Oliver—because… because… Don't look at me like that!' But her body was betraying her protest. 'This isn't part of the plan. You *like* plans. Have you forgotten?'

'Which just goes to show what a changed man I'm becoming.'

'You haven't changed, Raoul.' She flattened her hand against his chest to push him back, but just touching him weakened her defences. 'I told you—we've been there. We're not good for one another. We just need to be…to be friends…'

'Okay.' He straightened, and his voice was mild, but there was a glitter in his eyes that made her pulses race. 'If you're sure about that…'

He let his hand slide over her shoulder in a caressing, assured move that made her stomach flip and her breath catch in her throat. Then he backed off, and she was gulping in oxygen like a drowning person breaking the surface of the water.

Her heart was beating madly as she slipped into the passenger seat and turned to make sure that Oliver was strapped into his car seat. Over the years, her memories of Raoul had taken on a static form. Faced once again with the living, breathing, charismatic, dynamic and unbearably sexy Raoul, who could make her laugh and make her want to grind her teeth together in frustration in the next breath, had undermined all her defences.

Had he intuited this? Was that why he had made that

move? With the confidence of a predator knowing that it was just a matter of time?

The theme park was already packed by the time they got there. Oliver's excitement had been a slow burn, but his first sight of some of the rides, the chaos of the crowds, and the roar of the machines flying through the air with people dangling from them like rag dolls took his breath away.

'Does this live up to expectations?' Sarah asked Raoul halfway through, as he and Oliver descended from one of the child and parent rides. She was determined to keep her head and be as normal as possible. She *wouldn't* get in a flap.

It had warmed up, and his polo shirt exposed strong, muscled arms. She watched them flex and harden as he stooped to lift Oliver in one easy movement.

'Are you asking whether I've managed to discover my inner child yet? Nope,' he told her before she could say anything. 'I'm not one of those losers who gets wrapped up in that sort of thing.'

But, hell, he'd been doing quite a lot that was out of character for him. A picnic? Since when had he ever been the sort of guy who was interested in picnics? It was even more disquieting to realise that he had done it *for her*.

'Well, you should be.' Sarah saw a golden opportunity to strike out for independence and remind him that she had a life outside his many visits—that he couldn't just re-enter her life and take what he happened to want because it suited him.

Or maybe, she decided uneasily, it was to remind *herself* that she shouldn't be up for grabs, that she had a life outside his many visits. Although where exactly that life was she wasn't quite sure. The teaching assistant job which she had been due to start was now off the cards as they would be moving from the area, and she was caught in a limbo of not really knowing when she should start looking for something else. Should she wait until they had settled in their new house before she began registering with agencies?

With nothing on the agenda, it had been easy to slip into a comfortable pattern of just Oliver and Raoul. Really, it wasn't healthy.

'I mean,' she continued, as they began walking towards the next bank of rides. 'I don't think it's so much about getting in touch with your *inner child*. I think it's more about just being able to relax and have fun. I know you've been around us a lot, but that's not going to last for ever, and when you resume your hectic work schedule... Well, I can't imagine that you won't be stressed out. Having fun and taking time out can't be shoved into a few weeks before normal life resumes...'

'Why are you trying to engage me in an argument?'

'I'm just saying that there's nothing loser-like about someone who knows how to have a good time. In fact, I think it's a great quality in a guy. I'd go so far as to say that the kind of guy I would be interested in dating would be someone who really knew how to let his hair down and enjoy himself...'

When she tried to imagine this fictitious person, the image of Raoul annoyingly superimposed itself in her mind.

Raoul frowned and cast her a quelling look from under his lashes. He'd thought the subject of this so-called single life she envisaged leading had taken a back seat. He'd concluded that the matter had been shelved because she had seen the obvious—which was that there would be no single life for her while they were trying to sort out things with Oliver. It was disconcerting to think that she might have been biding her time, filling her head with thoughts of climbing back on the dating bandwagon when she was still attracted to *him*. He had *felt* it.

'Oliver's looking tired. I think we should have something to eat now,' he said coolly, turning abruptly in the direction of where the car had been parked.

'In fact,' Sarah continued, because this seemed as good a time as any to start talking about where they went from here, 'I think we need to have a little chat later.'

They had eased themselves out of the crowds now, and Raoul gently deposited Oliver on the ground. He had managed to win a stuffed toy at one of the stalls, and its furry head poked out from the top of his backpack. Insistent on having 'just one more ride', his attention was easily diverted at the promise of the chocolate cake which Raoul told him was waiting in the wicker basket.

'There's a lot to discuss now that the house has been bought. We have to talk about arrangements. I want to get my life in order and really start living it.'

'"Really start living it"?' Raoul's voice had become several shades cooler, and he kept it low because even though Oliver had yanked the stuffed panda out of his backpack and was currently engaged in conversation with it, he was fully aware that careless words could be picked up.

'Well, you have to admit that we've both been in a kind of hiatus over the past few weeks, and I suppose that might have led you to assume...well, the past few weeks have been peculiar...' Sarah took a deep breath. 'I bet you haven't had this much time off work since you started!' She gave a bright laugh at his juncture, although Raoul didn't seem amused. 'It's time for us *both* to come back down to reality...'

They were at the car, and Raoul began hauling stuff out of the boot. Having parked away from the main car park, they found themselves in a private enclosed spot, with shady overhanging trees that seemed designed to indulge prospective picnickers.

His mood had nosedived, although he was at pains not to let Oliver have any inkling of that. He unpacked a quantity of food sufficient to feed a small army, and stuck the chilled wine in the ice bucket which had thoughtfully been provided.

Oblivious of the atmosphere, Oliver attacked the picnic with enthusiasm, and awkward silences were papered over with his chatter as he relived every experience of every ride and tried his best to elicit promises of a return visit.

So she wanted to get back to the land of the living? Why shouldn't she? She was still young, and already she was changing as the worry eased off her shoulders. When he had bumped into her again she had been cleaning floors, and the stress of her situation had shown plainly on her face. Now the contours were returning to her body, and her features had lost the gaunt look that had originally caught him off guard. Why *wouldn't* she want to have some kind of fun? Go to clubs? Lead the life most young people her age were leading and which she had had to sidestep because of the responsibility of having to look after a child?

In every single detail it was a situation that should have suited him perfectly. He had left her once with the best of all possible intentions, and he had never deviated from his resolution to steer clear of the murky waters of matrimony. He was not one of those people who had ever thought that despite coming from no family background to speak of, despite a childhood rife with disillusionment and disappointment, he could somehow turn the tide and become a fully paid up member of the happy-ever-after crew. He had always sworn that the one thing he had taken from his experiences would be his freedom, and although he now had one other person to consider, he certainly wasn't going to go the whole hog and do anything that he would regret. If you only lived life for yourself, no one else had the power to disappoint. It was a credo in which he fully believed.

Okay, so he was still attracted to her. Yes, he hadn't had so many cold showers late at night in his life before. And, sure, she was attracted to him—whether she wanted to believe it of herself or not. But that surely wasn't enough to justify the rising tide of outrage at the thought of her *getting out there*.

Above all else he was practical, and taking this sizzling sexual attraction one step further would just add further complications to an already complicated situation. In fact he should be *urging* her to get out there and live a little. He should be heartily *agreeing* that the very thing they need to do now was plot a clear line forward and get on with it.

Within the next few days he anticipated that Oliver would be told by them, jointly, that he was his father. At that point the domestic bubble which they had built around themselves for a very essential purpose would no longer be required. She was one hundred percent right on that score. Gradually Oliver would come to accept the mundane business of joint custody. It wasn't ideal, but what in life ever really was?

Except he was finding it hard to accept any of those things.

There was a distinct chill in the air as the picnic was cleared away, and on the drive back Oliver, exhausted, fell into a soft sleep. To curtail any opportunity for Sarah to embark on another lengthy exposé of what she intended to do with her free time, Raoul switched on the radio, and the drive was completed in utter silence save for the background noise of middle-of-the-road music.

Twenty minutes from home, Sarah began chatting nervously. Anything to break the silence that was stretching like a piece of tautly pulled elastic between them.

The day which had commenced so wonderfully had ended on a sour note, and the blame for that rested firmly on her shoulders. But the realisation that she had been sliding inexorably back to a very dangerous place—one which she had stupidly occupied five years ago—had made her see the urgency of making sure that her barriers were up and functioning. She would never have believed it possible that time with Raoul could lower her defences to such an extent, but then he had always had a way of stealing into her heart and soul and just somehow *taking over*.

There were some things that she wanted to do to the house as soon as contracts had been exchanged. She wanted to do something lovely and fairly colourful to the walls. So she heard herself chattering inanely about paints and wallpaper while Oliver continued to doze in the back and Raoul continued to stare fixedly at the road ahead, only answering when it would have been ridiculously rude not to.

'Okay,' Sarah said finally, bored by the sound of her own voice droning on about a subject in which he clearly had next to no interest. 'I'm sorry if you think I wrecked the day out.'

'Have I said anything of the sort?'

'You don't have to. It's enough for you to sit there in silence and leave me to do all the talking.'

'You were talking about paint colours and wallpapers. I can't even pretend to manufacture an interest in that. I've already told you that I'll get someone in to do it all. Paint. Wallpaper. Furniture. Hell, I'll even commission someone to buy the art to hang on the walls!'

'Then it wouldn't be a home, would it? I mean, Raoul, have you ever really looked around your apartment?'

'What's that supposed to mean?'

'You have the best of everything that money can buy and it *still* doesn't feel like a home. It's like something you'd see in a magazine! The kitchen looks as though it's never been used, and the sofas look as though they've never been sat on. The rugs look as though nothing's ever been spilled on them. And all that abstract art! I bet you didn't choose a single painting yourself!'

Anger returned her to territory with which she was familiar. The hard, chiselled profile he offered her was expressionless, which made her even angrier. How could she not get to him when he got to her so easily? It wasn't fair!

'I don't *like* abstract art,' she told him nastily. 'In fact I hate it. I like boring, old-fashioned paintings. I like seeing stuff that I can recognise. I like flowers and scenery. I don't enjoying looking at angry lines splashed on a canvas. I can't think of anything worse than some stranger buying art for me because it's going to appreciate. And, furthermore, I don't like leather sofas either. They're cold in winter and hot and sticky in summer. I like warm colours, and soft, squashy chairs you can sink into with a book.'

'I'm getting the picture.' Raoul's mouth was compressed. 'You don't want help when it comes to interior design and you hate my apartment.'

Not given to being unkind, Sarah felt a wave of shame and embarrassment wash over her. She would never normally have dreamt of criticising anyone on their choice of décor for their home. Everyone's taste was different, after all. But the strain of having Raoul around, of enjoying his company and getting a tantalising glimpse of what life could have been had he only wanted and loved her, was finally coming home to roost. For all his moods and failings, and despite his arrogance, his perverse stubbornness and his infuriating ability to be blinkered when it suited him, he was still one hell of a guy—and this time round she was seeing so many more sides to him, having so many more opportunities to tumble straight back into love.

'*And* we still have to talk,' she said eventually, but contented herself with staring through the window.

If she had hoped to spark a response from him then she had been sorely mistaken, she thought sourly. Because he just didn't care one way or another what opinions she had about him, his apartment, or any other area of his life.

'Yes. We do.'

In an unprecedented move Raoul had done a complete U-turn. Thinking about her with some other man—pointlessly projecting, in other words—had been a real turn-off, and even more annoying had been the fact that he just hadn't been able to get his thoughts in order. Cool logic had for once been at odds with an irritating, restless unease which he had found difficult to deal with.

But her little bout of anger and her petulant criticisms had clarified things in his head, strangely enough.

Sarah wasn't like all the other women he knew, and it went beyond the fact that she had had his child.

It had always been easy for him to slot the *other* women who had come and gone like ships passing in the night into neat, tidy boxes. They'd filled a very clearly defined role and there were no blurry areas to deal with.

Yes, Sarah had re-entered his life, with a hand grenade in the form of a child, but only now was he accepting that her role in his life was riddled with blurry areas. He didn't know why. Perhaps it was because she represented a stage in his life before he had made it big and could do whatever he liked. Or maybe it was just because she was so damned open, honest and vibrant that she demanded him to engage far more than he was naturally inclined to. She didn't tiptoe around him, and she didn't make any attempts to edit her personality to please him. The women he had dated in the past had all swooned at their first sight of his apartment, with its rampant displays of wealth. He got the impression that the woman sulking in the seat next to him could have written a book on everything she hated about where he lived, and not only that would gladly have given it to him as a present.

The whole situation between them, in fact, demanded a level of engagement that went way beyond the sort of interaction he was accustomed to having with other women. Picnics? Home cooked meals? Board games? *Way* beyond.

He pulled up outside her house, where for once there was a parking space available. Oliver was rousing slowly from sleep, rubbing his eyes and curling into Sarah's arms. Taking the key from her, Raoul unlocked the front door and hesitatingly kissed his son's dark, curly mop of hair. In return he received a sleepy smile.

'He's exhausted,' Sarah muttered. 'All that excitement and then the picnic…he's not accustomed to eating so late. I'll just give him a quick bath and then I think he'll be ready for bed.'

She drew in a deep, steadying breath and firmly trod on the temptation to regret the fact that she had lashed out at him, ruined the atmosphere between them, injected a note of jarring disharmony that made her miserable.

'Why don't you pour yourself something to drink?' she continued, with more command in her voice that she felt. 'And when I come down, like I said, we'll discuss…arrangements.'

She was dishevelled. They had both shared the rides with Oliver, but she had done a few of the really big ones on her own. Someone had had to stay with Oliver, and Raoul had generously offered to babysit, seeing it as a handy excuse to get out of what, frankly, had looked like a terrifying experience. He might have felt sorely deprived as a boy at missing out on all those big rides, but as an adult he could think of nothing worse.

Her hair was tousled and her cheeks were pink, and he noticed the top two buttons of her checked shirt had come undone—although she hadn't yet noticed that.

'Good idea,' he murmured blandly, with a shuttercd expression that left her feverishly trying to analyse what he was thinking.

Raoul noted the hectic colour that had seeped into her cheeks, and the way her arms tightened nervously around a very drowsy Oliver. Arrangements certainly needed to be made, he thought. Though possibly not quite along the lines she anticipated.

She wanted to deal with the formalities, and there was no doubt that certain things had to be discussed, but he was running with a different agenda.

At long last he had lost that unsettling, disconcerting feeling that had climbed into the pit of his stomach and refused to budge. He liked having an explanation for everything and he had his explanation now. Sarah was still in his head because she was unfinished business. There were loose ends to their relationship, and he looked forward to tying all those loose ends up and moving on.

He smiled at her slowly, in a way that sent a tingle of maddening sensation running from the tips of her toes to the crown of her head.

'I'll pour you a drink too,' he said, his dark eyes arrowing onto her wary face, taking in the fine bone structure,

the wide eyes, the full, eminently kissable mouth. 'And
then we can…as you say…begin to talk about moving
forward…'

CHAPTER FIVE

SARAH took longer than she had planned. Oliver, for a start, had discovered a new lease of life and demanded his set of toy cars. And Raoul. In that order.

Determined to have a bit of space from wretched Raoul, in which she could clear her head and plan what she was going to say, Sarah had immediately squashed that request and then been forced to compensate for Raoul's absence by feigning absorption in a game of cars which had involved pushing them around the bed in circles, pretending to stop off at key points to refuel.

Forty minutes later she had finally managed to settle him, after which she'd taken herself off for a bath.

She didn't hurry. She felt that she needed all the time she could get to arrange her thoughts.

First things first. She would chat, in a civilised and adult fashion, about the impending necessity to talk to Oliver. She foresaw no problem there.

Secondly she would announce her decision to finally break the news to her parents that Raoul was back on the scene. She would reassure him that there would be no need to meet them.

Thirdly, they were no longer in a relationship—although they were *friends* for Oliver's sake. Just two people with a common link, who had managed to sort out visiting rights without the interference of lawyers because they were both so mature.

She would be at pains to emphasise how *useful* it had been doing stuff together, for the sake of his relationship with his son.

Downstairs, Raoul had removed himself to the sitting room, and Sarah saw, on entering, that he had poured himself a glass of wine. Ever since he had been on the scene her fridge had been stocked with fine-quality wines, and her cheap wine glasses had been replaced with proper ones—expensive, very modern glasses that she would never have dreamt of buying herself for fear of breakages.

He patted the space next to him, which wasn't ideal as far as Sarah was concerned but, given that her only other option was to scuttle to the furthest chair, which would completely ruin the mature approach she was intent on taking, she sat next to him and reached for her drink.

'I think we can say that was a day well spent,' Raoul began, angling his body so that he was directly facing her and crossing his legs, his hand on his thigh loosely holding his glass. 'Despite your rant about the state of my apartment.'

'Sorry about that.' She concentrated hard on sipping her wine.

He shrugged and continued to look at her, his brilliant dark eyes giving very little away. 'Why should you be?'

'I suppose it was a bit rude,' Sarah conceded reluctantly. 'I don't suppose there are very many people who are critical of you…'

'I had no idea you were being critical of *me*. I assumed you were being critical of the décor in my apartment.'

'That's what I meant to say.'

'Because you have to agree that I've taken every piece

of advice you've given and done everything within my power to build connections with Oliver.'

'You've been brilliant,' Sarah admitted. 'Have you... have you enjoyed it? I mean, this whole thing must have turned your world on its head...'

She hadn't actually meant to say that, but it was something they hadn't previously discussed—not in any depth at all. He had accepted the situation and worked with it, but she couldn't help but remember how adamant he had been all those years ago that the last thing he wanted was marriage and children.

'You had your whole life mapped out,' she continued, staring off into the distance. 'You were only a few years older than the rest of us, but you always seemed to know just what you wanted to do and where you wanted to be.'

'Am I sensing some criticism behind that statement?' Raoul harked back to her annoying little summary of the sort of thing she looked for in a man. 'Fun-loving' somehow didn't quite go hand-in-hand with the picture she was painting of him.

'Not really...'

He decided not to pursue this line of conversation, which would get neither of them anywhere fast. 'Good.' He closed the topic with a slashing smile. 'And, to get back to your original question, having Oliver has been an eye-opener. I've never had to tailor my life to accommodate anyone...'

And had he enjoyed it? He hadn't asked himself that question, but thinking about it now—yes, he had. He had enjoyed the curious unpredictability, the small rewards as he began making headway, the first accepting smile that had made his efforts all seem worthwhile...

'If it had been any other kid,' he conceded roughly, 'it would have been a mindless chore, but with Oliver...' He shrugged and let his silence fill in the missing words. 'And, yes, my life had been disrupted. Disrupted in a major way. But there are times when things don't go quite according to plan.'

'Really? I thought that only happened to other people.' Sarah smiled tightly as she remembered all the plans he had made five years ago—none of which had included her. 'What other times have there been in your life when things didn't go according to your plan? In your adult life, I mean? Things don't go according to plan when you let other people into your life, and you've *never* let anyone into your life.'

Okay, so now she was veering madly away from her timetable, but the simmering, helpless resentment she felt after weeks of feeling herself being sucked in by him all over again was conspiring to build to a head. It was as if her mouth had a will of its own and was determined to say stuff her head was telling it not to.

'I mean, just look at your apartment!'

'So we're back to the fact that you don't like chrome, leather and marble...'

'It's more than that!' Sarah cried, frustrated at his polite refusal to indulge her in her histrionics. 'There's nothing personal anywhere in your apartment...'

'You haven't seen all of my apartment,' Raoul pointed out silkily. 'Unless you've been exploring my bedroom when I haven't been looking...'

'No, of course I haven't!' But at that thought she flushed, and shakily took another mouthful of wine.

'Then you shouldn't generalise. I expected better of you.'

'Very funny, Raoul. I'm being serious.'

'And so am I. I've enjoyed spending time with Oliver.

He's my son. Everything he does,' Raoul added, surprising himself with the admission, 'is a source of fascination.'

'You're very good at saying all the right things,' Sarah muttered, half to herself.

Where had her temper tantrum gone? He was refusing to co-operate and now she was reduced to glowering. It took her a few seconds before she brought her mind to bear on the things that needed discussion.

'But I'm really glad that everything is going so well with Oliver, because it brings me to one of the things I want to say.' She cleared her throat and wished that he would stop staring at her like that, with his fabulous eyes half closed and vaguely assessing. 'Oliver has come to like you very much, and to trust you. When he first met you I really thought that it would be a huge uphill struggle for you two to connect. He had no real experience of an adult male in his life, and you had no experience of what to do around young children.'

'Yes, yes, yes. You're not telling me anything I don't already know...'

Sarah's lips tightened and she frowned. She had laid out this conversation in her head and she had already deviated once.

'It's terrific that you haven't seen it all as a chore.'

'If you're hoping to get on my good side, then I should warn you that you're going about it the wrong way. Derogatory remarks about where I live, insinuations that I'm too rigid for parenting...anything else you'd like to throw in the mix before you carry on?'

She thought she detected an undercurrent of amusement in his voice, which made her bristle. 'I think we should both sit down with Oliver and explain the whole situation. I'm not sure if he'll fully take it in, but he's very bright, and I'm hoping that he'll see it as a welcome development.

He's already begun to look forward to your visits.' She waited. 'Or, of course, I could tell him on my own.'

'No. I like the idea of us doing it together.'

'Good. Well…maybe we should fix a date in the diary?'

'*"Fix a date in the diary"?*' Raoul burst out laughing, which made Sarah go even redder. 'How formal do we have to be here?'

'You know what I mean,' she said stiffly. 'You're busy. I just want to agree on a day.'

'Tomorrow.'

'Fine.'

'Shall I get my phone out so that I can log it in?'

'I'm trying to be serious here, Raoul. After we talk to Oliver I can talk to my parents. I haven't breathed a word to them, but Oliver's mentioned you a couple of times when he's spoken to Mum.'

Nor had she visited her parents in nearly a month. She was used to nipping down to Devon every couple of weekends, and she was guiltily aware that it had been easier to fudge and make excuses because her mother would have been able to eke the truth out of her, and she hadn't wanted the inevitable sermon.

'But that's not your problem. You won't have to meet them at all. I'll explain the situation to them…tell them that we happened to bump into one another… They'll be pleased because it's always worried them that you were out there, not knowing that you had fathered a son. I'll have to explain that I haven't mentioned anything earlier because I wanted you to get to know Oliver, work through some of the initial difficulties. I think they'll understand that…'

'And I won't meet them because…?'

'Why should you? You'll be involved in Oliver's life, but you won't be in mine. Which is really what I want to talk to you about. Visiting rights and such. I don't think we have to go through lawyers to work something out, do we? I mean, the past few weeks have been fine. Of course I realise that it's not really been a normal routine for you, but we can work round that. I'm happy to be flexible.'

Raoul found himself recoiling from the deal on the table, even though it was a deal that suited him perfectly. Yes, he had taken a lot of time off work recently. In fact working late into the night, pretty much a routine of his, had been put on temporary hold, and even time catching up in front of his computer had been limited. Her willingness to compromise should have come as a relief. Instead, he was outraged at her easy assumption that he would be fobbed off with a night a week and the occasional weekend as Oliver's confidence levels in him rose.

'Visiting rights…' he repeated, rolling the words on his tongue and not liking how they tasted.

'Yes! You know—maybe an evening a week, whenever suits you. It would be good if you could set aside a specific day, although I know that's probably unrealistic given your lifestyle…'

Quite out of the blue she wondered when his lifestyle outside of work would recommence. His extra-curricular activities. Should she go over old ground? Repeat that she would prefer Oliver not to have to deal with any unfamiliar women? Or would Raoul be sensible enough to understand that without her having to spell it out in black and white?

It was all well and good, laying out these rules and regulations in a calm, sensible voice, but nothing could disguise the sickening thump of her heart when she thought about the longer term. The days when she would wave goodbye to Oliver and watch from the front door of her new house as Raoul sped him away to places and experiences of which she would be ignorant.

She had become accustomed to the threesome.

She had to swallow hard so that the smile on her face didn't falter. 'Aren't you going to say anything?' she prompted uncertainly.

'Let me get this straight,' Raoul intoned flatly. 'We arrange suitable days for me to pick Oliver up and drop him off a couple of hours later, and beyond that our relationship is severed…'

'I'd prefer it if you didn't call it a *relationship*.' She thought of the tingling way he made her feel, and tacking the word *relationship* onto that just seemed to make things worse.

'What would you like me to call it?'

'I'd like to think that we're *friends*. I never thought that I'd see the day when I could refer to you in that way, but I'm pleased to say that I can. Now.'

'Friends…' Raoul murmured.

'Yes. We've really worked well together on this…er… project…' That didn't sound quite right, and she lowered her eyes nervously, realising, with a start that she had managed to drink her glass of wine without even knowing it. She could feel his proximity like a dense, lethal force, and it was all she could do not to squirm away from him.

'And that's what you want, is it, Sarah?'

Dazed and confused, she raised her bright green eyes to his, and was instantly overwhelmed by a feeling of light-headedness.

The sofa was compact. Their knees were almost touching. The last rays of the sun had disappeared into grey twilight, and without benefit of the overhead light his wonderful face was thrown into half shadows.

'Yes, of course,' she heard herself mumble.

'Friends exchanging a few polite words now and again…'

'I think that's how these things go...'

'It's not what I want and you know that.'

A series of disconcerting images flashed through Sarah's mind at indecent speed. All the simple little things they had done together over the past few weeks...things that had shattered her confidence in her ability to keep a respectable distance from him. And now here he was, framing the very words she didn't want to hear.

'Raoul...' she breathed shakily.

Raoul homed in on the hesitancy in her voice with an unassailable feeling of triumph. It had shocked him to realise how much he still wanted her—until he had worked out the whole theory of unfinished business. With that explanation in his head, he could now easily see why he had been finding it difficult to concentrate at work—why images of her kept floating in his mind, like bits of shrapnel in his system, ruining his concentration and his ability to focus.

'I like it when you say my name.' Right now the lack of focus thing seemed to be happening big-time. His voice lacked its usual self assured resonance. He extended his arm along the back of the sofa and then allowed his hand to drop to the back of her neck, where he slowly caressed the soft, smooth skin.

Sarah struggled to remember the very important fact that Raoul Sinclair was a man who was programmed to get exactly what he wanted—except she didn't know why on earth he would want *her*. But she felt her body sag as she battled to bring some cool reasoning to the situation.

Her moss green eyes were welded to his, and the connection was as strong as a bond of steel.

'I really want to kiss you right now.' He sounded as unsteady as she looked.

'No. You don't. You can't. You mustn't...'

'You're not convincing me…'

She knew that he was going to kiss her, just as she knew that she should push him away. But she couldn't move. Her slender body was as still as a statue, although deep inside was a torrential surge of sensation that was already threatening to break through its fragile barriers.

The touch of his mouth against hers was intoxicating, and she fell back, weakened with fierce arousal. With an unerring sensual instinct that was uniquely his Raoul closed the small distance between them. Or maybe her treacherous body had done that of its own sweet accord. Sarah didn't know. She was ablaze with a hungry craving that had been building for weeks. She moaned softly, and then louder as he trailed an exploring hand underneath her top, sending electric shocks through her whole body.

The hand that had flattened against his chest, aiming to push him away, first curled into a useless fist and then splayed open to clutch the neck of his shirt, so that she could pull him towards her.

She was burning up, and her breasts felt tender, her nipples tightening in anticipation. She strove to stifle a shameless groan of pleasure as his hand climbed higher, caressing her ribcage, moving round to unhook her bra.

As sofas went, this sofa was hardly the most luxurious in the world, but Raoul didn't think he could make it up the stairs to her bedroom. He tugged the cotton top over her head, taking her bra with it in the process, and gazed at her, half undressed, her eyes slumbrous, her perfect mouth half parted on a smile while her breasts rose and fell in quick rhythm with her breathing.

He couldn't believe how much he wanted her. Pure, driven sensation wiped out all coherent thought. If the house had suddenly been struck by an earthquake, he wasn't sure he would have noticed.

The effect she had on him was instantaneous, and as he fluidly removed his clothes he marvelled at his incredible sense of recall. It was as if his memories of her had never been buried, as he had imagined, but instead had remained intact, very close to the surface. It proved conclusively that she was the one woman in his life he had never forgotten because what they'd shared had been prematurely concluded. He had never had time to get tired of her.

Sarah watched as his clothes hit the ground. For a businessman he still had the hard, highly toned, muscular body of an athlete. Broad shoulders narrowed to a six pack and...

Her eyes were riveted by the evidence of his impressive arousal.

'You still like looking at me,' Raoul said with a slow smile. 'And I still like you looking at me.'

The touch of her slight hand on his erection drew a shudder from him, and he curled his fingers in her hair as he felt the delicacy of her mouth and tongue take over from where her hand had been.

Sarah, in some dim part of her mind, knew that she should pull back, should tell him that this was now and not then. But she had always been achingly weak around him and nothing had changed.

The taste of him simply transported her. She found that she couldn't think. Everything had narrowed down to this one moment in time. Her body, which had spent the past five years in cold storage, roared into life and there was nothing she could do about it.

She wriggled out of the rest of her clothes.

She was barely aware of him moving to shut the sitting room door, then tossing one of the throws from a chair onto the ground. She *was* aware of him muttering something about the sofa not being a suitable spot for lovemaking for anyone who wasn't vertically challenged.

The fleecy throw was wonderfully soft and thick.

'This is much better,' Raoul growled, straddling her and then leaning down so that he could kiss her. At the same time he slid his hands under her back, so that she was arched up to him, her breasts scraping provocatively against his chest. 'There's no way that a five-foot sofa can accommodate my six foot two inches.'

'I don't recall you being that fussy five years ago,' Sarah said breathlessly. There was so much of him that she wanted to touch, so much that she had missed.

'You'll have to tell me if I've lost my sense of adventure,' he murmured. He felt her twist restlessly under him. It was a cause of deep satisfaction that he knew exactly what she wanted.

He reared back and began to caress her breasts, looking down at her flushed face as he massaged them, rolling his thumbs over the pouting tips of her nipples while she, likewise, attended to his throbbing erection.

This was a foreplay of mutual satisfaction between two people comfortable with each other's wants. It was like resuming the steps to a well-rehearsed dance.

He bent so that he could feather her neck with kisses—soft, tender nibbles that produced little gasps and moans—and then, taking advantage of the breasts offered up to his exploring mouth, he began to suckle the pink crests, drawing one distended nipple into his mouth, driving her crazy, and making her impatient for him to do the same to the other breast.

It was incredible to think that the body he was now touching had carried his child, and a wave of bitter regret washed over him. So the circumstances would have been all wrong, and he had never factored a child into his life plan, but he would have risen to the challenge. He would have been there right from the very start. He wouldn't have missed out on the first four years of his son's life. He wouldn't have been obliged to spend weeks playing catch up in the father stakes.

But regret was not an emotion with which Raoul was accustomed to dealing, and there was no value in looking at things with the benefit of hindsight.

He blocked out the fanciful notion of a different path and instead trailed his mouth over the flat planes of her stomach, maybe not quite so firm as it had once been, but remarkably free of stretch marks.

The taste of her, as he dipped his tongue to tease her most sensitive spot, was the most erotic thing he had ever experienced.

He smoothed his hands over the satin smoothness of her inner thighs and she groaned as he gave his full attention to the task.

Several times he took her so close to the edge that she had to use every ounce of will-power to rein herself back. She wanted him inside her. She found that she was desperate to feel that wonderful moment when he took one deep, final thrust and lost all his control as he came.

'Are you protected?'

Those three words penetrated her bubble, and it took a few seconds for them to register.

'Huh?'

'I haven't got any protection with me.' Raoul's voice was thick with frustration. 'And you're not on the pill. I can tell from the expression on your face.'

'No. I'm not.' It was slowly sinking in that, however wrapped up he was in the throes of passion, there was no way he would permit another mistake to occur. Look at what his last slip-up had cost him!

'Still, there are other ways of pleasing each other...'

'No, I can't... I'm sorry... I don't know what happened...'

She rolled onto her side, feeling exposed, and then sat up and looked around to where their clothes lay in random piles on the ground. Reaching out, she picked up her top and hastily shoved it on. This was followed by her underwear, while Raoul watched in silence, before heaving himself up on one elbow to stare at her with brooding force.

'Don't tell me that you've suddenly decided to have an attack of scruples now!'

'This was a mistake!' She backed away from him to take refuge on the sofa, drawing her knees up and hugging herself to stave off a bad bout of the shakes.

She dragged her eyes away from the powerful image of his nudity. She wished that she could honestly tell herself that she had just given in to a temporary urge that had been too strong. But the questions raining down on her were of an altogether more uncomfortable nature.

How far had she *really* come these past few years? Had she forgotten just how easily he had found it to dump her? To write her off as surplus to requirements when it came to the big plan of how he wanted to live his life?

A few weeks ago Raoul Sinclair had been the biggest mistake she had ever made. Seeing him again had been a shock, but she had risen above that and tried hard to view his reappearance in her life as something good for the sake of Oliver.

Yes, he had still been able to get to her, but her defences had been up and she had been prepared to fight to protect herself.

But he had attacked her in a way she had never planned for. He had won her over with the ease with which he had accepted what must have been a devastating blow to all his long-term plans. He had controlled his ego and his pride to listen to what she had to say, and he had thrown himself into the business of getting to know his son with enthusiasm and heart wrenching humility. Against her will, and against all logic and reason and good judgement, she had succumbed over the weeks to his sense of humour, his patience with Oliver, his determination to go the extra mile.

How many men who had never contemplated having a family, indeed had steadfastly maintained their determination never to go down that road, would have reacted to similar news with the grace that he had?

Sarah suspected that a lot would either have walked away or else would have contributed financially but done the absolute minimum beyond that.

He had reminded her of all the reasons she had fallen in love with him in the first place and more.

Was it any wonder that she had been a sitting target when he had reached out and touched her?

Sarah could have wept, because she knew that fundamentally Raoul hadn't changed. He might want her body, but he didn't want her dreams, her hopes or her romantic notions—which, it now seemed, had never abandoned her after all, because they were part and parcel of who she was.

'Of course this wasn't a mistake!' He raked impatient fingers through his hair and looked at her as he got dressed. Huddled on the sofa in front of him she looked very young—but then, of course, she *was* very young. Had he presumed too much? No. Of course he hadn't. Her signals had been loud and clear. She had given him the green light, and for the life of him he couldn't understand why she was backing away from him now. The past few weeks had been inexorably leading to this place. At least that was how he saw it.

It wasn't just that she still had the same dramatic effect

on his libido that she'd always had. It wasn't just that she could look at him from under those feathery lashes and make him break out in a sweat. No, they had connected in a much more fundamental area, and he knew that she felt the same way. Hell, he was nothing if not brilliant when it came to reading the signs.

And just then? Before she had decided to start back-tracking? She had been as turned on as him!

'In fact,' he said huskily, 'it was the most natural thing in the world.'

'How do you figure that?'

'You're the mother of my child. I happen to think that it's pretty damned good that we're still seriously attracted to one another.' He sat on the sofa, elbows on thighs, and looked sideways at her.

'Well, I don't think it's good. I think it just…complicates everything.'

'How does it complicate everything?'

'I don't want to get into a relationship with you. Oh, God—I forgot you don't like the word *relationship*. I forgot you find it too threatening.'

Raoul could feel her trying to impose a barrier between them and he didn't like it. It annoyed him that she was prepared to waste time dwelling on something as insignificant as a simple word.

'I want you to admit what's obvious,' he told her, turning so that he was facing her directly, not giving her the slightest opportunity to deflect her eyes from his. 'You can't deny the sexual chemistry between us. If anything, it's stronger than it was when we were together five years ago.'

It terrified Sarah that he felt that too—that it hadn't been just a trick of her imagination that she was drawn to him on all sorts of unwelcome and unexpected levels. In

Africa they had come together as two young people about to take their first steps into the big, bad world. They had lived in a bubble, far removed from day-to-day life. There was no bubble here, and that made the savage attraction she felt for him all the more terrifying.

'No…' she protested weakly.

'Are you telling me that if I hadn't interrupted our love-making you would have suddenly decided to push me away?'

Sarah went bright red and didn't say anything.

'I thought so,' Raoul confirmed softly. 'You want to push me away but you can't.'

'Don't tell me what I can and can't do.'

'Okay. Well, let me tell you this. The past few weeks have been…a revelation. Who would have thought that I could enjoy spending so much time in a kitchen? Especially a kitchen with no mod-cons? Or sitting in front of a television watching a children's programme? I never expected to see you again, but the second I did I realised that what I felt for you hadn't gone away as I had assumed it had. I still want you, and I'm not too proud to admit it.'

'Wanting someone isn't enough…' But her words were distinctly lacking in conviction.

'It's a damn sight healthier than self-denial.' Raoul let those words settle. 'Martyrs might feel virtuous, but virtue is a questionable trade off when it goes hand in hand with unhappiness.'

'You are just *so* egotistical!' Sarah said hotly. 'Are you really saying that I'm going to be unhappy if I pass up the fantastic opportunity to sleep with you?'

'You're going to be miserable if you pass up the opportunity to put this thing we have to bed. You keep trying to deny it. You blow hot and cold because you want to kid yourself that you can fight it.'

Sarah would have liked to deny that, but how could she? He was right. She wavered between wanting him to touch her, enjoying it madly when he did, and being repelled by her own lack of will-power.

'I don't like thinking of you going to clubs and meeting guys,' he admitted roughly.

'Why? Would you be jealous?'

'How can I be jealous of what, as yet, doesn't even exist? Besides, jealousy isn't my thing.' He lowered his eyes and shifted. 'You still have a hold over me,' he conceded. 'I still want you…'

'There's more to life than the physical stuff,' Sarah muttered under her breath.

'Let's agree to differ on that score,' Raoul contradicted without hesitation. 'And it doesn't change the fact that we're going to end up in bed sooner rather than later. I'm proposing we make it sooner. We're unfinished business, Sarah…'

'What do you mean?'

Raoul took her fingers and played with them idly, keeping his eyes locked to hers. 'Back then, I did what was right for both of us. But would what we had have ended had it not been for the fact that I was due to leave the country?'

'Yes, it *would* have ended, Raoul. Because you're not interested in long-term relationships. Oh, we might have drifted on for a few more months, but sooner or later you would have become tired of me.'

'Sooner or later you would have discovered that you were pregnant,' Raoul pointed out with infuriating calm.

'And how would that have changed anything? Of course it wouldn't! You would have stuck around for the baby because you have a sense of responsibility, but why don't you admit that there's no way we would have ended up together!'

'How do I know what would have happened? Do I have a crystal ball?'

'You don't need a crystal ball, Raoul. You just need to be honest. If we had continued our...our whatever you want to call it...would it have led to marriage? Some kind of commitment? Or would we have just carried on sleeping together until the business between us was finally finished? In other words, until you were ready to move on? I know I'm sometimes weak when I'm around you. You're an attractive guy, and you also happen to be the father of my child. But that doesn't mean that it would be a good idea to just have lots of sex until you get me out of your system...'

'What makes you think that it wouldn't be the other way around?'

'In fact,' she continued, ignoring his interruption, 'it would be selfish of us to become lovers because we're incapable of a bit of self-denial! I don't want Oliver to become so accustomed to you being around that it's a problem when you decide to take off! I'm sorry I've given you mixed signals, but we're better off just being...friends...'

CHAPTER SIX

SARAH wondered how she had managed to let her emotions derail her to such an extent that she had nearly ended up back in bed with Raoul. The words *unfinished business* rankled, conjuring up as they did visions of something disposable, to be picked up and then discarded once again the minute it suited him.

Had he imagined that she would launch herself into his arms in a bid to take up where they had left off? Had he thought that she would greet his assertion about still wanting her as something wonderful and complimentary? He didn't want her seeing anyone else—not because he wanted to work on having a proper relationship with her, but because he wanted her to fill his bed until such time as he managed to get her out of his system. Like a flu virus.

He was an arrogant, selfish bastard, and she had been a crazy fool to get herself lulled into thinking otherwise!

She had a couple of days' respite, because he was out of the country, and although he telephoned on both days she was brief before passing him over to Oliver, which he must have found extra challenging, given Oliver's long silences and excitable babbling.

'I think we'll tell him at the weekend,' she informed Raoul crisply, and politely told him that there would be absolutely no need for him to rush over the second he got back, because at that time of night Oliver would be asleep anyway.

On the other side of the Atlantic, Raoul scowled down the phone. He should never have let her think about what he had said. He should have kissed her doubts away and then just made love to her until she was silenced.

Except, of course, she would still have jumped on her moral bandwagon. What had been so straightforward for him had been a hotbed of dilemma for her. He told himself that there were plenty of other fish in the sea, but when he opened his address book and started scanning down the names of beautiful women, all of whom would have shrieked with joy at the sound of his voice and the prospect of a hot date, he found his enthusiasm for that kind of replacement therapy waning fast.

Whereas before he had been comfortable turning up at Sarah's without much notice, he had now found himself given a very definite time slot, and so he arrived at her house bang on five-thirty to find Oliver dressed in jeans and a jumper while she was in her oldest clothes, her hair wet from the shower and pinned up into a ponytail.

'I thought we could sit him down and explain the situation to him,' were her opening words, 'and then you could take him out for something to eat. Nothing fancy, but it'll be nice for him to have you to himself without me around. I've also explained the whole situation to Mum and Dad. They're very pleased that you're on the scene.'

Within minutes Raoul had got the measure of what was going on. She was making it perfectly clear that they would now be communicating on a need-to-know basis only. Her bright green eyes were guarded and detached, only warming when they had Oliver between them so that they could explain the situation.

Finally fatherhood was fully conferred onto him. He was no longer the outsider, easing himself in. He was a dad, and as she had predicted it was a smooth transfer. Oliver had had time to adjust to him. He accepted the news with solemnity, and then it was as though nothing had changed. Raoul had brought him back a very fancy but admirably small box of bricks and an enormous paint-box, both of which were greeted with enthusiasm.

'Take a few pictures when he starts painting in your living room,' Sarah said sarcastically. 'I'd love to see how your leather furniture reacts to the watercolours.'

'Is this how it's now going to be?' Raoul enquired coldly, as Oliver stuffed his backpack with lots of unnecessary items in preparation for their meal out.

Defiant pink colour suffused Sarah's cheeks. She didn't want to be argumentative. He was going to be on the scene, in one way or another, for time immemorial, and she knew that they had to develop a civil, courteous relationship if they weren't to descend into a parody of two warring parents. But she was truly scared of reaching the point they previously had, which had been one of such easy friendship that all the feelings she had imagined left behind had found fertile ground and blossomed out of control. She had let him crawl under her skin until the only person she could think about had been him, so that when he'd finally touched her she had gone up in flames.

'No. It's not. I apologise for that remark,' she responded stiffly, stooping down to adjust Oliver's backpack, whilst taking the opportunity to secretly remove some of the unnecessary stuff he had slipped in. 'Now, you're going to be a good boy, Oliver, aren't you? With your dad?' Oliver nodded and Sarah straightened back up to address Raoul. 'What time can I expect you back? Because I'm going out. I'll only be a couple of hours.'

'You're going out? Where?'

Raoul gave her the once-over. Sloppy clothes. Damp hair. She was waiting for them to leave before she got dressed.

'I don't think that's any of your business, actually.'

'And what if you're not back when I return?'

'You have my mobile number, Raoul. You could always give me a call.'

'Who are you going to be with?'

Raoul knew that it was an outrageous question. He thought back to his brief—very brief—notion that he might get in touch with another woman, go on a date. The idea had lasted less than ten seconds. So...who was *she* going out with? On the first evening he had Oliver? With a man? What man? She had claimed that there was no one at all in her life, that she had been just too busy with the business of trying to earn some money and be a single parent. She might not have had the time to cultivate any kind of personal life, but that didn't mean that there hadn't been men hovering on the periphery, ready to move in just as soon as she found the time.

The more Raoul thought about it, the more convinced he became that she was meeting a man. One of those sensitive, fun-loving types she professed to like. Had she made sure to appear in old clothes so that he wouldn't be able to gauge where she was going by what she was wearing?

He was the least fanciful man in the world, and yet he couldn't stop the swirl of wildly imaginative conclusions to which he was jumping. He was tempted to stand his ground until he got answers that satisfied him.

Sarah laughed incredulously at his question. 'I can't believe you just asked that, Raoul.'

'Why?'

'Because it's none of your business. Now, Oliver's beginning to get restless.' She glanced down to where he was beginning to fidget, delivering soft taps to the skirting board with his shoe and tugging Raoul's hand impatiently. 'I'll see you in a couple of hours, and you know how to get hold of me if you need to.'

Sarah thought that it was a damning indication of just how quickly their relationship had slipped back into dangerous waters—the fact that he saw it as his right to know what she was getting up to. They might not have become lovers, the way they once had been, but it had been a close call. Had she sent out signals? Without even being aware of doing so?

She was going out with a girlfriend for a pizza. Wild horses wouldn't have dragged the admission out of her. She would be gone an hour and a half, tops, and whilst she knew that she shouldn't care one way or another if he knew that her evening out was a harmless bit of catching up with a pal, she did.

So instead of her jeans she wore a mini-skirt, and instead of her trainers she wore heels. She wasn't quite sure what she was trying to prove, and she certainly felt conspicuous in the pizza parlour, where the dress code was more dressing down than dressing up, but she was perversely pleased that she had gone to the trouble when she opened the door to Raoul two and a half hours later.

Oliver was considerably less pristine than he had been when he had left. In fact, Sarah thought that she could pretty much guess at what they had eaten for dinner from the various smears on his clothes.

'How did it go?'

Raoul had to force himself to focus on what she was asking, because the sight of her tight short skirt and high black heels were threatening to ambush his thinking processes.

'Very well…' He heard himself going through the motions of polite chit-chat, bending down to ruffle Oliver's hair and draw him into the conversation. Crayons and paper had been produced at the restaurant, and he had drawn some pictures. Happy family stuff. There would be a psychologist somewhere who would be able to say something about the stick figure drawings of two parents and a child in the middle.

'Right… Well…'

Raoul frowned as she began shutting the door on him. He inserted himself into the small hallway.

'We need to discuss the details of this arrangement,' he told her smoothly. 'As well as the details of the house move. Everything's signed. I'll need to know what needs to be removed from this place.'

'Already?'

'Time moves on at a pace, doesn't it?'

Sarah fell back and watched him stride towards the sitting room. 'I'll get Oliver to bed and be back down in a sec,' she mumbled helplessly to his departing back.

Tempted to get out of her ridiculous gear, she decided against it. Whatever technicalities had to be discussed wouldn't take long, although she was surprised at how fast the house had become available. The last time she had seen it, it had been something of a derelict shell. At the time, she had confided in Raoul what she would like in terms of furniture, but that was the last she had heard on the subject, which had been a couple of weeks ago. She had assumed that the whole process would take months, and had deferred thinking about the move until it was more imminent.

'I can't believe the house is ready. Are you sure?' This as soon as she was back in the sitting room, where he was relaxed in one of the chairs, with his back to the bay window. 'I thought these things took months…'

'Amazing what money can do when it comes to speeding things up.'

'But I haven't really thought about what to fill it with. I mean, none of this stuff is mine…'

'Which is a blessing, judging from the quality of the furnishings.' Raoul watched as she nervously took the chair facing his on the opposite side of the tiny sitting room. She had to wriggle the short skirt down so that it didn't indecently expose her thighs and his lips thinned disapprovingly. The top was hardly better. A vest affair that contoured her generous breasts in a way that couldn't fail to arouse interest.

Sarah couldn't be bothered to react because she didn't disagree.

'It's going to be weird leaving here,' she thought out loud.

'Oliver's excited.' *Who had the short skirt and the tight top and the high heels been for?* 'He's looking forward to having a bigger garden. Complete with the swing set I promised him. Did you enjoy your evening?'

Sarah, who had still been contemplating the prospect of being uprooted sooner than she had expected, looked at Raoul in sudden confusion.

'You're dressed like a tart,' he expanded coolly, 'and I don't like it.'

Sarah gripped the arms of the chair while a slow burning anger rose inside her like red spreading mist.

'How *dare* you think that you can tell me how I can dress?'

'You never wore clothes like that when I was around. Yet the very first time you have a bit of free time without Oliver you're dressed to the nines. I'm guessing that you've used your time profitably by checking what's out there for a single girl.'

'I don't have to…to…*dignify* that with a response!'

No, she didn't, and her stubborn, glaring eyes were telling him that he was going to get nowhere when it came to dragging an explanation of her whereabouts out of her.

Hot on the heels of her rejection, her self-righteous proclamation that their sleeping together wasn't going to be on the cards, her strident reminders to him that she wanted commitment, Raoul finally acknowledged what had been staring him in the face.

When it came to Sarah he was possessive, and he wanted exclusivity. He didn't want her dipping her toe into the world of dating and other men. Seeing her in that revealing get-up, he realised that he didn't even want her dressing in a way that could conceivably attract them. If she had to wear next to nothing, then he wanted it to be for his benefit and his benefit only.

He had never been possessive in his life before. Was it because she was more than just a woman to him? Because she was the mother of his child? Did he have some peculiar dinosaur streak of which he had hitherto been unaware? He just knew that the thought of her trawling the clubs made his blood run cold.

So he had never been moved by the notion of settling down with anyone? Well, life wasn't a static business. Rules and guidelines made yesterday became null and void when situations changed. Wasn't flexibility a sign of a creative mind?

He wondered that he could have been disingenuous enough to imagine his perfectly reasonable proposition that they take what they had and run with it might be met with enthusiasm. Sarah would never settle for anything less than a full-time relationship. And would that even be with him? he wondered uneasily. It was true that the sexual chemistry between them was electrifying, but it certainly wouldn't be the tipping point for her.

'Let's just talk about the practicalities,' she continued firmly. 'If you give me a definite date as to when we need to be out of here... I haven't given notice to the landlord,' she said suddenly. 'I need to give three months' notice...'

'I'll take care of that.'

'And I suppose we should discuss what days suit you to come and see Oliver. Or should we wait until we're settled in the new place? Then you can see how easy it is for you to get to where we are. Public transport can be a little unreliable. Oops, sorry—I forgot that you wouldn't be taking public transport...'

Raoul was acidly wondering whether she was eager to get her diary in order, so that she knew in advance when she would be able to slot in her exciting single life. What the hell was going on here? He was *jealous*!

He stood up, and Sarah hastily followed suit, bemused by the fact that he seemed to be leaving pretty much as fast as he had arrived. Not only that, but he had somehow managed to make her feel like a cheap tart. Although she knew that he had no right to pass sweeping judgements on what she wore or where she went, she still had to fight the temptation to make peace by just telling him the truth.

'The house will be ready by the middle of next week.'

'But what about my things?'

'I'll arrange to have them brought over. If all this furniture is staying, then I can't imagine that what's left will amount to much.'

'No, I suppose not,' she said in a small voice, perversely inclined to dither now that he was on his way out.

Raoul hesitated. 'It's going to be fine,' he said roughly.

'The house will be entirely in your name. You won't have to be afraid that you could lose the roof over your head, and really, it's just a change of location.'

'It'll be great!' She tried a bright smile on for size. 'I know Mum and Dad are really thrilled about it. They haven't been too impressed with our rented house, what with the busy street so close to the front door and not much back garden for Oliver.'

'Which brings me to something I haven't yet mentioned. Your parents.'

'What about them?'

'I want to meet them.'

'Whatever for?' Sarah asked, dismayed. Try as she had, she couldn't stop feeling deeply suspicious that neither of them had really believed her when she had told them that Raoul was back on the scene but that it was absolutely fine because she had discovered that she felt nothing for him.

'Because Oliver's my son and it makes sense for me to know his grandparents. There will be occasions when they visit us in London and vice versa.'

'Yes, but…'

'I also don't want to spend the rest of my life with your parents harbouring misconceptions about the kind of man I am.'

'They don't have misconceptions,' Sarah admitted grudgingly. 'I told them how much time you'd spent with Oliver, and also about the house.'

'I'd still like to meet them, so you'll have to arrange that and give me a few days' advance notice.'

'Well, maybe when they're next in London…'

'No. Maybe within the next fortnight.'

With the house move a heartbeat away, and a date set in the diary for the three of them to visit her parents in

Devon, Sarah had never felt more like someone chucked onto a rollercoaster and managing to hang on only by the skin of her teeth.

Her possessions, once she had packed them all up, amounted to a few cardboard boxes, which seemed a sad indictment of the time she had spent in the rented house. Nor could she say, with her hand on her heart, that there was very much that she would miss about where she'd lived. The neighbours were pleasant enough, although she knew them only in passing, but the place was wrapped up in so many memories of hardship and trying to make ends meet that she found herself barely glancing back as the chauffeur-driven car that had been sent for them arrived to collect her promptly on Wednesday morning.

Oliver could barely contain his excitement. The back of the opulent car was strewn with his toys. Of course Raoul's driver knew who they were, because from the start Raoul had flatly informed her that he couldn't care less what other people thought of his private life, but she could see that the man was curious, and amused at Oliver's high spirits. Sarah wondered whether he was trying to marry the image of his boss with that of a man who wouldn't mind a four-year-old child treating his mega-expensive car with cavalier disrespect.

Sarah was charmed afresh at the peaceful, tree-lined road that led up to the house, which was in a large corner plot. Anyone could have been forgiven for thinking that London was a million miles away. It was as far removed from their small rented terraced house on the busy road as chalk was from cheese. Whatever her doubts and anxieties, she couldn't deny that Raoul had rescued them both from a great deal of financial hardship and discomfort.

Hard on the heels of that private admission she felt a

lump in her throat at the thought of them being *friends*. She had been so offended by his suggestion that they become lovers for no other reason than they were still attracted to one another, and so hurt that he only wanted her in his bed as a way of exorcising old ghosts… She had positively done the right thing in telling him just where he could take that selfish, arrogant proposal, and yet…

Had she reacted too hastily?

Sarah hurriedly sidelined that sign of weakness and scooped Oliver's toys onto her lap as the car finally slowed down and then swept up the picturesque drive to the house.

Raoul was waiting for her inside.

'I would have brought you here,' he said, picking up Oliver, who demanded to be put down so that he could explore, 'but I've come straight from work.'

'That's okay.' Sarah stepped inside and her mouth fell open—because it bore little resemblance to the house she had last seen.

Flagstone tiles made the hallway warm and colour-ful, and everywhere else rich, deep wood lent a rustic, cosy charm. She walked from room to room, taking in the décor which was exactly as she would have wanted it to be, from the velvet drapes in the sitting room to the re-stored Victorian tiles around the fireplace.

Raoul made a show of pointing out the bottle-green Aga which took pride of place in the kitchen, and the old-fashioned dresser which he had had specifically sourced from one of the house magazines which had littered her house.

'You had a crease in the page,' he informed her, 'so I took it to mean that this was the kind of thing you liked.'

Oliver had positioned himself by the French doors that led from the small conservatory by the kitchen into the garden, and was staring at the swing set outside with eyes as round as saucers.

'Okay,' Sarah said on a laugh, holding his hand, 'let's have a look outside, shall we?'

'I don't remember the garden being this well planted,' she said, looking around her at the shrubs and foliage that framed the long lawn. There was even a rustic table and chairs on the paved patio, behind which a trellis promised a riot of colour when in season.

'I had it landscaped. Feel free to change anything you want. Why don't we have a look upstairs? I can get my driver to keep an eye on Oliver,' he added drily. 'We might have a fight on our hands if we try and prise him off the swing.'

Raoul had had considerable input with the furnishings. He had hired the very same mega-expensive interior designer who had done his own penthouse apartment, but instead of handing over an enormous cheque and giving her free rein he had actually been specific about what he wanted. He knew that Sarah hated anything modern and minimalist. He'd steered clear of anything involving leather and chrome. He had stopped short of buying artwork, although he had been tempted by some small landscapes that would have been a terrific investment, but he had done his utmost with a bewildering range of colour options and had insisted that everything be kept period.

'I can't believe this is going to be our new home,' Sarah murmured yet again, as she ran her hands lovingly over the Victorian fireplace in what would be her bedroom. A dreamy four-poster bed dominated the space, and the leaded windows overlooked the pretty garden. She could see Oliver on the swing, being pushed by Raoul's very patient driver, and she waved at him.

'Did you choose all this stuff yourself?'

Raoul flushed. How cool was it to have a hand in choosing furnishings for a house? Not very. Especially when there had been a million and one other things clamouring for his attention at work. But he had been rattled by her rejection, and had realised that despite what he saw as an obvious way forward for them he could take nothing for granted.

'I think I know what you like,' he prevaricated, and received a warm smile in response.

Sarah squashed the temptation to hug him. He did things like this and was it any wonder that her will-power was all over the place? She had expected to find a house that was functioning and kitted out in a fairly basic way. Instead there was nothing that wasn't one hundred percent perfect, from the mellow velvet curtains in the sitting room to the faded elegant wallpaper in the bedroom.

Oliver's room, next to hers, was what any four-year-old boy would have dreamt of, with a bed in the shape of a racing car and wallpaper featuring all his favourite cartoon characters.

Yet again she had to remind herself that she had done the right thing in turning her back on what had been on offer. Yet again she forced herself back onto the straight and narrow by telling herself that, however good Raoul was at being charming, going the extra mile and throwing money at something with a generosity that would render most people speechless, he was still a man who walked alone and always would. He was still a man with an inbuilt loathing of any form of commitment, which in his head was the equivalent of a prison sentence.

Yet again she was forced to concede that his invitation to be his lover would have sounded the death knell for any ongoing amicable relationship they might foster, because she would have been the one to get hurt in the end. She knew that if she got too close to him it would be impossible to hold any of herself back.

But the steps he had taken to ensure that she walked into a house that was brilliant in every way moved her.

'We'll have to sit down and talk about visiting.' She strived to hit the right note of being convivial, appreciative but practical.

Raoul looked at her with veiled eyes. Had he hoped for a more favourable reaction, given the time and effort he had expended in doing this house up for her? Since when did *quid pro quo* play a part in human interaction? Was this the legacy that had been willed to him courtesy of his disadvantaged background?

He thrust aside that moment of introspection, but even so he knew that she was sliding further and further away from him.

'I don't want to have weekly visits,' he told her, lounging on the ledge by the window and surveying her with his arms folded.

'No…well, you can come as often as you like,' she offered. 'I just really would need to find out exactly when, so that Oliver isn't disappointed…I know your work life makes you unpredictable…'

'Have I been unpredictable so far?'

'No, but…'

'I've come every time I said I would. Believe me, I understand how important it is to be reliable when there's a child involved. You forget I have intimate experience of kids waiting by windows with their bags packed for parents who never showed up.'

'Of course…'

'I know how damaging that can be.'

'So…what do you suggest? He'll be starting school in September…maybe weekends might be a good idea. Just to begin with. Until he gets used to his new routine. Kids can be tetchy and exhausted when they first start school…'

'I'm not in favour of being a part-time father.'

'You *won't* be.'

'How am I to know that would be a continuing state of affairs?'

'I don't understand…'

'How long before you find another man, in other words?' He thought of her, dressed to kill, on the hunt for a soulmate.

Sarah stared at him incredulously. Slowly the nuts and bolts cranked into gear and she gave a shaky, sheepish laugh. 'Okay. I know what you're getting at. You think that I went somewhere exciting the last time you took Oliver out. You think that I got dressed up and decided to…I don't know…paint the town red…'

Raoul flushed darkly and kept his eyes pinned to her face.

'Do you really think that I'm the type of person who keeps her head down, bringing up a child, and then hits the clubs the very second she gets a couple of hours out of the house?'

'It's not that impossible to believe. Don't forget you were the one who made a big song and dance about wanting to be free to find your knight in shining armour! If such a person exists!'

'Oh, for heaven's sake!' She walked towards him, angry, frustrated, and helplessly aware that the only contender for the vacancy of knight in shining armour was standing right in front of her—the very last man on whom the honour should ever be conferred because he wasn't interested in the position. 'Look, I didn't go *anywhere* last Saturday. Well, nowhere exciting at any rate. I met my friend and we went out for a pizza. Are you satisfied?'

'What friend was this?'

'A girlfriend from Devon. She moved to London a few months ago, and we try to get together as often as we can. It's not always possible with a young child, and so I took advantage of having a night off to have dinner with her.'

'Why didn't you tell me at the time?'

'Because it was none of your business, Raoul!'

'Did it give you a kick to make me jealous?'

It was the first time he had ever expressed an emotion like that. Many times he had told her that he just wasn't a jealous person. His admission now brought a rush of heady colour to her cheeks, and she could feel her heart accelerate, beating against her ribcage like a sledgehammer. Suddenly conscious of his proximity, she widened her eyes and heard her breaths come fast and shallow. She feverishly tried to work out what this meant. Did he feel more for her than he had been willing to verbalise? Or was she just caving in once again? Clutching at straws because she loved him?

'You're telling me that you were *jealous*?'

Having said more than he had intended to, Raoul refused to be drawn into a touchy feely conversation about a passing weakness. He looked at her with stubborn pride.

'I'm telling you that I wasn't impressed by the way you were dressed.' He heard himself expressing an opinion that would have been more appropriate had it come from someone three times his age. 'You're a mother...'

'And so short skirts are out? I'm *not* getting all wrapped up in this silly business of you thinking that you can tell me what to wear or where to go or what to think!' Her temporary euphoric bubble was rapidly deflating. 'And I'm *not* about to start clubbing. I have too much on my plate at the moment,' she admitted with honesty, 'to even begin thinking about meeting a guy.'

'And I'm not prepared for that time to come,' Raoul said with grim determination. 'I don't want to be constrained to two evenings a week, and I don't want you telling me that this is about you. It's not. It's about Oliver, and you can't tell me that it's not better for a child to have both parents here.'

Sarah looked at him with dazed incomprehension. 'So...?'

'So you want nothing short of full time commitment? Well, you've got it. For Oliver's sake, I'm willing to marry you...'

CHAPTER SEVEN

FOR a few seconds Sarah wondered whether she had heard right, and then for a few more seconds she basked in the bliss of his proposal. Now that he had uttered those words she realised that this was exactly what she had wanted five years ago. His bags had been packed and she had been hanging on, waiting for him to seal their relationship with just this indication of true commitment. Of course back then his response had been to dump her.

'You're asking me to marry you,' she said flatly, and Raoul titled his head to one side.

'It makes sense.'

'Why now? Why does it make sense now?'

'I'm not sure what you're getting at, Sarah.'

'I'm guessing that the only reason you've asked me to marry you is because you don't like the thought of being displaced if someone else comes along.'

'Oliver's my son. Naturally I don't care for the thought of another man coming into your life and taking over my role.'

But would he have asked her to marry him if he hadn't happened to see her in a short skirt and a small top, making the most of what few assets she possessed, and jumped to all the wrong conclusions? He hadn't asked her to marry him when she had told him that she wanted the opportunity to meet someone with whom she could have a meaningful relationship, that there was more to life than sex...

Sarah reasoned that that was because, whatever she said, he had believed deep down that his hold over her was unbreakable. Historically, she had been his for the asking, and he knew that. Had he imagined that it was something she had never outgrown? Had he thought that underneath all her doubts and hesitation and brave denials she was really the same girl, eager and willing to do whatever he asked? Until it had been brought home to him, silly and mistaken though he was, that she might actually have *meant* what she said?

For Sarah, it all seemed to tie up. Raoul enjoyed being in control. When they had lived together on the compound all those years ago he had always been the one to take the lead, the one to whom everyone else instinctively turned when it came to decision making. Had the prospect of her slithering out of his reach and beyond his control prompted him into a marriage proposal?

'I didn't think that you ever wanted to get married,' she pointed out, and he gave an elegant shrug, turning to stare out of the window to where Oliver's appetite for the garden appeared to be boundless.

'I never thought about having children either,' he returned without hesitation, 'but there are you. The best-laid plans and so on.'

'Well, I'm sorry that Oliver's come along and messed up your life,' she said in a tight voice, and he spun round to look at her.

'Don't ever say that again!' His voice was low and sharp and lethally cold, and Sarah was immediately ashamed of her outburst because it hadn't been fair. 'I may not have planned on having children but I now have a child, and there is no way that I would wish it otherwise.'

'I'm sorry. I shouldn't have said that. But…look, it would be a disaster for us to get married.'

'I'm really not seeing the problem here. There's more than just the two of us involved in this…'

'So what's changed from when you first found out about Oliver?'

'I don't understand this. Are you playing hard to get because you think that I should have asked you to marry me as soon as I found out about Oliver?'

'No, of course not! And I'm not playing *hard to get*. I know that this isn't some kind of game. You don't *want* to marry me, Raoul. You just want to be in a position of making sure that I don't get involved with anyone else and jeopardise your contact and influence with Oliver, and the only way you can think of doing that is by putting a ring on my finger!'

She spun round on her heels and made for the door, but before she could reach it she felt his fingers on her arm and he whipped her back round to face him.

'You're not going to walk out on this conversation!'

'I don't want to carry on talking about this. It's upsetting me.'

Raoul shot her a look of pure disbelief. 'I can't believe I'm hearing this! I ask you to marry me and you're acting as though I've insulted you!'

'You want me to be grateful, Raoul, and I'm not. When I used to dream of being married it was never about getting a grudging proposal from a man who has an agenda and no way out!'

'This is ridiculous. You're blowing everything out of proportion. Oliver needs a family and we're good together.' But Raoul couldn't deny that the idea of her running around with other men had, at least in part, generated his urgent decision. Did that turn him into a control freak? No!

'In other words, all things taken into account, why not? Is that how it works for you, Raoul?' She couldn't bring herself to look at him. His hand was a band of rigid steel on her arm, even though he actually wasn't grasping her very hard at all.

Silence pooled around them until Sarah could feel herself beginning to perspire with tension. Why was it such a struggle to do what she knew was the right thing? Why was it so hard to keep her defences in place? Hadn't she learnt anything at all? Didn't she deserve more than to be someone's convenient wife, even though she happened to be in love with that *someone*? What sort of happy future could there be for two people welded together for the wrong reason?

'Look, I know that the ideal situation is for a child to have both parents at home, but it would be wrong for us to sacrifice our lives for Oliver's sake.'

'Why do you have to use such emotive language?' He released her to rake an impatient hand through his hair. 'I'm not looking at it as a *sacrifice*.'

'Well, how *are* you looking at it?'

'Haven't we got along for the past few weeks?' He answered her question with a question, which wasn't exactly an informative response.

'Yes, of course we have...' Too well, as far as Sarah was concerned. So well, in fact, that it had been dangerously easy to fall in love with him all over again—for which foolishness she was now paying a steep price. A marriage of convenience would have been much more acceptable were emotions not involved. Then she could have seen it as a business transaction which benefited all parties concerned.

'And I know you don't like hearing this particular truth,' Raoul continued bluntly, 'but we get along in other ways as well…'

'Why does it always come down to sex for you?' Sarah muttered, folding her arms. 'Is it because you think that's my weakness?'

'Isn't it?'

Suddenly he was suffocatingly close to her. Her nostrils flared as she breathed in his heady, masculine scent. Unable to look him in the face, she let her eyes drift to the only slightly less alarming aspect of his broad chest. The top two buttons of his shirt were undone, and she could glimpse the fine dark hair that shadowed his torso.

'There's nothing wrong with that,' Raoul murmured in a velvety voice that brought her out in goosebumps. 'In fact, I like it. So we get married, Oliver has a stable home life, and we get to enjoy each other. No more having to torture yourself with pointless Should we? Shouldn't we? questions…no more wringing of hands…no more big speeches about keeping our hands off one another while you carry on looking at me with those hot little eyes of yours…'

Although he hadn't laid a finger on her, Sarah felt as though he had—because her body was on fire just listening to the rise and fall of his seductive words.

'I don't look at you…that way…'

'You know you do. And it's mutual. Every time I leave you I head home for a cold shower.' He tilted her mutinous head so that she was looking up at him. 'Let's make this legal, Sarah…'

The sound of Oliver calling them from downstairs snapped Sarah out of her trance and she took a shaky step back.

'I can't drag you kicking and screaming down the aisle,' Raoul said softly as she turned to head down the stairs.

Sarah stilled and half looked over her shoulder. 'But think about what I've said and think about the consequences if you decide to say no.'

'Is there some sort of threat behind what you're saying, Raoul?'

'I have never used threats in my dealings with other people. I've never had to. Instead of rushing in and seeing everything insofar as it pertains to *you*, try looking at the bigger picture and seeing things insofar as they pertain to everyone else.'

'You're telling me that I'm selfish?'

'If the cap fits…'

'I'm just not as cynical as you, Raoul. That doesn't make me selfish.'

Raoul was stumped by this piece of incomprehensible feminine logic, and he shook his head in pure frustration. 'What's cynical about wanting what's best for our child? You need to think about my proposition, Sarah. Now, Oliver's getting restless, but just bear in mind that if *I* am not impressed by the thought of some guy moving in with you and taking over my role, how would *you* feel when some woman moves in with me and takes over *your* role…?'

Leaving her with that ringing in her head was the equivalent of a threat, as far as Sarah was concerned. Furthermore, for the rest of the day he treated her with a level of formality that set her at an uncomfortable distance, and she wondered whether this was his way of showing her, without having to spell it out, what life would be like should they go their separate ways, only meeting up for the sake of their child.

She resented the way he could so effectively narrow everything down in terms that were starkly black and white. Oliver needed both parents at home. They got along. There

was still that defiant tug of sexual chemistry there between
them. Solution? Get married. Because she had rejected
his original offer: *Become lovers until boredom sets in.*
Marriage, for Raoul, would sort out the thorny problem
of another man surfacing in her life, and also satisfy his
physical needs. It made such perfect sense to him that any
objection on her part could only be interpreted as selfishness.

Ridiculous!

But, whether he had intended it that way or not, his point
was driven home over the next few days, during which he
came at appointed and prearranged times so that he could
take Oliver out. He had asked her advice and laughed when
she had told him that any restaurant with starched white
linen tablecloths and fussy waiters should be avoided at
all costs, but there was a patina of politeness he now ex-
uded which Sarah found horribly unnerving.

Of course she wondered whether she was imagining
it. His marriage proposal was still whirring around in her
head. Had that made her hyper-sensitive to nuances in his
demeanour?

She had tried twice to raise the topic, to explain her
point of view in a way that didn't end up making her feel
as if she was somehow *letting the side down*, but in both
instances his response had been to repeat that she had to
think it through very carefully.

'Wait and see how this arrangement works,' he had
urged her, 'before you decide to rush headlong into a decision that you might come to bitterly regret.'

In a few well-chosen words he had managed to sum her
up as reckless, irresponsible, and incapable of making the
right choices.

Again Sarah had tried to get a toe hold into an argument, but he had expertly fielded her off and she had been left stewing in her own annoyance.

And at the bottom of her mind crawled the uncomfortable scenario of Raoul finding someone else. Now that he had taken on board the concept of marrying someone, would it prove persuasive enough for him to actually consider a proper relationship? He had had a congenital aversion to tying himself up with someone else. His background had predicated against it. But then Oliver had come along and a chip in the fortress of his self-containment had been made. Then he had taken the step of asking her to marry him.

Of course for all the wrong reasons as far as she was concerned! But he *had* jumped an enormous hurdle, even if he *did* see it only as a logical step forward, all things considered.

What if, having jumped that hurdle, he now allowed himself to finally open up to the reality of actually taking someone else on board? What if he *fell in love*?

When Sarah thought about that, she found herself quailing in panic. *She* could give him long, moralising speeches about the importance of not getting married simply for the sake of a child. *She* could scoff at the idea of entering into a union as intimate as marriage without the right foundations in place, because she was scared that she would not be able to survive the closeness without wanting much, much more. But how thrilled would she be if he took himself off to some other woman and decided to tie the knot?

It could easily happen, couldn't it? Having a child would have altered everything for him, even if he barely recognised the fact. She wondered whether he had been changed enough to consider the advantages of having a permanent woman in his life—someone who could be a substitute mother. Sarah felt sick at the prospect of having a *step-*

mother in the mix, but on the subject of things *making sense* it certainly would make sense, down the road, for him to get married.

He would surely find it difficult to continue playing the field, always making sure that Oliver and whatever current woman of the day didn't overlap. Would he want to live the rest of his life like that? And what about when Oliver got older and became more alert to what was happening around him? Would Raoul want to risk having his private life judged by his own child? No, of course he wouldn't. If there was one thing she had learnt, it was that Raoul was capable of huge sacrifices when it came to Oliver. He would never countenance his own son seeing him as an irresponsible womaniser.

Sarah found herself frequently drifting off into such thoughts as they settled into their new house and began turning it into a home.

There was absolutely nothing to be done, décor-wise, because everything was of an exquisite standard, but the show home effect was quickly replaced with something altogether more cosy as family pictures were brought out of packing boxes and laid on the mantelpiece in the sitting room. The fridge became a repository for Oliver's artwork as she attached his drawings with colourful little magnets, and the woven throws her mother had given her when she had first moved to London turned the sofa in the conservatory into a lovely, inviting spot where she and Oliver could watch television. They went on short forays into the nearby village, locating all the essentials.

On the surface, everything was as it should be. It was only her endlessly churning mind that kept her awake at night and made her lose focus when she was in the middle of doing something.

Raoul continued to behave with grindingly perfect, gentlemanly behaviour, and Sarah found herself wondering on more than one occasion what he was getting up to on the evenings when he wasn't around.

She hadn't realised how accustomed she had become to seeing him pretty much every day, or at least being given some explanation of where he was and what he was doing on those days when he hadn't been able to make it. On the single occasion when she had tried fishing for a little information he had raised his eyebrows, tutted, and told her that really it wasn't any of her business, was it?

Two days before they were due to go to Devon to visit her parents Raoul returned Oliver to the house after their evening at a movie and, instead of leaving, informed her that the time had come to have a chat.

'I'll wait for you in the kitchen.' He had given her two weeks, and two weeks was plenty long enough. He wasn't used to hanging around waiting for someone else to make their mind up—especially when the matter in question should really have required next to no deliberation—but Raoul had taken a couple of steps back.

Although she was attracted to him, she had refused to become his mistress, and he didn't think that she had done so because she had been holding out for a bigger prize. The plain and simple truth was that she was no longer his number one adoring fan. He had hurt her deeply five years ago, and that combined with the hardship of being a single mother without much money to throw around had toughened her.

Raoul knew that there was no way he could push her into marrying him. He was forced to acknowledge that in this one area, he had no control. But biding his time had driven him round the bend—especially when he kept remembering how easy and straightforward things had been between them before.

She returned to the kitchen forty-five minutes later. She had changed into a pair of loose, faded jeans that sat well below her waist and a tee shirt that rode up, exposing her flat belly, when she stretched into one of the cupboards to get two mugs for coffee.

'So...' she said brightly, once they were both at the kitchen table with mugs of coffee in front of them. This kitchen, unlike the tiny one in the rented house, was big enough to contain a six-seater table. He sat at one end, and Sarah deliberately took the seat at the opposite end. 'You wanted to talk to me? I know I've said this a thousand times, but the house is perfect. I can't tell you what a difference it makes, and there's so much to do around here. I've already found a morning playgroup we can go to! It's just so leafy and quiet.'

Raoul watched her and listened in silence, waiting until she had rambled on for a while longer before coming to a halting stop.

'Two weeks ago I asked you a question.'

Having spent the entire two weeks thinking of nothing else *but* that question he had posed, Sarah now looked at him blankly—and received an impatient click of his tongue in response.

'I'm not going to hang around for ever waiting for you to give me an answer, Sarah. I've waited so that you have had time to settle into the house. You've settled. So tell me—what's the answer going to be?'

'I...I don't know...'

'Not good enough.' Raoul contained his mounting anger with difficulty.

'Can I have a few more days to think about it?' Sarah licked her lips nervously. 'Marriage is such a big step,' she muttered, by way of extra explanation.

'Likewise having a child.'

'Yes…but…'

'Are we going to go down the same monotonous route of self-sacrifice?'

'No!' Sarah cried, stung by his bored tone of voice.

'Then what's your answer to be?' He looked at her fraught face and thought that he might have been sentencing her to life in prison—and yet five years ago she would have exploded with joy at such a proposal. 'If you say no then I *walk away*, Sarah.'

'Walk away? What do you mean walk away? Are you saying that you're going to abandon Oliver if I don't agree to marry you?'

'Oh, for God's sake! When are you going to stop seeing me as a monster? I will never abandon my own flesh and blood!'

'I'm sorry. I know you wouldn't,' Sarah said, ashamed, because sudden panic had driven her to say the first stupid thing in her head. 'So what *are* you saying?'

'I'll find someone else,' Raoul told her bluntly, 'and we will get in touch with lawyers, who will draw up papers regarding settlement and visiting rights. You will see me only when essential, and only ever when it is to do with Oliver. Naturally I will have no control over who you see, don't see, or eventually become seriously involved with, and the same would apply to me. Am I spelling things out loud and clear for you?'

The colour had drained from Sarah's face. Presented with such a succinct action-and-consequence train of events, she felt her wildly scattered thoughts finally crystallise into one shocking truth. She would lose him for ever. He really would meet another woman and the question of love wouldn't even have to arise. He would regulate his love-life because he would have to, and she would be left on the outside…watching.

She wouldn't conveniently stop loving him just because he'd removed himself from her.

He might not love her, but he would be a brilliant father—and she would be spared the misery of *just not having him around*. Who had ever said that you could have it all?

She was sadly aware that she would settle for crumbs. She wanted to ask him what would happen when he got bored with her. Would he begin to conduct a discreet outside life? It was a question to which she didn't want an answer.

She had thought that any marriage without love would be doomed to failure. She had never imagined herself walking down the aisle knowing that the guy by her side was only there because he had found himself in the unenviable position of having no choice. Duty and responsibility were two wonderful things, but she hadn't ever seen them as sufficient. Raoul, on the other hand, had moved faster towards the inevitable—and she had to catch up now, because the stark alternative was even more unpalatable and she hated herself for her weakness.

'I'll marry you,' she agreed, daring to steal a look at his face.

Raoul smiled, and realised that he had been panicked at the thought that she might turn him down. He *never* panicked! Even when he had been confronted with a child he hadn't known existed, when he had realised that his life was about to be changed irrevocably for ever, he hadn't panicked. He had assessed the situation and dealt with it. But watching her, eyes half closed, he had been aware of a weird, suffocating feeling—as if he had stepped off the edge of a precipice in the hope that there would be a trampoline waiting underneath to break his fall.

He stood up, thinking it wise to cover the basics and

then leave—before she could revert to her previous stance, reconsider his offer and tell him that it was off, after all. She could be bewilderingly inconsistent.

'I'm thinking soon,' he said, feeling on a strange high. 'As soon as it can be arranged, to be perfectly honest. I'll start working on that straight away. Something small...' He paused to look at her pinkened cheeks. Her hair was tumbling over her shoulders and he wanted nothing more than to tangle his fingers into it and pull her towards him.

'Although you are the one who factored marriage into your dreams of the future,' he murmured drily, 'so it's up to you what sort of affair you want. You can have a thousand people and St Paul's Cathedral if you like...'

Sarah opened her mouth to tell him that anything would do, because it wouldn't really be a *true* marriage, would it? Yes, they had known each other once. Yes, they had been lovers, and she had been crazy enough to think that he had loved her as much as she had loved him, even if he had never said so. But he hadn't intended marrying her then, or even setting eyes on her again once he had left the country. He hadn't wanted her then and he didn't want her now, but marriage, for him, was the only way he could be a permanent and daily feature in his son's life. Because she had rejected the first offer on the table, which had been to be his mistress.

Approaching the whole concept of their union in the way he might a business arrangement, maybe he had thought that living together would be the lesser of two evils. They would have learned to compromise without the necessity of having to take that final, psychologically big step and commit to a bond sealed in the eyes of the law. Or maybe he had just thought that if what they had fizzled out it would just be a whole lot easier to part company if they had merely been living together. And by then

he would have had a much stronger foothold in the door—
might even have been able to fight for custody if he'd chosen to.

Racked with a hornets' nest of anxieties, she still knew
that it would be stupid to open up a debate on the worth
of a marriage that had yet to happen. What would that get
her? Certainly not the words she wanted to hear.

'Something small,' she said faintly.

'And traditional,' Raoul agreed. 'I expect you would
like that, and so would your parents. I remember you saying something about a bracelet that your grandmother had
given your mother, which she had kept to be passed on to
you when you got married? You laughed and said that it
wasn't exactly the most expensive trousseau in the world,
but that it meant a lot to both of you.'

'Isn't there *anything* that you've forgotten?' Sarah asked
in a tetchy voice. All her dreams and hopes were being
agonisingly brought back home to her on a painful tide of
self-pity. She thought that she might actually have been
hinting to him at the time when she had said that. 'Anyway,
I think she lost that bracelet.'

'She *lost* it?'

'Gardening. She took it off, to…er…dig, and it must
have got all mixed up with soil and leaves…' Sarah
shrugged in a suitably vague and rueful manner. 'So, no
bracelet to pass on,' she finished mournfully.

'That's a shame.'

'Isn't it?' She suddenly frowned. 'So…we get married
and live here…'

'In this house, yes.'

'And what will you do with your apartment?'

Raoul shrugged. His apartment no longer seemed to
have any appeal. The cool, modern soullessness of the
décor, the striking artwork that had been given the nod by

him but bought as an investment, the expensive and largely unused gadgets in the kitchen, the imposing plasma screen television in the den—all of it now seemed to belong to a person with whom he could no longer identify.

'I'll keep it, I expect. I don't need to sell it or rent it, after all.'

'Keep it for what?'

'What does it matter?'

'It doesn't. I was just curious.'

They were going to be married. It wouldn't be a marriage made in heaven, and Sarah knew that her own suspicious nature would torpedo any hope of it being successful. As soon as Raoul had told her that he would keep the apartment she had foreseen an unpalatable explanation. An empty apartment would be very handy should he ever decide to stray.

She tried her utmost to kill any further development on that train of thought. 'I suppose you have some sort of sentimental attachment to it?' she prompted.

Raoul shook his head. 'Absolutely none. Yes, it was the place I bought when I'd made my first few million, but believe it or not it's been irritating me lately. I think I've become accustomed to a little more chaos.' He grinned, very relaxed now that he could see a definite way forward and liked what he saw.

Suddenly the reality of Raoul actually *living* with them made her giddy with apprehension. Would there be parameters to their marriage? It wouldn't be a *normal* one, so of course there must be, but was this something she should talk about now? Were there things she should be getting straight before she entered into this binding contract?

'Er…we should really talk about…you know…'

He paused and looked down at her. She had one small hand resting on his arm.

'What your expectations are…' Sarah said stoutly.

Raoul's brows knitted into a frown. 'You want a list?'

'Obviously not *in writing*. That would be silly. But this isn't a simple situation…'

'It's as simple or as difficult as we choose to make it, Sarah.'

'I don't think it's as easy as that, Raoul. I'm just trying to be sensible and practical. I mean, for starters, I expect you'd like to draw up some kind of pre-nup document?' That had only just occurred to her on the spur of the moment—as had the notion that laying down guidelines might confer upon her some sort of protection, at least psychologically. The mind was capable of anything, and maybe—just maybe—she could train hers to operate on a less emotional level. At least to outward appearances. Besides, he would be mightily relieved. Although, looking at his veiled expression now, it was hard to tell.

'Is that what you want?' Raoul asked tonelessly—which had the instant effect of making Sarah feel truly horrible for having raised the subject in the first place.

In turn that made her angry, because why should *he* be the only one capable of viewing this marriage with impartial detachment? What was so wrong if she tried as well? He didn't know what her driving motivation for doing so was because he wasn't in love with her, but why should that matter? He didn't have the monopoly on good sense, which was his pithy reason for their marriage in the first place!

'It might be a good idea,' she told him, in the gentle voice of someone committed to being absolutely fair. 'We don't want to get in a muddle over finances later on down the road. And also…' She paused fractionally, giving him an opportunity for encouragement which failed to materialize. 'I think we should both acknowledge that the most we can strive for is a really good, solid friendship...'

Her heart constricted as she said that, but she knew that she needed to bury all signs of her love. On the one hand, if he knew how she really felt about him the equality of their relationship would be severely compromised. On the other—and this would be almost worse—he would pity her. He might even choose to remind her that at no point, *ever*, had he led her to believe that lust should be confused with something else.

It would be a sympathetic let-down, during which he might even produce a hankie, all the better to mop up her overflowing tears. She would never live down the humiliation. In short, she would become a guilty burden which he would consider himself condemned to bear for the rest of his life. Whereas if she feigned efficiency she could at least avert that potential disaster waiting in the wings.

That thought gave her sufficient impetus to maintain her brisk, cheery façade and battle on through his continuing unreadable silence.

'If you think that we're embarking on a sexless marriage...' Raoul growled, increasingly outraged by everything she said, and critical of her infuriating practicality—although he really shouldn't have been, considering it was a character trait he firmly believed in.

Sarah held up one hand to stop him in mid-flow. This would be her trump card—if it could be called such.

'That's not what I'm saying...' Released from at least *that* particular burden—of just not knowing what to do with this overpowering attraction she felt for him—Sarah felt a whoosh of light-headed relief race through her. 'We won't take the one big thing between us away...'

The hand on his arm softened into a caress, moved to rest against his hard chest, and she stepped closer into him, arching up to him, glad that she no longer had to try and fight the sizzling attraction between them.

Raoul caught her hand and held it as he stared down at her upturned face,

'So tell me,' he drawled softly, 'why didn't you just agree to be my lover? It amounts to the same thing now, doesn't it?'

'Except,' Sarah told him with heartfelt honesty, 'maybe I just didn't like the notion of being your mistress until I went past my sell-by date. Maybe that's something I've only just realised.' She hesitated. 'Do you...do you want to reconsider your proposal?'

'Oh, no...' Raoul told her with a slow, slashing smile, 'this is exactly what I want...'

CHAPTER EIGHT

A WEEK and a half later and Raoul wasn't sure that he had got quite what he had wanted—although he was hard pressed to put a finger on the reason *why*.

Sarah's histrionics were over. She no longer vacillated between wanting him and turning him away. She had stopped agonising about the rights and wrongs of their sleeping together.

In fact, on the surface, everything appeared to be going to plan. He had moved in precisely one week previously. For one day the house had been awash with a variety of people, doing everything it took to instal the fastest possible broadband connection and set up all the various technologies so that he could function from the cosy library, which had been converted into a study complete with desk, printer, television screens to monitor the stock markets around the world and two independent telephone lines. Through the window he could look out at the perfectly landscaped garden, with its twin apple trees at the bottom. It was a far more inspiring view than the one he had had from his apartment, and he discovered that he liked it.

The wedding would be taking place in a month's time.

'I don't really care when it happens,' Sarah had told him with a casual shrug, 'but Mum's set her heart on something more than a quick register affair, and I don't like to disappoint her.'

Thinking about it, that attitude seemed to characterise the intangible change Raoul had uneasily noticed ever since she had accepted his marriage proposal.

True to her word, they were now lovers, and between the sheets everything was as it should be. Better. He touched her and she responded with fierce, uninhibited urgency. She was meltingly, erotically willing. With the lights turned off and the moonlight dipping into the room through a chink in the curtains they made love with the hunger of true sexual passion.

Just thinking about it was enough to make Raoul half close his eyes and stiffen at the remembered pleasure.

But outside the bedroom she was amicable but restrained. He came through the front door by seven every evening, which was a considerable sacrifice for him, because he was a man accustomed to working until at least eight-thirty most days. Yes, she asked him how his day had been. Yes, she would have cooked something, and sure she had a smile on her face as she watched him go outside with Oliver for a few minutes, push him on the swing, then return to play some suitably childish game until his son's bedtime beckoned. But it was almost as though she had manufactured an invisible screen around herself.

'Right. Have you got everything?' They were about to set off for Devon for their postponed visit to her parents. There was more luggage for this two-night stay than he would have taken for a three-week long-haul vacation. Favourite toys had had to be packed, including the oversized remote controlled car which had been his first and much ignored present for Oliver, but which had risen up the popularity ladder as the weeks had gone by. Drinks had had to be packed, because four-year-olds, he'd been assured, had little concept of timing when it came to long car journeys. Several CDs of stories and sing-a-long nursery rhymes had been bought in advance, and Sarah had drily informed him that he had no choice when it came to listening to them.

She had made a checklist, and now she recited things from it with a little frown.

'Is it always this much of a production when you go to visit your parents?' he asked, when they were finally tucked into his Range Rover and heading away from the house.

'This is a walk in the park,' Sarah told him, staring out of the window and watching the outskirts of London fly past. 'In the past I've had to take the train, and you can't believe what a battle *that's* been with endless luggage and a small child in tow.' She looked round to make sure that Oliver was comfortable, and not fiddling with his car seat as he was wont to do, and then stared out of the window.

Weirdly, she always felt worse when they were trapped in the confines of a car together. Something about not having any escape route handy, she supposed. With no door through which she could conveniently exit, she was forced to confront her own weakness. Her only salvation was that she was trying very hard, and hopefully succeeding, to instil boundaries without having to lay it on with a trowel.

She was friendly with him, even though under the façade her heart felt squeezed by the distance she knew she had to create. She couldn't afford to throw herself heart and soul into what they had, because she knew that if she did she would quickly start believing that their marriage was real in every sense of the word—and then what protection would she have when the time came and his attention began to stray? He didn't love her, so there would be no buffer against his boredom when their antics in the bedroom ran out of steam.

Daily she told herself that it was therefore important to get a solid friendship in place, because that would be the glue to hold things together. But at the back of her mind she toyed with the thought that friendship might prove more than just glue. Maybe, just maybe, he would become reliant on a relationship forged on the bedrock of circumstance. He had proposed marriage as a solution, and how much more he would respect her if she treated it in the same calm, sensible, practical way he did.

She was determined to starve her obsession with him and get a grip on emotions that would freewheel crazily given half a chance.

The only time she really felt liberated was when they were making love. Then, when he couldn't see the expression on her face, she was free to look at him with all the love in her heart. Once she had woken up to go to the bathroom in the early hours of the morning, and she had taken the opportunity, on returning to bed, to stare. In sleep, the harsh, proud angles of his beautiful face were softened, and what she'd seen wasn't a person who had the power to damage, but just her husband, the father of her child. She could almost have pretended that everything was perfect…

As they edged out of London, heading towards Devon along the scenic route rather than the motorway, Oliver became increasingly excited at the sight of fields and cows and sheep, and then at his favourite game of counting cars according to their colour, in which her participation was demanded.

After an hour and a half his energy was spent, and he fell asleep with the abruptness of a child, still clutching the glossy cardboard book which she had bought earlier in the week to occupy him on the journey down.

'I expect you're a bit nervous about meeting my parents…' Sarah reluctantly embarked on conversation rather than deal with the silence, even though Raoul seemed perfectly content.

Raoul gritted his teeth at the ever-bland tone of voice which she had taken to using when the two of them conversed.

'Should I be?'

'I would be if I were in your shoes.' Sarah's eyes slid over to absorb the hard, perfect lines of his profile, and then she found it was a task to drag them away.

'And that would be because…?'

'I'm not sure what they'll be expecting,' she told him honestly. 'I haven't exactly blown your trumpet in the past. In fact when I found out that I was pregnant… Well, put it this way: wherever in world you might have been, you ears would have been burning.'

'I'm sure that will be history now that I'm around and taking responsibility for the situation.'

'But they'll still remember all the things I said about you, Raoul. I could have held everything back, but finding out that I was pregnant was the last straw. I was hormonal, emotional, and a complete mess. I got a lot off my chest, and I doubt my mother, particularly, will have forgotten all of it.'

'Then I'll have to take my chances. But thank you for being concerned on my behalf. I'm touched.' His mouth curved into a sardonic smile. 'I didn't think you had it in you.'

'There's no need to be sarcastic,' Sarah said uncomfortably.

'No? Well, I hadn't intended on having this conversation, but seeing that you're up for a bit of honesty… I go to bed with a hot-blooded, giving, generous lover, and wake up every morning with a stranger. You'll have to excuse me for my assumption that you wouldn't be unduly bothered one way or another what your parents' reaction to me is.'

Hot-blooded, giving, generous... If only he knew that those words applied to her in bed and out of it, by night and by day.

'I hardly think that you can call me a *stranger*,' Sarah protested on a high, shaky laugh. 'Strangers don't... don't...'

'Make love for hours? Touch each other everywhere? Experiment in ways that would make most people blush? No need to worry, Sarah. We're not exactly shouting, and Oliver's fast asleep. I can see him in my rearview mirror.'

Sarah could feel her cheeks burning from his deliberately evocative language.

What do you want? she wanted to yell at him. Did he want her to be the adoring, subservient wife-in-waiting, so that he could lap up her adulation safe in the knowledge that she had been well and truly trapped? When he certainly didn't adore *her*?

'Well, aren't you pleased that you were right?' she said gruffly. 'I can't deny that I find you very attractive. I always have.'

'Call me crazy, but I can smell a *but* advancing on the horizon...'

'There *is* no but,' Sarah told him, thinking on her feet. 'And I really don't know what you mean when you accuse me of being a stranger. Don't we share all our dinners together now that we're living under the same roof?'

'Yes, and your increasing confidence in the kitchen continues to astound me. What I'm less enthusiastic about is the Stepford Wife-to-be routine. You say the right things, you smile when you're supposed to, and you dutifully ask me interested questions about my working day... What's happened to the outspoken, dramatic woman who existed two weeks ago?'

'Look, as you said yourself, what we're doing is the right thing and the sensible thing. I've agreed to marry you and I don't see the point in my carrying on arguing with you...'

'I'm a firm believer that sometimes it's healthy to argue.'

'I'm tired of arguing, and it doesn't get anyone anywhere. Besides, there's nothing to argue about. You haven't let us down once. I'm surprised no one's sent men in white coats to take you away because they think you've lost the plot—leaving work so early every evening and getting in so late every morning.'

'I'd call it adjusting my body clock to match the rest of the working population.'

'And how long is *that* going to last?' She heard herself snipe with dismay, but there was no reaction from him.

After a while, he said quietly, 'If I had a crystal ball, I would be able to tell you that.'

Sarah bit down on the tears she could feel welling up. There was a lot to be said for honesty, but since when was honesty *always* the best policy?

'Maybe I'm leaving work earlier than I ever have because I have something to leave for...'

Oliver. Paternal responsibility had finally succeeded in doing what no woman ever had or ever would, Sarah diplomatically shied away from dragging that thorny issue out into the open, because she knew that it would lead to one of those arguments which she was so intent on avoiding. Instead she remained tactfully silent for a couple of minutes.

'That's true,' she said noncommittally. 'I should tell

you, though, before we meet my mum and dad, that they'll probably guess the reasons behind our sudden decision to get married…'

'What have you told them?' Raoul asked sharply.

'Nothing…really.'

'And what does *nothing…really* mean, Sarah?'

'I may have mentioned that you and I are dealing with the situation like adults, and that we've both reached the conclusion that for Oliver's sake the best thing we can do is get married. I explained how important it was for you to have full rights to your son, and that you didn't care for the thought of someone else coming along and putting your nose out of joint…'

'That should fill them with undiluted joy,' Raoul said with biting sarcasm. 'Their one and only daughter, walking down the aisle to satisfy *my* selfish desire to have complete access to my son. If your mother hadn't lost that heirloom bracelet she'd been hoping to pass on to you she probably would have gone out into the garden, dug a hole and buried it just to save herself the hypocrisy of a gesture for a meaningless marriage.'

'It's not a *meaningless marriage*.'

Sarah knew she had overstepped the self-assertive line. It was one thing being friendly but distant. It was another to admit to him that she was spreading the word that their marriage was a sham. Not that she had. She hadn't had the heart to mention a word of it to her parents. As far as she knew they thought that her one true love had returned and the ring soon to be on her finger was proof enough of happy endings. They had conveniently forgotten the whole dumping saga.

Raoul didn't trust himself to speak.

An awkward silence thickened between them until

Sarah blurted out nervously, 'In fact, as marriages go, it makes more sense than most.'

More uncomfortable silence.

She subsided limply. 'I'm just saying that there's no need to pretend anything when we get to my parents.'

'I'm not following you.' Raoul's voice was curt, and for a brief moment Sarah was bitterly regretful that she had upset the apple cart—even if the apple cart *had* been a little wobbly to start with.

She was spared the need for an answer by the sound of little noises from the back seat as Oliver began to stir. He needed the toilet. Could they hurry? Their uncomfortable conversation was replaced by a hang-on-for-dear-life panic drive to find the nearest pub, so that they could avail themselves of the toilets and buy some refreshments by way of compensation.

Oliver, now fully revived after his nap, was ready to take up where he had left off—with the addition of one of the nursery rhyme tapes. He proceeded to kick his feet to the music in the back, protesting vehemently every time a move was made to replace it with something more soothing.

He was the perfect safeguard against any further foolhardy conversations, but as the fast car covered the distance, only getting trapped in traffic once along the way, Sarah replayed their conversation in her head over and over again.

She wondered whether she really *should* have warned her parents about the reality of the situation. She questioned why she had felt so invigorated when they had been arguing. She raged hopelessly against the horrible truth—which was that maintaining a friendly front was like drinking poison on a daily basis. She asked herself whether she had done the right thing in accepting his marriage proposal, and then berated herself for acknowledging that she had because she couldn't trust herself ever to be able to deal with the sight of him with another woman.

But what if he *did* stray from the straight and narrow? What if he found marriage too restrictive, even with Oliver there to keep his eyes firmly on the end purpose? She had attempted to give that very real possibility house room in her head, but however many times she tried to pretend to herself that she was civilised enough to handle it, she just couldn't bring herself to square up to the thought. Should she add a few more ground rules to something that was getting more and more unwieldy and complex by the second?

She nearly groaned aloud in frustration.

'I think I'm getting a headache,' she said tightly, running her fingers over her eyes.

Raoul flicked a glance in her direction. 'I sympathise. I'm finding that "The Wheels on the Bus" can have that effect when played at full volume repeatedly.'

Sarah relaxed enough to flash him a soft sideways smile. She was relieved that the atmosphere between them was normal once again. It was funny, but although her aim was to keep him at a distance the second she felt him really stepping away from her she panicked.

'We'll be there before the headache gets round to developing.'

Sure enough, twenty minutes later she began to recognise some of the towns they passed through. Oliver began a running commentary on various places of interest to him, including a sweet shop of the old-fashioned variety which they drove slowly past, and Sarah found herself pointing out her own landmarks—places she remembered from when she was a teenager.

Raoul listened and made appropriate noises. He was

only mildly interested in the passing scenery. Small villages in far-off rural places did very little for him. If anything they were an unwelcome reminder of how insular people could be in the country—growing up as one of the children from the foster home in a town not dissimilar to several they had already driven through had been a sure-fire case of being sentenced without benefit of a jury.

Mostly, though, Raoul was trying to remain sanguine after her revelation that she had already prejudiced her parents against him.

His temper was distinctly frayed at the seams by the time he pulled up in front of a pleasant detached house on the outskirts of a picturesque town—the sort of town that he imagined Sarah would have found as dull as dishwater the older she became.

'Don't expect anything fancy,' she warned him, as the car slowed to a halt on the gravelled drive.

'After the build-up you've given your parents, believe me—I'm not expecting anything at all.'

Sarah flinched at the icy coldness in his voice.

'I did you a favour,' she whispered defensively, because she could think of no way of extricating herself from her lie. 'It saves you having to pretend.'

'There are times,' Raoul said, before launching himself out of the car, 'when I really wonder what the hell makes you tick, Sarah.'

He moved round to the boot, extracting their various cases, and slammed it shut—hard—just as Oliver, released from the restrictions of his car seat, flew up the drive towards the middle-aged couple now standing on their doorstep to throw himself at them. Sarah was following Oliver, arms wide open to receive their hugs.

Raoul took it all in through narrowed eyes as he began walking towards the house. Her father was stocky, his hair thinning, and her mother was an older version of Sarah, with the same flyaway hair caught in a loose bun, tendrils escaping all over the place just as her daughter's did, and wearing a long flowered skirt and a short-sleeved top with a thin pink cardigan. She was as slender as her husband was rotund, and she had Sarah's smile. Ready, warm, appealing.

So, he thought grimly, these were the people she had decided to disabuse. Two loving parents who had probably spent their entire lives waiting for the day their much loved only daughter would get married, settle down...only to hear that the getting married and settling down wasn't quite the kind they had had in mind.

Making his mind up, he walked towards them. The smile on his face betrayed nothing of what was going through his head.

'So nice to meet you...' He slung his arm over Sarah's shoulder and pulled her against him, feeling the tension in her body like a tangible electric current. Very deliberately, he moved his hand to caress the back of her neck under the tumble of fair hair. 'Sarah's told me so much about you both...' He looked down at her and pressed his thumb against the side of her neck, obliging her to look up at him. Her big green eyes were wary. 'Haven't you, sweetheart...?'

What was he playing at? Whatever it was, he was managing to blow a hole in her composure.

The gestures of affection hadn't stopped at the front door.

Yes, there had been moments of reprieve during the course of the afternoon, when Oliver had demanded attention and when she'd gone into the kitchen to help prepare the dinner with her mother, but the rest of the time...

On the sofa he was there next to her, his arm along the back, his fingers idly brushing her neck, while he played the perfect son-in-law-to-be by engaging her parents in all aspects of conversation which he knew would interest them.

She realised how much she had confided in him about her background, because now every scrap of received information had come home to roost. He quizzed them about her childhood. He produced anecdotes about things he remembered having been told like a magician pulling rabbits from a hat. He recalled something she had said in passing about her father always wanting to do something with bees, and much of their time, as they sat at the dinner table, was taken up with a discussion on the pros and cons of bee-keeping, about which he seemed to be indecently well informed.

Even if she *had* told her parents the truth about their relationship they would have been hard pressed to believe her based on Raoul's performance.

He engaged them on every level, and when she showed signs of taking a back seat he made sure to drag her right back into the conversation—usually by beginning his remark pointedly with the words, 'Do you remember, darling…?'

Every reminder brought back a fuzzy familiarity that further undermined her composure. He talked at length about the compound in Africa, and revealed what she had known from that random communication she had glimpsed ages ago—that he contributed a great deal to the compound. He listed all the improvements that had been made over time, and confided that he had actually employed someone to oversee the funding.

'Those were some of the most carefree months in my

entire life,' he admitted, and she knew that he was telling the absolute truth.

The complex, three-dimensional, utterly wonderful man she had fallen deeply in love with was well and truly out of the box in which she had tried, vainly, to shove him. Holding back the effect he had on her was like trying to shore up a dam with a toothpick.

The bedroom in which they had been put—her old bedroom newly revamped, but with all the mementoes of childhood still in evidence—did nothing to repair her frayed nerves.

She was as jumpy as a cat on a hot tin roof when, at a little after ten, they were shuffled off upstairs—because surely they must be exhausted after that long drive from London?

'And don't even *think* about getting up for Oliver,' her mother carolled as Sarah was leaving the kitchen. 'Your dad and I want to spend some time with him, so you just have yourselves a well-deserved lie-in! Lots planned for the weekend!'

Sarah crept upstairs to find Raoul already showered and waiting for her on the bed, where he was sprawled, hands folded under his head, wearing nothing but for a pair of dark boxer shorts. Instantly all thought left her head. Her body reacted the way it always did: liquefying and melting, and already anticipating the feel of his fingers on it.

But her emotions were all over the place, and she informed him that she was going to take a shower.

'I'll be waiting for you when you return,' Raoul told her, following her with his eyes as she disappeared into the adjoining shower room, which was small but perfectly adequate.

She reappeared twenty minutes later. He watched her

walk towards him, wearing nothing, and swiftly whipped the duvet over him—because a man could lose his mind at the sight of that glorious body, with its full, pouting breasts and smooth lines, and his mind was precisely what he needed at this very moment.

Sarah slid under the covers and turned towards him, covering his thigh with hers and splaying her fingers across his broad chest.

The shower had helped cool her down, but there was still a desperation in her as she slid further on top of him and felt the rock-hardness of his erection press against her. With a soft moan she parted her legs and moved sinuously against the shaft, her body aching and opening up for him. As the sensitised, swollen bud of her clitoris rasped against him she had to stop herself from groaning out loud.

Raoul shuddered, fighting the irresistible impulse to spin her onto her back and sate his frustration by driving into her.

'No,' he said unevenly.

Sarah wriggled on top of him. 'You don't mean that,' she breathed, panicked by that single word.

She dipped her head, covered his mouth with hers, felt him groan as he kissed her back. Hard. He flipped her onto her back and straddled her so that he could carry on kissing her.

Sarah arched away. Her breasts ached and tingled. She wanted the wetness of his mouth on her nipples, suckling them, driving her crazy. She desperately needed to feel his mouth licking and exploring between her legs, sending her to greater and greater heights until she needed him to thrust into her. She wanted the fragile balance she had forced onto their relationship restored, because without it she was all at sea, lost and struggling to find a foothold in stormy waters.

'*No*, Sarah! God!' Raoul sprang back from her, literally leapt off the bed and walked tensely towards the window, to stare outside until his body began to damn well do as it was told. 'Cover yourself up,' he told her harshly, because the distraction of her nudity was doing his head in.

Sarah squirmed until she was sitting up and drew her knees up, pulling the covers right the way to her chin while he continued to loom over her in the semi-darkness like a vengeful god.

She felt cheap and dirty, and the ramifications of how she had tackled her own wayward emotions slammed into her with the savagery of a clenched fist.

How could she ever have thought that she could separate herself? Peel away her emotions and leave intact the deep craving of her body to be satisfied under cover of darkness? She wasn't built like that. She was engulfed with a sudden sense of shame.

'This isn't working,' he told her with harsh condemnation.

'I don't know what you're talking about.'

'You know damn well what I'm talking about, Sarah!' He raked his fingers through his hair. He wanted to punch something.

'No, I don't! I thought today went really well! I mean, they like you...'

'Against all odds?' His mouth curled cynically.

'I didn't exactly *say* all those things I told you,' Sarah confessed in a small voice. 'I didn't really tell them about the state of our relationship. Of course they know how it ended between us five years ago, but I didn't tell them that we were only together now because of Oliver. I just couldn't face telling them the truth—at least not just yet...'

'Why are you only now coming clean on that score?'

'What difference does it make whether they know or

not? It's true, isn't it? One chance meeting,' she said bitterly, 'and both our lives changed for ever. What's that they say about the butterfly effect? Half an hour later and I would have finished cleaning that part of the office. Half an hour later and you would have left without even knowing that I was only metres away from you, in another part of the building...'

'I prefer not to dwell on pointless *what if?* scenarios.'

Sarah gazed down at her interlinked fingers. Raoul's reappearance in her life might have turned her world upside down, but for Oliver it had been nothing but the best possible outcome.

Her heart was beating so furiously inside her that she could scarcely breathe.

'That bracelet...'

Sarah looked up at him quickly, so aggressively dominant in the small bedroom. 'What about it?'

'Gold rope? With some kind of inscription on the outside? Your mother was wearing it. Looks like the gardening accident wasn't quite as terminal for the piece of jewellery as you imagined.'

'I...I... Maybe I was mistaken...'

'No,' Raoul told her coldly, 'maybe *I* was mistaken. I stupidly thought that you were willing to give this marriage a try, but you're not.'

His lack of anger was terrifying.

'I *am* giving it a try...'

'Really? Because you're sleeping with me?'

Sarah felt the slow boil of anger thread its way through her panic and confusion. Suddenly he was dismissive of the fact that they were sleeping together? What a noble guy! Anyone would have thought that making love was way down on his agenda, when it was the *only* thing he had placed any value on! The only thing he had *ever* placed any value on. How dared he stand there, like a headmaster in front of a disappointing and rebellious student, and preach to her that he wasn't satisfied?

'Weren't *you* the one who made such a great big deal about our *mutual attraction*? Our *sexual chemistry*?' she flung at him. 'Didn't you tell me that we had *unfinished business* and the only way we could possibly sort that out was by *jumping into bed together*? You have a very convenient memory when it comes to things you don't want to remember, Raoul!'

'Am I to be forever punished for being honest when we first reconnected, Sarah?'

'And am *I* to be punished for being honest now?' she returned just as quickly. '*You* made it clear what this marriage was going to be all about, didn't you?'

She hated the shard of hope inside her that still wanted to give him the chance to say something—to tell her that she was wrong, that it wasn't just about the fact that they had a child together.

His silence shattered her.

'I'm playing by *your* rules, Raoul, and I'm finding that they suit me just fine! In fact, I think you were right all along! Having sex and lots of it is really working wonders at getting you out of my system!'

She sensed his stillness and wanted to snatch the words back. But they were out in the open now, and she didn't know what to do with his continuing lack of response. She tried to recapture some of her anger but it was disappearing fast, leaving in its wake regret and dismay.

'So the sex is all that matters to you, I take it?'

'Yes, of—of course it is…' she stammered, bewildered by that remark. 'Just like it is to you. And responsibility too, of course… We're doing this for Oliver, because it's always better for a child to have both parents at home. We're being sensible…practical…'

'What story are you going to spin your mother when it comes to the heirloom bracelet?'

'Wha…?'

'I one hundred percent agree with you. Heirlooms to be handed over are for brides who actually *want* to be married.'

'You're not being fair, Raoul.'

'I'm being perfectly fair. I had actually thought we had more going for us than just physical attraction, but I was wrong.' He began walking towards the door.

Sarah watched him, frantically trying to process what he had said.

His voice was flat and composed and as cold as ice. 'I've got your message loud and clear, Sarah. It's always good to have the rules laid bare…'

CHAPTER NINE

SARAH lay frozen for a few minutes. Now that she wanted to recall everything he had said, so that she could sift through his words and get them to make sense, she found that her thoughts were in a jumble. Her heart was beating so furiously that she could scarcely catch her breath, and she had broken out in a film of perspiration. Her nakedness was a cruel reminder of how she had attempted to drown her misery in making love.

She could get herself worked up at the thought of Raoul using *her*, but only now was she appreciating that she had been equally guilty of using *him*—even if she had tried to tell herself that that couldn't possibly be the case, because wasn't sex all he had wanted from her from the very start?

Where had he gone?

His self-control was such a part and parcel of his personality that to see him stripped of it had shaken her to her core.

Or had she been mistaken? Was he just angry with her?

With a little cry of horror and shaky panic, Sarah flung the covers off her and scrambled around the room to fling on a pair of jogging bottoms and an old long-sleeved jumper—a left-over reminder of her teenage years, when she had been in the school hockey team.

The house was dark and quiet as she tiptoed into the

hall. Her parents had never been ones to burn the midnight oil, and they would be fast asleep in their bedroom at the far end of the corridor. Oliver's door was ajar, and she peeped in, through habit, to see him spread flat on the bed, having kicked off his quilt, a perfect X-shape, lightly snoring.

Just in case, though, she made sure not to turn on the lights, and so had to grope her way down the stairs until her eyes adjusted to the darkness and she could move more quickly, checking first the kitchen, then the sitting room.

It wasn't a big house, so there was a limited number of rooms she could check, and her anxiety increased with each empty room. After twenty minutes, she acknowledged that Raoul just wasn't in the house.

The temperature had dropped, and she hugged herself as she quietly let herself outside.

At least his car was still there. She hurried down to the road and glanced in both directions. Then, as she headed back towards the house, a faint noise caught her ears and she stealthily made her way to the back of the house.

The garden wasn't huge, but it backed onto fields so there was an illusion of size. To one side was her mother's vegetable plot, and towards the back, through a wooden archway that had been planted with creeping wisteria, was a gazebo. Her father's potting shed was right at the very bottom of the garden. Trees and shrubbery formed a thick perimeter.

Walking tentatively through the archway, she spotted Raoul immediately. He was in the gazebo, sitting with his head in his hands. She paused, and then walked quietly towards him, feeling him stiffen as she got nearer although he didn't look up at her.

'I'm really sorry,' she said helplessly.

Just when she thought that he wasn't going to reply at all, he looked up and shrugged his broad shoulders.

'What for? You were being honest.'

'I was just trying to be mature about the whole thing...'

Raoul flung his head back and stared up, away from her, and in the fierce, proud, stubborn set of his features she could see the little boy who'd grown up in a foster home, learning young how to hide himself away and build a fortress around his emotions.

She rested her hand on his forearm and felt him flinch, but he didn't pull it away and for some reason that seemed like a good sign.

'I gave you what you wanted,' Raoul said, his eyes still averted. 'At least I gave you what I thought you wanted. Don't you like the house?'

'I love it. You know I do. I've told you so a million times.'

'I've never done that before, you know. I've never let myself be personal when it comes to choosing things for another person, but I made it personal this time.'

'I know. You wanted Oliver to have the very best.'

'I very much doubt whether Oliver cares that there's a bottle-green Aga in the kitchen or not.'

Her heart skipped a beat. 'What are you trying to say?'

'Trying? I thought it had been obvious all along.' He glanced across at her and her breath caught painfully in her throat. 'I wanted you to marry me. Maybe at the beginning I didn't think it was necessary. Maybe at the beginning I was still clinging to the notion that I was a free, independent guy who happened to have found himself with a child. It took me a while to realise that the freedom I'd spent my life acquiring wasn't the kind of freedom I wanted after all.'

'I don't want to tie you down,' Sarah said quietly. 'I did.

Once. When we were out there. I thought you were just the most wonderful thing that had ever happened to me in my entire life. I built all sorts of castles in the air, and then when you dumped me my whole world fell to pieces.'

'I did what I thought was right at the time.'

'And I understand that now.'

'Do you? Really? I look at the way you are with your family, Sarah, and I see how badly you must have been affected by our break-up. You've grown up with security and a sense of your own place in the world. I grew up without either. I never allowed myself to get too close to anyone, and even when we met again, even after I found out that I was a father, I kept holding on to that. It was different with Oliver. Oliver is my own flesh and blood. But I still kept holding on to the belief that I wasn't to let anyone else in.'

'I know. Why do you think it's been so hard for me, Raoul? You've no idea what it's been like, standing on the side, wondering if the time will ever come when I can just get inside that wall you've spent a lifetime building around yourself.' She sighed and dragged her eyes away from him. The moon was almost full and it was a cloudless night. 'Look, you're not the only one who was afraid of getting hurt.'

Raoul opened his mouth to protest that he wasn't scared of anything, and then closed it.

'I know you hate the thought of anyone being able to hurt you.'

'God, it's ridiculous how well you seem to know me.'

There was wry, accepting amusement in his voice and, heartened by that, Sarah carried on.

'I spent so many years thinking of you as the guy who broke my heart that when we met again I *still* wanted to think of you as the guy who broke my heart. Yes, there was Oliver, and there was never any question that I would tell you about him and accept the consequences, but it was so important for me to keep you at a distance. And you kept looking at me and reminding me how much I still wanted you.'

'And yet you could never come right out and say it,' Raoul inserted gruffly. 'You were driving me crazy. I wanted to sleep with you and I knew you wanted to sleep with me, and you carried on fighting it. Every time I looked at you it was as though we had never been separated by five years. I didn't even know it at the time, but I let you into my life five years ago, Sarah, and you shut the door behind you and never left. I only thought you did.' He groped for her hand and linked her fingers through his. 'Asking you to marry me was a very big deal for me, Sarah.'

'You said that we were unfinished business…'

'If that's all you were to me I would never have asked you to marry me, because it wouldn't have bothered me if eventually you found another man.'

'You were worried about losing Oliver.'

'I think I knew, deep down, that that wouldn't happen. You would have allowed me all the access I wanted—and, let's face it, it's not as though children of parents who don't live together end up forgetting who the absent parent is. No, I asked you to marry me because I wanted you in my life and I couldn't envisage life without you in it.'

'Oh, Raoul.' Tears gathered in the corners of her eyes and she smiled at him, a smile of pure joy.

'I love you, Sarah. That's why I asked you to marry me. Like a fool, I'm only now admitting it to myself. I loved you five years ago and I never stopped. I love you and want you and need you, and when you retreated into that shell of yours and only came out at night when we were making love, it was as though the bottom of my world had dropped out.'

Sarah flung her arms around him, almost sending them both toppling off the narrow seat, and buried her head in the crook of neck.

'Are you telling me that you love me too?'

She heard the broken quality of his voice and knew that underneath the self-assurance there was still uncertainty– a legacy that he hadn't yet left behind.

'Of *course* I love you, Raoul!' She kissed his cheeks, his eyes, and her hands fluttered across his harshly beautiful face until he captured them and kissed the tips of each of her fingers. 'I was so scared of getting hurt all over again,' she admitted, with a catch in her voice. 'I thought I'd be able to handle our relationship, *us*, without getting involved. I mean, I was so shocked when I saw you again. But I told myself that I'd grown up and learnt lessons from the way things had turned out between us. I told myself that I was free of whatever influence you had over me…'

She thought back to those many weeks when he had infiltrated her life and shown her flimsy notions up for the nonsense they had been from the very beginning.

She lay back against him and stared up at the bright constellations. 'When Oliver met you and the two of you didn't…um…'

'Exactly hit it off?' It seemed like a very distant memory now.

'Yes… Well, I realised that the two of you would have to learn to interact, and I knew that the only way that would happen would be if I intervened. I just didn't take into account how devastating it would be to have you back in my life, virtually full-time… We were both older…somehow it felt like I'd started seeing the real you…and I fell in love with you all over again.'

'Was that why you broke my heart by pushing me away?'

'Stop teasing. I didn't really break your heart…'

'You did. Into a thousand pieces. I came here intending to give you everything. I wasn't going to let you get away with being my woman by night and a person I barely recognised by day.'

'And you thought I'd rejected you…'

'Somehow just wanting me for my body didn't work.' He laughed with incredulity. 'I can't believe I've just said that.'

'Of course,' Sarah breathed, in a lingering, seductive voice, 'wanting you for your body isn't *such* a terrible thing…especially now that you know that I want you for so much more…'

They were married a month later, at the little village church. It was a quiet affair, with friends and family mingling easily and getting to know one another, and Sarah had never felt happier than when Raoul slipped that ring on her finger and whispered how much he loved her.

And then her parents had Oliver for ten days while they had a blissful honeymoon in Kenya. For their last three days they went back to the compound in Mozambique where they had first met, so that they could both see the changes that had taken place over the five years. And there were many changes, thanks to Raoul's generous contributions over the years, although the house with all the steps, which they had shared along with the other gap year students, was still there, and a moving reminder of where it had all begun.

Even the log was still there—the very same log she had sat on, filled with misery and despair. It had survived the punishing weather, and she wondered who else had sat on it and thought about their loved ones.

The new batch of students working there seemed so young that it made her laugh.

They finally returned to London, and the very first thing Raoul said, on walking through the front door, was that they needed a house in the country.

'I never thought I'd step outside London again,' he confessed as they lay in bed on their first night back. 'But I'm beginning to think that there's something quite appealing about all that open space…'

He gently smoothed her hair back from her face, and she smiled at him with such tenderness and love that he felt, once again, that feeling of safety and a sense of completion.

'We could go there on weekends…somewhere in Devon…it's not that far…'

'Yes,' Sarah replied seriously, 'that might not be a bad idea. I mean, it would be great to see more of Mum and Dad—especially now that you've managed to convince Dad that he should take up the bee-keeping thing, with lots of help from you—and the children would like it…'

'Already planning an extension to our family?' Raoul laughed softly, and slipped his hand underneath her lacy top.

They had made love less than an hour ago, but just the feel of her swollen nipple between his fingers was sufficient to rouse him to an instant erection. He pushed the top up, licked the valley between her breasts, which was still salty and damp with perspiration, and settled himself to suckle on the sweet pink crests.

'I thought we were talking,' Sarah laughed.

'Fire away. I'm all ears.'

'I can't talk…when…' She gave up, arching her body to greet his eager mouth as he sucked and teased her breasts, then moved lower down to torment the little bud already swollen in anticipation.

The flicking of his tongue stifled all hope of conversation, and it was a long time before she whispered drowsily, 'Not so much *planning* an extension to our family as thinking there might be one arriving in the next few months or so…'

Raoul propped himself up and looked at her with urgent interest.

'You're pregnant?'

'I was going to tell you as soon as I did a test—but, yes, I think I am. I recognise all the signs…'

And she *was* pregnant.

She had almost stopped believing in fairytales, but now she had to revise that opinion—because whoever said that fairytales *didn't* come true…?

* * * * *

THE CHANGE IN DI NAVARRA'S PLAN

LYNN RAYE HARRIS

One more time for my sweet cat, Miss Pitty Pat (MPP). This is the last book we wrote together before she succumbed to heart disease. Which, of course, means I wrote it and she lay on my feet or legs or lap, depending on her mood. I miss her like crazy.

CHAPTER ONE

"YOU, GET UP."

Holly Craig looked up at the man standing so tall and imposing before her. Her heart skipped a beat at the sheer masculine beauty of his face. He had dark hair, piercing gray eyes and a jaw that had been chiseled out of Carrara marble. His nose was elegant, tapered, and his cheekbones were so pretty that supermodels must surely swoon in envy at the sight.

"Come on, girl, I don't have all day," he said, his tones sophisticated and clipped. And Italian, she realized. He had an accent that wasn't thick. Rather, it was refined and smooth, like fine wine. Or fine perfume.

Holly clutched her case—a secondhand case that wasn't even real leather—to her chest and shifted on the couch. "I—I'm not sure you have the right—"

He snapped his fingers. "You are here to see me, yes?"

Holly swallowed. "You are Mr. Di Navarra?"

He looked irritated. "Indeed."

Holly jumped up, her heart thrumming a quick tempo. Her skin flushed with embarrassment. She should have known this man was the powerful head of Navarra Cosmetics. It wasn't as if she'd never seen a photo of the man who might just hold her entire future in his hands. Everyone knew who Drago di Navarra was.

Everyone except her, it would seem. This meeting was

so important, and already she'd got off on the wrong foot. *Easy, ma belle,* her grandmother would have said. *You can do this.*

Holly stuck her hand out. "Mr. Di Navarra, yes, I'm Holly—"

He waved a hand, cutting her off. "Who you are isn't important." His gaze narrowed, dropped down over her. She'd worn her best suit today, but it was at least five years out of season. Still, it was black and serviceable. And it was all she had. She lifted her chin, confused by the strange meeting thus far, but not yet willing to ruin it by calling him on his rudeness.

"Turn around," he ordered.

Holly's cheeks flamed. But she did it, slowly turning in a circle until she faced him again.

"Yes," he said to an assistant who hovered nearby. "I think this one will do. Let them know we're coming."

"Yes, sir," the woman said, her manner cool and efficient as she turned and strode back toward the office they'd both emerged from.

"Let's go," Drago said. Holly could only stand and watch him stride away from her, bewilderment muddling her head and gluing her feet to the floor.

He seemed to realize she wasn't with him, because he stopped and turned around. He looked impatient rather than angry, though she suspected angry was next on the agenda.

"Are you coming or not?"

Holly had a choice. She could say no, she wasn't coming. She could tell him he was rude and appalling and she'd come here for an appointment, and not to be talked down to, scrutinized and ordered around.

Or she could go, figure out what his strange manner was all about and get her chance to pitch him her ideas. The case in her hands was warm, fragrant with the samples she'd tucked inside. It reminded her of home, of her grand-mother and the many hours they'd spent together dreaming about taking their perfumes to the next level, instead of only blending them for the friends and townspeople who purchased their custom combinations.

She'd come a long way to see this man. She'd spent every bit of savings she had getting here, with only enough for her lodging and the return trip home again. If she lost this opportunity, she lost far more than money. She lost her dream. She lost Gran's dream. She'd have to go home and start over again.

Because Gran was dead and the house would soon be gone. She couldn't afford to keep it any longer. Unless she convinced Drago di Navarra that she had something worth investing in. Something worth taking a chance on.

And she would do whatever it took to get that oppor-tunity.

"Yes," she said firmly. "I'm coming."

Drago could feel her eyes upon him. It was nothing he wasn't accustomed to. Women often stared. It was not something he felt was an inconvenience. No, it was an advantage, especially for a man in the business he was in.

In the business of making people more beautiful, it did not hurt to be attractive yourself. If much of that was genetics, well, it was not his fault.

He still used Navarra products— soap, cologne, skin care, shampoo—and he would always maintain, to who-ever would listen, that they benefited him greatly.

Now he sat in the back of the limousine with his projec-tions and printouts, and studied the focus-group informa-tion for the newest line of products NC was bringing out this fall. He was pleased with what he saw. Very pleased.

He was not, it should be noted, pleased with the agency that had sent this girl over. She was the fourth model he'd seen this morning, and though they'd finally got it right, he was angry that it had taken four attempts to get the correct combination of innocence and sex appeal that he'd desired for this ad campaign.

He was selling freshness and beauty, not a prepackaged look that many of the models he'd seen recently came with. They had a hard edge about them, something that looked out from their eyes and said that, while they might appear innocent, they had actually left innocence in the rearview mirror a thousand miles ago.

This girl, however…

He looked up, met her gaze boldly, appraisingly. She dropped her eyes quickly, a pink stain spreading over her cheeks. A sharp feeling knifed into him, stunning him. He had a visceral reaction to that display of sweetness, his body hardening in a way it hadn't in quite some time. Oh, he'd had sex—plenty of it—but it had become more of a box to check off in his day rather than an escape or a way to relax.

His reaction just now interested him. His gaze slipped over her again, appraised what he saw, as he had the first time. She was dressed in a cheap suit, though it fit her well. Her shoes were tall, pink suede—and brand-new, he realized, looking at the sole of one where she'd turned her legs to the side. The price tag was still on the shoe. He tilted his head.

$49.99

Not Jimmy Choo shoes or Manolo Blahnik shoes, certainly. He didn't expect her to be wearing thousand-dollar shoes, or even the latest designer fashions, but he had rather expected she would be more…polished.

Which was odd, considering that polish was precisely what he did not want. Still, she was a model with a highly respected New York City firm. He'd have thought she might be a bit more prepared. On the other hand, perhaps she was fresh from the farm and they'd sent her over straightaway in desperation.

"How many of these jobs have you done before?" he asked.

She looked up again. Blinked. Her eyes were blue. Her hair was the most extraordinary shade of strawberry-blond, and a smattering of light freckles dotted her pale skin. He would have to tell the photographer not to erase those later. They added to her fresh look.

"Jobs?"

Drago suppressed a stab of impatience. "Modeling jobs, *cara*."

She blinked again. "Oh, I, um…"

"I'm not going to send you away if this is your first time," he snapped. "So long as the camera loves you, I couldn't care less if you've just come up from the family farm."

Her skin flushed again. This time, her chin came up. Her eyes flashed cool fire, and he found himself intrigued at the play of emotions across her face. It was almost as if she were arguing with herself.

"There's no need to be rude, you know," she snapped back. "Manners are still important, whether you've got a billion dollars or only one."

Drago had a sudden urge to laugh. It was as if a kitten had suddenly hissed and swatted him. And it had the effect of making some of his tension drain away.

"Then I apologize for being rude," he said, amused.

She folded her arms over her breasts and tried to look stern. "Well, then. Thank you."

He set the papers down on the seat beside him. "Is this your first time to New York?"

Her tongue darted out to moisten her lower lip. A slice of sensation knifed into his groin. "Yes," she said.

"And where are you from?"

"Louisiana."

He leaned forward then, suddenly quite certain he needed to make her feel comfortable if he was going to get what he wanted out of this shoot. "You'll do a fine job," he said. "Just be yourself in front of the camera. Don't try to act glamorous."

She dropped her gaze away and slid her fingers along the hem of her jacket. "Mr. Di Navarra—"

"Drago," he said.

She looked up again. Her blue eyes were worried. He had a sudden urge to kiss her, to wipe away that worried look and put a different kind of look there. He gave himself a mental shake. Highly uncharacteristic of him. Not that he didn't date the models—he did sometimes—but this one wasn't his usual type. He liked the tall, elegant ones. The ones who looked as if ice cubes wouldn't melt in their mouths.

The ones who didn't make him think of wide-eyed idealists who chased after dreams—and kept chasing them even when they led down self-destructive paths. Women like this one were so easily corruptible in the wrong hands. His protective instincts came to the fore, made him want to send her back to Louisiana before she even stepped in front of the camera.

He wanted her to go home, to stop chasing after New York dreams of fame and fortune. This world would only disappoint her. In a few months, she'd be shooting drugs, drinking alcohol and throwing up her food in order to lose that extra pound some idiotic industry type had told her made her look fat.

Before he could say anything of what he was thinking, the car came to a halt. The door swung open immediately. "Sir, thank goodness," the location manager said. "The girl isn't here and—"

"I have her," Drago said. The other man's head swung

around until his gaze landed on the girl—Holly, was it? Now he wished he'd paid more attention when he'd first seen her outside his office.

"Excellent." The man wiggled his fingers at her. "Come along, then. Let's get you into makeup."

She looked terrified. Drago smiled encouragingly. "Go, Holly," he said, trying the name he was fairly certain was correct. He didn't miss the slight widening of her eyes, and knew he'd got it right. Clearly, she hadn't expected him to remember. "I will see you again when this is over."

She looked almost relieved as her eyes darted between him and the location manager. "Y-you will?"

She seemed very alone in that moment. Something inside him rose to the fore, made him ask a question he knew he shouldn't. "Are you busy for dinner?"

She shook her head.

Drago smiled. He shouldn't do this, he knew it, and yet he was going to anyway. "Then consider yourself busy now."

Holly had never been to a fancy restaurant in her life, but she was in one now—in a private room, no less—sitting across from a man who might just be the most handsome man she'd ever seen in her life. The longer she spent in Drago di Navarra's company, the more fascinated she was.

Oh, he hadn't started out well, that was for sure—but he'd improved tremendously upon further acquaintance. He'd actually turned out to be…nice.

There was only one problem. Holly frowned as she listened to him talk about the photo shoot earlier. She wasn't a model, but she'd stood there in Central Park and let people fuss over her, dress her in a flowing purple gown, paint her with makeup, tease her hair—and then she'd stepped in front of the camera and froze, wondering how she'd let this thing go so far.

She'd only wanted a chance to tell Drago di Navarra about her perfumes, but she hadn't known where they were going or what he expected until it was too late. She'd choked when she should have explained. But she'd been worried that if she explained who she was and what she wanted, he would be angry with her.

And that wasn't going to work, was it?

Still, as she'd stood there, frozen, she'd known it was over. Her dream was dead, because she was going to have to explain to all these people watching her that she truly had no idea what she was doing.

But then Drago had walked onto the shoot and smiled at her. She'd smiled back, and suddenly the photographer was happy. She was certain she'd still been awkward and out of place, but everyone had seemed delighted with her. They'd changed her clothes, her hair, her makeup several times. And she'd stood in front of that camera, thinking of her perfumes and wondering how on earth she was going to explain herself to Drago, until someone finally told her they were done.

Then Drago had whisked her off for dinner and she'd clammed up like a frightened schoolgirl. She was still wearing the last dress they'd put on her, a pretty, silky sheath in eggplant and a pair of gold Christian Louboutin pumps. This entire experience was a fantasy come to life in many ways. She was in New York City, being wined and dined by one of the most eligible bachelors in the world, and she wanted to remember every moment of it.

And yet everything about this day was wrong, because she'd come here to pitch her perfume, not model for Navarra Cosmetics. How could she tell him? How could she find the perfect moment to say "Oh, Drago, thank you for the dinner, but what I really want to talk to you about is my perfume"?

Still, she had to. And soon. But every time she tried to

open her mouth and tell him, something stopped her. There were interruptions, distractions. When he reached across the table and took her hand in his, every last thought in her head flew out the window.

"You were fabulous today, Holly," he said. And then he lifted her hand to his lips and pressed them against the back of her hand. A sizzle of electricity shot through her, gathered in her feminine core and made her ache in ways she'd never quite experienced before.

She'd had a boyfriend back home. She'd been kissed. They'd even gone further than that—but she'd never felt the moment was right to go all the way.

And then he'd broken up with her. Taken up with that catty Lisa Tate instead. It still stung.

You're too selfish, Holly, he'd said. *Too focused on your damn perfume.*

Yes, she was focused. Holly dragged herself back to the present, tried so hard to ignore the skittering of her pulse and the throbbing deep in her core. She knew what this was. She might not have had sex before, but she wasn't stupid. She'd experienced desire with Colin, but she'd just never got to the point where she'd tumbled over the edge into hedonism.

She could imagine it with this man. Her heart skipped as she met Drago di Navarra's smoky gray eyes. *Tell him, Holly. Tell him now....*

"Thank you," she said, dropping her gaze from the intensity of his as her pulse shot forward again.

"You're quite a natural. I predict you will go far in this business if you don't allow yourself to be corrupted by it."

She opened her mouth to speak, but his cell phone rang. He glanced down at the display, and then said something in Italian that could have been a curse.

"You must excuse me," he said, picking up the phone. "This is important."

"Of course," she replied, but he'd already answered the call. She sat with her hands in her lap and waited for him to finish.

Holly gazed at the silk wallpaper and the gilt fixtures, and felt as if she'd landed on another planet. What was she doing here? How had she ended up in the company of a billionaire, having dinner with him as if it were a daily occurrence?

Everything about her trip to New York thus far was so different from her usual experience that she could hardly get her bearings.

Why couldn't she seem to say what she needed to say? She'd feel better if she had her samples. With those, she could find her way through this strange landscape. But her samples were in her case, which was stowed in his car. That had given her pause, but he'd convinced her that her belongings would be fine while they ate dinner.

If only she had her case, she could open it up and pull out her samples. She could explain her concepts, sell him on the beauty of Colette, the last perfume she and her grandmother had worked on together. It was the best one, though her ideas for others were infinite. She got a tingle of excitement just thinking about the blend of smooth essences, water and alcohol that produced the final product.

Drago finished his call and apologized for the interruption. "Forgive me, *bella mia*," he said. "But the beauty industry never sleeps."

"It's fine," she told him, smiling. Her heart was beating fast again, but she'd finally settled on a plan of action. Once she was reunited with her case, she would explain to this man why she was really here. She was certain he couldn't say no once she'd given him a whiff of Colette.

Their dinner came then, and Holly found herself relaxing in Drago's company. He was completely charming. He was attentive, sending most of his calls to voice mail, and interested in what she had to say.

She told him about Louisiana, about her grandmother— without mentioning perfume, since that had to wait for her samples—and about the trip to New York on the bus.

He blinked. "You came all this way on a bus?"

Holly dropped her gaze to her plate as heat seared her cheeks. "I couldn't afford to fly," she said. But she had spent nearly everything she had scraping together the money for this brief trip. Just to talk to this man, for pity's sake.

Which she was doing, but not in the way she needed to. Not yet. She took a sip of her white wine and let it sit on her tongue for a moment while she sorted the flavors—the base notes were of wood and smoke while the top notes were floral. Delicious. Her nose was far better than her taste buds, but she could still sort flavors fairly well by taste.

"You really are fresh off the family farm," he said.

But it wasn't an insult, not this time, and she didn't take it as such. He seemed rather...wondering, truthfully. "I suppose I am," she replied.

"With big New York dreams." His tone was a bit less friendly this time, but she didn't let it bother her. Or maybe it was the wine that didn't let it bother her.

She shrugged. "Doesn't everyone have dreams?"

His gaze slipped over her face, and she felt heat curling in her belly, her toes. Oh, how she never wanted this night to end. She wanted to drink champagne under the stars, and she wanted to dance in his arms until dawn.

His hand settled over hers, and a shiver prickled down her spine. A delicious shiver. Her entire body seemed to cant toward him, like a flower turning to the sun. His fingers skimmed along her bare arm. Fire danced in their wake, and Holly wasn't certain she could pull in her next breath.

"I have a dream," he said softly, his body so close to hers now, his beautiful mouth within reach if only she leaned a bit farther forward. His fingers slid along her cheek, into her hair, and she felt as if she were melting. She ached and wanted and didn't care what tomorrow brought so long as this man kissed her now. Tonight.

His lips hovered over hers and her eyes slid closed. Her heart was beating so hard he must surely see the pulse in her throat. But she didn't care. She was too caught up in the beauty, the wonder, the perfection of this night. It was like a fairy tale, and she was the princess who'd finally been found by the prince.

His laugh was soft and deep. It vibrated through her, made her shudder with longing.

And then his mouth claimed hers in a tender kiss that stole her breath away. It was so sweet, so perfect—

But she wanted more. She leaned closer, and he laughed again, in his throat this time, before he parted her lips and thrust his tongue into her mouth. Holly couldn't stop the moan that vibrated in her throat.

The kiss suddenly changed, turned more demanding then as his mouth took hers in a hot, possessive kiss unlike anything she'd ever experienced before. Their tongues met, tangled, dueled. She could feel the strength of that kiss in her nipples, between her legs. Her sex throbbed and her panties grew damp.

She wanted to be closer to him. Needed to be closer. She wrapped her arms around his neck, clinging to him, losing herself in this kiss, this moment.

Drago finally dragged himself up, away from her, breaking the kiss. Her mouth tingled with the memory of his. Her eyes settled on his mouth, and a thrill went through her.

"My dream," he said, his voice a sensual purr in her ear, "is that you will accompany me back to my apartment."

Holly could only stare at him as he stood and held his hand out. Everything in her wanted to be with him. She wasn't ready for this night to end, no matter that a tiny corner of her soul urged her to be cautious. She wanted more of this excitement, this exhilaration.

More of Drago.

Holly put her hand in his, and her skin sizzled at the contact. This was right, she knew it deep down. So very right.

"Yes," she said shyly. "I want that, too."

CHAPTER TWO

One year later...

"I DON'T KNOW why you don't march right into his office and demand he help you out."

Holly looked up at her best friend and roommate. Gabriella was holding little Nicholas, rocking him back and forth. He was, thankfully, asleep for a change. Poor Gabi was such a saint, considering that Nicky hadn't slept a whole night through since Holly had brought him home from the hospital.

Holly picked up a tester and sniffed it. Attar of roses. It filled her mind with a profusion of fat red blooms like the ones that her gran had grown. Bushes that now belonged to someone else, since she'd lost the property months ago. Her mouth twisted as bitterness flooded her throat with scalding acid.

She set the tester down and pushed back from the table where she mixed her fragrances. "I can't go to him, Gabi. He made it very clear that he wanted nothing more to do with me."

Holly still felt the sting of Drago di Navarra's rejection as if it was yesterday. She also—damn him—felt the utter perfection of his lovemaking as if it had happened only hours ago. Why did her body still insist on a physical response at the thought of that single night they'd shared?

At least her brain was on the right track. The only response her brain had was rage. No, that wasn't quite true. Her mental response was like a fine perfume. The top note was rage. The middle, or heart note, was self-loathing. And the base note, the one that had never yet evaporated, was shame.

How had she let herself be so damn naive and needy? How had she fallen into Drago's arms as if it were the easiest thing in the world when it was nothing like her to do so? Holly pressed her teeth together. She would never be that foolish again. She'd learned her lesson, thanks to Drago, and she would never forget it.

She'd been so easily led, so gullible and trusting. She hated thinking about it, and yet she couldn't quite stop. And maybe that was a good thing, because it meant she would never be that foolish again. The world was a cold, hard, mean place—and she was a survivor. Drago had taught her that.

He'd taught her to be suspicious and careful, to question people's motives—especially men's. He'd made her into this cold, guarded creature, and she hated him for it.

But as she looked at her son in her friend's arms, she was overcome with a sudden rush of love. Nicky was perfect. He made her world full and bright and wonderful. Every single inch of him was amazing, regardless that his father was an arrogant, evil, heartless bastard. Drago might have been the worst thing to ever happen to her, but Nicky was the best.

Irony at its most potent.

"But if he knew about Nicky," Gabi started.

"No." Holly knew her voice was hard. Thinking about Drago did that to her. But she couldn't take it out on Gabi. She tried again, sighing softly, spreading her hands wide in supplication. "I tried to tell him. His secretary said he did not want to speak to me. Ever. I wrote a letter, but I never got a reply."

Gabi looked militant. "These are the modern ages, honey bun," she said. "Put it on Facebook. Tweet the crap out of it. He'll see it and come."

Holly shuddered. As if she would expose herself that way. "He won't. Not only that, but do you want me to die of shame?" She shook her head emphatically. "No way. He had his chance."

Gabi gazed down at the cherubic face of Holly's son. "I know. But this little guy ought to have the best that money can buy."

Holly felt the truth of that statement like a barb. She couldn't help but look around their tiny apartment. Tears pricked her eyes. Since returning home to New Hope, she'd lost Gran's home, failed in her goal to become a respected perfumer and had to move sixty miles away to New Orleans so she could support herself. She'd taken a job as a cocktail waitress in a casino. It wasn't ideal, but the tips were good.

Gabi had moved last year, before Gran had died, and when Holly found out she was pregnant, Gabi had encouraged Holly to come join her.

Holly had gratefully done so.

There was no way she could stay in New Hope. Her grandmother had been a well-respected member of the community. And though Gran would have stood beside her if she'd still been alive, she wasn't. And Holly wouldn't shame her memory by causing the tongues of New Hope's citizenry to wag.

In New Hope, everyone knew everyone. And they didn't hesitate to talk about anyone so silly as to fall from grace in such a spectacular manner. Besides, no way was she subjecting Nicky to the town's censure when there was absolutely no reason for it. This was the twenty-first century, but there were those in her hometown who acted as if a single mother was a disgrace.

"I'm doing the best I can," Holly said.

Gabi's big blue eyes widened. "Oh, honey, of course you are. I'm sorry for being such an insensitive bitch." She kissed Nicky's tiny forehead. "I just forgot myself in my fury for this precious little thing. What a stupid father he has. Hopefully, when he grows up one day to be president of the United States, he won't be hampered by that side of the family tree."

Holly laughed. Leave it to Gabi to find just the thing to make her giggle when she was so angry. She went over and squeezed her friend's arm. "You're the best, Gabi. I'm not mad at you, believe me. It'll all be fine. I'm going to make a fragrance that knocks *someone's* socks off, and then I'm going to get noticed. Drago di Navarra isn't the only cosmetic king in the world, no matter what he might think."

"He messed up when he sent you home without sampling your fragrance."

The heat of shame bloomed inside her chest again. Yes, he'd sent her home without even sampling the first fragrance. After their gorgeous night together, he'd made her breakfast and served it to her in bed. She'd felt so happy, so perfectly wonderful. They'd talked and eaten and then he'd had her case delivered to her when she'd remembered to ask for it. That was when he'd noticed the scent.

"What is this, *cara*?" he'd asked, his beautiful brows drawn down in confusion as he'd studied the case in his hands.

"Those are my samples," she'd said, her heart beginning to trip in excitement.

"Samples?"

"Yes, my fragrances. I make perfume."

She'd missed the dangerous gleam in his eye as he'd set the case down and opened it. He'd drawn out a bottle of Colette and held it up, his gray eyes narrowed as he'd studied the golden fragrance.

"Explain," he'd said, his voice tight.

She'd been somewhat confused, but she had done so. Because they'd spent a beautiful night together and she knew he wasn't really an ogre. He was a passionate, sensual, good man who felt things deeply and who didn't open up easily.

Holly resisted the urge to clutch her hand over her heart, to try to contain the sharp slice of pain she still felt every time she thought of what had happened next. Of how stupid she'd been not to see it coming. She could still see his handsome face drawn up in rage, his eyes flashing hot as his jaw worked. She'd been alarmed and confused all at once.

Then he'd dropped the bottle back into the case with a clink and shoved it toward her.

"Get out," he'd said, his voice low and hard and utterly frightening.

"But, Drago—"

"Get the hell out of my home and don't come back." And then, before she could say another word, he'd stalked from the room, doors slamming behind him until she knew he was gone. A few minutes later, a uniformed maid had come in, her brow pleated in mute apology. She'd had Holly's suit—the suit she'd worn to see Drago in the first place—on a hanger, which she'd hung on a nearby hook.

It had seemed even shabbier and sadder than it had the day before.

"When you are ready, miss, Barnes will take you back to your lodgings."

Holly closed her eyes as she remembered that moment of utter shame. That moment when she'd realized he wasn't coming back, and that she'd failed spectacularly in her task to convince him of her worth as a perfumer.

Because she'd let herself get distracted. Because she'd been a mouse and a pushover and a foolish, foolish idiot.

She'd let Drago di Navarra make love to her, the first man ever to do so, and she'd gotten caught up in the fantasy of it. She'd believed that their chemistry was special, that the things she'd felt with him were unique, and that he'd felt them, too.

Fool.

But he'd kicked her out of his house as though she'd been a common prostitute.

And hadn't you?

A little voice always asked her that question. She wasn't blameless, after all. She'd spent close to twenty-four hours pretending to be something she wasn't in the single hope of convincing the high and mighty CEO of Navarra Cosmetics that she had what it took to design a signature perfume for his company.

She'd had opportunity enough to tell him why she was really there, and she'd kept silent each and every time. She'd treated it all like an adventure. The country mouse goes to the city and gets caught up in a comedy of errors. Except, she wasn't a mouse and she had a voice.

Worse, she'd complicated everything when she'd fallen for his seduction. She knew very well how it must have looked to him, a powerful man who held the key to her dream in his hand.

He'd thought her the worst kind of liar and gold digger—and the evidence had been stacked against her.

She gazed at her son and her heart felt so full with all the love swelling inside it. Yes, she should have told Drago who she was and what she wanted. But if she'd opened her mouth sooner, she wouldn't have Nicky. What a thought that was. Life might have been easier, but it certainly wouldn't have been sweeter.

Holly's eyes prickled with tears. Gran would have told

her that the past was just that and it did no good to dwell on it, because you couldn't change it without a time machine. Holly knuckled her tears away with a little laugh—but then her gaze caught on the digital display on the microwave.

"I have to get to work," she said to Gabi. "Will you be all right until Mrs. Turner comes to collect him?"

Gabi looked up from where she was still cradling Nicky. "It's a couple of hours before my shift yet. Don't worry."

Holly always worried, but she didn't say that to Gabi. She worried about providing for her baby, worried that he was only three months old and she had to work so much. She worried that she'd been unable to breast-feed him—some women couldn't, the nurse had told her after the zillionth failed attempt—and he had to drink formula, and she worried that he needed so many things and she could barely provide any of them.

Holly kissed her son's sweet soft skin before changing into her uniform of white shirt, bow tie and tight black skirt. Then she stuffed her heels into her duffel and slipped on her tennis shoes. She made it to the bus stop in record time. With twenty minutes to spare, she got to the casino, put on her heels and touched up her makeup before stashing her things and heading to the floor for her shift.

In all her wildest imaginings, she'd never pictured herself serving drinks in a casino. But here she was, arranging her tray with cocktail napkins, pen and pad, stirrers, and then gliding through the crowd of people hovering around tables and machines, asking for drink orders—and enduring a few pats to the bottom in the process.

Holly gritted her teeth, hating that part of the job but unwilling to react, because she needed the money too badly. The rent was due next week, and it was always a struggle to make up her portion along with buying diapers and formula and groceries.

Holly pushed a hand through her hair, anchoring it behind her ears, and approached the group of men hovering around one of the baccarat tables. They were rapt on the game, and most especially on a man who sat at one end of the table, a dark-haired beauty hanging over his shoulder and whispering something in his ear. His face was remarkable, beautiful and perfectly formed—and all too familiar.

For a moment, Holly was stunned into immobility. What were the chances Drago di Navarra would walk into this casino and sit at a table in her section? She'd have guessed they were something like a million to one—but here he was in all his arrogant, rotten glory.

Just her miserable luck. She glanced behind her, looking for Phyllis, hoping to ask the other waitress to take this table. Holly's belly churned and panic rose in her throat at the thought of waiting on Drago and his mistress.

But Phyllis was nowhere to be seen, and Holly had no choice. The moment she accepted that, another feeling began to boil inside her: anger.

She suddenly wanted to march over to Drago's side and slap his handsome face. She'd endured a twenty-three-hour labor, with Gabi as the only friend by her side. Other women had happy husbands in the delivery room, and masses of family in the waiting room. But not her. She'd been alone, with only Gabi holding her hand and coaching her through.

By the time Nicky had been born and someone handed him to her, she'd felt as if the little crying bundle was an alien life-form. But she'd fallen into deep love in the next moment. She had seen Drago in her son's face, and she'd felt a keen despair that he'd tossed her out the way he had. That he'd refused to take her calls. He was missing out on something amazing and perfect, and he would never know it.

Now, seeing him in this casino, sitting there so arrogant and sure with a woman hanging on him, all Holly felt was righteous anger. Her heart throbbed in her chest. Her blood beat in her brain. She knew she should turn around and walk away, find Phyllis no matter how long these people had to wait for drinks, but she couldn't seem to do it. Instead, she moved around the table until she was standing beside the man who sat at a right angle to Drago.

"Something from the bar, sir?" she asked when the play had finished. She pitched her voice louder than she normally would and looked over at Drago. The woman with him sensed a disturbance in the perfumed air around her—much too heavy a scent, Holly thought derisively, like something one would use in a brothel to cover the smells of sex and sweat—and brought her head up to meet Holly's stare.

Sweat and sex. Holly swallowed as a pinprick of hot jealousy speared into her at the thought of this woman and Drago tangling together in a bed.

Holly sniffed. No, not jealousy. As if she cared. *Honestly.*

She was irritated, that was what. Irritated by the haughty look of this woman, and the outrageous presence of the man sitting at the table, oblivious to the currents whipping in the air around him.

The woman's dark eyes raked over her. And then she did the one thing Holly had both hoped and feared she would do. She said something to Drago. He looked up, his gaze colliding with Holly's. Her heart dived into her toes at the intensity of that gray stare. A hot well of hate bubbled inside her soul. It took everything she had not to throw her tray at him and curse him for the arrogant bastard he was.

"Dry martini," the man beside her said, and Holly dragged her attention back to him.

"Yes, sir," she said, writing the drink on her pad.

When she looked up again, Drago was still looking at

her, his brows drawn together as if he were trying to place her. He didn't know her? He couldn't remember?

That was not at all the reaction she'd expected, and it pierced her to the core. She'd had his baby, and he couldn't even remember her face....

That, Holly decided, stiffening her spine, was the last straw. She turned and marched away from the table, perilously close to hyperventilating because she was so angry—and because the adrenaline rush of fear was still swirling inside her. She went over to the bar and placed her orders, telling herself to calm down and breathe.

So he didn't recognize her. So what? Had she really thought he would?

Yes.

She shook her head angrily. He was a rich, arrogant, low-down, lying son of a bitch anyway. He'd wined her and dined her and seduced her. Yes, she'd fallen for it. She wasn't blameless.

But he'd promised to take care of the birth control, and she'd trusted him to do it right. But he must have done something wrong, because she'd gotten pregnant. And he hadn't cared enough about the possibility to take her calls.

Rotten, selfish, self-serving *bastard!*

Holly grabbed her tray once the drinks were ready. She would march back over there and deliver her drinks as usual. She would *not* pour them in Drago's lap, no matter how much she wanted to.

"Thanks, Jerry," she said to the bartender. She turned to go—and nearly collided with the slickly expensive fabric of Drago di Navarra's tailored suit.

Drago's nostrils flared as he looked at the woman before him. The color in her cheeks was high as she righted her tray before spilling the contents down the front of his

Savile Row suit. Her eyes snapped fire at him and her mouth twisted in a frown.

"If you will excuse me, sir, I have drinks to deliver."

Her voice was harder than he remembered it. Her face and body were plumper, but in a good way. She'd needed to round out her curves, though he'd thought she was perfectly well formed at the time. This extra weight, however, made her into a sultry, beautiful woman rather than a naive girl.

A girl who'd tried to trick him. He hadn't forgotten that part. His jaw hardened as he remembered the way she'd so blissfully confessed her deception to him. She'd come to New York armed with perfume samples that she hoped to sell to his company, and she'd cost him valuable time and money with her pretense. It wasn't the first time a woman had tried to use him for her own ends, but it had been a pretty spectacular failure on his part. He'd had to scrap every picture from the photo shoot and start again with a new model, which had been a shame when he'd seen the photos and realized how perfect she'd been in the role.

He'd wondered in the weeks after she'd gone if he'd overreacted. But she'd scraped a raw nerve inside him, a nerve that had never healed, and throwing her out had been the right thing to do. How dare she remind him of the things he most wanted to forget?

Still, it had taken him weeks to find the right model. Even then, he hadn't actually been the one to do it. He'd been so discouraged that he'd delegated the task to his marketing director. It wasn't like him to let anything derail him for long, but every time he'd tried to find someone, he kept thinking about this woman and how she'd nearly made a fool of him.

How she'd taken him back to a dark, lonely place in his life, for the barest of moments, and made him remember what it was like to be a pawn in another's game. He shook those feelings off and studied her.

The model they'd hired to replace her was beautiful, and the fragrance was selling well, but he still wasn't satisfied. He should be, but he wasn't.

There was something about this woman. Something he hadn't quite forgotten over the past year. Even now, his body responded with a mild current of heat that he did not feel when Bridgett, whom he'd left fuming at the baccarat table, draped herself over him.

"The perfume business did not work out for you, I take it?" he asked mildly, his veins humming with predatory excitement. She was still beautiful, still the perfect woman for his ad campaign. It irritated him immensely.

And intrigued him, as well.

Her pretty blue eyes were hard beneath the dark eye makeup and black liner, but they widened when he spoke. She narrowed them again. "Not yet," she said coolly. "I'm surprised you remembered."

"I never forget a face." He let his gaze fall to her lush breasts, straining beneath the fabric of the tight white shirt the casino made her wear. "Or a body."

Her chin lifted imperiously. He would have laughed had he not sensed the loathing behind that gaze. Her plan hadn't worked and now she hated him. How droll.

"Well, isn't that fortunate for you?" she said, her Southern accent drawing out the word *you*. "If you will excuse me, sir, I have work to do."

"Still angry with me, *cara*? How odd."

She blinked. "Odd? You seduced me," she said, lowering her voice to a hiss. "And then you threw me out."

Drago lifted an eyebrow. She was a daring little thing. "You cost me a lot of money with your deception, *bella mia*. I also had to throw out a day's worth of photos and start over. Far more regrettable than tossing you out the door, I must admit."

The corners of her mouth looked pinched. But then she snorted. "I'm waiting tables in a casino and you talk to me about money? Please."

"Money is still money," he said. "And I don't like to lose it."

She was trembling, but he knew it wasn't fear that caused it. "Let me tell you something, Mr. Di Navarra," she began in a diamond-edged voice. "I made a mistake, but it cost me far more than it cost you. When you spend every last penny you have to get somewhere, because you've staked your entire future on one meeting with someone important, and then you fail in your goal and lose your home, and then have to provide for your—"

She stopped, closed her eyes and swallowed. When she opened them again, they were hot and glittering. "When you fail so spectacularly that you've lost everything and then find yourself at rock bottom, working in a casino to make ends meet, then you can be indignant, okay? Until then, spare me your wounded act."

She brushed past him, her tray balanced on one hand as she navigated the crowd to deliver her drinks. Drago watched her go, his blood sizzling. She was hot and beautiful and defiant, and she intrigued him more than he cared to admit.

In fact, she excited him in a way that Bridgett, and any of the other women he'd dated recently, did not. And, damn her, she was still perfect for the ad campaign. She wasn't quite as fresh-faced as she'd been a year ago, but she now had something more. Some quality he couldn't quite place his finger on but that he wanted nevertheless.

And he always got what he wanted, no matter the cost. He stood there with eyes narrowed, watching her deliver drinks with a false smile pasted on her face. There was something appealing about Holly Craig, something exciting.

He intended to find out what it was. And then he intended to harness it for his own purposes.

CHAPTER THREE

HOLLY'S SHIFT ENDED at one in the morning. She changed her shoes and grabbed her duffel before heading out to catch the streetcar. Once she'd ridden the streetcar as far as she could go, she would catch the bus the rest of the way home. It was a long, tiring ride, but she had no choice. It was what she could afford.

She exited the casino and started down the street. A car passed her, and then another pulled alongside. Her heart picked up, but she refused to look. The streetcar wasn't far and she didn't want to cause trouble for herself by glaring at a jerk in a sedan. It wasn't the first time some guy thought he could pick her up, and it probably wouldn't be the last.

"Would you like a ride?"

Holly's heart lurched. She stopped and turned to stare at the occupant of the gleaming limousine. He sat in the back, the window down, an arm resting casually on the sill.

"No," she said, starting to walk again. Her blood simmered. So many things she'd wanted to say to this arrogant bastard earlier, but she'd held her tongue.

Which was necessary, she realized. It would do no good to antagonize Drago di Navarra. Not only that, but there was also a little prickle of dread growing in her belly at the thought of him learning about Nicky. No doubt he would think she'd done that on purpose, too.

Which was ridiculous, considering he'd been the one to assure her that birth control was taken care of.

"It's late and you must be tired," he said, his voice so smooth and cultured. Oh, how she hated those dulcet Italian tones!

"I am tired," she told him without looking at him. The limo kept pace with her as she walked, and it irritated her to think of him sitting there so comfortably while she trod on aching feet across the pavement. "But I'm tired every night and I manage. So thanks anyway."

Drago laughed softly. "So spirited, Holly. Nothing at all like the girl who came to New York with starry-eyed dreams of success."

A bubble of helpless anger popped low in her belly. She stopped and spun around, marching over to the car. It was completely unlike her, but she couldn't seem to stop herself. The urge to confront him was unbearable. The limo halted.

"I might have been naive then, but I'm not now. I know the world is a cruel place and that some people who have absolutely everything they could ever want are even crueler than that." She tossed a stray lock of hair over her shoulder with trembling fingers. "So if I'm *spirited*, as you say, I had to learn to be that way. It's a dog-eat-dog world, and I don't want to be eaten."

Spirited? She hardly thought of herself that way at all. No, more like she was a survivor because she had to be. Because someone else depended on her. Someone tiny and helpless.

Drago opened the car door and stepped out, and Holly took a step back. He was so tall, so broad, so perfect.

No, not perfect. A jerk!

"Get in the car, Holly," he said, his voice deep and commanding. "Don't be so stubborn."

Holly folded her arms beneath her breasts and cocked a

hip. "I don't have to do what you order me to do, Drago," she said, using his name on purpose. Reminding him they'd once been intimate and that she wasn't an employee—or, heaven forbid, a girlfriend—to be ordered around. It felt bold and wicked and brave, and that was precisely what she needed to be in order to face him right now. "Besides, won't your lady friend be angry if you drag me along for the ride?"

His nostrils flared in irritation. One thing she remembered about Drago di Navarra was that he was not accustomed to anything less than blind obedience. It gave her a sense of supreme satisfaction to thwart that expectation.

"Bridgett is no longer an issue," he said haughtily, and Holly laughed. He looked surprised.

"Poor Bridgett, tossed out on her gorgeous derriere without a clue as to what she did wrong."

Drago left the door open and came over to her. He was so tall she had to tilt her head back to look up at him. Her first instinct was to flee, but she refused to give in to it. Not happening. She'd been through too much to run away at the first sign of trouble. She told herself that she was far stronger than she'd been a year ago. She had to be.

She *was*.

"Get in the car, Holly, or I'll pick you up and toss you in it," he growled. It surprised her to realize that she could smell his anger. It was sharp and hot, with the distinct smell of a lit match.

"I'd like to see you try," she threw at him, heedless of the sizzle in his glare. "This is America, buddy, and you can't just kidnap people off the street."

Holly didn't quite know what happened next, but suddenly she was in the air, slung over his shoulder before she could do a thing to stop him.

"Put me down!" she yelled, beating her fists against his back as he carried her over to the car. The next instant, she was tilting downward again, and she clung to him as if he was going to drop her. But he tossed her into the car instead, tossed her bag in after her, and then he was inside and the door slammed shut.

Holly flung herself at the opposite door, but it was locked tight. The limo began to speed down Canal Street. Holly turned and slammed her back against the seat, glaring at the arrogant Italian billionaire sitting at the opposite end. He looked smug. And he didn't have a hair out of place, while she had to scrape a tangle of hair from her face and shove it back over her ears.

"How dare you?" she seethed. Her heart pounded and adrenaline shoved itself into her limbs, her nerves, until she felt as if she were wound so tight she would split at the seams. If his anger was a lit match, hers was a raging fire. "If anyone saw that, you're in big trouble."

"I doubt it," he said. He leaned forward then, gray eyes glittering in the darkened car. "Now, tell me where you live, Holly Craig, and my driver will take you home. Much easier, *no*?"

Holly glared.

"Come, Holly. It's late and you look tired."

She wanted to refuse—but then she rattled off her address. What choice did she have? It *was* late, she *was* tired, and she needed to get Nicky from Mrs. Turner. If she had to let this man take her there, so be it. At least she would arrive far earlier than if she took the bus. And that would make Mrs. Turner happy, no doubt.

"Do you have a guilty conscience?" she asked when he'd given the driver the address.

He laughed. "Hardly."

That stung, but she told herself she should hardly be surprised. He'd thrown her out without a shred of remorse, and then refused all attempts to contact him. Heartless man.

"Then why the sudden chivalrous offer of a ride home?"

His gaze slid over her, and her skin prickled with telltale heat. She gritted her teeth, determined not to feel even a sliver of attraction for this man. Before she'd met Drago di Navarra, she'd thought she was a sensible woman in control of her own emotions. He'd rather exploded that notion in her face.

And continued to explode it as her body reacted to his presence without regard to her feelings for him. Feelings of loathing, she reminded herself. Feelings of sheer dislike.

Her body didn't care.

"Because I need you, *cara mia*."

She swallowed the sudden lump in her throat. He'd said something similar to her that night in his apartment. And she, like an idiot, had believed him. Worse, she'd wanted it to be true. Well, she wasn't that naive anymore. Italian billionaires did not fall in love with simple, unsophisticated virgins in the space of an evening.

They didn't fall in love at all.

"Sorry, but the answer is no."

His long elegant fingers were steepled together in his lap. "You have not yet heard the proposition."

"I'm still sure the answer is no," she said. "I've been propositioned by you before, and I know how that works out for me."

He shook his head as if he were disappointed in her. "I liked you better in New York."

Her skin stung with heat. "Of course you did. I was a mouse who did whatever you told me to do. I've learned better now."

And she was determined to prove it.

"You like being a cocktail waitress, *bella*? You like men touching you, rubbing up against you, thinking you're for sale along with the drinks and the chips?"

The heat in her cheeks spread, suffusing her with an

angry glow. "No, I don't. But it's just about all I'm qualified for."

"And if I were to offer you something else? A better way to earn your money?"

Her stomach was beginning to churn. "I won't be your mistress."

He blinked at her. And then he laughed again, and she felt the hot, sticky slide of embarrassment in her veins. Oh, for pity's sake. After the way the woman he'd been with tonight looked, did she truly think he was interested in her?

But he had been once. She hadn't dreamed it. Nicky was proof she had not.

"Charming, Holly. But I don't need to pay a woman to be my mistress. If I were to choose you for that…position…I am certain you would not refuse."

Holly could only gape at his utter self-confidence. "It's a wonder you bother with casinos when you have such bad instincts. I'm surprised you haven't lost everything when you reason like that in the face of such overwhelming evidence to the contrary."

"*Dio*," he said, "but you are a stubborn woman. How did we end up in bed together again?" He didn't wait for her reply. He nodded sagely as if answering his own question. "Ah, yes, that's right. You were deceiving me."

Shame suffused her at that mention of their night together. But she didn't bother to deny it. He wouldn't believe it anyway. "Clearly, you like your women to shut up and do as they're told."

"Which you seem to be incapable of doing," he growled.

"Fine," she snapped. "Tell me what you want so I can say no."

His stare was unnerving. But not because it made her uncomfortable. More likely because she wanted to drown in it. "I want you to model for the Sky campaign."

Holly's mouth went dry. Sky was the signature fragrance from NC, the one she'd modeled for in New York when she hadn't been able to tell Drago why she was really there. "That's not funny," she said tightly.

His expression was dead serious. "I'm not joking, Holly. I want you for Sky."

"I did that already," she said. "It didn't work out, as I recall."

He shrugged. "A mistake. One we can rectify now."

The trembling in her belly wasn't going away. It was spreading through her limbs, making her teeth chatter. She clamped her jaw tight and tried not to let it show. Thankfully, the car was dark and the lights from the city didn't penetrate the tinted windows quite as well as they otherwise would have.

"I don't think it's possible," she said. And it wasn't. How would she go to New York with a three-month-old baby in tow? She didn't think that was what Drago had in mind at all.

"Of course it is. I will pay you far more than you earn in that casino. You will do the shoot and any appearances that are needed, and you will be handsomely rewarded. It's a win for you, Holly."

She thought of her baby in his secondhand crib, of the tiny, dingy apartment she shared with Gabi. The air conditioner was one window unit that rattled and coughed so badly she was never certain it would keep working. The carpet was faded and torn, and the appliances were always one usage away from needing repairs.

It was a dump, a dive, and she would do just about anything to get out of there and take her baby to a better life.

But what if he didn't mean it? What if he was toying with her? What if this was simply another way to punish her for not telling him the truth in New York?

She wouldn't put it past him. A man who threw her out and then refused all contact? Who didn't know he had a son, because he was so damn arrogant as to think she would want to contact him for any other reason than to tell him something important?

He was capable of it. More than capable.

"I want a contract," she said. "I want everything spelled out, legal and binding, and if it's legit, then I'll do it."

Because what choice did she have? She wasn't stupid, and she wasn't going to turn this opportunity down when it could mean everything to her child. Once she had a contract, signed and ironclad, she would feel much more in control.

"Fine."

Holly blinked. She hadn't expected him to agree to that.

"I hope you're certain about this," she said, unable to help herself when her teeth were still chattering and her body still trembling. What if this was a mistake? What if she were opening up Pandora's box with this act? How could she *not* be opening Pandora's box, when she had a three-month-old baby, and this man didn't know he was a father? "You know I'm not a model. I have no idea what I'm doing."

"Which is precisely why you're correct for the campaign. Sky is for the real woman who wants to recapture a certain something about her life. Her youth, her innocence, her sex appeal."

Irritation slid into her veins. "I've smelled Sky. It's not bad, but it's not all that, either."

The match-scent of anger rolled from him again. Why, oh, why did she feel the need to antagonize him? *Just take the money and shut up*, she told herself. The silence between them was palpable. And then he spoke. "Ah, yes, because you are an expert perfumer, correct?"

Sarcasm laced his voice. It made her madder than she already was, regardless that she knew she shouldn't push him.

"You have no idea. As I recall, you threw me out before I could show you."

He sat back in the limo then, his long limbs relaxing as if he were about to take a nap. She knew better, though. He was more like a panther, stretching out and pretending to relax when what he really planned was to bring down a gazelle.

"It takes years to learn how to blend perfumes. It also takes very intense training, and a certain sensitivity to smell. While you may have enjoyed mixing up essences you've ordered off the internet for all your friends, and while many of them may have told you how fabulous you are, that's hardly the right sort of training to create perfume for a multinational conglomerate, now, is it?"

Rage burned low in her belly, along with a healthy dose of uncertainty. It wasn't that she wasn't good, but she often felt the inadequacy of her origins in the business. She had no curriculum vitae, no discernable job experience. How could she communicate to anyone that she was worthy of a chance without backing it up with fragrance samples?

She glanced out the window, but they weren't quite to her neighborhood yet. So she turned back to him and tried very hard not to tell him to go to hell. He was so arrogant, so certain of himself.

And she suddenly burned to let him know it.

"It's gratifying that you know so much about me already," she said, a razor edge to her voice. "But perhaps you didn't know that my grandmother was born in Grasse and trained there for years before she met her husband and moved to Louisiana. She gave up her dreams of working for a big house, but she never gave up the art. And she taught it to me."

It wasn't the kind of formal instruction he would expect, but Gran had been extremely good at what she did. And Holly was, too.

She heard him pull in a breath. "That may be, but it still does not make you an expert, *bella mia*."

The accusation smarted. "Again, until you've tried my scents, you can't really know that, can you?" She crossed her arms and tilted up her chin. Hell, why not go for it? What did she have to lose? "In fact, I want that in the contract. You will allow me to present my work to you if I model for your campaign."

He laughed softly. The sound scraped along her nerve endings. But not quite in a bad way. No, it was more like heated fingers stroking her sensitive skin. She wanted more.

"You realize that I will say yes to this, don't you? But why not? It costs me nothing. I can still say no to your fragrances, even if I agree to let you show them to me."

"I'm aware of that."

She believed him to be too good a businessman to turn her fragrances away out of spite. He hadn't built Navarra Cosmetics into what it was today by being shortsighted. She was counting on that.

And yet there was much more at risk here, wasn't there? They were getting closer and closer to her home, and she had a baby that was one half of his DNA.

But why should that matter?

He was the sperm donor. *She* was the one who'd sacrificed everything to take care of her child. She was the one who'd gone through her entire pregnancy alone and with only a friend for support. She was the one who'd brought him into the world, and the one who sat up with him at night, who worried about him and who loved him completely.

This man hadn't cared enough about the possibility of a child to allow her even to contact him. He'd thrown her out and self-importantly gone about his life as if she'd never existed.

A life that had included many trysts with models and actresses. Oh, yes, she'd known all about that even when she hadn't wanted to. His beautiful, deceptive face had stared out at her from the pages of the tabloids in the checkout line. While she'd been buying the few necessities she could afford to keep herself alive and healthy, he'd been wining and dining supermodels in Cannes and Milan and Venice.

She'd despised him for so long that to be with him now, in this car, was rather surreal. She had a baby with him, but she didn't think he'd like that at all. And she wasn't going to tell him. He'd done nothing to deserve to know.

Nothing except father Nicky.

She shoved that thought down deep and slapped a lid on it. Yes, she absolutely believed that a man ought to know he had a child. But she couldn't quite get there with Drago di Navarra. He wasn't just any man.

Worse, he'd probably decide she was trying to deceive him again, and then her chances of earning any money to take care of her baby would be nullified before she ever stepped in front of a camera. He'd throw her and Nicky to the wolves without a second thought, and then he'd step into his fancy limo and be ferried away to the next amazingly expensive location on his To See list.

No, she couldn't tell him. She couldn't take the chance when there was finally a light at the end of the tunnel.

The car pulled to a stop in front of her shabby apartment building. Drago looked out the window—at the yellow lights staining everything in a sickly glow, the fresh graffiti sprayed across the wall of a building opposite, the overflowing garbage bins waiting for tomorrow's pickup, the skinny dog pulling trash from one of them—and stiffened.

"You cannot stay here," he said, his voice low and filled with horror.

Holly sucked in a humiliated breath. It looked bad, yes, but the residents here were good, honest people. There were drugs in the neighborhood, but not in this building. Mr. Boudreaux ran it with an iron fist. It was the safest thing she could afford. Shame crawled down her spine at the look on Drago's face.

"I *am* staying here," she said quietly. "And I thank you for the ride home."

His gaze swung toward her. "It's not safe here, *bella mia.*"

Holly gritted her teeth. "I've been living here for the past seven months," she said. "It's where I live. It's what I can afford. And you have no idea about safe. You're only assuming it's not because it's not a fancy New York neighborhood like you're used to."

He studied her for a long moment. And then he pressed an intercom button and spoke to the driver in Italian. After that, he swung the door open and stepped out.

"Come then. I will walk you to your apartment."

"You don't have to do that," she protested, joining him on the pavement with her duffel in tow. "The door is right here."

The building was two stories tall, with three entrances along its front. Each stairwell had two apartments on each floor. Hers was on the second floor, center stairwell. And the driver had parked the limo right in front of it. A dog barked—not the one in the garbage, but a different one— and a curtain slid back. She could see Mrs. Landry's face peering outside. When her gaze landed on the limousine, the light switched out and Holly knew the old woman had turned it off so she could see better.

She was a nosy lady, but a sweet one.

"I insist," Drago said, and Holly's heart skipped a beat. She had to take her things to her apartment, and then she had to go to Mrs. Turner's across the hall and get Nicky.

"Fine," she said, realizing he wasn't going away otherwise. If she let him walk her to the door, he'd be satisfied, even if he walked her up the steps to her apartment. And it wasn't as if her baby was home.

She turned and led the way to the door. She reached to yank it open, but he was there first, pulling it wide and motioning for her to go inside.

"Better be careful you don't get your fancy suit dirty coming inside here," she said.

"I know a good cleaner," he replied, and she started up the stairs—quietly, so as not to alert Mrs. Turner, who might just come to the door with her baby if she heard Holly arrive.

He followed her in silence until she reached the landing and turned around to face him. He was two steps behind her, and it put him on eye level with her. The light from the stairwell was sickly, but she didn't think there was a light on this earth that wouldn't love Drago di Navarra. It caressed his cheekbones, the aristocratic blade of his nose, shone off the dark curls of his hair. His mouth was flat and sensual, his lips full, and she remembered with a jolt what it had felt like to press her lips to his.

Dammit.

"This is it," she whispered. "You can go now."

He didn't move. "Open the door, Holly. I want to make certain you get inside."

He didn't whisper, and she shot a worried glance at Mrs. Turner's door. She could hear the television, and she knew her neighbor was awake.

"Shh," she told him. "People are sleeping. These walls are thin, which I am sure you aren't accustomed to, but—"

He moved then, startling her into silence as he came up to the landing and took her key from her limp hand. "You'd be surprised what I have been accustomed to, *cara*," he said shortly. "Now, tell me which door before I choose one."

Her skin burned. She pointed to her door and stood

silently by while he unlocked it and stepped inside. Humiliation was a sharp dagger in her gut then. A year ago, he'd dressed her in beautiful clothes, made her the center of attention, taken her to a restaurant she could never in a million years afford and then taken her back to his amazing Park Avenue apartment with the expansive view of Central Park. None of those things was even remotely like what he would see inside her apartment and she burned with mortification at what he must be thinking.

He turned back to her, his silvery eyes giving nothing away. "It appears to be safe," he told her, standing back so she could enter her own home. A home that, she knew, would have fit into the foyer of his New York apartment.

She slid the door quietly closed behind her, not because she wanted to shut him in, but because she wanted to keep her presence from Mrs. Turner until he was gone.

Fury slid into her bones, permeating her, making her shake with its force. She spun on him and jerked her keys from his hand. "How dare you?" she sputtered. "How dare you assume that because I live in a place that doesn't meet with your approval, you have a right to think I need your help to enter my own home?"

"Just because you've entered without incident in the past doesn't mean there won't come a night when someone has broken in to wait for you," he grated. "You're on the second floor, *cara*. You're a beautiful woman, living alone, and—" here he pointed "—these windows aren't precisely security windows, are they? So forgive me if I wanted to make sure you were safe. I could no more allow you to come in here alone than I could jump out that window and fly. It's not what a man does."

"First of all, I don't see why you care. And second, I don't live alone," she grated in return, her heart thrumming at everything he'd just said.

He blinked. "You have a boyfriend?"

"A best friend, if you must know. And she's at work right now."

He glanced around the room again. Gabi had left a lamp burning, as she always did, but it was a dim one in order to save electricity. Drago flicked a switch on the wall, and the overhead light popped on, revealing the apartment in all its shabby glory.

It was clean, but worn. And there was no way to hide that. His gaze slid over the room—and landed squarely on the package of diapers and jars of baby food sitting on the dinette. Holly closed her eyes and cursed herself for not putting everything away this afternoon. She'd been too caught up with her fragrances in the little free time she'd had after returning from the store.

Drago's brows drew down as he turned his head toward her. "You have a baby in this apartment?"

Before she could answer him, tell him she was collecting for charity or something, there was a knock on the door.

"Holly?" Mrs. Turner called. "Are you home, sweetie?"

CHAPTER FOUR

DRAGO WATCHED AS the color drained from Holly Craig's face. She pushed her hair behind her ear and turned away from him, toward the door.

"Coming, Mrs. Turner," she said sweetly, and he felt a flicker of annoyance. She'd been nothing but cross with him since the moment he'd first spoken to her in the casino. He understood why she would be angry with him, since he'd ruined her plans last year, but she should be perfectly amenable now that he was offering her the job of modeling for Sky. If she was ambitious, and she must be to undergo the deception she had, why wasn't she softening toward him?

His gaze landed on a table tucked into one corner of the room. It was lined with testers and other paraphernalia she must use to make her fragrance. Clearly, she was serious about it. And her grandmother was from Grasse, the perfume capital of the world. That didn't mean the woman had had any talent, or that she'd been a *nez*. Those were highly prized. If she'd been a nose, she would have gone to work in the industry, husband or no.

But Holly was certainly convinced she had what it took to succeed in his business. He glanced at the shabby furnishings and wasn't persuaded. If she had talent, why was she here? Why hadn't she kept trying even after he'd turned her down? There were other companies, other opportunities. They weren't the best, but they were a leg up.

Which she desperately seemed to need, he admitted. He refused to feel any remorse for that. She might have spent all her money coming to New York, but he was not responsible for her choices.

And yet, this place depressed him. Made him feel jumpy and angry and insignificant in ways he'd thought he'd forgotten long ago. He hadn't always lived the way he did now—with everything money could buy at his fingertips—and this dingy apartment was far too familiar. He thought of his mother and her insane quest for something he'd never understood—something she'd never understood, either, he'd finally come to realize years after the fact.

Donatella Benedetti had been looking for enlightenment, the best he could figure. And she'd been willing to drag her only son from foreign location to foreign location, some of them without electricity or running water or any means of communicating with the world at large. He'd held a hat while she'd busked on the streets, playing a violin with adequate-enough skill to gain a few coins for a meal. He'd curled up in a canoe while they'd floated down an Asian river, moving toward a village of mud huts and deprivation. He'd learned to beg for money by looking pitiful and small and hungry. He'd known how to count coins before he'd ever learned to read.

Holly took a deep breath and opened the door to greet an older woman standing on the other side. The woman held a baby carrier, presumably containing a baby, if the way Holly bent down and looked at it was any indication.

The beginnings of a headache started to throb in Drago's temple. Babies were definitely not his thing. They were tiny and mysterious and needy, and he hadn't a clue what to do with them.

"I thought I heard you come up," the woman was saying. "He was a good baby tonight. Such a sweetie."

"Thank you, Mrs. Turner. I really appreciate you helping out like this."

The other woman waved a hand. "Pish. You know I'm a night owl. It's no problem to keep him while you work." She looked up then, her gaze landing on him. Drago inclined his head while her eyes drifted over him. "Oh, my, I didn't know you had company," she said.

Holly turned briefly and then waved a hand as if to dismiss him. "Just an old acquaintance I ran into tonight. He's leaving now."

He was not leaving, but he didn't bother to tell her that. Or, he was leaving, but not just yet. Not until he figured out what was happening here.

There was a baby, in a carrier, and Holly was taking it from the woman. Was it her baby? Or her roommate's? And did it matter? So long as she modeled for Sky, did he care?

"Go ahead and take care of the baby," he said evenly. "I can go in a moment, once everything is settled."

The woman she'd called Mrs. Turner nodded approvingly. "Excellent idea. Get the little pumpkin settled first."

Mrs. Turner handed over a diaper bag, as well as the carrier, and Drago stepped forward to take the bag from Holly. She didn't protest, but she didn't look at him, either. A few more seconds passed as Holly and Mrs. Turner said their goodbyes, and then the door closed and they were alone.

Or, strike that, there were three of them where there'd been four. Drago gazed at the baby carrier as the child inside cooed and stretched.

"He's hungry," Holly said. "I have to feed him."

"Don't let me stop you."

She gazed at him with barely disguised hatred. "I'd

prefer you go," she said tightly. "It's late, and we need to get to bed."

"Whose baby is this?" he asked curiously. He thought of her in New York, sweet and innocent and so responsive to his caresses, and hated the idea she could have been with another man. He'd been her first. Yet another thing about her that had fooled him into thinking she hadn't had ulterior motives.

Drago tried very hard not to remember her expression of wonder when he'd entered her fully for the first time. She'd clung to him so sweetly, her body opening to him like a flower, and he'd felt an overwhelming sense of honor and protectiveness toward her. Something she'd been counting on, no doubt.

Dio, she had fooled him but good. She'd gotten past all his defenses and made him care, however briefly. Anger spun up inside him. But there were other feelings, too, desire being chief among them. It rather surprised him how sharp that feeling was, as if he'd not had sex in months rather than hours. Quite simply, he wanted to spear his hands into her hair and tilt her mouth up for his pleasure.

And then he wanted to strip her naked and explore every inch of her skin the way he once had, and let the consequences be damned.

Her expression was hard as she looked at him, and he wondered if she knew what he was thinking. Then she walked over to the couch—a distance of about four steps— and set the baby carrier on the floor. She grabbed the diaper bag from him and began to rummage in it. Soon, she had a bottle in her hands and she took the baby out of the carrier and began to feed it.

Drago watched the entire episode, a skein of discomfort uncoiling inside him as she deliberately did not answer his question.

It wasn't a hard question, but she looked down at the

baby and made faces, talking in a high voice and ignoring him completely. Her long reddish-blond hair draped over one shoulder, but she didn't push it back. He let his gaze wander her features, so pretty in a simple way, and yet earthy somehow, too.

She had not been earthy before. Now she bent over the child, holding the bottle, her full breasts threatening to burst from the white shirt, her legs long and lean beneath the tight skirt of the casino uniform. The only incongruous items of clothing were the tennis shoes she'd changed into.

Drago suddenly felt out of his element. Holly Craig nursed a child and turned every bit of love and affection she had on it, when all she could spare for him was contempt. Watching her with the baby, he had a visceral reaction that left a hole in the center of his chest. Had his mother ever focused every ounce of attention she had on him? Had she ever looked at him with such love? Or had she only ever looked at him as a burden and a means to an end?

"Holly," he said, his voice tight, and she looked up at him, her gaze defiant and hard. If he'd been a lesser man, he would have stumbled backward under that knife-edged gaze of hers. He was not a lesser man. "Whose child is that?"

He asked the question, but he was pretty certain he knew the answer by now.

"Not that it's any of your business," she told him airily, "but Nicky is mine. If this changes your plan to have me model for Sky, then I'd appreciate it if you'd get out and leave us alone."

Holly's heart hammered double-time in her chest. She hadn't wanted him to know about Nicky at all, not yet, not until the contract he'd agreed to provide was signed and she knew she'd get her money for doing the Sky campaign at the very least.

But of course her luck had run out months ago. First, she'd gone to New York, spent every dime she had and come home empty-handed. Then she'd lost the house and property—and found out she was pregnant. God, she could still remember her utter shock when her period hadn't started and she'd finally worked up the courage to buy a pregnancy test.

And she'd driven two towns over to do so, not wanting *anyone* in New Hope to wonder why she needed a pregnancy test.

She looked down at the sweet, soft baby in her arms now and knew for a fact he was not a mistake. But he'd definitely been a shock on top of everything else she'd had to deal with just then.

And now, of course, when all she wanted was the absolute best for him, when she needed to protect him and provide for him and keep him secret until she had this job sewn up, Mrs. Turner had heard her come home and brought him to her. What if Drago figured it out? What would happen then? She'd lose the opportunity to provide a better life for her baby.

Drago was looking at her with a mixture of disdain and what she thought might be utter horror. Resignation settled over her. She'd already lost the opportunity then.

But you can still tell him the truth.

Would he ignore his child's needs if he knew? Could she take that chance?

"How old is the child?" he asked, brows drawn low, and her heart did that funny squeeze thing it did when she was scared.

"A couple of months," she said vaguely, ignoring the voice. She couldn't tell him. How could she take the chance after everything that had happened? Not only that, but why did he deserve to know when he'd thrown her out and left her to fend for herself?

Guilt and fear swirled into a hot mess inside her belly. She'd always done the right thing. But what was the right thing now?

"You wasted no time, I see," he said coolly.

"I'm sorry?"

He looked hard and cool, remote. "Finding another lover," he spat at her.

A hard knot of something tightened right beneath her breastbone. Of course he thought she'd gone home and gotten pregnant by someone else. Of course he did. Holly closed her eyes and willed herself to be calm.

It didn't work.

My God, the man was arrogant beyond belief! Resentment flared to life in her gut, a hot bright fire that seared into her. "Why should I have waited? Thanks for showing me what I'd been missing, by the way. It was ever so easy to go home and climb back on the horse."

She gazed down at Nicky, who was sucking the bottle for all he was worth, and willed the irrational tears gathering behind her eyelids to melt away. Drago di Navarra not only thought she'd intended to use her body to get what she wanted out of him, but he also thought she'd been so promiscuous as to run straight home and get pregnant by another man. As if she could have borne another man's touch after she'd had his.

"Perhaps you should have been more careful," he said, and a fresh wave of hatred pounded into her. Her head snapped up. She didn't care what he saw in her gaze now.

"How dare you?" she said, her voice low and tight. "You know nothing about me. *Nothing!*" She sucked in a shaky breath. "Nicky is a gift, however he got here. I wouldn't trade him for a million Sky contracts, so you can take your disdain and your contempt and get the hell out of my home."

She was shaking, she realized, and Nicky felt it. He started to kick his little arms and legs, and his face scrunched up. The bottle popped out of his mouth, but before she could get it back in, he turned his head and started to wail.

"Shush, sweetie, Mommy's here," she crooned, her eyes stinging with tears and gritty from lack of sleep. She just wanted to put her head down and not get up again for a good long time.

But that wasn't possible. It wasn't ever possible these days.

"Forgive me. I shouldn't have said that."

Holly cuddled Nicky, rocking him softly, and looked up at Drago. Shock coursed through her system at those quiet words, uttered with sincerity. It was a glimpse of the man she'd found so compelling last year, the one who'd made her feel safe and who'd made her laugh and sigh and then shatter in his arms.

She'd liked that man, right up until the moment he'd proven he didn't really have a heart after all. And while she told herself not to be fooled now, she was moved by the apology. Or maybe she was just too exhausted to keep up the anger.

Nicky continued to wail, and Holly stood and bounced him up and down in her arms. "Hush, baby. It's okay."

"You need help," Drago said.

She didn't look at him. "I have help. You saw Mrs. Turner. Gabi helps, too. It's my turn now."

"You're tired, Holly. You should get some sleep."

"I can't sleep until he does." She paced the floor, giving Drago as wide a berth as possible in the small room. "You should probably go. Your driver will be wondering if I bashed you over the head and took your wallet."

"I doubt it," he said. He eyed the room again and she could feel the strength of his contempt for their surroundings.

"Drago." He looked at her, his nostrils flaring. He was acting as if he'd been caught with his hand in the cookie jar. "You should go. We'll be fine. We've been fine for months. Nicky will fall asleep soon, and then I'm going to crash, too. I have another shift tomorrow at noon."

"I'm afraid I can't do that," he said, and her stomach flipped. He took a step closer to her and she bounced Nicky a little more frantically. It seemed he didn't mind the movement at all. His little eyes were starting to close.

"Of course you can," she said. "You can't stay here, for God's sake. Nor would you want to, I'm sure. I'm afraid we don't have silk sheets, milord, or room service—"

"Shut up, Holly, and listen to me," he commanded.

And, as much as she wanted to tell him to go to hell, she did as he told her. Because she was tired. And scared he would walk out and take her last opportunity with him.

"I'm listening," she said when he didn't immediately continue.

"I'm returning to New York in the morning. You're coming with me."

Reflexively, she held Nicky a little tighter. "I'm not leaving my baby. Nor am I going anywhere without a contract," she said tightly. Because she didn't trust him. Because, as much as she wanted it to be true, she was too accustomed to bad luck to believe it was finally turning around for her.

Drago di Navarra wasn't suddenly being nice and accommodating for no reason. Did he suspect? Or was he just planning to drop her from an even greater height than he had the last time?

"No, you aren't leaving him," Drago said. "And you aren't returning to that casino, either. Pack what you need for the night. I'll send someone by for the rest of your things tomorrow."

Holly could only gape at him, her skin flushing hot with hope and fear and shame all rolled into one. *Don't trust him, don't trust him....*

And yet she wanted to. Needed to. He was the only way out of this hellhole.

Except, she had obligations.

"I can't just leave," she said. "This is my home. Gabi isn't even here. I can't quit the casino without notice—"

"You can," he said firmly. "You will."

Pressure was building behind her forehead. What should she do? What would Gran have said? Thoughts of Gran threatened to bring a fresh flood of tears, so she bit down on her lip and pushed them deep. *Think, Holly.*

"You're asking me to turn my life upside down for nothing more than a promise," she said. "How do I know you aren't planning some elaborate scheme to put me in my place once more?"

He blinked. And then he laughed, while she felt her skin turn even redder. "Honestly, *cara*, do you think I've spent a year plotting how to pay you back for deceiving me in New York? Until tonight, I had not given you another thought."

Well, all righty, then.

His words stung in ways she hadn't imagined possible. There wasn't a day since he'd thrown her out that she hadn't thought about him in some capacity or other—and here he was telling her so offhandedly that he hadn't thought of her at all.

"How flattering," she murmured, keeping her eyes on her baby so as not to reveal her hurt.

"It's not personal," he told her, all gorgeous Italian playboy. "I am a busy man. But when I saw you again, I remembered those photos and how right you were in them. All I want is your face on my campaign."

Nicky was finally asleep now. Holly turned and took him into her bedroom, where she placed him in his crib near her bed. When she straightened, Drago was standing in the door.

"I'll go," she told him quietly, making her decision. "But not tonight." She turned to look back at her baby before gazing at Drago again. "He can't be moved right now. It'll wake him up. And I'm too tired to pack a thing."

She joined Drago in the entry to her room. He was gazing down at her in frustration, his brows drawn down over his beautiful gray eyes.

"You're a very stubborn woman, Holly Craig," he said softly, his eyes dipping to her mouth before coming back up again. Her lips tingled. She told herself it was because she'd been biting them.

"I will always do what's best for my baby," she said. "He comes first. I'm sorry if you find that inconvenient."

She could feel the heat of Drago's body enveloping her, smell the cool scent of his cologne—a home run for Navarra Cosmetics, at least where he was concerned. Scents smelled different on different people, but this one seemed tailored to him. It was light, so light she'd not really noticed it before now, but it was also intoxicating.

There was sandalwood, which was to be expected in male cologne. But there were also pears, which was surprising, as well as moss. It was fresh and clean and she liked it. And she would forever associate the smell of NC's signature male cologne with its ruthless CEO.

Drago's mouth flattened for a moment, as if he were annoyed. But then he shook his head slightly.

"An admirable trait in a mother, I imagine," he said, and there was a piercing pain in her heart that she did not understand. Did he sound wistful just then? Lonely? Lost?

"I will send a car for you in the morning, *cara*. Say your goodbyes and pack your things. You won't need to return to this dwelling ever again."

Her heart hammered. "I can't leave Gabi in the lurch. She will need enough money to cover a couple of months' rent at least."

He didn't even blink. "I will take care of it."

And then he was gone, his footsteps echoing in the stairwell as he left her life once more.

CHAPTER FIVE

DRAGO'S APARTMENT IN New York was somehow even grander than she remembered it. Holly lay back on a bed that was almost as big as her entire room had been in New Orleans and stared up at a ceiling that had actual frescoes painted on it. Frescoes, as if this were a grand church instead of a personal dwelling.

Stunning. And completely surreal.

It was late afternoon and she needed to get out of bed, but she didn't want to. Early this morning—far earlier than she would have liked—Nicky had been awake and ready for his bottle. While she'd fed her baby, she'd done a pretty good job of convincing herself that Drago wasn't coming back. That she'd dreamed the whole thing.

Gabi had stumbled home at six, and Holly had told her the whole story—including the part where she was supposed to leave New Orleans and never have to worry about living in squalor again.

Gabi's face had lit up like the Fourth of July. "Oh, my God, Holly, that's amazing! You have to go! You *are* going, right?"

Holly had frowned. "I'm not sure." Then she'd raked a hand through her tangle of hair. "I mean, last night I was pretty sure. But how can I leave you? And how can I possibly deal with that man again? He's not nice, Gabi. He's selfish and arrogant and only concerned with his bottom line and—"

"And handsome as sin," Gabi had interrupted. "As well as richer than God. Not to mention he's the father of your baby."

Holly had frowned. "That's what worries me the most."

Gabi had sat down and taken her hand, squeezing it. Her blue eyes had been so serious. "This is a once-in-a-lifetime opportunity, Holly. You have to go. There's a reason this is happening now, and you have to go see what it is."

In the end, Holly had gone. Drago had arrived at eight, and by then Holly had packed everything she needed into three suitcases and a diaper bag. It was everything she owned. Drago had looked over her belongings coldly, and then his driver had carried them all down to the limo. Holly had hugged Gabi goodbye, crying and promising to call. She'd been terrified to leave her friend alone, but Drago had handed Gabi a fat envelope and told her to use it wisely.

Holly had bitten her lip to keep from saying something she might regret. It was up to Gabi to accept or decline the money, and in the end she'd accepted. She'd had no choice, really. Without Holly to help with expenses, she would have had to hustle to find another roommate or take on extra hours at work. The money was the better choice.

Within an hour, they'd been on a plane to New York. Within two hours, they'd landed. And, an hour later, she'd found herself in this room. She didn't know what she'd expected, but staying at Drago's had not been it. When she'd turned to him, he'd known what she was going to say, because he'd preempted her.

"There's no sense putting you in a hotel with a baby when this place is so big."

Nicky was in an adjoining room—the situation was going to take some getting used to. He had a nice crib and a play area with plenty of appropriate toys for a young baby. When she'd put him down for his afternoon nap, she'd come straight in here and climbed into bed. She always tried to snatch a few moments' sleep while Nicky was out—but he usually woke her before she was fully rested.

A prickle of alarm began to grow in her belly as she reached for her cell phone. She blinked at the display, certain she wasn't seeing it right. Because, if she was, that meant she'd been asleep for nearly three hours now.

Holly scrambled off the bed and ran into the adjoining room. Panic slammed into her when she realized Nicky was not in the crib. She tore open the door and raced down the hall, skidding into the palatial living area, with its huge windows overlooking Central Park. A woman sat on the floor and played with her baby. Nicky was on his belly, twisting the knobs of a toy, and the woman made encouraging noises as he did so.

"Who are you?" Holly demanded. She was trembling as she stood there. Part of her wanted to snatch her baby up and take him away from this woman, but the rational part told her not to alarm him when he was perfectly happy with what he was doing. And clearly safe and well.

The woman got to her feet and smiled. She was older, a bit plain, dressed in jeans and a T-shirt. She held out her hand. "I'm Sylvia. Mr. Di Navarra hired me to help with your son."

Holly's throat tightened painfully. She would *not* allow him to interfere. "I don't need help," she said. "He made a mistake."

Sylvia frowned. "I apologize, Miss Craig, but Mr. Di Navarra seems to think you do."

"I will speak to Mr. Di Navarra," she said tightly.

"Speak to me about what?"

Holly spun to find Drago standing in the door. Her heart did that little skip thing she wished it wouldn't do at the sight of him. But he was beautiful, as always, and she couldn't help herself. How had this splendid creature ever been interested in her for even a moment? How had they managed to make a baby together when she was so clearly not the class of woman he was accustomed to?

He wore faded jeans that she knew were artfully faded rather than work faded, and a dark shirt that molded to the broad muscles of his chest. His feet were bare. Something about that detail made her heart skitter wildly.

"I don't need help to take care of my son," she said. "You've wasted this woman's time."

He came into the room then and she saw he was holding a newspaper at his side. He tossed it onto a table and kept walking.

"I beg your pardon." He was all arrogance and disdain once more. "But you definitely do."

He stopped in front of her and put two fingers under her chin. She flinched. And then he turned her head gently this way and that, his eyes raking over her.

"I intend to pay a lot of money for this face to grace my ads. I'd prefer if you truly are rested instead of having you edited to look that way."

She pulled out of his grip and glared at him. Of course he was concerned about the campaign. What had she expected? That he'd hired a nanny because he cared? He didn't care. He had never cared.

Strike that: he only cared about himself.

"You could have asked me. I didn't appreciate waking up and finding my baby gone."

"My mistake, then," he said, his eyes searching hers. "I told Sylvia to take him when he cried. I knew you didn't get enough sleep last night."

Holly didn't dare think the fact he'd noticed she didn't get enough sleep meant anything other than he wanted to protect his investment. But she couldn't remember the last time someone had paid attention to how much sleep she was getting. It made a lump form in her throat. Gabi would have noticed if she weren't in the same boat.

Gran would have, too. Gran would have put her to bed and taken the baby for as long as she needed. Holly bit the inside of her lip to stop a little sob from escaping. It wasn't even eighteen months since Gran had died, and it still hurt her at the oddest times.

Holly glanced at Sylvia, who had gotten back down on the floor to entice Nicky with a new toy. There was a tightness in her chest as she watched her baby play. She'd greatly appreciated Mrs. Turner's help, and she was certain the woman was kind and gentle, but she was almost positive Mrs. Turner had spent her time watching television instead of playing on the floor with Nicky.

Sylvia clearly knew what she was doing—in fact, Holly thought sadly, the woman seemed to know more than she did, if the way she encouraged Nicky to play with different shapes was any indication. Holly had been satisfied when he'd been occupied and happy. She'd never really considered his play to be a teaching moment.

Holly put a hand to her forehead and drew in a deep breath. She wasn't a bad mother, was she? She was simply an overworked and exhausted one, but she loved her son beyond reason. He was the only thing of value she had.

"You need to eat," Drago said, and Holly looked up at him.

"I'm not hungry." As if to prove her a liar, her stomach growled. Drago arched an eyebrow. "Fine," she said, "I guess I am after all."

"Come to the kitchen and let the cook fix you something."

Holly looked doubtfully at her baby and Sylvia. It wasn't that she didn't trust the woman, but she didn't know her. And she was nervous, she had to admit, with this change in circumstances. The last time she'd been here, it had all been ripped away from her without warning. She wasn't certain it wouldn't be again. "I'd rather stay here."

Drago frowned. "He's not going anywhere, Holly. He'll be perfectly fine."

Holly closed her eyes. She was being unreasonable. She'd left Nicky with Mrs. Turner for hours while she rode a bus and a streetcar halfway across town and went to work. Was it really such a stretch to go into another room and leave this woman alone with her child?

"All right," she said. Drago led her not to the kitchen but to a rooftop terrace with tables and chairs and grass—actual grass on a rooftop in New York City. The terrace was lined with potted trees and blossoming flowers, and while she could hear the city sounds below, her view was entirely of sky and plants and the buildings across the tree-tops in Central Park. Astounding, and beautiful in a way she found surprising.

"This is not the kitchen," she said inanely.

Drago laughed. "No. I decided this was more appropriate."

They sat down and a maid appeared with a tray laden with small appetizers—olives, sliced meats, tiny pastries filled with cheese, cucumber sandwiches, ham sandwiches and delicate chocolates to finish. It wasn't much, but it was precisely the kind of thing she needed just now.

Holly dug in to the food, filling her plate and taking careful bites so as not to seem like a ravenous animal. She might not be accustomed to fancy New York society, but her grandmother had at least taught her the art of being graceful. The maid appeared again with a bottle of wine. Holly started to protest, but Drago shushed her. Then he poured the beautiful deep red liquid into two glasses.

"You should appreciate this," he said. "A Château Margaux of excellent vintage."

As if she even knew what that meant. But she did understand scents and flavors. Holly lifted the wine and swirled it before sniffing the bowl. The wine was rich and full and delicious to the nose. She took a sip, expecting perfection. It was there. And she knew, as she set the glass down again, it was the sort of thing she could never afford.

When she glanced up, Drago was watching her. His gray eyes were piercing, assessing, and she met them evenly. So unlike the Holly of a year ago, who'd stammered and gulped and been a nervous wreck in his presence. It took a lot to meet that stare and not fold, but she was getting better at it.

"Describe the wine to me," he said, his voice smooth and commanding. As if he were accustomed to telling people what to do and then having them do it. Which, of course, he was.

Holly bristled, though it was a simple request. She was tired and stressed and not in the mood to play games with him. Not in the mood to be devoured like a frightened rabbit.

"Taste it yourself," she said. "I'm sure you can figure it out."

She didn't expect him to laugh. "You have made it your mission in life to argue with me, it seems."

"I wouldn't say it's a mission, as that implies I give you a lot of thought. But I'm not quite the same person you ordered around last year. I won't pretend I am."

She was still more of that person than she wanted to be, but she was working very hard on being bold and brave. On not letting his overwhelming force of a personality dominate her will.

Not that he needed to know that.

He leaned back and sipped his wine. "I didn't force you to do anything you didn't want to do, Holly. As I recall, you wanted to do the same things I did. Very much, in fact."

Holly tried to suppress the heat flaring in her cheeks. Impossible, of course. They were red and he would know it. "The wine is delicious," she said, picking up the glass and studying the color. "The top notes are blackberry and cassis. The middle might be rose, while the bottom hints at oak and coffee." A small furrow appeared between Drago's brows.

"Ah, you are embarrassed by what happened between us," he said softly.

Her heart skipped a beat. "Embarrassed? No. But I see no need in discussing it. It's in the past and I'd like to just forget the whole thing."

As if she could.

His nostrils flared, as if he didn't quite like that pronouncement. "Forget? Why would you want to forget something so magnificent, Holly?"

She picked up the wine and took another sip, kept her eyes on the red liquid instead of on him. "Why not? You did. You refused to listen to me and threw me out. I'm sure you promptly forgot about me once I was gone."

His handsome face creased in a frown. "That doesn't mean I didn't enjoy our evening together."

"I really don't want to talk about this," she said. Because it hurt, and because it made her think of her innocent child in the other room and the fact that his father sat here with her now and didn't even know it. Hadn't managed to even consider the possibility.

No, he thought she'd spent the night with him in order to sell her fragrances. And then, when that didn't work, he thought she'd run home and got pregnant right after. As if she had the sense of a goat and the morals of an alley cat.

Yes, she could tell him the truth…but she didn't know him, didn't trust him. And Nicky was too precious to her to take that kind of chance with.

"What you see here is not who I have always been," he

said, spreading an arm to encompass the roof with its expensive greenery. "It may appear as if I were born with money, but I assure you I was not. I know what it's like to work hard, and what it's like to want something so badly you'd sell your soul for it. I've seen it again and again."

Holly licked suddenly dry lips. Was he actually sharing something with her? Something important? Or was he simply trying to intimidate her in another way? "But Navarra Cosmetics has been around for over fifty years," she said. "You are a Navarra."

He studied the wine in his glass. "Yes, I am a Navarra. That doesn't mean I was born with a silver spoon, as you Americans say. Far from it." He drew in a breath. "But I'm here now, and this is my life. And I do not appreciate those who try to take advantage of who I am for their own ends."

Holly's heart hardened. She knew what he was saying. What he meant. Her body began to tremble. She wanted to tell him how wrong he was. How blind. But, instead, she pushed her chair back and stood. She couldn't take another moment of his company, another moment of his smugness.

"I think I'm finished," she said, disappointment and fury thrashing together inside her.

Of course he wasn't telling her anything important. He was warning her. Maybe he hadn't been born rich, maybe he'd been adopted or something, but she didn't care. He was still a heartless bastard with a supreme sense of arrogance and self-importance. He could only see what he expected to see.

If she didn't need the money so much, she'd walk out on *him*. Let him be the one to suffer—not that he would suffer much if she didn't do the Sky campaign. He'd find another model, like he had last year, and he'd eventually give up the idea of her being the right person for the job.

No, the only one who would suffer if she walked out was Nicky. She wasn't walking out. But she wasn't putting up with this, either. She was going back inside and collecting her baby. Then she was going to her room and staying there for the evening.

Before she could walk away, Drago reached out and encircled her wrist with his strong fingers. They sizzled into her, sending sparks of molten heat to her core. Her body ached when he touched her, and it made her angry. Why hadn't she ached when Colin had touched her? Why hadn't she wanted him the way she wanted Drago di Navarra?

Life would be so much easier if she had. Lisa Tate would have never entered the picture. Nicky might be Colin's son, and they might be married and living in her cottage in New Hope while he worked his lawn-care business and she made perfume for the little shop she'd always wanted to open.

They could have been a happy little family and life could have been perfect. She might have never gotten a chance to sell her fragrances to a big company, but Gran would have understood. Gran had only ever wanted her to be happy. She knew that now. A year ago, she'd thought she had to succeed in order to carry on Gran's legacy. That Gran was counting on her somehow.

But she knew Gran wouldn't have wanted her to suffer. She wouldn't have wanted Holly to work so hard, to scrape and scrape and barely get by. She'd have wanted Holly happy, living in their cottage and making her perfumes.

Except that living in the cottage hadn't been an option, had it? Gran's health had suffered in the last few years and she'd had to borrow against the house to pay her bills. Holly had hoped to save the only home she'd ever known when she'd gone to New York.

What a fool she'd been. She'd left the big city broke and pregnant and alone.

"So long as we know where we stand, there's no need to get upset," Drago said, his voice smooth and silky and hateful to her all at once. "Sit. Finish eating. You'll need your strength for the coming days. I can't afford for you to get sick on me."

Her wrist burned in his grip. She wanted to pull away. And she wanted to slide into his lap and wrap her arms around his proud neck. Holly blinked. Was she insane? Had she learned absolutely nothing about this man?

She hated him. Despised him.

Wanted him.

Impossible. Wanting him was a threat to her well-being. To her baby's well-being.

Holly closed her eyes and stood there, gathering her strength. She would need every bit of it to resist his touch. So long as he didn't touch her, she could remain aloof. She could remember the hate. Feel it. Soak in it. That was how she would survive this. By remembering how it had felt when he'd kicked her out. How she'd felt when she'd lost everything and given birth with only Gabi and the medical staff for company.

There'd been no happy new father, no roses, no balloons for the baby. No joy, other than what she'd felt when she'd held Nicky.

"I am finished," she said coolly. "And I'd appreciate it if you'd let go of me."

Drago's jaw was tight. He looked as if he were assessing her. Cataloging her flaws and finding her lacking, no doubt. "Sit down, Holly. We have much to discuss."

"I'd rather not right now, thanks."

His grip tightened on her wrist. Then he let her go abruptly, cursing in Italian as he did so. "Go, then. Run away like a child. But we will have a discussion about what I want from you. And quite soon."

Holly gritted her teeth together and stared across the beautiful terrace to the sliding-glass doors. Freedom was almost hers. All she had to do was walk away. Just go and get Nicky and go to her room for the night.

But it was simply postponing the inevitable. She knew that. It was what she wanted to do, and yet she couldn't. She had to face this head-on. Had to fight for this opportunity before he changed his mind.

Holly Craig wanted to be the kind of woman who didn't back down.

She *would* be that kind of woman. She sank down in her chair like a queen and crossed her legs, in spite of her racing heart. Then she picked up the still-full wineglass and leveled a gaze at Drago.

"Fine. Talk. I'm listening."

CHAPTER SIX

DRAGO HAD NEVER met a more infuriating woman in his life. Holly Craig sat across from him at the table, with golden sunlight playing across her face and her pale hair, setting flame to the strands, and looked like a sweet, innocent goddess.

An illusion.

She was not sweet. She was most definitely not innocent. Remembering the ways in which she was not innocent threatened to make him hard, especially after he'd just had his hand on her soft skin. He forced the memory of making love to her from his mind and focused on the stubborn set of her jaw.

So determined, this woman. So different compared to last year. He sometimes had glimpses of that innocent girl under the veneer, but mostly she was hard and weary. Changed.

Or perhaps last year had been nothing more than an act. Perhaps she'd been just as hard then but had pretended not to be. He'd learned, over the years, that women would do much in an attempt to snare a wealthy man. Holly might have been a virgin, but that didn't mean she hadn't been a virgin with a plan. Innocence in sexual matters did not imply innocence overall.

Nevertheless, he still wanted her for Sky. She had the face he needed. An everywoman face, but pretty in the way every woman wanted to be. No, she was not perfect. She wasn't the sort of gorgeous that a top supermodel was.

But she was perfect for what he wanted her for.

And that was why he put up with her, he told himself. With her hostility and her loathing and her refusal to co-operate.

Drago had worked his way up the ladder at Navarra Cosmetics, because his uncle had insisted he start at the bottom to really know the business, but one of the things he'd always had—and had honed into a fine instrument these days—was a gut feeling for what was right for the company. Holly Craig was right for Sky, and he intended to have her.

Even if he had to suffer her hostility and a baby in his house. When they went to Italy, he would put her and the child in another wing of the estate. Then he would cheerfully forget about her until the shoot was completed and he went over the photos.

She took a sip of the wine and he thought of the way she'd described it to him. She'd never had Château Margaux, he'd bet on that, but she'd described it perfectly after one sip. She knew scents and flavors, he had to give her that.

Whether or not that made her a good perfumer was an entirely different matter.

"Tell me what you expected when you came to New York last year."

Her eyes widened. And then narrowed again, as if she were trying to figure out the trick.

"I'm not sure what you mean," she said carefully.

Her eyes dropped and a current of irritation sizzled into him. "Are you not? You had a case of perfume samples. You pretended to be a model. What was your intent? What did you think would happen once you had my undivided attention?"

She colored, her eyes flashing hot. He didn't know why, but that slice of temper intrigued him. "Because I had intent, right? You never gave me a chance to explain that morning, if I recall. It was a misunderstanding, but you didn't stay for that part."

He sipped the wine. "How did I misunderstand you, *cara*? You were not mute. You spent the entire evening with me. Not only that, but you stood in front of the cameras for two hours and never corrected the impression you were there to model."

Her color remained high. She closed her eyes for a moment. A second later, she was looking straight at him, her eyes shiny and big in her pale face. "I know. I should have. But you assumed I was a model, and I was too scared to say otherwise. Scared I'd lose my chance to talk to you."

"You had my undivided attention all evening," he bit out.

"Hardly undivided," she threw back at him. "You took a dozen phone calls at least. How anyone could have a conversation with you under those circumstances is beyond me."

"Ah, so this is your excuse. What about later, *cara*?"

He didn't think it possible, but her color heightened. Her cheeks were blazing now. She picked up her untouched glass of water and took a deep draft. Drago almost wanted to laugh, but he was too irritated. Still, her blushes made him think of how inexperienced she'd been—and how eager at the same time.

Basta, no. Not a good thing to think about.

"We were, um, busy later. I didn't think it was appropriate." Her head came up then and her eyes glittered. "Haven't you ever stopped to wonder how I could have possibly known you needed a model that day? How I just happened to be sitting there in your waiting room? It wasn't planned, Drago. I had an appointment." She cleared her throat. "Or I thought I did. A university friend of the mayor's wife said she knew you and could arrange a brief meeting. I was told the day and time and that I would have ten minutes. So I went."

It could be true, certainly. He had no recollection. But that did not change what she'd done. How she'd lied. "And yet you took advantage of the situation when I mistook you for the model."

She let out an exasperated breath. "I did. I admit it! But you ordered me to go with you and you didn't give me a chance to explain. I made a decision that it was best to go along with you until I could."

Drago studied her for a long moment. Did he really believe Holly Craig had masterminded the entire situation?

No, he didn't. But she had taken advantage of it. Of him. And that was unforgivable.

"It's possible you were on the schedule. But that was a bad day, as I recall. All the models were wrong. I told my secretary to reschedule the meetings."

She looked unhappy. "Since I didn't schedule it, it wasn't my contact information she would have had. Besides, I'd already come all that way. I couldn't go back without talking to you."

Yes, and she'd been sitting there in his waiting room, looking so fresh and out of place at the same time. He still remembered the black suit and the pink heels with the price tag. A twinge of something sliced into him, but he didn't want to examine it. And he definitely wasn't revisiting what had happened next. It might have been a mistake, but she'd had ample opportunity to tell him the truth.

Instead, she'd seen a way to gain advantage—and she'd taken it. Then she'd kept the pretense going until she'd thought she had him right where she wanted him. He could still see her face that morning, still see how pleased she'd been with herself when he'd questioned her about the case.

His reaction had been inevitable. He'd experienced all those old feelings of despair and fear and loneliness he'd had as a boy, and he'd hated her for doing that to him. For making him remember what he'd worked hard to bury. He'd had no choice but to walk out.

Because she'd blindsided him and he hadn't seen it coming. He'd thought she was someone she wasn't, and he'd felt something with her that he hadn't felt in a long time. He had almost—almost, but not quite—let himself relax with her. She'd been so guileless, unlike the women he usually dated. His fault for always choosing sophisticates, but until he'd experienced someone like Holly Craig, he'd not realized he might enjoy less artifice.

That she'd fooled him, that she'd been as scheming as the most seasoned gold digger, still rankled. He did not regret throwing her out.

But he did regret that he'd let her escape without first seeing the photos. He'd thought about tracking her down once she was gone, but he'd ultimately decided it was best if he did not.

"And what did you hope to gain from a meeting with me? A job?"

She shook her head. "I had hoped you would want Colette."

"Colette?"

"It's named after my grandmother. It's the last fragrance we created together. The finest, I might add. I had hoped you would buy it and market it."

"Surely you know this is not how huge companies work." He slid his fingers along the stem of his wineglass. "At Navarra, we employ several perfumers. We brainstorm concepts and give directions. The perfumers work to create something that meets our expectations. Sometimes, we create fragrances in tandem with celebrities. We do not, however, buy fragrances from individuals."

Her chin lifted. "Yes, but this one is good enough you might have. And I had to try."

He could almost admire her determination. Almost. "Why?"

She turned her head and put her fingers to her lips. He wondered if she was thinking about her answer, but when she turned back to him, he could see the sheen of moisture in her eyes. "Because my gran was gone and I didn't want to lose her house. I wanted to honor her memory and save my childhood home at the same time."

Inside, a tiny flicker of unease reared its head. "And did you lose the house?" He knew the answer because of how he'd found her. If she'd still had her childhood home, would she have been a cocktail waitress in a casino? Especially with a baby?

There were two fresh spots of color in her cheeks. "I did. I couldn't make the payments against the debt, so it was sold. A nice couple lives there now."

He hadn't had a childhood home. The thought made him feel raw inside. But he'd wanted one. He'd been eleven when his uncle had finally wrested him from his mother's capricious grip. Eleven when he'd first entered the Di Navarra estate in Tuscany. It was as close to a childhood home as he had.

Except, he had no memories of a mother's love or of warmth and belonging in a place. His uncle had been good to him, and he was grateful, but he'd spent a lot of time alone—or with tutors—because Uncle Paolo had spent so much time working.

"Where are your parents?" he asked her.

"I never knew them. My father is a mystery man, and my mother died when I was a baby." She said it so unemotionally, but he knew it had to hurt. He'd never known his father, though of course he knew his identity. He hadn't been that lucky with his mother. She had left her imprint deep. He was still trying to cover the scars of what she'd done to him.

"And what about the father of your child?" he asked, shaking away painful thoughts of his mother. "Why didn't he step up and help?"

Her lips flattened and she took a deep breath. "He didn't want to be burdened, I imagine," she finally said, her voice soft and brittle at once.

He imagined her pregnant and alone, without a home, and felt both anger and sympathy. Anger because she reminded him of his mother and sympathy because she'd lost so much. Was that what had happened to his mother? He'd never understood why she'd been so flighty, why she'd moved from place to place, always searching for something that eluded her.

She might have had to settle down if not for him. If not for the money he represented. The money his uncle gave for his care, but which she would spend taking him someplace remote and hiding him from the Di Navarras. When she would run out, she would emerge again, hand outstretched until Uncle Paolo filled it—and then they would disappear once more.

Clearly, Holly wasn't doing that with this child—but she had been living in that dingy building and leaving the baby with strangers. His mother had done the same thing, time and again. If Holly got money from the baby's father, would she spend it all recklessly in the pursuit of filling some emptiness inside herself? Or would she settle down and take care of the baby the way he should be taken care of?

"I am given to understand you can sue for child support in this country," he said mildly. "At the least, you could have gotten a bit of help for your child. I wonder that you did not do it."

Her eyes flashed hot. "You make it sound so simple.

But I would have needed money for a lawyer, wouldn't I? Since I couldn't afford to make the mortgage payments, I couldn't afford a lawyer, either."

"So you got a job as a cocktail waitress." There was condemnation in his tone. He knew it, and so did she. Certainly she could have found something else. Something safer for a child.

Her chin came up. "After I left New Hope, yes. I went to New Orleans and got a job in the casino. The tips were good and I needed the money."

"But not good enough to afford you a decent place to live."

"Not everyone is so fortunate as you."

"I have had nothing handed to me, *cara*. I worked for everything I have."

"Yes, but you had all the advantages."

"Not quite all," he said. For the first eleven years, he'd had no advantages. Hell, he hadn't even been able to read until Uncle Paolo had taken him away from his mother and gotten him an education that didn't require him to count out coins for supper. "Besides, when you are done here, you'll have enough money to take your baby somewhere safe."

"How dare you suggest I would put my baby in danger?" she said tightly. "Just because I couldn't afford a home that meets *your* standards, Your High and Mightiness, doesn't mean my son wasn't safe."

She was tightly strung, her body practically trembling with nervous energy. Her eyes flashed fire and her jaw was set in that stubborn angle he'd oddly come to enjoy. Such a firecracker, this girl.

They'd burned together before. What would it be like now?

He shoved the thought away and let his gaze slide over

her lovely face. She was going to make Navarra Cosmetics a lot of money, if his gut was any judge. And it usually was.

He didn't need to screw it up by getting involved with her again, however enticing the thought. Instead, he thought of where he'd found her, of the utter desolation of that apartment building, and his anger whipped higher.

"Do you really want your child to grow up there, Holly? Do you want Mrs. Turner keeping him every night, while he cries and asks where his mother is? Do you want him to only see you for a few minutes a day while you do whatever it is you plan to do with the money?"

She blinked at him, and he knew his voice had grown harsh. But he wouldn't take any of it back. She had to consider these things. She had to consider the child.

"Of course I don't want that," she said. "I want a house somewhere, and a good school. I want Nicky to have everything I had growing up. I intend to give it to him, too."

Everything inside him was tight, as if someone had stretched the thinnest membrane over the mouth of a volcano. He didn't know why she got to him so badly, but he didn't like it. Drago worked to push all the feelings she'd whipped up back under the lid of the box he kept them in.

"Perhaps you can give him those things," he finally said when he no longer felt so volatile. "Do you have any idea what the going rate is on a cosmetics campaign?"

She shook her head.

"It could be in the six figures, *cara*. But we'll need to see how the test shots go first." Because, no matter how bad he felt for her and the baby, he wouldn't hand over that kind of money for nothing. He'd go out of business if he allowed sympathy to get in the way of his decisions.

Her eyes were huge. Then she swallowed and fixed him with a determined look. "I expect to see that contract, spelling it all out, before anything happens."

Irritation lashed into him. "You don't trust me?" he asked, a dangerous edge to his voice.

She was nobody. She had nothing. She needed this job—and she needed his goodwill, after what she'd pulled last year.

But she didn't hesitate to push him. To demand her contract. He had to admit that a grudging part of him admired her tenacity even while she maddened him.

"Should I?" she said sweetly.

"Do you have a choice?"

Her jaw worked. Hardened. "No, I don't suppose I do."

"Precisely." He shoved back from the table and stood. "You will get your contract, Holly, because that is what businesses do."

Then he leaned down, both hands on the table, and fixed her with an even look. "And if you don't like the terms, you will be taken back to where I found you and left there without the possibility of ever seeing a dime."

Holly was restless. She was so accustomed to being on the go, to working hard for hours every day and then scrambling to get home and take care of her child, that being in this apartment with a nanny and no schedule felt surreal.

She'd tried to read a book. She'd tried to watch television—what was with all these people airing their private business in front of a TV judge for public consumption, anyway?—and she'd tried to listen to music. Nothing made her feel settled for more than a few moments.

She thought about going for a walk, but she was a little too intimidated by the prospect of roaming New York City streets alone. She'd walked the short distance from the casino to the streetcar stop in the dark—risky enough in some ways, but she'd never felt intimidated doing it.

Here, she thought if she went outside, she might never find her way back again.

So, she sat with the television remote and skipped through a variety of shows. And she finally had to admit to herself that the source of her restlessness wasn't just that her life had gone from two hundred miles an hour to a full stop in the space of a heartbeat.

No, it was also Drago di Navarra. He'd been angry at her earlier, and he'd threatened to drop her back in New Orleans, where he'd found her. The thought had chilled her. Yes, she was murderously furious with him—with his high-handedness and his arrogance and his certainty she'd been out to dupe him—but she couldn't let her anger get in the way of this job. She couldn't let him send her away before she'd earned that money.

It frightened her that she was suddenly so dependent on the promise of so much money. Yesterday, she'd nearly thrown a tray of drinks in his face. She'd been hostile to him and she'd wanted him gone—but he'd seduced her with words, with the promise of a better life for her child, and now she'd bought into it so thoroughly that the prospect of not having it threatened to make her physically ill.

She'd pushed him during their conversation. She'd been angry and she'd lashed out. Part of her regretted it—and part of her was glad. Damn him and his smug superiority anyway!

As if thinking of the devil conjured him, Drago walked into the living room, dressed in a tuxedo and looking every inch the gorgeous tycoon. Holly's heart thumped. Her jaw sagged and she snapped it closed again when she realized she was gaping at him.

Of course he was going out. Of course.

She didn't know where he was going, or who he was going with, but the thought of him out there dancing with some beautiful woman pierced her.

Why?

She did not care what he did. Holly lifted her chin and

stared at him, waiting for him to speak. Because, clearly, he'd come in here to say something to her. Perhaps he'd decided she wasn't worth the trouble after all. Perhaps he'd come to tell her to gather her things because a car was waiting to take her back to the airport.

"I have to go out," he said without preamble, and she let her gaze drop over him.

"I can see that. Have a wonderful time."

He ignored her and came over to perch on the arm of the chair facing where she sat. The TV was behind him, so she tried to focus on it.

Impossible, of course.

"We need to talk," he said, and her heart skipped. He was going to send her home. It was over. Well, she'd known it couldn't last. But he was going to have to pay her for her inconvenience, damn him. She'd left her job, for heaven's sake.

He lifted his arm, tugged the cuff of his sleeve. Adjusting. Making her wait for it. He was so cool, so unconcerned. His gaze lifted, bored into hers.

"Do you have a passport?" he asked, and Holly blinked.

"I— Um, no." Well, that wasn't what she'd expected.

He frowned. "Then we'll need to take care of it. As soon as possible."

"Why?"

"Because we are going to Italy, *cara*."

Italy? Her pulse throbbed with a sudden shot of fear. "Why?"

He looked annoyed. "Because this is where the Sky shoot will take place. Because I am the boss and I say so."

Holly shifted on the couch. "You aren't my boss," she pointed out, and then berated herself for doing so. But why should she let him get away with being so pointedly arrogant? He'd asked her to do the campaign. She'd said yes— but they hadn't started yet and she didn't have a contract.

He lifted one eyebrow. "Am I not? Somehow, I thought the one paying the salary would be in charge."

"You haven't paid me a single penny yet," she said.

"Haven't I? You did not get to New York by magic, Holly. Nor does Sylvia work for free."

Her ears felt hot. Well, yes, those things did cost money. "I did not ask you to hire her."

"No, but a baby on the hip was not quite what I had in mind for the ad."

"I won't go to Italy without a contract." She said it belligerently, and then winced at her tone. What was the matter with her? Did she want him to send her home? Back to nothing?

"These things take time to draft," he said coolly. "I don't keep a sheaf of contracts in my desk and whip one out as needed. Rest assured, Holly, you will get a contract. But you still need a passport, and so does the baby."

Her heart slid into her stomach. She'd never filled out paperwork for a passport before, but she imagined it required information she'd rather not share with Drago. Information that might make him ask questions.

"I don't understand why we can't do the shoot here. We did before. The park is lovely, and —"

"Because it's not what I want this time," he said. "Because I have a vision, and that vision takes place in Italy."

She dropped her gaze to the tips of her tennis shoes, where they rested on the ottoman in front of her. Jeez, he sat there in a tuxedo, and she was wearing jeans and tennis shoes as if she was still a teenager or something.

It reminded her starkly of the difference in their circumstances.

"It seems like a waste of money," she said softly. "The park is here, and it was so pretty the last time."

He stood and she could feel his imposing gaze on her. She looked up, and her heart turned over at the intensity of his stare. There was something in that gray-eyed gaze, something hot and secret and compelling.

Holly swallowed.

"I appreciate you thinking about the bottom line," he said with only the mildest hint of sarcasm, "but the fact is I can afford to do what I want. And what I want is you in Italy."

Holly twisted her fingers together in her lap. "Then I suppose we'll have to get passports."

"Yes," he said. "You shall. I'll make arrangements." He looked at his watch and frowned. "And now, if you will excuse me, I have a date."

A date.

Holly's stomach twisted, but she forced herself to give him a wan smile. Really, she didn't care at all—but being here made her remember what it had been like between them. The heat and passion and pleasure, the utter bliss of his possession.

Another woman would experience that tonight, while Holly lay in a bed in his apartment, only steps from the room where he'd first shown her what it was like between a man and a woman. She would twist and turn and imagine him with someone else. She would burn with longing, the way she'd done during the lonely nights when she hadn't been able to stop thinking about him no matter how much she'd wanted to.

Holly picked up the remote and flipped through the channels. She didn't see what was on the screen, couldn't have focused if her life depended on it, but it was something to do while she waited for him to walk out.

"Have fun," she said, because she had to say something.

He stood there a moment more, hands thrust in pockets. And then he turned and walked out and her heart slid to the bottom of her toes. Her eyes stung with unshed tears that she angrily slapped away.

She was furious because she was helpless. Because she had to do what he wanted or lose the money. That was the reason she wanted to cry.

The *only* reason.

Drago was not enjoying himself. He'd been expected to attend this event for the past month—a charity gala at the Met—but his attention was elsewhere. The woman on his arm—a beautiful heiress he'd met at a recent business dinner—bored him. He didn't remember her boring him when he'd met her only a few weeks ago. He remembered that he'd been interested.

She was lovely and articulate, and she had her fingers in many causes. But he saw beneath that veneer tonight. She had causes because she needed something to do with her money and her time.

She didn't care about the people she helped. She did it because it was expected of her. And because it brought her attention. He remembered seeing her in the paper only a couple of days ago, being interviewed about some fashion show she'd attended in Europe.

Even that wouldn't have been enough to make him think she didn't really care. No, it was her behavior tonight. Her need to be seen on his arm and her ongoing *catty* chatter about some of the other people in the room. As if she were better than them. As if he were, too, and needed to be warned about them.

The disconcerting thing was this: he wasn't quite certain any of these things would have truly bothered him just a few days ago. But now he thought of Holly sitting in that squalid apartment and feeding her baby a bottle, and a hot feeling bloomed in his chest.

Holly knew what it was like to struggle. To have almost nothing. She'd lost her home, and she'd gone to work as a waitress to make ends meet. His mother had done much the same, though for reasons of her own that had made no sense to anyone but her.

This woman—Danielle, was it?—wouldn't know the first thing about what struggling really meant.

He did. Even if he hadn't been a part of that world in a very long time, he knew what it was to have nothing. To rely on the kindness of strangers to eat. To beg and struggle and do things you didn't want to do, simply because you needed to survive. He'd only been a child, but the memory was imprinted deep. It was also usually buried deep—but not since Holly Craig had come back into his life.

"Drago, did you hear anything I said?"

He looked down at the glittering creature by his side—and a wave of disgust filled him. He didn't want this artifice. Not tonight. He didn't want to spend his time in the company of a woman who was superficial and selfish. She had millions, but she was still a user. A user of a different kind than his mother had been, but a user nonetheless. It dismayed him that he'd never seen it before.

Tonight, he wanted a woman who would look at him like he wasn't a god, a woman who would refuse to accept his pronouncements as if they were from some exalted place and, therefore, not to be questioned.

He wanted Holly. He wanted a woman who was direct with him. Oh, she hadn't always been. But she was now. She knew where she stood with him, so she was no longer trying to scam him. There was no need for pretense between them. She glared and huffed and stubbornly tried to get her way. She did not cajole. She spoke her mind.

No one spoke their mind to him. Not the way Holly did. She didn't even seem to like him much—but she did want him.

He knew that from the way her breath shortened when he was near, the way her eyes slid over him and then quickly away, as if she didn't want to be caught looking at him. Her skin grew pink and her breathing shallow.

That wasn't hatred, no matter what she claimed. It was desire.

"I heard you," he said to the woman at his side. "And I am terribly sorry, but I have to leave. I'm afraid I have another engagement tonight."

Danielle's mouth opened, as if she couldn't quite believe it. "But I thought…"

Drago lifted her limp, cool hand to his mouth and pressed a kiss there. "*Ciao, bella.* It was lovely to see you again."

And then, before she could utter another word, he strode from her side, out the front doors and down the sidewalk. His apartment wasn't far. His driver would have come to pick him up, but he wanted to walk. He needed to walk if he were to quench this strange fire for Holly Craig, before he stormed into his home and took her into his arms.

It was inconvenient to want a woman he'd once thrown out of his life. But he couldn't seem to stop himself.

He reached his building in less than fifteen minutes. The doorman swung the entry open with a cheery good-evening. Drago returned the greeting, and then he was in his private elevator and on his way up to the penthouse.

It was quiet when he let himself in. He glanced at his watch. It wasn't late, only nine-thirty. But his apartment was just as always. There was no television blaring, no one sitting in the living room, no baby on the floor surrounded by toys.

He found that oddly disappointing. He didn't care much for babies, but when he'd walked in earlier and seen Sylvia playing with the child while Holly made up a bottle, he'd had an odd rush of warmth in his chest. He'd dismissed it as something minor; a physical malady like acid reflux.

But now he felt strangely hollow, as if that warmth

would rush back if Holly were here with her son. He strode through the living room and toward the hall where the bedrooms were, his heart pounding. What if she'd left? What if she'd changed her mind and taken her opportunity to leave while he was out?

He'd taken the precaution of informing his driver—and the doorman—to alert him if she did, but no one had called. So why did he feel anxious?

A sound came from the direction of the kitchen, and he stopped, his heart thumping steadily as his ears strained to hear it again. It was late enough that the staff he employed would have gone home for the day, so he didn't expect to find any of them lurking about the kitchen.

He stopped abruptly as his gaze landed on the figure of a woman standing at the counter, her long blond hair caught in a loose ponytail. She was wearing yoga pants and a baggy T-shirt that looked as if it had been washed so frequently the color had faded to a flat red, one shade removed from pink.

She reached up to open the microwave and took out a bowl of something. Then she set a baby bottle inside it. Something about watching her warm the bottle hit him square in the gut. He'd never considered his life to be lacking, never felt as if he were missing out by not having a wife and children. He didn't know how to be close to anyone, not really, and he didn't know how to bridge that gap.

He'd always been on the outside looking in. And it had never bothered him until this moment. It was not a pleasant sensation to feel like an outsider in his own house.

But he did. And it made him feel empty in a way he had not in a very long time.

CHAPTER SEVEN

SOME SIXTH SENSE told Holly she wasn't alone. The skin on the back of her neck prickled and heat gathered in her core. She knew who it was. She didn't have to see him to know. She could feel him. Smell him.

She turned slowly, nonchalantly, her heart pounding in her breast. The sight of him in that tuxedo nearly made her heart stop. He was dark, beautiful, his gray eyes heated and intense as he watched her. He looked…broody, as if he'd had a bad evening. As if something had gone awry.

Was it wrong that her heart soared to think his date might not have worked out?

"You're back early," she said, keeping her voice as even as she could. Hoping he didn't hear the little catch in her throat.

"Perhaps I am not," he said, moving toward her, all hot handsome male. His hands were in his pockets and his jacket was open to reveal the perfect line of studs holding his shirt closed. His bow tie was still tight, as if he were going to an event instead of coming from one. "How would you know which it is?"

Holly turned to check the bottle. Not quite ready yet, so she dropped it back in the water. Then she shrugged. "I wouldn't. I'm just guessing. You don't strike me as the 'home and in bed by ten o'clock' type."

The moment she said it, she wished she could call the

words back. Heat flared in her cheeks, her throat, at the mention of Drago and a bed. Good grief, what was the matter with her?

Drago arched one eyebrow, and she knew he wasn't about to let her get away with that statement without comment.

"Oh, I most definitely am the 'home and in bed' type. Sometimes, I like to skip the evening out and go straight to bed."

Holly deliberately pretended not to understand. "How tragic for you. I would have thought the rich and dynamic CEO of a major corporation dedicated to making people beautiful would like to see and be seen."

"There's a time for everything, *cara mia*," he said, his voice low and sexy and relentless in the way it made vibrations of pleasure move through her body.

She'd spent the past few hours thinking about him. Wondering what he was doing tonight, if he was waltzing under the stars with some beauty, captivating her the way he'd once captivated Holly. He was a mesmerizing man when he set his mind to it. It had depressed her to think of him turning his charm onto another woman.

She told herself the only reason for her feelings was because she was here, in his apartment again, where he'd made love to her and created a baby. Her feelings were only natural in this setting. They would abate as soon as she was gone from this place.

He came closer, until she could smell him. Until her senses were wrapped in Drago di Navarra and the cool, clean, expensive fragrance of him. It wasn't just his cologne, which was subtle as always. It was him. *His* fragrance.

She wanted to turn and press her cheek to his chest, wanted to slide her fingers along the satin of his lapels, and just pretend for a moment that he was hers.

"Yes, and now it's time to feed Nicky," she said, her voice trembling more than she would have liked as she checked the bottle again. It was almost ready, but not quite. She set it back in the water with shaking fingers and then turned to lean against the marble counter. "So tell me all about your evening. Was it fun? Did you see anybody cool?"

He blinked. "Anybody cool?"

"You know. A movie star or something."

He shrugged. "There might have been. I wasn't paying attention."

Holly could only shake her head. Drago was a law unto himself, a man unimpressed with such fickle things as fame. It would take a very great deal to impress him, she imagined.

"Oh, yes, I suppose these things are ever so tedious for you," she said, with more than a little sarcasm. "Dress up in expensive finery, drink champagne, eat fancy hors d'oeuvres and hobnob with celebrities. What a life."

"Actually," he said, "it is tedious sometimes. Especially when the people one is with are shallow and self-absorbed."

Holly wanted to say something about how he was shallow and self-absorbed, but she suddenly couldn't do it. She should, but she couldn't seem to make the words come out. Because, right now, he looked a little lost. A little bleak. She wasn't sure why, but from the moment she'd turned around and seen him there, she'd been thinking of a lost and lonely soul.

Completely incongruous, since Drago di Navarra didn't *have* a soul. She tried to call up her anger with him, but it wouldn't surface.

She shrugged. "There are shallow people everywhere. I could tell you tales about the casino, believe me."

His eyes were hot and sharp. "And then there are people like you."

Her heart sped up. She swallowed the sudden lump in her throat. "What does that mean?"

He came and put his hands on her shoulders, stunning her. A shiver slid down her spine, a long slow lazy glide that left flame in its wake. Her body knew the touch of his. Craved it.

Holly felt frantic. *No, no, no.* It had hurt too much the last time she'd let him touch her. Not during, but after. When he'd sent her away. When she'd known she would never see him again. When he'd shattered her stupid, innocent heart into a million pieces. She hadn't been in love with him—how could she have been in only one night?—but he'd made her feel special, wonderful, beautiful. And she'd mourned because his rejection meant she hadn't been any of those things.

She could not endure those feelings again.

"What do you think it means?" he asked.

Holly sucked in a breath as doubt and confusion ricocheted through her head. "I think it means you're trying to seduce me again."

He laughed, and warmth curled deep inside her. She loved his laugh. He seemed a different man when he laughed. More open and carefree. He was too guarded, too cold otherwise. She could like him when he laughed.

"*Dio*, you amuse me, *cara*. Perhaps I was too hasty last year."

She refused to let those words warm her or vindicate her. "Perhaps you were," she said shakily.

His hands moved up and down her arms. Gently, sensually. She wanted to moan with everything he made her feel. "And yet here we are, with an entire evening to kill."

His voice was heady, deep and dark, and it made her think of tangled limbs and satiny skin. Of pleasure so intense she must have surely exaggerated it in her mind. Nothing could be that good. Could it?

Holly dug her fingernails into her palms, reminding herself there was pain in his proposition. Because it hadn't ended well the last time, and she didn't expect it would end any better now. She could take no risks.

"I'm sorry, but it's too late, Drago. You lost your chance to make me your sex slave. I am slave to only one man now, and he's pint-size and ready for his bottle."

Drago let his hands slide down her arms before he dropped them to his sides. Perversely, it stung her pride that he accepted her pronouncement so easily. As if he hadn't really wanted her after all.

"He's lucky to have a mother so dedicated."

Holly's pulse thumped. She let her gaze drop as a wave of hot shame rolled through her. "I do my best. I could probably do better."

Drago put a finger under her chin and lifted her gaze to his. His eyes bored into hers. "What makes you say this, Holly?"

Tears sprang to life behind her eyes and she closed them briefly, forcing herself to push them down again. She would not cry. She would not show a single moment of vulnerability to this man. She had to protect herself. To do that, she had to be strong. Immovable.

She wasn't so good at that, but she was learning. She had no room for softness anymore. Not for anyone but her son.

"I've worked so much," she said, her voice hoarse. "I haven't always been there for him. I hated leaving him with a babysitter every day. And I hated where we lived, Drago, but it was the best I could do."

He sighed again. "Things could have been far worse, believe me. You did what you had to do."

She didn't like the look in his eyes just then. Bleak. Desolate. As if he knew firsthand what those worse things were.

"I did the best I could. We weren't homeless and we had enough to eat."

A dark look crossed his face, and her heart squeezed in her chest. She almost reached up, almost put her palm on his jaw and caressed it as she'd done once before so long ago. But he took a step backward and put distance between them again.

"And now you are doing better. Working for me will give you a fresh start, Holly. You'll have more options."

She let out a shaky breath. "That's why I'm here."

He was frowning. Holly gripped the counter behind her until her fingers ached from the effort. She suddenly wanted to go to him, slip her arms around his waist. The only thing stopping her was the stone in her hands, anchoring her.

"You should have demanded help from his father," Drago said tightly. "He shouldn't have let you struggle so hard."

A shiver rolled through her then, stained her with the unmistakable brush of guilt. Oh God. "I couldn't," she choked out. "H-he made himself unavailable."

Drago looked suddenly angry. "Is he married, Holly?"

She was too stunned to react. And then, before her brain had quite caught up to her reflexes, she nodded once, quickly. A voice inside her shrieked in outrage. What was she doing? Why was she lying? Why didn't she just tell him the truth?

He would understand. He'd just said he knew she'd done her best. He would help her now, he would be a father to their child—

No. She knew none of those things. He was so intense, so powerful, and she had no idea what he would do if she told him the truth. What if he didn't believe her? What if he threw her out again, before she could earn the first cent? She needed this money too badly to risk it. And she needed to protect her child.

Until she had the contract, that ironclad promise of money, she couldn't risk the truth. She had to protect Nicky. He came first.

Drago's gaze was hard and her heart turned over in her chest. It ached so much she thought she might crumple to the floor in agony.

Your fault, her inner voice said.

"I'm sorry if that disappoints you," she told him, her voice on the edge of breaking. She shouldn't care what he thought, but she found that she did.

His eyebrows rose. "Disappoints me?" He shook his head. "I wasn't thinking that at all, Holly. I was thinking what a bastard this man is for leaving you so vulnerable."

Oh, goodness. He looked fierce, angry, as if he would go to battle for her and Nicky right this moment. It made the guilt inside her that much deeper, that much thicker and harder to shake off. She could endure him better when he was arrogant and bossy. She couldn't endure his empathy.

"I didn't tell him," she blurted, and Drago's expression turned to one of surprise.

She dropped her gaze to the floor. Holy cow, she was digging herself a hole, wasn't she? A giant hole from which she'd never escape.

"Didn't tell him? You mean, this man has no idea he has a son?"

She nodded, her heart pounding. "I tried, b-but he wouldn't listen. He didn't want to know."

Drago looked stunned, as if that thought had never occurred to him, and the quicksand under her feet shifted faster. Blindly, she turned and reached for the bottle. She couldn't stand here another minute. Couldn't sink deeper into the mire of lies and half-truths.

"I have to go feed Nicky."

She started to bolt from the room, but Drago's hand on her elbow caught her up short. "It's not too late to make this man meet his obligations—"

"It is," she said sharply. "It just is."

Drago sat at his desk and thought of Holly's face when she'd told him about the father of her baby the night before. She'd seemed so ashamed, so vulnerable. He'd wanted to pull her into his arms and tell her it was all right. Tell her she didn't need to worry. He'd considered, briefly, finding this man and forcing him to acknowledge his child.

But Holly's reaction told him everything he needed to know. She was scared of this man, whoever he might be. And as much as that angered him, as much as it made him want to find the bastard and thrash him for hurting her, Drago wasn't going to press the issue.

Besides, if this man came forward, there'd be someone else in Holly's life. Someone besides him. He wasn't quite sure why that thought bothered him, but it did. He didn't want to share her with another man.

Drago closed his eyes and pulled in a deep breath. No, it wasn't that he didn't want to share her. What an absurd thought. They'd had a hot night together, a fabulous night, but she had a baby now and he didn't see himself getting involved with a woman who had a baby.

The idea was fraught with pitfalls. Yes, he'd certainly like to have sex with her again. He wanted to take her to his bed and see if it was as good as he remembered.

But he couldn't. She'd shown him a vulnerability last night that had sliced into his chest and wrapped around his heart. She'd been frightened and confused—and worried. He didn't want or need that kind of intimacy. He wanted the physical without the emotional—and Holly Craig wasn't capable of that right now.

Drago ran both hands through his hair and turned to stare out across the city. He loved the city, loved the hustle and bustle, the sense of life that permeated the streets every hour of every day. New York City truly was the city that never slept.

But, right now, he wanted to be somewhere that slept. He wanted to be somewhere quieter, where life was more still. He wanted to take Holly and her infant to Italy.

But if he were going to get her to Italy, he had to get the passports taken care of. Drago opened an email from his secretary, who had informed him of what they would need to expedite the process. He made notes of what was required and went on to the next email.

This one contained sales figures for the quarter. Navarra Cosmetics was doing fabulously, thanks to a new skin-care line aimed at the middle-aged consumer. They had also debuted a new palette of colors for eyes, lips and cheeks that was doing quite well.

The numbers on fragrances were good. But Sky wasn't doing quite as well as he wanted for the new signature fragrance. Other CEOs would be perfectly happy with these numbers. But he wasn't. Because he *knew* they could be better.

Drago sat there a moment longer, thinking. And then he logged off his computer and informed his secretary he was leaving for the day. How could he concentrate when he was eager to revamp the Sky campaign? In order to do that, he needed passports for Holly and her child.

By the time Drago walked into his apartment, nearly half an hour later, he was no closer to understanding this strange pull Holly Craig had on him or why he was taking off in the middle of the day to do something he could have sent any number of assistants to do.

But when he strode into the living room and saw her on the floor with her baby, he got that same strange rush of warmth he'd had the first time. She looked up, her eyes wide and wounded, and his chest felt tight.

"*Ciao,* Holly," he said, dropping his briefcase on a nearby table.

She smiled, but it didn't reach her eyes. "I didn't expect to see you for hours," she said.

He shrugged. "I am the boss. I make my own hours."

She looked at her baby and smiled, only this time it was genuine. He tried not to let that bother him. "It must be nice," she said, her voice a little higher and singsongy as she directed it at the baby.

"Indeed."

The baby gurgled in response, his little lips spreading in a grin. Drago watched as he picked up a fuzzy toy cat and put the ear in his mouth. Drago had been around babies before, in the commune his mother had once dragged them to on some tiny island somewhere he'd tried to forget, but he'd never really had anything to do with them. The older children had been expected to take care of the babies while their parents worked in the vegetable gardens—and got high in the evenings—but Drago's one major act of rebellion, before his mother had left the commune and tried to use him to get money from the Di Navarras again, had been to refuse to help with the babies.

Instead, he'd had to pick vegetables and hoe rows. He suppressed a shudder and folded himself into a nearby chair. Holly's brows rose. And then she turned toward her baby and started to gather him up.

"Why don't I take Nicky and get out of your way—"

"No. Stay." She stiffened, and he sighed. "Please stay. I need to talk to you."

She let the baby go and he threw the cat. Then he picked up a toy banana and started to chew on that.

"I'm all ears," she said brightly, though her eyes were wary.

"Do you have a copy of his birth certificate?"

The color drained from her face. "Why?"

Drago felt there was something he was missing here, but he wasn't quite sure what it could be. "For his passport. We have to take him to the passport office and apply in person, because he is a baby and it's his first."

She dropped her gaze. "All right," she said quietly.

"Is his father named on the certificate?"

Her head snapped up again. There was definitely fear in those pretty blue eyes. A wave of violence washed over him. He wanted, more than anything in that moment, to make her feel safe from the bastard who'd abandoned her and her child.

"If he is, then he must approve of you taking the baby from the country," he explained. "If not, it does not matter."

Holly seemed to wilt as she shook her head. "No, he's not named. He would have had to be there to sign it, and that wasn't going to happen."

Drago smiled to reassure her. "Good. Then you are safe. All will be well."

"Yes, I—I suppose so."

She turned to look at her baby, and his heart pinched. She loved the child so much. What would it have been like to have a mother who'd loved him that way? A mother who did everything for his benefit instead of for her own?

He would never know

"There's nothing to worry about, Holly," he said. "Everything will be fine."

"Of course," she said. But she didn't sound reassured.

CHAPTER EIGHT

EVERYTHING WAS NOT going to be fine. Holly sat in the limo with Drago, Nicky tucked into his carrier, as they whisked their way through the streets of New York City on the way to the passport office. In her bag, she had Nicky's birth certificate and the forms she'd filled out for their passports.

She could still see the box that had made her heart drop to her toes: parents' names. She'd filled in only her side, because in Louisiana a father had to sign the birth certificate in order to be named. Drago wasn't on Nicky's birth certificate. No one was.

Still, it made her nervous. What if the passport office wanted more information? What if Drago were sitting beside her when they demanded it? How would she answer? How *could* she?

Holly pressed a hand to her stomach and concentrated on breathing in and out. There was still no sign of a contract, and they were on their way to get passports. It could all fall apart here. She could find herself on a plane home in just a few hours.

She would never see Drago again. That thought twisted her belly tighter than before. The scent of her fear was sharp, like cold steel against her tongue. She tried to ignore it, tried to focus on the other scents in the car. Warm leather, soft powdery baby, sensuous man. She closed her eyes and savored that last one as if it would soon be gone.

"What's the matter, Holly?"

She whipped around to look at Drago. His sharp gaze raked her. Belatedly, she smiled, trying to cover her distress. "Nothing at all."

One eyebrow rose in that superior manner of his. "I don't believe you."

She clasped her hands together in her lap. "Believe what you like, but I'm fine."

His frown didn't go away. "Would it help you to know that my lawyers have finished drafting your contract?"

Her heart did a slow thump against her chest. The contract. If only she had that already signed, she wouldn't worry as much. *Wrong.* Of course she would. Because she'd been lying to Drago from the moment he'd walked back into her life.

And, as she knew from bitter experience, he didn't handle deception very well.

"Oh? That's good."

His brows drew down. "You don't sound very enthused. Considering how insistent you've been, I find this rather odd."

Holly swallowed. "I'm very enthused," she said with false brightness. "What do you want from me? A happy dance right here in my seat?"

"Not precisely."

She rolled her eyes, tried to play it off. "I'm happy, Drago. Ecstatic."

He watched her a moment more. "Fine," he said, before dropping his gaze to his tablet once more.

Holly turned to look out the window at the traffic, her heart thrumming. She had to tell him the truth. Not right now, certainly, but soon. It was the right thing to do, no matter how much it terrified her. Once she had the contract, once it made sense to do so, she would have to find a way.

Provided it didn't all fall apart before she got that far.

The car pulled to a stop in front of a building on Hudson Street, and Drago opened the door. When they were standing on the sidewalk, Holly holding Nicky's carrier, she looked over at Drago, who was getting the diaper bag from the limo.

"You can come back and get us," she said. "I'll call when I'm done."

He looked imposing as he straightened to his full height and gazed down at her. He was dressed in a custom suit, navy blue, with a crisp white shirt and no tie. The pale blue diaper bag with the smiling monkey on it looked completely out of place against that elegant backdrop.

And yet he held it as though he could care less that the rich and entitled CEO of one of the most important cosmetics companies in the world might look just a little ridiculous. Or a little too appealing for a tabloid photo.

Holly cast her gaze up and down the street, but nobody with a camera emerged to snap a shot. Thank goodness.

"I'm going with you," Drago said.

"I don't see why," she returned. "I can handle it alone. Or you could send a lackey. Surely you have work to do."

"I have a cell phone and a tablet, Holly. I can work, I assure you."

She tried to swallow down her fear. It tasted like bitter acid. "I won't run away, Drago, if that's what you're worried about."

A preposterous suggestion that he'd be worried about her leaving, but it was the only thing she could think of.

"Holly, for goodness' sake, just turn around and walk into the building. We have an appointment and you're going to make us late."

She glared at him a moment more, her stomach dancing with butterflies—and then she heaved a sigh. "Fine, but don't blame me if it takes six hours and you're bored silly. I told you not to come."

Thankfully, it did not take six hours. But Holly's fear refused to abate while they waited. When they were finally shown into an office and it was time to hand over the paperwork, Holly snatched the diaper bag from Drago and fished out the papers with trembling hands. Then she handed them directly to the clerk.

The clerk was a typical bureaucrat, going over everything in triplicate. At one point, the woman looked up at Drago. He was flipping through files on his tablet and didn't seem to notice, but Holly's heart climbed into her throat as she waited for the woman to say something.

Then the clerk met Holly's gaze for a long moment. Finally, she seemed to give a mental shrug, and the moment was over. A short while later, they were on their way back to Drago's apartment, the passports safely tucked away in Holly's purse.

Holly felt a little shell-shocked over the whole thing. When they arrived at Drago's, she took Nicky and put him down for his nap. Then she climbed into bed and lay there, staring at the ceiling, her stomach still churning with guilt and fear. It wound its way through her belly, her bones, her heart, curling and squeezing until she thought she would choke on it.

She'd overcome another obstacle, gotten one step closer to the goal. Her luck was holding, but for how much longer?

She needed to tell Drago the truth before her luck ran out, but she was caught in an infinite loop of her own making. There was no scenario in which she could envision telling him and it not exploding in her face.

Once she signed the contract, she would tell him. Once she had the guarantee that she'd have money to take care of her baby, she could admit the truth. And then, even if he threw her out again when it was over, it would be fine. Everything would be fine.

But she couldn't quite make herself believe it.

When Holly finally emerged from her room a couple of hours later, it was because she was hungry and couldn't stay hidden any longer. She hoped that Drago would have gone out for the evening, so she didn't have to face him right now, but of course nothing ever went the way she hoped.

He looked up as she tiptoed into the kitchen. Her stomach slid down to the marble floor and stayed there.

"I was just looking for something to eat," she said casually.

"There's Chinese takeout," he said. "It's in the warming drawer."

She couldn't help but look at him in surprise. "You eat Chinese takeout?"

He shrugged. "Doesn't everyone?"

Not billionaires, she thought. She expected they ate lofty meals in the kinds of restaurants he'd taken her to the last time she was in New York. Or meals prepared at home by their personal chefs. Which he did happen to have.

"I figured that would be too, um, basic for you."

He laughed and a trickle of warmth stirred inside her. She loved that laugh more than she should. He was sitting at the expansive kitchen island with papers arrayed around him and an open laptop off to one side. Just a tycoon and his paperwork. Quite a different picture from the one she usually made at her worn Formica table every month, trying to make too little money stretch too far.

Chinese takeout had been a luxury. And Gabi was usually the one who'd bought it, against Holly's protests.

Save your money, Gabi. Don't waste it on me.

It's not a waste. Eat.

The memory of her and Gabi perched on the sofa in

front of the television, eating from containers, made her feel wistful. And lonely.

"Holly, I'm a man like any other," Drago said. "I like lobster and champagne, I like Kobe beef, I like truffles—but I also like Chinese takeout, hotdogs from a cart and gyros sliced fresh at a street fair."

She very much doubted he was like other men. But the idea of him eating a hot dog he'd bought from one of the carts lining the city streets fanned the warmth inside her into a glow.

"Next you'll be telling me you like funnel cakes and deep-fried candy bars."

"Funnel cakes, yes. Candy bars, no."

She pictured him tearing off bites of funnel cake, powdered sugar dusting his lips, and fresh butterflies swirled low in her belly. "Will wonders never cease?"

He grinned and then stood and walked over to the warming drawer. He wore faded jeans and a dark T-shirt, and his feet were bare. It was entirely too intimate and sexy, especially since the sky was dark and the city lights sparkled like diamonds tossed across the horizon.

She didn't know why that made it more intimate, but it did.

Drago pulled open the drawer and took out several containers of food. "There's a variety here. Mu shu pork, sweet-and-sour chicken, Mongolian beef, kung pao shrimp, black-pepper fish, lo mein, fried rice..."

Holly could only gape at him. "Gracious, was there a party tonight and I missed it?"

He shrugged, completely unselfconscious. "I didn't know what you liked, so I ordered several different things."

He set the containers on the counter, and Holly walked over to peer at the contents. Her stomach rumbled. It all looked—and smelled—wonderful. Drago set a plate and some wooden chopsticks on the counter.

"Thank you," she said softly. And then, though it embarrassed her, "But I'll need a fork."

He pulled open a drawer and took out a variety of silverware—forks and spoons so she could dip out the food—and set them down without a word about her inability to use chopsticks. It was a silly thing, but she was ridiculously grateful that he didn't tease her about it.

He walked back to his seat at the island, and Holly started to fill her plate. She thought about retreating to her room with the food, but he'd been so nice to order it all and she didn't want to be rude.

Holly turned and set the plate on the island. But instead of sitting, she stood and dug her fork into the kung pao shrimp. The flavors exploded on her tongue—spice and tang and freshness. Far better than anything she'd ever had from the lone Chinese restaurant in New Hope, where everything was either hidden under too much breading or soaked in sauce.

"I have your contract here," Drago said softly, and her belly clenched. "When you're done, we'll go over it."

She wanted to shove the food away and see it now, but she forced herself to keep chewing. She'd been unable to eat breakfast or lunch and now she was starving. If she didn't eat now, she didn't know if she would be able to. Her nerves swirled and popped like ice dropped on a hot grill. She was so close to having security for her baby. So close.

She put the fork down. "I have to see it now," she said. "I'll never be able to wait."

Drago frowned. "Only if you promise to keep eating," he said, picking up a sheaf of papers from the pile next to him.

"I will."

He came over and stood beside her, and her body was suddenly made of rubber. She wanted to lean into him, into his heat, and rest there while he explained what was in the papers. But she didn't. She forced herself to remain stiff, forced herself to keep forking food into her mouth while Drago pulled up the top sheet and laid it down.

"This is a basic contract," he said. "You'll appear in the ads, if all goes well with the test shots, for the next year. You'll be available for appearances to promote the perfume—industry functions, parties, etc.—and for more shoots as necessary. In exchange, you'll receive five hundred thousand dollars—"

Holly nearly choked on a bite of Mongolian beef. Drago glanced down at her, one brow lifted curiously.

"Sorry," she said a few moments later, after she'd gulped water from her glass and coughed enough to embarrass herself thoroughly.

"If the test shots aren't good," Drago continued while she mentally reeled over the sum he'd just named, "if we decide you aren't right after all, you'll receive a fifty-thousand-dollar severance fee and all your expenses for returning home."

Fifty thousand was still a lot of money. She could do something with fifty thousand. She could find a decent job, afford a better apartment. But half a million? Heavens above.

It was far more than she'd hoped—and yet a part of her was oddly disappointed. This wasn't how she'd envisioned her future. She wanted to work for a top company like Navarra Cosmetics. But she didn't want to stand in front of a camera and be the face of a fragrance. She wanted to *create* the fragrance.

But she had no choice. Since Nicky had come into her life, her desires took a backseat.

"What about my perfume?" she asked.

He flipped a couple of pages and tapped his finger on a line. "It's here. You get a half-hour appointment. Nothing more, and there are no guarantees."

"Do I get the appointment even if you decide not to keep me for the campaign?"

"Yes."

Her heart took up residence in her throat. "All right." She set down her fork and wiped her fingers on her napkin. "Can I read it?"

He pushed the contract toward her. "Take your time. But it needs to be signed tonight, *cara*. We leave for Italy tomorrow."

She'd thought her chest couldn't get any tighter, but she was wrong. "So soon?"

Drago looked so imposing standing there, hands in pockets, watching her. "*Sì*. There is no time to waste."

Holly perched on a bar stool and began to read the contract from beginning to end. There was a lot of legalese, but it was straightforward enough for her to understand. If the test shots went well, she got a lot of money. If they didn't, she still got money. And she got a chance to present her perfume to the head of Navarra Cosmetics, which was all she'd ever wanted in the first place.

When she finished reading, Drago laid a pen down in front of her. She glanced up at him, met his gaze. He seemed…very self-satisfied. The heated look on his face sent a sizzle of sensation straight to her core.

Her body softened, her insides melting as if she'd drunk a glass of wine. She felt fluid, languid. And intensely in need of his touch.

Holly picked up the pen, concentrated on the warm, smooth feel of the expensive barrel in her fingers. Anything that would take her attention from Drago. Anything that would make her heart stop tripping along as though it was running a marathon. Finally, she took a deep breath and pushed the pen across the signature line. Then she laid it on the table.

"*Grazie, cara,*" Drago said, reaching for the documents.

He shoved them into an envelope and then made a quick call to someone. A moment later, a man appeared in the doorway to the kitchen. Holly blinked as Drago handed him the envelope.

"You had someone waiting?" she asked when the man was gone.

"It is a courier, and yes, he was waiting to take these back to my attorney."

"But I was in my room," she said inanely.

"This I know," he replied. "But he only just arrived before you came out. I was coming to get you in five more minutes."

"Oh."

He was still looking at her, his gaze somehow both hot and assessing at the same time. "Feel better?" he asked.

Holly swallowed. Her mouth was dry. "Truthfully, I'm not sure. I'm not a model," she added, as if he didn't know.

His eyes sparkled with humor as he went back to his seat. "What is a model, except someone who advertises a product? You are not a professional, no. But you will learn."

"I don't want to be a model," she told him truthfully. "I want to make perfume."

She wondered if he was irritated with her for mentioning it, because he picked up his pen and tapped it on the island. "Ah, yes. And I have promised to let you present your fragrances to me. It seems to me as if you are gaining your chance in exchange for your participation."

Her heart thumped and her skin tingled with a different kind of excitement. "You won't be sorry," she said. "I know you won't."

She wasn't arrogant, but she knew her fragrances were good. And she wanted him to know it, too. She was confident in her ability, even if sometimes she felt like a total failure on the business side of things.

And a total failure elsewhere, as well. A cloud of doubt and fear drifted through her happiness, and she shivered. He was the father of her child and he did not know it. And she didn't know how to tell him. If not for that, everything would be perfect.

The thought made her want to giggle hysterically.

"What is wrong, Holly?" Drago asked, and she realized that something of her mood must show on her face.

"It's nothing," she told him carefully. "Nerves. Just a few days ago, I was taking drink orders. Now I'm here, in New York City again. With you. I keep waiting for the bottom to fall out."

He reached across the island and touched her hand. A shockingly strong current of heat flashed through her. Skin on skin. It was heavenly. Her entire body concentrated its attention on the limited surface area where they touched. It wasn't enough, and it was too much.

When he traced his thumb over her knuckles, she thought she would moan. She bit her lip to keep it from happening. *It's just skin*, she told herself. But it was his skin, his hand.

"You worry too much, *cara mia*," he said, his voice a sensual rumble deep in her core. "We're tied to each other now. For the foreseeable future."

He was talking about the contract and the Sky campaign. Though, for a single dangerous moment, she envisioned a different kind of bond. A bond between two people who wanted to be together. Two people who shared a child.

Holly licked her lips nervously. Her chest rose and fell as her breath came in short bursts. She wanted to run. She wanted to shove back from the island and flee before she fell any deeper into the morass. Before the truth came out and everything fell apart again.

Her life had been on the brink of disaster since Gran had died. She was accustomed to it. She was not accustomed to having hope. It terrified her. She tugged her hand away and tucked it into her lap.

Storm clouds fought a battle in Drago's expression. He looked frustrated and confused, and then he looked angry, his eyes hardening by degrees. Finally he sat back again. Incongruously, she wanted to reach out to him, beg him to touch her again.

"You have no reason to be scared of me," Drago said, shoving his chair back and standing. "I'm not a monster."

She tilted her head up to meet his hard gaze. But it stunned her to realize there was something more in his eyes. He looked…lost, alone. Her breath razored into her lungs.

"I don't think you're a monster," she said softly.

"I'm not sure I believe you."

Impulsively, she put her hand on his arm. His skin was warm beneath his sleeve, the muscle solid. His eyes were hooded as he stared at her, and a wave of fire sizzled through her body, obliterating everything in its path except this feeling between them.

This hot, achy feeling that made her body sing.

She dropped her hand away, suddenly uncertain. Why did she want to tempt fate again? Why did she want to take the risk and immolate herself in his flame?

Drago tilted her chin up when she would have looked away. "I don't understand you, Holly Craig. You are hot and cold, fierce and frightened. One minute I think you want…" He shook his head. "But then you don't. And I'll be damned if I can figure it out."

She tried to drop her chin, but he wouldn't let her. He forced her to meet his gaze. It was unflinching, penetrating. She trembled inside, as if he were reaching deep inside her soul and ferreting out all her secrets.

Except, he wasn't. He couldn't know what she kept hidden.

"It didn't end so well the last time," she told him. "Maybe that's what scares me."

He blew out a breath and closed his eyes for a long moment. "I make no apologies for what happened, Holly. You lied to me."

"I know. And I'm sorry for it. But I already told you why."

"Yes, you did." He sank onto the stool beside her and rubbed his palms along his jeans. "I don't like being lied to. And I don't like being used."

She wondered if he could see her pulse throbbing in her throat. Her palms were damp, but she didn't dare to wipe them dry while he watched her.

"I understand," she said.

"I don't think you do," he replied. He picked up a glass of some kind of liquor that had been sitting beside his paperwork and took a drink. She watched the slide of his throat, wondered how on earth such a thing could make her gut clench with desire.

"I've always been a Navarra, but I haven't always lived as one," he said quietly, after a long moment of silence.

Holly wrapped her arms around herself, her gut aching with the loneliness of his words.

"My parents were not married. My father was a playboy, a wastrel. My mother was easily corrupted, I think. When he wouldn't marry her, she might have had a bit of a breakdown." He shrugged, and she wondered what he did not say. "They were together for a couple of years, at least. I was a baby when he left her. He died in a car accident not too long after that. And that's when my mother started trying to use me to get things from his family. She spent years trotting me out in front of my uncle, demanding money and then spending it all foolishly."

"Babies need a lot of things," she said. "Maybe she didn't have enough, and…"

The fire in his eyes made her words die. She swallowed, her soul hurting so much for him. And for the woman who'd tried to raise him alone.

"She had enough, Holly. But not enough for her to get what she wanted."

"What did she want?"

His throat worked. "I wish to hell I knew." He threaded a hand through his hair, dropped it to his side again. "My uncle offered to take me in, but she refused to give me up."

Holly's stomach tightened. "I understand that. I wouldn't give Nicky up, either."

Drago leaned toward her. His expression was filled with pain and confusion. "She refused because she knew what she had. I was the golden goose, and periodically I brought her a golden egg. Eventually, my uncle offered her enough to let me go."

Holly's heart thudded painfully for him. But she understood why a mother wouldn't give up her child. Why she tried and tried to make it work before she finally gave in. What must Drago's mother have felt when she'd realized she couldn't keep him? That he would be better off with the Di Navarras than with her?

And why wouldn't Drago's uncle take them both? Why didn't he provide them with a home instead of an unthinkable option for a mother?

"I'm so sorry, Drago." What else could she say?

His features were bleak, ravaged. She wanted to put her arms around him and hold him tight. But she didn't. She didn't know if he would welcome it. If she could be strong enough to do it without confessing her own sins.

Oh, God, how could she ever tell him about Nicky now? He would *never* comprehend why she'd kept it a secret.

"I don't like to be used, Holly. I don't like the way it makes me feel."

"I understand," she said, her throat aching, her eyes stinging with tears. "And I'm sorry."

For so many things.

He sighed again. And then he shook his head as if realizing how much he'd said. "You should finish your dinner."

She looked at the food congealing on the plate. There was no way she could eat another bite. "I'm finished."

He stood again, shoved his hands into his pockets. He looked more lost than she would have ever thought possible.

"Do you see your mother much now?" she asked tentatively, imagining him as a little boy who must have felt so alone and confused when his mother had finally given in to his uncle's demands.

His eyes glittered as he turned to look at her. "I have not seen her since I was eleven and my uncle finally convinced her to sign over custody. And I never will again. She committed suicide six years ago."

Holly's heart hurt. "I'm sorry."

He shrugged with a lightness he could not possibly feel. "This is life."

"But…your mother," she said, her throat aching.

He reached out and slid his finger over her cheek, softly, lightly. "I believe you are a good mother, Holly Craig. But not all women are as dedicated as you."

His words pierced her in ways he would never know. What kind of mother kept a son from his father? What kind of mother struggled to raise him, to provide for him, when he could be the heir to all of this wealth? When he could have everything?

"Drago, I—" But she couldn't say it. Her throat closed up and nothing would come out.

He smiled, but it was not a real smile. It didn't reach his eyes. "Go to bed, Holly. Tomorrow will be a long day."

Like a coward, she fled.

CHAPTER NINE

HOLLY DIDN'T SLEEP very well. She kept waking up for myriad reasons. First, she couldn't stop thinking about Drago telling her, his eyes stark and lonely, that his mother had given him to his uncle and that he'd never seen her again. Then she kept worrying about Nicky, wondering if he was safe in his crib or if he was awake and crying and feeling alone.

She knew he wasn't crying, because she had a baby monitor. But every time she'd drift off to sleep, she'd hear him crying. Lost little boy. Lonely little boy. So she'd pop awake to silence—or as silent as the city could be with the cars rolling by far below, the honk of horns and squealing of brakes reaching high into the sky and finding her ears even in this protected environment.

She thought about Drago and Nicky and wondered how she would ever—or could ever—broach that topic. And she thought about getting on a plane and flying across a vast ocean to a place she'd never been. A place where she knew no one. Where she would be as lost as if she'd been plunked down on another planet.

Finally, Holly gave up and got out of bed. She showered and dressed in her best pair of jeans and a silky top with a cardigan she could put over it if she got chilled. She looked at herself in the mirror and felt woefully inadequate in her simple clothes.

Unsophisticated. Plain.

She leaned closer to the mirror, peering into it, trying to figure out what it was about her face that Drago wanted for his perfume. Freckles? She had a few of those, but she thought of them as imperfections rather than characteristics.

Her nose was small and straight, her cheekbones were on the plump side these days, and her mouth wasn't exactly a supermodel mouth. Her lips weren't luscious. They were average. Two pink lines that formed a pretty pout if she pursed her lips.

Her eyes were blue, but not spectacular. They weren't cornflowers or sapphires or any of those other things. They were just blue. Maybe sky-blue. Maybe just plain blue.

Holly brushed her hair into a ponytail and went to check on Nicky. He was awake, looking up at the mobile above him and kicking his little legs. Holly took him out of his crib and went into the kitchen to fix his bottle.

Drago looked up as she entered. He was sitting at the tall table facing the view, drinking coffee and reading the newspaper. Her heart flipped at the sight of him. She was getting a little tired of reacting so strongly to him, but she knew it wasn't going away. It had been there from the first moment, and would likely always be there.

"*Buongiorno, cara*," he said.

"Good morning," she replied. Nicky pumped his arms and made a loud noise, and she laughed, unable to help herself. When she looked at Drago, he was smiling, though he looked tired. Perhaps he'd had trouble sleeping, too.

"He is rather, uh, energetic, yes?"

Holly nodded. "Oh, yes. He keeps me on my toes."

She rummaged in the refrigerator for the formula she'd mixed in the wee hours. Nicky hadn't drunk it all, so she'd put it away. Now she needed to heat it up. Which was hard to do with a squirming baby in her arms. She tried to shift him around, but he kept wiggling.

"Let me," Drago said, coming over and holding out his hands.

Holly's heart skipped several beats as she gazed up at him. Then she handed over his son. It felt as if someone had wrenched her child from her arms, so much did it hurt to give him to Drago at this very moment.

A ridiculous notion, but there it was. And then it was gone as Drago stood there with Nicky in his arms, looking suddenly uncertain. He held the baby out from his body with both hands, and Nicky kicked his legs back and forth.

"You won't break him," Holly said. "Cradle him to your chest and be sure to support his head."

Drago dragged his gaze from the baby to her. "That's it?"

Holly nodded. "That's it."

Drago did as she said, and she turned back to the counter, getting a bowl and filling it with water. She popped it into the microwave to heat and turned back to where Drago stood, looking down at Nicky warily.

She would have laughed if her heart hadn't been breaking.

"He's so small," Drago said.

"But getting bigger every day."

Nicky started to fuss and Drago shot her a panicked look.

"Bounce up and down a little bit," she said. Drago looked doubtful, but then he started to do as she said, and Nicky quieted. Holly bit her lip to keep from smiling at the sight of strong, handsome Drago di Navarra—playboy, billionaire cosmetics king—bouncing awkwardly with a baby in his arms.

But then her smile faded when she considered that Nicky was *his* baby and she still needed to tell him so.

After last night, after she'd understood how lonely his life had been, it felt terribly wrong not to tell him he had a son.

But the moment had to be right. And it wasn't now.

She turned to the microwave and took the water out, setting the bottle inside and then reaching for her baby. Drago seemed relieved as he turned him over. Holly bounced Nicky and said nonsensical things to him while Drago went back to his coffee and paper. But rather than pick up the paper, he watched her. She met his gaze, saw the confusion and heat in his beautiful gray eyes.

"You make me want the strangest things, Holly Craig," he said softly, and a hot feeling bloomed in her belly, her core.

"It's probably just indigestion," she said flippantly, and he laughed. But her heart thrummed and her blood beat and a fine sheen of sweat broke out on her upper lip and between her breasts.

What she really wanted to know was what kind of things. That was the question she wanted to ask, but was too scared to. *Coward.*

Yes, she was a coward, at least where Drago was concerned. Because there was something about him, something she desperately desired. And if she angered him, if he sent her away, then she wouldn't get that thing, would she? It wasn't just sex, though it was that, too.

It was…*something.*

He folded the paper and sat back to sip his coffee with one arm folded over his body. He wore faded jeans and a dark button-down shirt, and his muscles bulged and flexed as he moved his arm. Her knees felt weak.

"Yes, perhaps you are right," he said. "Perhaps I just haven't had enough coffee yet." He glanced at his watch and frowned. "We need to leave for the airport in an hour. Will you be ready?"

Her stomach spun. "Yes."

"Good." He stood then. "I have some paperwork to attend to first. I'll let you know when it's time."

He left her in the kitchen alone, and she fed Nicky while looking out over the early-morning mist wreathing Central Park. She grabbed a cup of coffee and a bagel from the bag of fresh ones sitting on the counter.

Soon, they were in the car and on their way to JFK airport. Traffic was insane in New York and they spent a lot of time sitting still. Drago worked on his laptop, and Holly gazed out the window while Nicky slept.

She must have dozed, because suddenly Drago was shaking her awake and she was clawing back the fog in her brain while trying to process what he was saying.

"Passports," she finally heard him say. "I need your passports."

She fished in her bag and dug them out. Drago took them from her and then she leaned back and closed her eyes again. It was several minutes before the uneasy feeling in her belly finally grabbed her brain and shook hard enough to drag her into alertness.

But it was already too late. She sat up ramrod straight to find Drago looking at her, his gaze as hard as diamonds, his face some combination of both disgust and rage.

She'd had every chance in the world, and she'd blown it. Drago wasn't stupid. He would have realized by now she hadn't told him the truth. And he would never believe she hadn't meant to deceive him.

He held a blue passport in his hand, opened to the first page. He turned it toward her. She didn't need to look at it to know what it said.

"Tell me, Holly, precisely how old your child is again. And then I want you to tell me once more about this married man you had an affair with."

* * *

Drago felt as if someone had put a vise around his neck and started twisting. He couldn't breathe properly and he had to concentrate very, very hard on dragging each breath in and then letting it out again. It was the only thing keeping him from raging at her and demanding a definitive answer right this instant.

He held the passport in a cold grip and watched the play of emotions across her face. Her eyes were wide, the whites showing big and bright, and her skin was flushed. Her mouth was open, but there was no sound coming out.

Then she went deadly pale as all that heat drained away. He kept waiting for her to explain. To tell him why her baby was three months old and not two. Not that it meant anything that the child was three months old. It didn't make the boy his. He kept telling himself that.

Drago hadn't noticed the baby's real age at first. Hadn't realized the implications. She'd been soft and sleepy and he hadn't wanted to wake her, but he'd needed the passports for when they went through the checkpoint to reach the private jets. She'd handed them to him and gone back to her nap, and he'd flipped them open, studying the details as the car crawled closer to the guard stand. He was a detail-oriented man.

Holly was twenty-four, which he already knew, and she'd been born in Baton Rouge. Nicholas Adrian Craig had been born in New Orleans a little over three months ago.

That detail had meant nothing to him at first. Nothing until he started to think about how long ago it had been that he'd first met Holly when she'd come to New York. It was a year ago, he remembered that, because he remembered quite well when he'd had to scrap all the photos from the false shoot and start over. The numbers were imprinted on his brain.

Even then, he'd had a moment's pause while he'd pictured pretty, virginal Holly rushing home to Louisiana and falling into bed with another man. He didn't like the way that thought had made him feel.

But then, as he'd pondered it, as he'd watched her sleep and let his gaze slide over to the sleeping baby in his car seat—the baby with a head of black hair and impossibly long eyelashes—another thought had taken hold.

And when it did, Drago felt as if someone had punched him in the gut. He'd struggled to breathe for the longest moment.

There was no way. No way this child could be his. Black hair and long lashes meant nothing. He'd used protection. He always used protection.

But there'd been that one time when the condom had torn as he was removing it, and he started to wonder if it had perhaps torn earlier.

And as that thought spiraled and twisted in his brain, doubt ignited in his soul. If it were true, how could she do such a thing? How could anyone do such a thing?

But he did not know that she had, he reminded himself. He did not know.

"Whose child is he, Holly?" Drago demanded, his voice as icy cold and detached as he could make it. Because, if he did not, it would boil over with rage and hurt.

She'd lied to him. And she'd used him, used the opportunity to get what she wanted from him. He thought of the contract she'd insisted on, the money he'd agreed to pay her, and his blood ran cold.

Her gaze dropped and a sob broke from her. She crammed her fist against her mouth and breathed deeply, quickly. And then, far quicker than he'd have thought possible, she faced him. Her cheeks and nose were red, and her eyes were rimmed with moisture.

"I tried to tell you," she said, and his world cracked

open as she admitted the truth. Pain rushed in, filling all the dark and lonely corners of his soul. The walls he'd put up, the giant barriers to hurt and feeling—they tumbled down like bricks made of glass. They shattered at his feet, sliced deep into his soul.

"What does that mean?" he snapped, still hoping she would tell him it was a mistake, that this child was not his and she hadn't kept that fact hidden from him for the past three months. For nine long months before that.

But he already knew she wouldn't. He knew the answer as certainly as he knew his own name. This child was a Di Navarra, and Drago had done exactly as his father had done—he'd fathered a child and abandoned it to a mother who thought nothing of living in squalor and leaving her baby with strangers.

He wanted to reach out and shake her, but he forced himself to remain still.

"It means," she said, her voice soft and thready, "that I wrote you a letter. That I called. That you turned me away and refused all contact."

He was still reeling from her admission.

"And I will wager you didn't try hard enough," he growled. "I never got a letter."

It staggered him to think she'd spent all those months carrying his child, and he hadn't even known it. He hadn't specifically refused contact with her, but he had a long-standing policy of not accepting phone calls from people—especially women—not on his approved list of business associates. As for the letter, who knew if she'd even sent one?

"Well, I sent it. It's not my fault if you didn't get it."

His vision was black with rage. "How convenient for you," he ground out. "You say you sent a letter, but what proof do I have? You could be lying. And you could have done more, if you'd really wanted to."

"Why would I lie about this? I was alone! I needed help! And not only that, but what else would you have had me do?" she snapped tearfully. "Fly to New York with my non-existent credit cards and prostrate myself across the floor in front of your office? I tried to get in touch with you, but it was like trying to call the president of the United States. They don't just let anyone in—and no one was letting me in to you!"

The moment she finished, her voice rising until it crackled with anger, the baby started to cry. Drago looked at the child—Nicky, Nicholas Adrian—and felt a rush of confusion like he hadn't known since he was a boy, when his mother would come into his bedroom and tell him they were leaving whatever place he'd finally gotten settled into.

He didn't like that feeling. If they were still in the apartment, he would have stalked out and gone for a run in the park. Anything to put some distance between him and this lying, treacherous woman. But he was stuck in this car and his head was beginning to pound.

Holly bent over and started trying to soothe the baby, ignoring him as she did so. She talked in a high voice, offered the child a pacifier and made shushing noises. A tear slipped down her cheek, and then another, and her voice grew more frantic.

"Holly."

She looked up at him, her eyes so full of misery. He felt a rush of something akin to sympathy, but he shoved it down deep. Locked it in chains. How could he feel sympathy for her when she'd lied to him? When she'd used him?

He hated her. And he would *not* let her get away with keeping his child from him. Not any longer.

"Calm down," he ordered tightly. "He senses your distress."

"I know that," she snapped. She turned back to the baby—his son—and began to unbuckle the straps holding him in the seat. Then she pulled him out and cradled him against her, rocking and shushing until his tears lessened. Finally, he took a pacifier and Holly seemed to wilt in relief.

"You've been in my house for nearly a week now," Drago said, his voice so icy it made him cold. "And you've kept the truth from me. You had every chance to tell me, Holly. Every chance. Just like before."

She didn't look at him, and he wanted to shake her until she did. The violence whipping through his body frightened him, though he knew he would never give in to it.

But he'd never been this shocked, this betrayed, before. His mother had sold him in the end, sold him for money and freedom to do as she liked, and even the pain of that didn't quite compare to this.

He had a child, a baby, and the only reason he knew it was because he could do math. If he hadn't figured it out, would she have ever told him? Or would she have done the job, taken the money and disappeared with his child?

Until she'd spent it all and needed more....

Drago shook himself. "You have nothing to say to me?" he demanded. "You would sit there after what you've done and refuse to explain yourself?"

Her head came up then. Her eyes were red-rimmed. "I didn't know how to tell you. I thought you might throw me out again."

He reeled. She was unbelievable. A user. A schemer. First it was perfume; now it was a child.

He despised her.

"I might still," he growled. He wouldn't be as tender as his uncle had been. He knew what could happen when you let a woman keep a child she couldn't take care of properly, and he would never allow that to happen to his own son. He would use the might and money at his disposal to make sure she never saw this boy again.

Her eyes widened with fear. God help him, he relished it. He wanted her to wonder, wanted her to suffer as he was suffering.

"You would do that to your own son?" she asked, her voice wavering.

The violence in his soul whipped to a frenzy. "Not to him, Holly. To *you*."

Fear was an icy finger sliding down her spine. It sank into her body, wrapped around her heart and squeezed the breath from her. Drago sat beside her, his handsome face far colder than she'd ever seen it before.

He hated her. She could see it clearly, and her heart hurt with the knowledge that any sort of closeness they might have been building was lost. Crushed beneath the weight of this new reality.

She was frozen in place, frightened with the knowledge that he could kick her out of his life and keep her son. That he would even try.

And then, like the sun's rays sliding from behind the clouds to melt an ice-encrusted landscape, the first fingers of flame licked to life inside her belly. They were weak at first, vulnerable to being crushed out of existence.

But Nicky stretched and reached up to curl his fingers into the edge of her cardigan, and a wave of pure love flooded her with strength.

She met Drago's cold stare with a determined look of her own. Her heart was a fragile thing in her chest, but she didn't intend to let him know it. "You will not separate me from my son. Not ever."

"You forget who has the power here, *cara*," he said tightly.

"And you forget who Nicky's legal parent is," she threw back at him.

His jaw was a block of granite. "There are ways of remedying that," he said, and her stomach dropped through the floor.

"No," she choked out. "No. There's nothing you can do to change it."

She would fight him with every ounce of strength she had left in her body to prevent it. He would never take Nicky away. Never.

He was not the same man she'd spent the past few days with. This man was infinitely darker, more frightening. "Everyone has a price, Holly. Even you."

She hugged her baby's little body to her. "You're wrong, Drago. I'm sorry if you had a bad childhood, and I'm sorry you think your mother traded you for money. But I love my son and I'm not giving him up. You don't have enough money to even make me think about it, much less ever do it."

His eyes glittered and she shivered. "We'll see about that, *cara*."

He didn't say another word to her for the rest of the car trip. Instead, he got on the phone and started talking in rapid Italian. He made two or three calls before they reached the jet parked on the tarmac, and Holly's nerves were scraped raw by that time.

She wondered who he was talking to, what he was saying and what he planned to do. Was he talking to his lawyers? To someone who would bar her from the plane while he took Nicky and jetted off for Europe?

She held her baby tighter. She would never let him take this child from her. She wouldn't let anyone bar her from the plane and she would never accept money in exchange for Nicky.

There simply wasn't enough money in the world to make it worth her while.

When they reached the jet, Drago told her to hand Nicky over to Sylvia, who stood at the bottom of the stairs, smiling warmly. Holly cradled her baby close and refused, her heart hammering in spite of Sylvia's friendly greeting.

"You could fall on the steps," he said sharply, and her stomach banged with fear.

"I won't fall," she said. And then she started up the steps, one arm around her son, the other holding the metal railing until she was at the top and walking onto the plane. Drago was right behind her, so close she could smell his scent over the lingering aroma of jet fuel and the new smell of the plane's interior.

She could also smell the sharp scent of his anger, steely and cold. His body, however, was hot at her back, and she stepped away quickly, emerging into a spacious cabin.

The plane was much larger than the jet they'd flown on just a few days ago. This one was also incredibly luxurious. The interior gleamed with white leather, dark shiny wood finishes and chrome. There was a bar at one end, a couch with a television, and several other plush chairs.

"There are two bedrooms," Drago informed her. "And several bathrooms."

In the end, it turned out that one of the bathrooms was bigger than her entire bedroom had been in New Orleans. She knew Drago was wealthy—he was the head of a multinational corporation and heir to a cosmetics fortune—but she'd never quite realized the impact of all that money until this very moment, when she feared it was about to be arrayed against her. Yes, she'd signed a contract for half a million dollars, but she now realized how very tiny a drop in the ocean of wealth that was to a man like Drago di Navarra.

And it worried her. What if he did try to take Nicky away? She flinched as the door to the Jetway closed with a solid thump. Panic bloomed. She wanted off this plane. She wanted to take her baby—who she'd finally handed over to Sylvia now that they were firmly inside—and run down the stairs and into the terminal. Away from Drago. Away from the vessel that was about to take her across an ocean and put her somewhere she knew no one.

And had no power. Holly swallowed hard. She turned to go after Sylvia, to find her baby and at least be with him for the duration of the trip, since escape was now impossible.

But Drago was there, tall and commanding and so very distant as he gazed down at her, his handsome features set with disdain. An aching sadness unfolded itself within her as she thought back to last night and the Chinese food. She'd almost felt close to him then.

Almost.

"You will need to sit and buckle up," Drago said. "We'll be off the ground in a few minutes."

"I want to be with Nicky."

"Sylvia is taking care of him. That is what she is paid to do."

Holly tossed her ponytail over her shoulder. She could not let him see that he intimidated her, no matter how much he did. "My idea of how to raise a child isn't paying people to take care of him. Nicky needs me."

His eyes narrowed and she had a sudden, visceral feeling that she'd crossed a line somewhere.

"He will have only the best from now on, Holly. Sylvia is the best."

"And I am his mother," she said, her heart stinging with pain. She'd given Nicky everything she had, but of course it wasn't the best money could buy. She tilted her chin up. She had to be brave, assertive. "There's more to taking care of a child than money. He needs love and attention, and I give him that."

"Ah, yes," he said. "Such as when you dropped him with your neighbor and went to work in a casino. I'm sure he had plenty of love and attention then."

She felt as if he'd hit her. "I did the best I could," she

told him. "It wasn't as if you were there to help. And you weren't going to *be* there because I couldn't get in touch with you. You made it very clear that I was never to do so."

He shot up out of his seat and she took a step back instinctively. "To sell me perfume," he thundered. "You were never to contact me about your damn perfume!"

Her breath razored in and out of her lungs. "And how was I supposed to make sure you knew the difference if you'd already ordered your secretary to deny my calls?" she yelled back. "Was I supposed to send you mental signals and hope that did the trick?" She picked up a pretend phone and held it to her ear. "Oh, look," she mimicked, "it's Holly Craig calling. But this time it's *important*!"

His teeth ground together and anger clouded his features. Out of the corner of her eye, she saw a flight attendant moving carefully around them. That was when she realized they were making a spectacle.

She turned and flung herself down in a plush club chair and buckled her seat belt. Her cheeks sizzled with heat and her nerves snapped with tension. Her fingers trembled as she gripped the arms of the seat.

Drago dropped into a chair beside her, though there were plenty of other empty seats, and buckled himself in. Anger rolled off his body like fallout from a nuclear explosion.

"If you had wanted to tell me," he snarled, "you would have found a way. Instead, you let me believe this baby belonged to another man. A married man who abandoned you and left you to starve in the cold. You lied to me, Holly. And you would have kept on lying if I hadn't figured it out."

"I didn't say it was a married man. You *assumed*—"

"And you agreed!" he shot back. "What else was I to think, the way you acted?" His voice sliced into her. "You were worried about getting caught in your lies."

She whipped around to face him. "Yes, I was worried, Drago! I was worried because you promised me a way out of my situation. And if you learned the truth, and reacted the way you had the last time, I'd be back at square one. Only, this time I had my son to think about. And no way in hell was I letting you hurt *him*."

His eyes narrowed dangerously. She realized then, looking at him, that the roiling surface of his anger went far, far deeper than she'd ever thought. He was civilized—but barely.

"Did you ever consider for one moment, for one damn moment, that I might have a wholly different reaction to the knowledge I'd fathered a child? Especially when I told you about my own circumstances as a boy?"

She swallowed. "Not at first," she said. She'd endured the humiliation of being thrown out of his life before, when she'd done nothing wrong, and she couldn't take that chance with her child. "But I was going to tell you. I wanted the time to be right."

He leaned in toward her, his gray eyes hard and angry. "And why should I believe a word you say?"

Her eyes felt gritty. "No reason," she whispered.

"Precisely." He leaned back again, his body stiff with anger as the jet began to move. "You are going to regret your silence, Holly Craig," he told her. "You are going to regret it very much when I am through with you. This I promise."

CHAPTER TEN

THEY LANDED IN Italy late that night. It was dark and Holly couldn't see anything. She had no idea where they were, though she thought she'd read that the Di Navarras were from Tuscany. She didn't get a chance to ask Drago, because he got into a different car than she did. She was with Sylvia and Nicky, which was a great relief after the tension-filled flight over the Atlantic.

As soon as they'd been airborne, Drago had disappeared. He'd ripped open the seat belt and shot up from his chair like a hunted creature. Then he'd stalked toward the rear of the plane and hadn't returned. When she'd inquired of a flight attendant, she'd learned that Drago had an office. She didn't see him again until right before they landed.

He'd still glared at her with the same fury as he had hours before. His anger had not abated in the least, and that chilled her.

The cars wound their way through the night until they reached a grand estate that seemed to sit on a hill of its own. There were tall pencil pines and arbors of bougainvillea they passed on their way up the drive.

Holly wasn't even certain she'd been taken to the same place as Drago until she got out of the car and saw him gesturing to a man, who eventually bowed and then turned to give quick orders to the line of men and women standing behind him. Suitcases were hefted into many hands, and then they disappeared behind the tall double wooden doors of the villa.

Drago didn't spare her so much as a glance as he entered the house. Holly's heart pinched. And then she sniffed. She told herself that she did *not* miss the way he'd looked at her this morning when he'd told her she made him want things he'd never wanted before. It had been an illusion, nothing more. The sooner she forgot about it—the sooner she armed herself for this new reality—the better.

She was shown to a large corner room filled with antiques, Oriental carpets, gilded mirrors and overstuffed couches and chairs. There was a television in a cabinet, and a huge four-poster bed against one wall.

"I will need a crib," she said to the woman who was explaining how the television worked.

The woman blinked. "There is no need, Signorina Craig," she began in her perfect English. "The child is to stay in the nursery."

For the first time, Holly realized Sylvia was not right behind her, carrying Nicky. She'd been so tired, so lost in her own thoughts, that she hadn't noticed they were no longer with her. Holly's blood beat in her ears as fresh panic shot through her. "The nursery? And where is that?"

The woman, a pretty woman with dark hair coiled on her head, continued to smile. As if she'd been told to always be polite to the guests, no matter how frantic they sounded.

"It is not far," she said.

Ice formed in Holly's veins. "Not far? I'm afraid that's unacceptable."

The woman inclined her head in that slight manner that reeked of studied politeness. "Signore Di Navarra has ordered it, Signorina Craig. I cannot contravene *il padrone's* orders."

Holly didn't even bother to argue. She simply turned on her heel and strode from the room. There was a shocked silence behind her, and then the woman called her name, rushing after her. Holly picked up her pace, roving blindly through the corridors, taking turns that led into dead ends and empty rooms, doubling back on herself and trying again.

She didn't realize she was crying until she stopped in a hallway she'd already been in once before, looking right and left, and heard a sound like a sob. It took her a minute to realize the sound had come from her.

She squeezed her eyes shut, gritted her teeth. She would *not* lose control. She would not. She would find Nicky— or she would find Drago and give him a piece of her mind he wasn't likely to ever forget.

Holly came upon a set of stairs and dashed down them until she found herself in the huge circular entry. The foyer was quiet now, compared to just a few minutes ago, but she stood in the cavernous space until she heard a sound. A footstep, the clink of a glass, something. She moved toward it until it she heard a voice.

And then she burst into a room ringed with tall shelves that were lined with books. It took her a moment to realize the damn man had a library. A light burned softly on a desk, and a man stood behind it, his back to her, talking on a phone.

Drago.

Rage and longing filled her, rushing through her body in twin waves. She didn't understand how she could be so angry and so needy at the same time. How she could want to rage at him and hold him at once. She took a step forward, and Drago turned at the sound, his silvery eyes gleaming with anger when he saw her. He finished the call and set his phone on the desk.

"What do you want, Holly?"

She took another halting step forward, her lungs burning, her chest aching. "How dare you?" she spat. "How *dare* you!"

Drago looked bored. "How dare I what, *cara mia*? You must say what you mean. Or get out until you can."

"Nicky. You've put him in the nursery. Away from me." She could hardly get the words out she was so angry.

A muscle leaped in his jaw. "He is a baby. The nursery is where he belongs."

"He is my son, and I want him with me," she growled.

"He is my son, too, and I want him in the nursery. He is safe there."

Violence rocked through her. "Are you trying to say he's not safe with me?"

"And if I am?"

She couldn't answer that. Not without committing violence. "Why do you even have a nursery? You aren't married, you don't have children—"

The look on his face could have melted steel. "I do now, don't I?"

Holly swallowed. "You know what I mean."

"I do indeed."

She ignored the taunt in his voice. He was doing this deliberately. Trying to prove his mastery over her. His power. He wanted her scared. "How can you have a nursery?"

He came around the desk, too cool for words, and leaned against it. Then he folded his arms over his chest, and the fabric of his dark shirt bulged with muscles. Where had he gotten a physique like that? Clearly, he worked out— but she had no idea when he had the time, since he always seemed to be running his business.

Holly shook her head to clear it. She did *not* need to worry about Drago's muscles. They weren't hers to explore. Nor did she care.

"This estate has been in my family for generations,

cara. There has always been a nursery. It's been in disuse for quite some time, but a phone call fixed that. Did you think my son would have nowhere to stay once we arrived? Did you believe I would not even think to see to his comfort and care? Such a low—and dangerous, I might add—opinion you have of me."

There was menace in his voice. And heat. Oddly, it was the heat that interested her. She studied his face, the hard planes and angles of his perfectly sculpted features, and her pulse thrummed.

She needed to focus, and not just on this man before her. "I want my baby with me. He's not used to being alone."

"He is not alone, Holly. He has a nanny."

"He doesn't need a nanny," she blurted. "He only needs me."

Drago straightened to his full height. She wanted to take a step back, but she held her ground. "He needs more than a mother who struggles to make ends meet." His voice was like a whip. "More than a mother who leaves him with strangers while she works twelve to sixteen hours a day."

Pain exploded in her chest. She sucked in a deep breath and willed herself not to cry. Of course he would hit her where it hurt the most. Of course. "I gave him the best I could, Drago. I will always give him the best I can."

"Yet I can give him more. Better. How can you wish to deny him that?"

"I never said I did. But you will not separate us. Not ever."

His eyes narrowed. "Such conviction. And yet I wonder where this conviction stems from. Have you found your own golden goose, Holly? Will you cling to this child until you've bled as much money from his existence as you can?"

Holly didn't even think before reacting. The distance between them shrank too quickly for her to be aware of what she was doing. The next thing she knew, she was standing right in front of him and Drago was holding her wrist in an iron grip. Her open hand was scant inches from his face.

She jerked in his grasp, but he didn't let her go. Instead, he yanked her closer, until their bodies were pressed together, breast to belly to hip. It was the first time they'd been this close in a year, and the shock ricocheted through her.

Her palms came up to press against his chest—that hard, masculine chest that had filled her dreams for months. Holly forced herself to concentrate on her anger, not on the way it felt to be this close to Drago again—as if she'd come home after years away. As if she'd found water in the desert after going without for so long.

It was an illusion.

"You're a cruel bastard," she spat. "I love my son more than my own life. There is nothing I wouldn't do for him. *Nothing!*"

"Prove it."

She blinked up into his cold, handsome face. "What do you mean?"

"Walk away, Holly. Give him to me, and I will make sure he has the best money can buy for the rest of his life."

A shudder racked her. And then the heat of anger filled her. How dare he try to manipulate her emotions this way?

"I won't," she said. "No matter what you do to me, I won't."

His eyes glittered. One dark eyebrow lifted. "Are you certain?"

Her heart thumped. "Very."

Drago pushed her away and walked back around the desk. Then he sat down and opened a drawer, ignoring her for the moment. Her nerves stretched tight.

Finally he looked up, his handsome face cold and blank.

"There is a party tomorrow night for some industry people. You will attend."

Holly folded her arms across her chest, hugging herself as the wind dropped from her sails. "A party?"

His gaze was sharp, hard. "Yes. You signed a contract. You are the new face of Sky. You will be by my side tomorrow night."

Her throat ached. She couldn't very well refuse, and they both knew it. "Where is my son?"

Drago's look changed to one of supreme boredom. "The nursery is down the hall from your room. To the right. I imagine you went left when you departed, yes?"

She felt like a fool. How did he do that to her? "Yes."

His gaze dropped to his papers. "We are done. Good night."

When she was gone, Drago dropped his head into his hands and sat there at his desk, being very quiet and very still. Quite simply, she turned him upside down. This morning, his world had been right. He'd enjoyed having Holly in his home, oddly enough. He'd looked forward to talking to her. To watching her mother her baby.

His baby.

Drago swallowed. It felt like razor blades going down his throat. His entire day on the plane had been spent working in his office, making calls, viewing reports, talking until his voice gave out. He'd tried to distract himself, but all the while his chest had been tight and his eyes had stung and he'd wanted to go back into the main cabin and wrap his hands around Holly Craig's pretty neck.

And then he'd wanted to strip her naked and take her up against the wall. Bend her over a table. Lay her spread-eagled on the floor.

He hadn't cared how he would have her. He'd just wanted her.

And it angered him. How could he want a woman like her? A woman who'd lied to him, who'd kept his child hidden from him for the sake of a damn contract? She'd had every chance to tell him the truth, starting from the first moment when he'd walked into that hovel of an apartment and ending with the moment he'd discovered the truth for himself.

She hadn't done so, and he didn't believe she'd had any intention to—or at least not until it most benefited her. When she needed more money, when she'd spent everything she had, just like his mother had always done, she'd come with her hand out.

But even if she'd wanted to tell him, even if he gave her the benefit of the doubt, how could he forgive her for the lie for the past year? She said she'd written to him—who the hell wrote letters these days?—and tried to call.

He wasn't easy to get in touch with—but it wasn't impossible. Just last month, a woman he'd met at a party had managed to get a call through to his home number. He was not impossible to find. And Holly Craig had been to his home, unlike most of the women he went out with.

What if he'd never gone to New Orleans? When would she have come to him?

Drago shuddered. His mother hadn't taken him to his uncle for money until he'd been nearly four years old. He could still remember the look on Paolo's face when they'd shown up here at the villa. Shock, anger and confusion. And then Uncle Paolo and his mother had gone into his uncle's office while he was supposed to have played outside.

Instead, he'd stood in the foyer and listened to the raised voices. He'd been too young to know what they were fighting about, but he remembered the tension—and he remembered being scared and feeling as if it was his fault.

He would *never* allow his son to feel that way. As if he

was the source of everyone's problems. As though he was a commodity to be bartered again and again.

Drago shoved back from the desk and stood. One way or the other, he was taking control of his child's life immediately. Holly Craig had stood in his way long enough. No more.

He would own her completely—or he would send her away for good.

Holly was nervous. She stood just inside the house, listening to the sounds of laughter and music and chatter on the terrace outside, and felt as if her heart would pound from her chest. Drago had informed her only this morning that the party was taking place here, at his villa—and all her plans to beg out of the event with a headache or a stomachache or something else had come crashing down around her head.

She'd had no idea how she was supposed to attend a party when all she had were jeans and tennis shoes, but a tall, elegant woman—accompanied by three assistants— had arrived immediately after Drago's announcement with a selection of gowns and shoes and jewelry. Within two hours, Holly had a gown for the event and all the accessories to match—even down to the fine, lacy underwear.

She'd wanted to wear her own undergarments, but the woman—Giovanna—had looked at her in horror when she'd suggested it. When everything arrived that afternoon, Holly had still intended to wear her own things— until she'd taken a good look at the dress and realized the underwear was designed to go with it, and that her own would not be flattering to the cut of the gown at all. Vanity won out over stubbornness, and now she stood there in the shadows in a strapless flowing white gown, sewn with iridescent cream sequins, and felt so very out of her element that it frightened her.

She'd never worn anything so beautiful or expensive in her life. Her senses, already highly tuned, were sharpened tonight. Every scent bombarded her with sensation until she was afraid she'd have a pounding headache before the night was through. After she'd dressed, she'd taken one sniff of the bottle of Sky that Drago had sent up for her and knew she couldn't wear it.

There was nothing wrong with the fragrance, but it wasn't her. Instead, she spritzed on Colette and, head high and heart pounding, left her room and made the descent to the first level. She'd thought Drago would be waiting for her, but there was no one. The party was outside, in the glowing Tuscan evening. The sun was behind the horizon, but the sky was still golden and the landscape below undulated in darkening shadows of green and black.

Holly felt like a spy watching through the windows. And she felt as if she didn't belong. She wanted to go back upstairs to the nursery and curl up on the couch there with Nicky. Holly lifted her head. She was doing this for Nicky. For his future.

"I don't especially like crowds, either," a voice said, and Holly spun around to find a man standing behind her. He hadn't been in the room when she'd walked in. He was tall, handsome—not so handsome as Drago—and he was smiling at her. He held out his hand as he walked up. "I don't believe we've met. I am Santo Lazzari."

Holly held out her hand as butterflies swirled in her belly. Santo Lazzari of House of Lazzari was powerful in his own right. House of Lazzari wasn't a cosmetics firm, though they did sell a selection of designer perfumes in their stores to go along with their clothing and handbags. "Holly Craig. But how did you know…"

"That you weren't Italian?" He laughed. "My dear, Drago has spoken of nothing else since this party began."

His eyes narrowed as he studied her. "You are the new face of Sky."

Holly dropped her gaze as a blush spread over her cheeks. She was going to have to get used to this, even if she felt like an imposter. Even if she felt as if Santo Lazzari was mocking her, picking her apart and finding her lacking.

"I did tell Drago I'm not a model, but he seems to believe I'm what he wants." Her skin heated further as she realized what she'd said. "For the campaign," she added hastily.

Santo laughed. "Yes, Drago is like that." He took a step closer, sniffing the air around her. "Is this the perfume? It smells different from how I remembered."

"Um, well, no," she stammered. "I mean, yes, it's perfume. But it's not Sky."

Santo's gaze sharpened. "A new fragrance? Drago has not mentioned this before."

Beads of moisture rose on Holly's skin. Should she tell this man what she was wearing? Or should she change the subject? But how could she let a chance like this go by, especially when Drago was threatening to take her baby away? Telling Santo Lazzari about Colette could be insurance against the future. Drago was certain not to buy her perfume now, no matter that she had an ironclad appointment to pitch it to him.

"It's my own blend."

Santo's eyebrows lifted. "Is it, now?" His eyes gleamed with sudden interest. He held out his arm to her. "Come, Holly Craig, tell me more about this scent as we enter the party. I want to hear all about it."

Holly hesitated a moment longer. What would Drago think if she entered the party on another man's arm? But then the truth hit her, and it made her ache.

Drago would not care in the least. He despised her now.

No doubt he would think she was searching for another rich victim.

She told herself she did not care what he thought. She told herself it didn't matter, that the tentative closeness she'd thought they were building had been only an illusion. Drago did not care about her. He cared only about punishing her.

Holly smiled and put her arm through Santo's.

Drago stood with some of his best clients, telling them about his plans for Sky, when a collective hush fell over the gathering. Male eyes gleamed with appreciation as they gazed at a point beyond his shoulder. Drago turned to see what new arrival had caught their attention so thoroughly—

And gaped in stunned silence at the vision in white gliding across the terrazzo on the arm of Santo Lazzari. For a moment, he wondered who the woman was—but he knew. He knew it in his bones, his blood. He knew it in his soul.

Holly Craig did not look like the Holly Craig he knew. The Holly Craig he preferred, he realized with a jolt. No, this Holly was sleek and lovely, with her blond hair piled on her head to reveal her elegant neck, and her body-hugging dress shimmering in the torches that were beginning to glow on the perimeter of the terrazzo.

She moved like liquid silk. And she clung to Santo Lazzari in a way that made him see red. Her hand rested easily on Santo's arm and her head was turned to gaze up at Santo as if he was the most wonderful thing she'd ever seen.

Drago wanted to rip her from the other man's grip and claim her as his in front of all these people. So no man would dare to touch her again.

Instead, he tamped down on the urge to fight and strode toward the laughing couple. Holly sobered instantly when she glanced over and saw him, but Santo continued to gaze down at her for a long minute before he looked up to meet Drago's gaze.

"*Grazie, bella mia*," Santo said as he took Holly's hand and kissed it. "It's been a pleasure talking with you."

"And you," she replied, her voice soft and sweet in a way it never was with him. With everyone else—Nicky, Sylvia, the passport clerk, a flight attendant—but never him. That thought grated on his mind as he took Holly's hand and gripped it tight.

"*Amore,*" he said. "I have been waiting for you to arrive."

She smiled, but he knew it was false. "And here I am."

"Yes, here you are."

He wanted to drag her back inside and lock her in her room, but instead he turned and led her into the gathering. He introduced her to many people as they circulated. He made sure she had wine and food, and he kept her moored at his side. Much of the time, her hand was anchored in his, until he could concentrate only on that small area of skin where they touched. Until his senses were overrun with sensation and desire.

As soon as he could do so without drawing attention, he dragged her through another door and into his office. He closed the door behind them and turned to face her. She stood in the darkness, her dress catching the light from outside and shimmering like white flame. He closed the distance between them, until he stood before her, dominating her space.

Her scent stole to him and he stiffened as he finally realized what had puzzled him for the past hour. "You are not wearing Sky."

"No."

"Why not?"

"Because I'm doing everything else you want of me."

"Everything else is not quite as good as everything," he grated.

She shrugged. "I will wear it the next time."

His blood beat in his ears. "How do you know there will be a next time?"

That made her pause. "I don't."

"What were you talking to Santo about?"

She seemed taken aback. "We talked about many things. You, the campaign, the weather."

His eyes narrowed. "That's all?"

Her chin lifted in the darkness. "Why do you care, Drago? You aren't interested in me as anything more than a face for your campaign, so what does it matter what I talk about with another man?"

"You are the mother of my child."

"Oh, so that's important to you now? I thought I was an obstacle, a situation to be dealt with."

The truth of her words slid beneath his skin. "And I will deal with you, *cara mia*. Whatever you thought before you came here, whatever ideas you might have had, you can forget. Nicky is my son, and my heir, and I will not allow you to withhold him from me or to use him to control me. Are we clear?"

"You're disgusting, do you know that?" She flung the words like poisoned darts. "I'm sorry for whatever hell you might have gone through in your life, but I am not your mother and I won't abandon my son. You can't buy me off, and you can't make me go away. I'll fight you, Drago. I'll fight you to the bitter end, and I won't do it cleanly. If you force me, I'll take to the internet. Then I'll call the media and I'll smear you and Navarra Cosmetics from one end of this planet to the other."

Fury rose to a dull roar inside him—but there was something else, too. Excitement. He recognized it in the way his body quivered, the way his nerve endings twitched and tingled.

Every cell in his being was attuned to her, attuned to her softness, her scent, her heat. He suddenly wanted to touch her. He wanted to thrust inside her body, wanted to feel her cling to him, shape herself around him, gasp and moan and shudder beneath him as he made her come again and again.

He dragged himself back from the brink, back from that irretrievable moment when he would claim her mouth for his own and then not cease until he'd had her body, too.

"Try it," he said. "I have the money to make it go away."

He could employ an entire team to counteract anything she tried online or with the media.

Sure, all it took was a sound bite and the idea that powerful, wealthy Drago di Navarra was being unfair to this poor woman, and he could suffer some bad publicity. But he'd weathered bad publicity before. He wasn't afraid of it.

"Of course you do," she said. "That's how you operate, isn't it? You buy people off. You threaten and yell and order, and people do what you want. Well, not me, Drago. We have a contract, and don't think I won't take you to court if you break it."

He could have laughed if he weren't so angry. She had no idea how powerless she was. How he could tie her up in court until she had nothing left to battle him with. She would win, but she would have nothing once she paid her lawyers.

Suddenly, he was tired of this. He was tired of battling with her—of battling with himself—when what he really wanted was to have her beneath him. There was no reason he could think of to fight this attraction a moment longer.

He reached for her and she gasped. But then he tugged her in close, until their bodies were pressed tightly together, his fingers spread across the skin of her back where the dress dipped down. She was warm, and his fingers tingled as if electricity flowed beneath her skin.

"Your threat is as frightening as a swat from a kitten," he murmured, his gaze focusing on her lips—those lush, pretty lips that had dropped open in surprise.

Her head tilted back, her eyes searching his. The heat of her burned into him. His cock leaped against the confines of his trousers, and he knew she felt it by the widening of her eyes. She did not try to move away, and he experienced a surge of triumph. Her palms on his chest became fistfuls of his shirt. Her eyes filled with sexual heat.

Oh, yes, he'd not read this wrong at all. She wanted him. Desperately.

"I'm not a kitten, Drago," she said, her gaze on his mouth. "I mean what I say."

"Yes," he said, his hands sliding down her back, cupping her bottom and pulling her in closer to the heat and hardness of his body. "I know you do."

She gasped. And then she moved her hips. It was a slight movement, the whisper of an arch, but he knew in that moment that she was lost. As lost and helpless to this pull between them as he was.

"I hate you," she said, the sound halfway to a moan as he held her to him and slid the hardness of his body along the sensitive heart of her.

"Yes," he said. "You hate me, *bella mia.* I can feel it so strongly."

She gasped again. "This is so wrong," she said. "I shouldn't feel like this, not after the things you've said...."

Neither should he. But he lowered his head and slid his mouth along the sweet curve of her jaw anyway. Her fingers flexed convulsively in his shirt.

"Don't think, Holly. Just feel. Feel what we do to each other...."

CHAPTER ELEVEN

A CORNER OF Holly's brain told her she needed to stop this. That she needed to push this man away and let him know, once and for all, that she was not his to command.

But she couldn't do it. Because she was his. She wanted him to command her, at least in this. She wanted to feel his heat and hardness and strength. Wanted to lose herself in him, in the way he made her feel.

He confused her, and excited her. He frightened her, and challenged her. She hated him—and she wanted him. She'd spent the past hour trying to focus on the conversations around her, trying to smile and be the Sky spokesmodel, but all her senses kept coming back to one immutable fact: Drago's hand on hers was driving her insane.

Now she had much more than his hand. His mouth moved along her jaw, slid to her ear. He nibbled the tender flesh of her earlobe, and she could feel the erotic pull all the way to her toes. She'd long since passed the mark where she was ready for him. Her sex felt heavy between her thighs, achy. She was wet and hot. She *needed.*

She slipped her arms around his neck and he rewarded her with a lick of his tongue on the tender flesh behind her ear.

Then he growled something in Italian and his hands went to her waist. He found the zipper at her back and slid it down slowly, until the bodice of her strapless dress gaped. His fingers found the clasp of her bra and then her breasts were free from their confinement.

Holly instinctively covered herself. "There are people outside," she said in a panic. "They will notice we've gone."

"Yes, they will notice. But they won't search for us, *bella mia*. They are well fed, plied with the best wines and dishes I have to offer. They will stay and listen to the musicians, they will eat and drink and talk. They will not follow us."

She felt so wicked standing here in his office, naked from the waist up, and hearing the strains of music and voices coming from the gardens. Drago covered her hands with his, gently pulled them away until her breasts were bare and gooseflesh rose on her skin.

Then his palms found them, shaped them, and her heart shuddered in her chest.

"So lovely," he said. "So tempting."

And then he dropped his head and took one tight nipple in his mouth. Holly thought she would come unglued right then. She clutched his head, cried out with the sweet torture of his lips and tongue and teeth on her breast. She hadn't been touched like this in a year. Not since he'd been the one to show her how beautiful and perfect it could be.

"Drago," she gasped. "I don't know—"

"I do," he said. Then he pressed her breasts together in his hands, moved between them, licking and sucking her nipples while she arched her back and thrust them into his hot mouth. She felt every tug, every pull between her legs, as if her nipples were somehow attached to her sex.

He made her utterly crazy. She shouldn't be doing this, shouldn't be succumbing to the sensual power he had— but she didn't want to stop. It had been too long, and she'd been too lonely.

If he wanted her this way, if he couldn't help himself,

either, then maybe there was a chance for them. A chance they could work out their differences and be good parents to their child for his sake.

"I want to touch you," she cried at the next sweet spike of pleasure.

"Then touch me."

Holly shoved his tuxedo jacket from his shoulders, then tugged his shirt from his waistband. Her hands slipped beneath the fabric until her palms were—finally, finally—on his hot flesh. His skin quivered beneath her touch, and it made her bold.

She found his nipples, pinched them between her thumbs and forefingers while he sucked on hers. He groaned low in his throat. And then he pushed her back, ripped open his tie and shirt, studs scattering across the floor.

His chest was so perfect, so beautiful. He wasn't muscle-bound, like a body builder who didn't know when to quit. But he had a hard physique that made her mouth water. His eyes, when she finally dragged her gaze away from his firm pectorals, sizzled into her.

"Do you want me, Holly?"

She should tell him no. She knew she should, but she couldn't. She nodded mutely.

"Then come to me." He opened his arms and she went into them. When their skin touched, she wanted to moan with the pleasure. Drago's fingers roamed over her flesh, his thumbs gliding over her sensitive nipples again and again. Holly spread her hands on his chest, slid her fingers over the firm planes of muscle.

She looked up, into his eyes, her heart turning over at the heat she saw there. She wanted him to kiss her. It was odd to think he'd had his mouth on her breasts, but had not yet kissed her. She moved restlessly in his arms, stretched up on tiptoes to find his mouth, but he dropped his lips to the side of her neck again.

The fire between them spun up quickly. Drago pushed the dress down her hips until it pooled at her feet. "It will wrinkle," she said.

"I don't care."

She reached for his zipper. It didn't take her a moment to free him from his trousers. She wrapped her hand around his hot, hard flesh, her heart thrumming hard, making her dizzy.

His groan made her want to do things she'd never done before. She dropped to her knees and put her mouth around him, her tongue curling and gliding over his hot flesh.

Drago swore. She glanced up at him, and his eyes were closed tight. His jaw flexed as if he were in pain.

But she knew it wasn't pain—or not the bad kind, anyway.

Still, he didn't let her explore him the way she wanted. Too soon, he dragged her up into his arms and speared his hand into her hair. This time—oh, yes, this time—his mouth came down on hers.

And that was when she knew that nothing in her life would ever be the same again.

Holly's knees buckled when Drago's tongue touched hers. It was a silly reaction, and yet she couldn't control it. She'd forgotten just how drugging his kisses were. How necessary.

He caught her around the waist, and then he lifted her and turned until she was sitting on his desk. The wood was cold on her bare bottom. She was still wearing the lacy thong that went with the dress, but it didn't protect her skin from the coolness.

Not that she wanted to be protected. It was a welcome coolness, since the heat of their bodies threatened to incinerate her.

Drago tugged at her panties until she lifted her bottom and he could yank them off. Then he spread her knees wide and stepped between them. Instinctively, Holly curled her legs around his waist. Together, they fell backward—she heard the crash of many things hitting the floor and realized that Drago had swept them away with his arm as he'd laid her down on the desk. She only hoped there was nothing breakable—

And then she didn't care. Drago's mouth was thorough, demanding. His hard erection rode the seam of her body, gliding against her wetness with the most deliciously pleasurable friction imaginable.

It wasn't enough. She wanted more, wanted him inside her. Her hands kneaded the flesh of his back, skated down his sides, over his hips. She tried to reach between them, tried to guide him into her, but he pulled back with a muttered curse.

"Condom," he said. And then somehow he found one in the desk. He pulled away and rolled it on. She lay on the desk and watched him, feasted her eyes on the sheer beauty of his body. He put his hand over the mound of her sex, and she bit her lip to keep from crying out. Then he slid a finger down, into all that wetness. He hissed, as if she'd burned him—and then he skimmed over her damp skin while she whimpered.

Drago traced her, the plumpness on the outside, the delicate ridges on the inside, and all the while her heart beat a crazy rhythm in her chest. When he touched her most sensitive spot again, she cried out as sensation rocked her.

"You're so ready for me, *cara*," he said. "And it is everything I can do not to take what you offer right this very moment."

Her eyes snapped open. "Take it. Please."

He shook his head, and her heart dropped. Was this some crazy act of revenge? Was he going to deny this heat between them now that they'd come so far? Was he going to send her away before anything happened?

Disappointment tasted bitter. So bitter.

But then he spoke and her heart soared once more. "Not yet. First, I want to make you come." He stroked her again, and she shuddered. "I want you to sob my name, Holly. I want you to beg me for release."

"I'll beg now," she told him, her body on fire. "I have no shame."

And she didn't. Not where he was concerned. The only shame she'd ever felt was when he'd kicked her out. She'd not felt one moment of guilt for what she'd done with him. She might not have always realized that, but it was the truth. There was no shame in these feelings, no shame in this fire between them.

He laughed, a deep sensual purr that reverberated through her. "Patience, *cara*. Some things are worth the wait."

"I've been waiting a year," she said heatedly, and his eyes darkened. But it wasn't an angry darkening. No, instead she sensed he was on the edge of control. He was every bit as eager as she was. He just didn't want to admit it. Or perhaps it was better to say that Drago di Navarra was accustomed to being in control. Taking his time meant he could govern his need. Meant that he was superhuman, not prey to the usual vicissitudes of emotion.

But Holly wanted him to lose control. She didn't know why it was important to her, but if she was committed to doing this with him—and she was—she wanted it to be something he couldn't shape into what he wanted it to be. She wanted it to be as wild and chaotic for him as it was for her.

Holly lifted herself on her elbows and reached for him. His breath hissed in when she closed her hand around him. He was so hot and hard that she wondered how he could stand it.

Because she could barely stand the empty ache in her core. The only way to ease that ache was to fill it with him.

"I'm begging you now, Drago," she said, hardly recognizing the note of desperation in her voice. "I'm begging you."

His eyes darkened again. Then he lowered his head slowly, so slowly, that she thought he would deny her. But then he kissed her, his lips fusing with hers so sweetly and perfectly that she let go of him and wrapped her arms around his neck.

The kiss was hotter than any she'd ever experienced with him. He took her mouth completely, utterly, and she gave herself up to him as if she'd been born to do so. Her legs went around his waist again, locked tight to keep him from leaving her.

But he had no intention of doing so. He found her entrance—and then he slid inside her. Slowly, but surely. Exquisitely. Holly gasped at the fullness of his possession. She hadn't remembered it being this way before, but of course it had been.

She closed her eyes. No, it would have been somewhat more intense simply because she'd been a virgin. She was no longer a virgin, and while she had no experience of sex beyond that single night with Drago, she was more than ready for this moment.

Drago groaned as he seated himself fully inside her. "Look at me, *bella*."

Holly opened her eyes again, met the intensity of his hot stare. The look on his face made her stomach flip. He was so intense, so beautiful. And, for this moment at least, he was hers.

"You excite me, Holly. You make me…"

Whatever he was going to say was lost as he closed his eyes and gripped her hips. His head tilted back, the muscles in his neck cording tight. And then he shifted his hips, withdrawing almost completely before slamming into her again.

Holly licked her lips as sensation bloomed in her core. A moment later, Drago was there, sucking her tongue into his mouth. She wrapped her arms around him and held on tight while he held her hips in two broad hands and pumped into her again and again.

She'd forgotten how amazing it was between them. How incredible. How necessary. The tension in her body wound tighter and tighter—until finally it snapped and flung her out over infinite space.

She fell forever, her body shuddering and trembling as she cried out her pleasure. Her senses were so keen, so sharp. She could smell their passion, a combination of flame and sweat and sex, and she could smell the flowers in the garden, the wine, the food, the mingled perfumes of dozens of people.

But, mostly, she smelled him—sandalwood, pears, moss and man. He was warm and hard and vibrant, and he owned her body in this moment.

When she thought she would never move again, when she was boneless and liquid in his arms, he withdrew from her body. And then he turned her so that she was sprawled over the desk, her bottom in the air, her breasts pressed against the wood

She spread her arms and gripped either edge of the desk as Drago entered her again. It was different this time, though just as delicious. The pressure was exquisite as he stroked into her. She didn't think she could come again but he slid his hand around her body, found her sweet spot. Holly moaned and bucked against him as the spring began to tighten once more.

Too quickly, she shattered, coming in a hot, hard rush of feeling that left her limp and weak.

Drago rocked into her body again and again—and then

he stiffened. Her name was a broken groan in his throat. A moment later, his lips settled on her shoulder and a shiver went through her. He was still inside her, still hard. She tilted her hips up, and Drago gasped.

"*Dio*, Holly. What you do to me should be illegal."

She couldn't help but laugh, though it didn't sound like her usual laugh. No, this was the laugh of a sensual woman. A satisfied woman. It was low and sexy and sultry. She liked it. "Maybe it is illegal," she said. "Maybe I like it that way."

He withdrew from her body and helped her up, turning her until they were pressed together from breast to hip. Her heart beat hard, dizzily. Drago tilted her chin up with a finger and kissed her thoroughly.

Then he broke the kiss and pressed his forehead to hers. "I'm taking you to bed, Holly. *My* bed. Any complaints?"

She thought about the party in the garden, about her baby tucked away in his room, and about the man standing before her. "Not a single one," she said.

Drago grinned. "This is what I like to hear."

"Obedience?" she asked as she searched for her underwear in the darkened room. But she said it teasingly for once.

He laughed. "In this instance, absolutely." He came over and helped her into her dress, his mouth dropped to her shoulder as he slid her zipper up again. "But I promise to make it worth your while, *amore mia.*"

Drago awoke in that early hour before dawn. Something felt different, and it took him a moment of lying there in the darkness and processing everything to realize what it was.

He was happy.

He frowned. But he shouldn't be happy. Not at all.

He should be murderously angry with the woman lying beside him. He had been angry. Violently so. But then he'd lost himself in her body and he hadn't been the same since. He couldn't seem to dredge up the fury he'd felt earlier. All he had now was hurt and sadness and desire. Plenty of desire.

Dio, what they'd done to each other last night. He was worn-out, sated. He couldn't remember the last time he'd felt so utterly drained after sex. Except, perhaps, the last time he'd been with her.

Drago threw the covers back and got out of bed. Quietly, so as not to wake Holly. She lay on her side, curled up, with her buttocks thrust toward him.

He had an urge to lean down and nip her.

Drago resolutely turned away from the woman in his bed and tugged on a pair of jeans he'd thrown over a chair when he'd been changing into his tuxedo. He had no idea when the party had ended or when the last guest had left. He was confident, however, they'd had a good time, regardless of his absence.

He left the room and padded down to the nursery, which was a few doors away on the same corridor. He'd originally planned to put Holly and her baby in another wing of the house—until he'd discovered the truth about the child.

Now the baby was his son and he had no idea what that meant to him other than it meant something important. He stepped into the nursery and walked over to the crib. The boy lay on his back, eyes closed, little chest rising and falling evenly.

Drago stood there and gazed down at the sleeping child while an emotional tornado whirled inside his soul. This was *his* flesh, *his* blood. He could see it now. In the dark hair, in the shape of the mouth, in the impossibly long lashes. This child was stamped with the Di Navarra signature traits like a piece of fine art was signed by the maker.

He felt a rush of feeling in his gut. He wanted to pick the boy up and hold him, but of course he wasn't about to do so. Even if he knew what he was doing, he didn't want to wake the baby when he slept so peacefully.

Drago might not know much about babies, but he knew they didn't sleep on command or at the convenience of others. If this one was asleep now, best to leave him that way. He watched the boy and thought of his own mother. Had she ever stood over him and felt this rush of emotion and protectiveness like he felt right now?

Probably not. What he didn't understand was how she couldn't feel those things. He didn't even know this child, not really, and he already knew he would never allow anyone to harm this baby. Not ever.

His eyes stung with tears. It stunned him, but he wiped them away and stood there a moment longer, clutching the sides of the crib and watching Nicky's little mouth move in his sleep. So beautiful. So perfect.

When he finally turned to leave, he drew up short. Holly stood in the doorway, her long reddish-blond hair hanging in disarray over her shoulders and down her back. She was bare-legged, having slipped into his discarded shirt. She looked so fresh and pretty, so innocent and sensual all at once.

Something twisted in his chest. He wanted to grab her and hold her close, but he didn't act on the urge.

"How is he?" she whispered.

"Asleep."

Holly glided over to his side and gazed down at her son. A smile curved the corners of her mouth and Drago felt a strong desire to kiss her. To own her and own that smile, too.

"He's so sweet," she said softly. "A very good baby." Then she looked up at him, and his heart clenched at the sadness on her face. It surprised him how much she affected him. How much he wanted to protect her and their baby, too.

He'd never felt this kind of possessiveness toward anyone. He knew it was because his feelings for her were all tangled up with the knowledge he'd fathered this child, but he couldn't quite seem to separate them.

He'd told her to walk away earlier. To take his money and walk away.

Now he couldn't imagine letting her go. He didn't *want* to let her go. And that frightened him.

Her brows drew together as she reached up and ran her hand along his jaw. "Don't worry," she said, and he knew that some of what he was feeling must have shown on his face. "You'll be fine with him. He will love you to pieces."

His heart seized. "I'm sure you're right," he said.

She slipped her arms around his waist and laid her head on his chest. "I am right. You'll see. Everything will be perfect."

He wanted to believe it, but he'd learned a long time ago that nothing was perfect.

CHAPTER TWELVE

TIME WAS FLUID. It moved like a river, rolling smoothly and inexorably forward. Sometimes there were rocks. Sometimes there weren't.

Holly sighed and looked up from her work. There had been no rocks for days now. She liked it this way. Life with Drago had been one long, immensely pleasurable ride along smooth water these past two weeks.

The days were pleasant—she played with Nicky, read books and mixed her perfumes. Drago had supplied her with everything she needed, just as he'd promised. He worked from home much of the time, though sometimes he got up early and took a helicopter to his office in Rome. She missed him when he wasn't at the house. Because when he was, he often came searching for her in the middle of the day.

They'd made frantic love against the wall of a closet once. He'd come looking for her and found her heading for her workroom. Instead of leading her back to the room they shared, he'd opened the nearest door—a closet—and dragged her inside. It had been incredibly erotic, fumbling with their clothes among the linens, mouth seeking mouth. He'd had to put his hand over her mouth to stop her cries when he'd buried himself deep inside her, their bodies sweating and writhing as they'd flown toward that perfect release. She'd bitten him, and he'd laughed.

There were other times, too, wonderful times, when they retreated to their room in the middle of the day and made love while the world moved by outside. She loved those moments, when it seemed as if they were the only two people who existed.

But of course she loved it when Drago came to play with Nicky, too. He'd been wary at first, nervous, but now he was a natural. And Nicky loved him, laughing whenever Drago picked him up and swooped him around the room, pretending he was a bird or a superhero.

She laughed, too, loving the sound of her two men enjoying each other's company.

But, as perfect as life had been lately, she wasn't worry-free. She and Drago avoided discussing anything to do with the future. What happened now?

She had no idea, and it worried her. For all her bravery, there were certain things she still couldn't manage to be vocal about. And the future was one of them.

There had been delays on the Sky campaign, so she'd told herself to stop thinking about it. Instead, she spent time working on her scents.

She tested the latest batch of Colette. Then she leaned back, satisfied it was perfect. She'd given some to the maids, and then she'd given some to the cook when she'd expressed an interest. Several of Drago's staff were now wearing her fragrances, not his. If he'd noticed, he hadn't said anything.

And she didn't think he could help but notice, since she wore the same fragrance herself. Colette was light, fresh and floral. There was lavender, verbena, vanilla, and a few secrets she wouldn't divulge to anyone. But it was unmistakable, and it tended to flatter most body chemistries. No one had been unable to wear it yet.

She sniffed the tester again, closing her eyes as she did so. It made her think of home, of Gran's lovely face. Of

the fat blooms in Gran's garden, and the delicious gumbo
on Gran's stove. She missed Gran so much.

A tear fell and she dashed it away, sniffling. She was
happy, dammit. Happy.

She had a wonderful baby and a man she loved—

Holly froze. *Love?* How could she love Drago di
Navarra? What they had was hot, physical and addictive.
It was also volatile and chaotic in many ways.

But it wasn't emotional. It was sex.

When it was over, she could walk away and not miss
a thing....

Holly hung her head as a sharp pain carved into her
at the thought. Oh, dear heaven, it *was* emotional. For
her anyway. Because the thought of leaving Drago, of not
being a part of his life anymore, felt as if she were trying
to slice off an arm or leg. She couldn't imagine life without him. Didn't want to.

That didn't mean it was love, though. He was the father
of her baby, and it was inevitable she felt something tender for him, especially as they spent time together and as
he doted on his son. In spite of his childhood, in spite of a
mother who'd given him up and made him feel unloved, he
was capable of so much love when it came to his little boy.

But what about her? How did he feel about her?

"Holly."

She turned at the sound of his voice, her heart leaping.
A single tear spilled down her cheek and she hurriedly
wiped it away.

"What's wrong?" he said, coming over to her side and
kneeling down. He looked so concerned, and her heart
turned over.

"I was thinking of Gran," she said huskily. It was true.

He reached up and wiped away another tear that escaped. "I'm sorry you lost her, Holly."

She shrugged, though she felt anything but lighthearted at the moment. "That's life, right?"

He stood and pulled her into his arms. She went willingly, burying her head against his chest and breathing him in. Oh, how she loved the smell of him. He wasn't wearing cologne today, but he still smelled like pears to her. Not sweet, but not tart, either. Delicious and crisp and inviting. That was Drago.

"It is life, but that doesn't make it hurt any less."

They stood that way for a long while, and then she pushed back and looked up at him, smiling through her tears. "I'm fine, Drago. I just miss her sometimes."

He took her hand and led her out onto the terrace. They sank onto a settee that was shaded from the sun by a vine-covered arbor. Fat grapes hung down, waiting for someone to pick them.

"Tell me about her," he commanded. She would have laughed at his imperious tone if she weren't touched by his desire to make her feel better.

"She raised me. I told you that before. I never knew my father, and my mother died when I was young. Gramps had died years before, so it was just me and Gran in her little cottage. She grew so many things, Drago. Vegetables, herbs and flowers. We ate well and we made essences. I had a wonderful childhood. I never thought I was missing out on anything."

"And then she died, and you couldn't keep her home."

She nodded. "Gran didn't have insurance, so when she got sick with cancer she had to borrow against the house. She didn't want to do it at first, but she really had no choice. And I was positive we'd find a way, once she was cured, to pay the money back."

She sucked in a pained breath. "But she wasn't cured, and I didn't find a way. After I buried her, there was hardly anything left. The cottage was repossessed. Someone else lives there now." She swallowed a fresh load of tears, her emotions whirling. "I just hope they love it the way I did."

His thumb skated rhythmically over the back of her hand. "I don't think they can, Holly. But I bet they love it in their own way."

Her throat was tight with emotion. He'd put it so perfectly. "Yes, I'm sure you're right. It would be impossible not to appreciate its beauty. The house isn't very big, but Gran had an acre of land and all of it planted and carefully tended. The wife was a gardener, so I'm sure she's in heaven with all the plants."

One of the maids came outside then and asked if they'd like something to drink. Drago asked for a bottle of wine and some water. Holly could smell the scent of Colette in the air. Drago watched the maid walk away.

"Don't think I haven't noticed that everyone smells similar to you," he said mildly.

She shrugged. "I was certain you must have. Are you angry?"

He laughed. "No one who works here is required to wear Navarra products, *cara*. For all I know, the housekeeper mixes up her own scents in her kitchen."

"She might, but that's not what she's wearing right now," Holly said.

"It's…different. I assume it's your Colette?"

Joy washed through her. "Yes. Gran and I made it together."

He looked thoughtful. "I think I like it. It's fresh, not overwhelming. Floral, but not cloying."

Holly nodded eagerly. "Yes, that's it exactly. I haven't found a woman yet whose body chemistry didn't complement the fragrance. It's different on everyone, but the same, too. If that makes sense."

He laughed. "You are talking to a man who hears a hundred different pitches a week for things that are the same but different. Sometimes it makes sense. Often, it's—how do you Americans say it?—bullshit."

"And is it bullshit this time?"

He pursed his lips in thought. "Perhaps not. But I will need more information." His gaze slid down her body, back up again, and she tingled everywhere he looked. "I will need a thorough, *private* demonstration, Holly Craig."

"I think I can arrange that," she told him. "Let me speak to the research-and-development department. I'll get back with you."

His eyes sparkled. "Mmm, and if I'm unwilling to wait that long?"

She tipped her head to the returning maid. "I think you must, Mr. Di Navarra. Your wine has arrived."

"Ah, but wine is portable," he said with a wink.

Drago was gone the next morning when Holly woke, off to Rome to tend to his business. She lay in the bed alone and thought about everything that had happened these past few weeks. She was happier than she'd have ever thought she could be, and she was frightened, too.

Drago did not talk about the future. Not ever. She had no idea what she meant to him, if anything. Oh, sure, they were lovers and she was the mother of his child—but what did that mean to him, beyond the here and now? He seemed to need her as much as she needed him—but he never said any tender words, never talked about what the future might hold for them.

She was under contract for a year, but only if the test shots went well. So far, there had been no test shots. There had been no shoot. Drago said it took time to do what he wanted and not to worry, but she worried nevertheless.

He did things like ask her about Gran and express his sorrow for her loss, and she wondered endlessly if that meant he felt something. Or if he was just being polite.

Yesterday, he'd said he'd needed more information about Colette. But once they'd been alone, perfume had been the furthest thing from his mind. He'd stripped her naked and made her mindless with pleasure. But when it was over, when they were sated and lying together in the bed, he'd pulled her close and fallen asleep. He'd not asked her one question about her fragrance.

She'd told herself it was ridiculous to be disappointed, especially after the way he'd held her and caressed her and wrung every drop of pleasure from her body, but she couldn't help herself. She wanted to be taken seriously, and Drago only wanted to use her body.

Not that she minded that part. But she wanted more. She wanted to know he thought about more than having sex with her. And she wanted to know what would happen when the campaign was over. Or if he didn't like the test shots and it never began.

He had to know she'd meant what she said about not giving up Nicky. But he had so much money and power. Did he really care what she said? He could fight her for custody. He might even win.

Holly's heart squeezed tight. She couldn't let that happen.

She flung the covers back and went to take a shower. After, she dressed in jeans and a T-shirt and went to find Sylvia and Nicky. They were in the garden, and Holly went to join them, her heart swelling with love for her baby. He sat on a blanket in the shade, playing with his toys, while Sylvia read a book. When he saw her coming, he threw the toy and began babbling excitedly. His little arms stretched up to her, and Holly bent to pick him up.

"Hello, precious," she said, sticking her nose against his neck and breathing in his soft baby scent.

She greeted Sylvia warmly, though she was still wary

of having anyone else take care of her son. It felt as if he wasn't hers as much, and she knew that was silly, but since Gran had died, she'd been so alone in the world with no other family. She had Gabi, of course, but Gabi didn't share DNA with her. This little guy, however, had become her world. She couldn't lose him. Not ever.

Holly spent the rest of the morning with Nicky and Sylvia, and then she put Nicky down for his nap and went to the room set up with her supplies. She had an idea for something new that she wanted to play with. When she'd been sitting in the grass earlier, the scent of sun-warmed cherries had seemed to waft over her from nowhere. They combined with the scent of the grapes in the arbor and the grass and soil beneath her to make her think of summer afternoons. It didn't mean she would get anything out of combining essences, but it was fun to play.

And it kept her mind occupied.

Sometime during the afternoon, there was a knock at her door. Her heart skipped when she thought it might be Drago, but then she realized he usually strode in without knocking.

"Yes," she called, and a maid opened the door.

"Signorina," she said, "there is a man here to see you."

Holly blinked. "Me? Are you certain?"

"Sì. It is Signore Lazzari, and he says he wishes to speak to you."

She hadn't thought about Santo Lazzari in two weeks, so to have him here now was a bit of a surprise. Still, she didn't have any reason not to see him. He knew she was the new face of Sky, and he was one of Drago's business associates.

"I'll be there in a minute," she said.

The maid inclined her head and left. Holly stoppered her essences, made a few quick notes and then went out to greet Santo.

* * *

Drago sat at his desk in his office in Rome and tried to concentrate on the numbers in front of him. But he couldn't seem to focus. He kept coming back to Holly, to the way she clung to him, the way she felt beneath him when their bodies were joined, the way he felt inside when he was with her.

She made him want to be a better man. She made him want to try to open his heart and trust someone. He'd never trusted anyone, not since he was little and had learned he could rely only on himself. That he was responsible for his own well-being instead of the woman who should have been taking care of him. He'd never had that freedom other kids had had, that freedom to play and have fun and not *think* about survival and belonging.

He'd always had to think about those things. About his place in his mother's world, and his place in the world at large. He had always been worth a lot of money. He still was, even more so now that he was in charge of it. His money enticed people to try to use him for their own purposes, to try to chip off just a little bit for themselves.

Holly had had his child, but she hadn't tried to get money from him. She hadn't shown up on his doorstep, threatening him with a paternity suit, threatening him with selling her story to the tabloids if he didn't pay up. She'd never tried to use Nicky to get anything from him.

She had kept him secret, though. And she had kept that knowledge hidden while she'd negotiated for a contract with him. She said it was because she wanted to secure her child's future. Because she was afraid he would kick her out again.

If he were honest with himself, she'd had every reason to think he might do just that.

He had not handled her betrayal quite so well the first time. In fact, he'd reacted in a way he never did. Blindly, emotionally. He'd thrown her out instead of listening to her pitch, politely telling her "no, thanks," and then sending her on her way.

But she'd blindsided him. Or, rather, his own feelings had blindsided him. In a single moment, Holly Craig had reminded him what it had felt like to be worth nothing as a person and everything as an entity. He'd hated her for making him feel that way.

And how did he feel now?

Drago sighed. That was the problem. He didn't know. He only knew that since taking her to his bed, he'd felt a sense of relief and joy that he hadn't experienced in a very long time. It made no sense, especially when he considered that she'd lied to him for so long—but maybe he was tired of being suspicious, tired of letting the past dictate the future.

He had a child with her, a wonderful, adorable child. And he wanted that child to have the things he hadn't had: a stable home, a father, love. Holly loved Nicky, and he loved Nicky. Shouldn't they work together to give their boy everything they could?

They hadn't had the best beginning, but they could have a good future together. All he had to do was take a chance. It took him a few more hours of thinking and considering and weighing all the options, but in the end he made a decision.

He picked up the phone and started to make a few calls. When he got home tonight, he would take the first step toward the future.

CHAPTER THIRTEEN

Excitement bubbled and popped in Holly's veins like fine champagne poured into a crystal flute. Santo Lazzari wanted her to make perfume for House of Lazzari. He wanted to buy Colette. It was everything she'd ever dreamed, everything she'd wanted when she and Gran had been mixing their blends together—and then, after, when Gran was gone and Holly had been determined to save her home and introduce the world to Gran's perfume.

But there was also an undercurrent of sadness in her joy. Drago. She'd wanted *him* to want Colette. She'd wanted him to be the one who was excited about the possibilities, who praised her for her skill and who mapped out a potential campaign that showed what he could do with her fragrance.

Except, he didn't seem interested. Yesterday, she'd thought he finally would talk to her about it, but he'd kissed her instead. And then he'd taken her to bed and made love to her and all thoughts of perfume had flown out the window.

Now she stood in her workroom and waited for him to return from Rome. She'd told Santo she had to think about it overnight, but what she really wanted to know was how Drago felt. Did he want Colette? Or was that nothing more than a dead end?

Finally, when the shadows grew long on the tall pencil

pines, she heard the *whop-whop* of the rotors as Drago's helicopter returned. Her heart lodged in her throat as she went outside to greet him. He came walking up from the helipad, clad in a custom suit and handmade loafers, carrying a briefcase and looking lost in thought.

She watched him for a long moment, her breath catching at the sheer masculine beauty of him. Santo Lazzari was handsome, and he'd even flirted with her a little bit, but she'd been unmoved. When Drago walked across a room—or a lawn—she felt as if she were slowly burning up from the inside out. Every sense attuned to him. Every cell of her body ached for him.

He saw her, finally. His expression grew serious and her blood slowed to a crawl in her veins. What was he thinking?

"Holly," he said when he drew near. And then, before she could ask him what was on his mind, he dropped the briefcase and dragged her into his arms. He kissed her thoroughly, completely, until she was boneless in his embrace.

"I have something for you," he said when he finally lifted his head. His eyes sparked with heat and passion, and a throbbing ache set up shop in her core.

"I think I know what it is," she said teasingly, her heart thrumming fast.

He laughed. "I doubt it." Then he reached into his pocket and pulled out a small velvet box.

Holly's heart lodged in her throat. "What is it?"

"Open it."

No one had ever given her jewelry—and certainly not something in a velvet box. She knew the size, the shape, knew what it usually meant in commercials and movies. But what did it mean here?

Her hands stayed anchored at her sides as the world spun crazily around her. "I don't think I can."

He stood there so tall and handsome in the golden light. She could hear birds in the trees now that the helicopter was gone again. Inside the house, she heard the clink of dishes and knew the chef was preparing dinner. Drago's scent assailed her nostrils, along with the freshness of the evening breeze and the dampness of an approaching storm.

She felt everything so keenly, and she was afraid to move beyond this moment. Afraid it wouldn't mean what she wanted it to mean. Afraid it would end and she'd be brokenhearted again.

"Then I will do it for you," he said, flipping back the lid as he stood so close to her she could feel his heat enveloping her senses.

The ring wasn't huge by billionaire standards, but it was undoubtedly bigger than anything she'd ever thought she would have. And it was unmistakably an engagement ring. The center diamond was at least three carats, and the band held more diamonds, which enhanced the center and made it sparkle all the more. She didn't think the setting was white gold. Platinum most likely, unless there were a more rare metal she didn't know about.

"Marry me, Holly," he said. "We'll make a home for Nicky, and one day he'll inherit all of this."

Her chest ached as tears filled her eyes. "I don't know what to say."

He looked uncertain for a moment, as if he hadn't anticipated that answer. "Say yes."

She wanted to. Desperately. But she couldn't until she asked a question. He'd never given any indication of his feelings, and she needed to know. "Do you love me, Drago?"

He swallowed. "I care about you," he said, and her heart fell slowly, so slowly, until it hit the floor and shattered into a million pieces.

She told herself it was silly to feel sad or disappointed.

It was too soon to ask for more. He was proposing to her. Offering to make a home for Nicky, to give him a family. She knew how important that was to him. A man who'd never had a stable home life until he was nearly a teenager.

What more could she ask for right this moment? It was a start. And yet she was more hurt by his offer than cheered. She wanted *more*. She wanted him to feel the way she felt. She wanted him to feel as if he would burst trying to contain all these hot, bright feelings inside the shell of his skin, and she wanted him to care about the things she cared about.

She told herself this was enough, for now. But it wasn't.

"Santo Lazzari wants to buy Colette," she said on a whisper, because she couldn't say the other things she was thinking. She couldn't put her heart on the line when she was more and more certain he didn't feel the same way.

Drago's face changed. She watched the emotions crossing his features and knew she'd said the wrong thing. There was disbelief, hurt, loneliness and, finally, fury. He snapped the box closed and she jumped at the finality of the sound.

"And what does Lazzari have to do with this, Holly?" he gritted. "With what I am asking you right now? Are you hoping for a better offer from *him*?"

Shock hit her like a lightning bolt sizzling across a clear blue sky. "What? No! But you said you care about me, and this is something I care about. And you haven't spoken of it, though I keep waiting—"

His expression grew darker, if that were possible, more thunderous. His lips curled back from his teeth and she shrank away from him. "You think mentioning Lazzari to me will make me buy your perfume?" He held up the box in his clenched fist. His knuckles were white where he gripped it so hard. "I'm offering you more than you could have ever dreamed possible—money, position, even power—and you still care about your trite little scents?"

His words stabbed into her. *Trite little scents.* He thought her dreams were beneath his notice. No, he thought she wanted to make perfume only so she could make money. That she was driven by ambition and greed rather than joy and love.

He didn't really know her if he thought that. He'd spent these past few weeks with her, and he had no idea who she was. It hurt more than she'd ever thought possible.

Blindly, she turned away from him. Everything was blurry as she started across the terrace. She had to get away, or scream.

"Where are you going?" he thundered. "Holly? Holly!"

She didn't turn around. She didn't stop. She kept going until she was inside her room, the door locked to the outside. Until she could cry for everything she'd lost, and everything she would never have.

Drago went back to Rome. When he reached his apartment, he slammed inside and threw his briefcase on the couch. And then he took the velvet box from his trousers, where it had sat like a hard lump of marble, and wanted to howl in frustration.

He'd misjudged her again. He'd thought she wanted him, wanted this life, but she wanted him to buy her perfume and she didn't mind using Santo Lazzari to get him to do it. And she wanted him to proclaim his love for her, as if that would make a difference somehow.

Love. *Dio*, what kind of fool would love her?

Drago raked a hand through his hair. He didn't understand love. He didn't understand how anyone could let go enough to feel love. In his mind, it was a dangerous emotion that made people unstable. When you loved someone, you gave them the keys to your soul. The means with which to destroy you.

He'd spent years loving a mother who hadn't loved him back—or hadn't loved him enough. It had taken him years to get over the neglect, and he was not about to open himself up for that kind of experience ever again.

Holly knew, damn her. She *knew* how hard this was for him, how damaged a life he'd had. She knew and she insisted on pushing him.

Santo Lazzari. *Christo!* It had been only a few weeks, and they hadn't even begun the Sky shoot yet. Already she was scheming to get her perfume in front of another company. It infuriated him that she would betray him, that she would talk to Santo instead of to him.

Why hadn't she just asked him what he thought? Why hadn't she come to him instead of going behind his back?

The answer was obvious: because she didn't trust him.

Hot feelings swirled inside him. He wanted to punch something. Wanted to rage and howl and ask why he wasn't good enough for her.

He went over to the liquor cabinet and poured a shot of whiskey. His fingers shook as he poured and he stopped, stared at them. *Why wasn't he good enough for her?*

That was the kind of question he'd asked as a child. It was a question for his mother, not for Holly. He set the whiskey down and stared at a window across the street, a little lower than his. A man and woman danced together, the woman smiling up at him, the man saying something that made her smile.

Holly was not his mother. And she very likely hadn't gone to Santo. He remembered Santo escorting her onto the terrace a couple of weeks ago. Santo could have asked her about the scent she was wearing then. And she would have told him the truth.

And even if she'd pitched it herself, why should that matter to him?

If he were truthful with himself, he hadn't shown much interest, though he knew she worked hard on her fragrances. He'd been in the room she'd set up as a work area, he'd smelled her concoctions and he'd seen her notes. She was a professional. And she was good.

But he'd never told her that. *Why not?*

Drago stood in the darkness of his Rome apartment, with the city sounds wafting up from below and the lights of Rome's ancient ruins and sacred domes glittering before him, and felt more alone than he'd ever felt in his life.

What was he doing? Why was he here instead of back at his villa, with his beautiful son?

And with Holly.

A cold, sinking feeling started in his gut, spread through his limbs. What if he'd ruined it this time? What if he'd gone too far? He tried to imagine his life without her in it. Emptiness engulfed him.

It was more emptiness than he'd ever thought he could feel. Somehow, she had become important to him. To his life. If he had to live without her in it, how could he ever laugh again?

He was a fool. A blind fool, driven by things that had happened to him over twenty years ago instead of by the things that his life had become. Inside, he was still lost and alone and frightened. And he was waiting—waiting for betrayal. He expected it, looked for it, congratulated himself when it happened. Because it was what he knew was supposed to happen to him.

But what if it wasn't? What if the problem was all him? What if Holly was exactly what she seemed to be? A somewhat naive, trusting woman who'd had to learn how to survive on her own when she'd found herself pregnant and alone.

Drago turned away from the window, panic bubbling up from a well inside him that he'd kept capped for far too long. He was an idiot. And not for the reasons he'd supposed. No one had made him into a fool. He'd done it all by himself.

Holly woke in the middle of the night, her eyes swollen, her throat aching, and knew she had to leave. There could be no Sky. There could be no Drago. She would do whatever it took to arrange for him to see his son, but right now Nicky belonged to her and she wasn't leaving here without him.

She dressed in the dark, tossed some things into a bag and went to gather Nicky from his crib. Somehow she managed to get him into his carrier without waking him, and then she crept down the stairs and stood in the empty foyer, undecided about what to do. On the hall table, there were several sets of car keys in a box. She took one—a BMW—and went out to the garage.

It took her nearly forty-five minutes to get the car, find the nearest train station on the GPS and drive to it. She could have gone to the airport, but for now she figured she'd get a train to Rome, call Santo Lazzari and arrange to meet with him about Colette, and then get a one-way ticket back to Louisiana. If she could just get an advance, she'd be all right. She had some money, but not enough to get her very far.

Holly purchased a ticket to Rome and went to sit on a bench. She studied her ticket and studied the boards, hoping she'd found the right track. Her eyes were gritty and tired, and she suddenly just wanted to go back to sleep. Nicky stirred in his carrier, but he was too sleepy to wake just yet. She prepared a bottle and hoped it would keep him quiet once he did.

Eventually, her train arrived—or she hoped it was her train—and she boarded it, finding a seat in a corner and leaning her head against the window. It throbbed with the remnants of her crying fit, and the early-morning coolness felt good against her skin.

She dozed a bit and then the train lurched and started to glide down the tracks. Her heart ached with such a profound sadness that she could hardly acknowledge it. How could she go back to the life she'd left behind? How could she forget Drago this time?

The last time, she hadn't been in love with him—or maybe she had, but it had been so easy to convince herself she hated him instead. This time, her heart mourned for everything that could never be. They would see each other again. Because of Nicky. She couldn't get out of it and she didn't want to.

But she would have to figure out how to survive those moments when she had to face him for the sake of their child.

The train lurched again, and then began to slow. They hadn't quite made it out of the station when it stopped completely. The Italians on board seemed unperturbed about it all, but her pulse hummed along a little bit faster. She just wanted to get away, before Drago discovered she was gone. She figured she had time, since he'd presumably returned to Rome last night, but she was nervous nevertheless.

There was a commotion in the car behind her, raised voices, and she turned to look along with the other passengers. Her heart seemed to stop beating then. She could see Drago's face, determined and hard, and her legs turned to mush. She reached for her bag, slid out of her seat and grabbed the carrier. She was on her way down the car when the door behind her opened and a man shouted her name.

She spun, her hair whirling into her face, and confronted him—because there was no escape now.

"Go away, Drago," she said. "Just leave me alone."

He looked wild-eyed as he moved into the car. The

other passengers glanced between them with interest, eyes bouncing back and forth as if they were at a tennis match.

"Holly, please." He held his hand out, and she saw that it shook. She steeled her heart against him and shook her head. What a good actor he was.

"Stop it," she said coldly. "You're only pretending so these people won't think you're some kind of unfeeling monster. But we both know the truth, don't we?"

He looked taken aback. "No, that's not true." He tried to smile, but it wasn't a very good attempt. "Besides, since when do I care what anyone else thinks about me?"

He had a point there, but if she allowed it to penetrate, her shield would crumble. She had to be strong. For her baby. For herself.

"You don't care about anyone."

He took another step forward, one hand out in supplication. "I care about you."

Panic bloomed in her soul. "You don't. You're only saying that because I tried to leave. Well, guess what, Drago, you can't force me to stay! I won't prevent you from being a part of Nicky's life, but I won't stay here and let you ruin my life, either."

His hand dropped to his side. "I don't want to ruin your life, Holly. I want to make it better."

She laughed bitterly. "By locking me up in a gilded cage? By not trusting me? By belittling my dreams and my interests? By telling me I'll never be good enough for the likes of you?"

His expression was stark. And then he said something that stunned her. "You're too good for me, Holly. I'm the one who isn't good enough."

Anger seeped from her like air from a balloon. Confusion took up residence in her brain. She wanted to believe him, but how could she? "Is this a trick?"

He shook his head, and she finally saw that lost, lonely

man that lurked inside him. "It's not a trick. I'm a fool, Holly. I need you too much, and it scares me."

Holly stared at him for a long moment, studying his face. Her heart thundered and her blood pounded and her skin felt hot and tight.

"I think he tells the truth," a woman said, and Holly glanced over at her. She was a pretty woman, with dark hair and eyes shiny with tears. "It is *amore, signorina.*"

Holly's heart skipped. "Is that true, Drago? Do you love me? Or is this all an elaborate ruse to get me to go back with you so you can take our son away?"

He stood there before her, so tall and commanding—and then he drew in a sharp breath and she heard the pain in it.

"I don't know what love is, Holly. I loved my mother. I know I did, and yet she didn't seem to care. She left me. I meant nothing at all to her. What if I am incapable of love? Of being loved?"

There was a huge lump in her throat. "You aren't incapable of being loved."

His eyes were filled with so much pain. "How do you know?"

She felt a tear spill over, and then another. How could she let him think such a thing when she knew the truth?

"Because I love you." The words felt like razor blades coming up, but once they were free, she was glad she'd said them.

She didn't know what would happen, but he moved then, an inexorable wave coming for her. Then he swept her up in his arms, her and Nicky, and held them tight, burying his face against her neck.

"I don't know what love is," he said, his voice a broken whisper in her ear. "But if it's this feeling that I would die without you, then yes, I love you. If you leave me, Holly, I will be more alone than I've ever been in my life."

The tears flowed freely down her cheeks now, and the train's inhabitants clapped and cheered.

"I want to stay with you, Drago. But I'm afraid. You hurt me, and I'm afraid."

His grip didn't ease. "I know. I've been an ass, Holly. I want you to come home with me, and I want you to marry me. And I want Colette, and whatever other perfume you want to make for me. I want you to be happy, to do what you love—and I'm sorry I said it was trite. It's not. Nothing you do is trite. I was just…afraid."

Holly drew in a shaky breath. And then she pulled back and put her hand on his cheek—his beloved cheek—and caressed him. "I love you, Drago. You can't make me stop. It has nothing to do with your money or your stupid cosmetics company. Even if you had nothing, I would love you."

He wiped away the tears on her cheeks with shaky fingers. His eyes shimmered with moisture, though he grinned to try to hide it. "That's a pretty speech, considering I am worth somewhere in the neighborhood of eighty billion dollars. It's easy to love a rich man, *amore mia*."

She laughed then. "Perhaps it is, but not when that rich man is you. Do you have any idea what a pain in the ass you can be? Sometimes it would be easier to love a cactus."

His laugh was broken, and it tore her heart to hear it. "You are too much, Holly Craig. You and that smart mouth." He drew in a breath. "Please marry me. Please come home and bring our son and let me spend the rest of my life making it up to you for being so blind and stupid."

"Yes," she said simply. Because it was right. Because there was nowhere else she'd rather be than in this man's arms for the rest of her life.

His smile was filled with relief and tenderness. "Then let me do this right," he said. Before she knew what he was about, he pulled a box from his pocket and dropped to one knee. "Marry me, Holly Craig. Fill my life with light and happiness. Tease me, exasperate me, challenge me—and never give up on me."

"Do it, *signorina,*" the dark-haired woman urged.

Holly laughed. As if she could do anything else when she had the great Drago di Navarra on his knees in front of her. As if she wanted to.

"It's a deal," she said softly. "No contract required."

Drago slipped the ring on her finger. Then he got to his feet and kissed her right there in the middle of the train as everyone cheered.

EPILOGUE

DRAGO LOOKED UP from the photos he'd been studying and found his wife standing in his office, looking amazingly gorgeous in a simple dress and flats.

"I didn't hear you come in," he said.

"Obviously." She came and looked over his shoulder. And then she sighed. "Are you sure about these?"

"Of course. You are the most gorgeous model to ever grace a fragrance ad."

"I think your colleagues are going to think you've lost your mind," she grumbled.

He turned and put his hands on her waist. "Holly, you are precisely what I wanted for this campaign. You're gorgeous but approachable. Women will buy this perfume in droves."

She ran her hands through his hair. And then she kissed him. "I think they'll buy Colette in greater droves."

He laughed. "You could be right. I guess we'll see when we launch it in the spring, yes?"

She arranged herself on his lap. He did not mind. His arms went around her and held her tight. How had he ever, *ever* thought he could live without her?

"I'm perfectly confident," she said. And then she frowned. "But, Drago, I'm afraid I can't work in your fragrance development lab as first planned."

He studied her face, shocked at this news. "But you

insisted you wanted this. You've proved to me how good you are, and I've been counting on adding your expertise to the staff."

She toyed with the lapel of his collar. "Yes, well, you can still have that expertise. But I'm afraid the scents will be too much for me. In a lab. At home, I can do it when I'm feeling well. But all those scents? No, not happening."

Drago shook his head. She'd left him about a mile back, standing on the side of the road and staring at her dust cloud. "I'm not following you," he told her.

She leaned down and kissed his nose. "Oh, you darling man. No, I suppose it wouldn't make a lick of sense to you. The smells, my darling, will be too much for a woman in my condition."

He felt as if his brain was stuck in the mud, spinning tires—

And then he came unstuck and her meaning dawned. "You're pregnant?"

Her smile could have lit up the grid. "Yes."

Drago squeezed her tight, unable to say a word. And then he panicked and let her go again. "I'm sorry, was that too much?"

"No, of course not." She squeezed him back and they sat together, holding each other and laughing.

"I almost forgot," he said. He pulled open a drawer and took out some papers. "I just got these. I wanted to surprise you."

Holly took the papers and opened them. Tears filled her lovely blue eyes as she read the deed. "Gran's house."

"Your house," he said, the lump in his throat nearly too big to get the words past.

"*Our* house," she said, squeezing him tight. "Oh, Drago, thank you."

He pushed her hair back from her face, tucking it behind her ears. And then he drew her down and kissed her sweetly. "Anything for you, Holly. Anything."

She made his life complete. Her and Nicky. And this new baby, whoever he or she turned out to be. Drago's heart was full as he kissed her again. Life was full.

And it always would be. In that, he had complete faith.

* * * * *

LET'S TALK
Romance

For exclusive extracts, competitions
and special offers, find us online:

f facebook.com/millsandboon

🐦 @MillsandBoon

📷 @MillsandBoonUK

Get in touch on 01413 063232

For all the latest titles coming soon, visit
millsandboon.co.uk/nextmonth

MILLS & BOON

THE HEART OF ROMANCE

A ROMANCE FOR EVERY KIND OF READER

MODERN

Prepare to be swept off your feet by sophisticated, sexy and seductive heroes, in some of the world's most glamourous and romantic locations, where power and passion collide.
8 stories per month.

HISTORICAL

Escape with historical heroes from time gone by. Whether your passion is for wicked Regency Rakes, muscled Vikings or rugged Highlanders, awaken the romance of the past.
6 stories per month.

MEDICAL

Set your pulse racing with dedicated, delectable doctors in the high-pressure world of medicine, where emotions run high and passion, comfort and love are the best medicine.
6 stories per month.

True Love

Celebrate true love with tender stories of heartfelt romance, from the rush of falling in love to the joy a new baby can bring, and a focus on the emotional heart of a relationship.
8 stories per month.

Desire

Indulge in secrets and scandal, intense drama and plenty of sizzling hot action with powerful and passionate heroes who have it all: wealth, status, good looks…everything but the right woman.
6 stories per month.

HEROES

Experience all the excitement of a gripping thriller, with an intense romance at its heart. Resourceful, true-to-life women and strong, fearless men face danger and desire - a killer combination!
8 stories per month.

DARE

Sensual love stories featuring smart, sassy heroines you'd want as a best friend, and compelling intense heroes who are worthy of them.
4 stories per month.

To see which titles are coming soon, please visit

millsandboon.co.uk/nextmonth